THE SEDUCTION OF PETER S.

Lawrence Sanders

THE SEDUCTION OF PETER S.

G. P. PUTNAM'S SONS / NEW YORK

Printed in the United States of America

THE SEDUCTION OF PETER S.

1

My name is Peter Scuro. I am the kind of man who goes through life asking: Is this all there is?

I said: "Do you know the answer to all the heavy questions that have baffled the world since Adam? I have the answer: Think of God as a clown, the Divine Clown. That solves everything. Undeserved suffering. Injustice. Pain. It all suddenly makes sense if you think of God as a clown. An earthquake kills a thousand people? Slapstick. A bridge collapses in Bolivia and thirty innocents are drowned? A great shtick. Are you following me? An infant born with leukemia? Hard act to top. The Divine Clown. Think about it. When the idea sinks in, you can sit back and applaud the performance."

Sol Hoffheimer's massive face sagged in a smile. "Peter, if you believed half of what you say, you'd be amused. But you're not; you're indignant. A nice distinction. You're not a true cynic; you're just peevish."

"That's right," I said. "I try to be hard as flint, but inside I'm just tapioca."

We were in my agent's littered office on West 45th Street. Outside, a gutsy wind and coughs of snow. Inside, a clanking radiator and the smell of dead cigars.

"So," Hoffheimer said, "I gather the audition didn't go too hot."

"Audition?" I said. "What audition? They took one look at me, and I was o-u-t. They're looking for a younger type."

"It happens," the agent said philosophically. "The director gets a mental image of the guy he wants, and—"

I gave a finger to the world. "I've been trying to match somebody's mental image—*anybody's!*—for twelve years now. I've worked hard. Made the rounds. Knocked down doors. Grabbed anything that came along. And what have I got to show for it? Some shitty credits and about eight thousand bucks over twelve years. That's the sum total of my theatrical career."

"Too many people," Hoffheimer said, shrugging. "Not enough jobs."

"Don't tell *me*. What hurts is that every year a new crop of kids shows up. I saw boys at that so-called audition today, I swear to God I could have been their father. And a lot of them handsome, rugged, with plenty of brio. Next January I'll be thirty-six. Where does that leave me, Sol—reading for the English butler with muttonchop whiskers? Yes, m'lord. No, m'lord. I'm getting to the breaking point."

"Listen," the agent said. "I can match you kvetch for kvetch. Me, I'm forty-eight. In the business almost twenty-five years. When I started, I had dreams of million-dollar deals. You know, calling the Coast: 'Hi, baby, this is Sol. Have I got a hot property for you!' Beautiful starlets. Champagne dinners. That's what I thought it would be like. Peter, I don't even *know* anyone on the Coast. And the only starlets I know are hookers."

I laughed. "We're a great couple of failures, Sol."

"No," the agent said. "That door could open tomorrow and a new Clark Gable or Marilyn Monroe could walk in."

"On the other hand, it could be your landlord with your overdue rent bill."

"Yeah," Hoffheimer said morosely. "That too."

The agent stripped the cellophane from a cheap cigar. He lighted it with a dented Zippo, blew a plume of smoke at the ceiling. He put his feet up on the desk. Stared at the one sooted window, the gusts of snow.

Sol Hoffheimer had grown into his face. Years ago, his head had seemed too large, his features gross. But as he aged, time had given him authority, a certain heavy elegance.

"One of the lesser Roman emperors," Jenny Tolliver had commented. "Picture him in a toga and see if I'm not right."

"You think you're a failure, Peter?" the agent asked suddenly.

"Close to it," I said. "I'm trapped. What else am I trained to do? Sell Jockey shorts in men's boutiques or demonstrate potato peelers in five-and-tens? I have no skills outside the theater. And they don't seem to want me *in* the theater."

"If you give up," Hoffheimer said, "you'll regret it for the rest of your life."

"I may have to live with that," I said. "If I want to eat."

The agent took his feet down, leaned across the desk to stare at me.

"I can let you have ten," he said.

I rose and began to gather up hat, coat, scarf, gloves.

"Thanks, Sol," I said, "but no thanks. I'm into you too deep now." I moved to the door, then turned back to face him. "By the way, if I don't see you before, Merry Christmas."

"Yeah," Hoffheimer said. "Merry Christmas to you, too."

I had my hand on the doorknob when I turned back again.

"I'll take that ten, Sol," I said, trying to smile.

2

Spring may belong to all the world, but winter is Manhattan's own. As I walked uptown on Fifth Avenue through the steely light I thought, despite my woes, that I wanted to be *there,* that moment.

The sky was a brittle blue, the wind edged. Snow blown from rooftops and ledges made sparkles in air as sharp as ether. Shoppers jostled. Flags snapped. Horns blared, and carols boomed from loudspeakers. It was all *alive,* and no one in that painting would ever die.

I strode with my tweed Burberry trenchcoat (a mite shabby at cuffs and collar) open and whipping. About my neck was a long vermilion cashmere scarf (bought at a discount from my last employer), casually looped. And cocked rakishly on my head, a knitted Irish field hat. (It was easy to steal a hat. You walked into a busy store hatless and emerged hatted.)

I had a tight, hawkish face, all corners and edges. Hair so black it was purple. An olive skin, and teeth as white and square as sugar cubes. A faint smile slicked with irony. To be honest, more Iago than Hamlet.

I was tall, lithe, with a bounce in my step and an arrogant posture. There was a thrusting forward against the crowd, against the knifing wind, against life.

I glanced occasionally at my reflection in the shop windows as I passed: In another time, I might have been a buccaneer, a courtier, a titled dandy. I saw myself as dashing—except sometimes at 3:00 A.M. when I wondered if I plodded.

My pace slowed at 48th Street, where the luxury shops began. Leather and silk. Hammered silver and molded gold. The world's riches gracefully wrought and artfully displayed, with the added attraction of uselessness.

I longed for the power to just walk in, point, laugh, and say, "I'll take that!" What a joy, to buy for no reason and discard at whim. To contemptuously show your superiority to those glittering baubles.

I paused to look into a shop that sold only imported foods: caviar and truffles, pâté and hearts of palm. A mob of shoppers waved fistfuls of bills at harried clerks.

I turned away, aching for a place in this moneyed world.

3

On West 54th Street, near Eighth Avenue, was the Losers' Place, a busy bar and moribund restaurant, frequented mostly by unemployed actors and off-duty cops.

It was a dim, musty hangout, boasting an alley for dart-throwing, an enormous TV set suspended by chains from the pressed tin ceiling, and Bass Ale on tap. The walls were covered with autographed photos of famous actors, none of whom would be caught dead in the joint.

The scarred bar was against the far wall. I wandered in, waved negligently at two acquaintances tossing darts, and headed directly for the bar. Planting one foot on the tarnished brass rail, I tipped my hat to the back of my head.

Jimmy, the bartender, came over and wiped away the cigarette ashes and pretzel crumbs on the bar in front of me.

"Peter," he said. "Merry the fuck Christmas."

"Ah shure," I said in a rank Irish brogue. "And I'll be wishin' the same to you and yours. Give us a wee Dickens, will ye, m'lad?"

And if you, a first-timer, had summoned the courage to ask Jimmy what a "Dickens" was, he would have muttered, "Oliver Twist"—a martini with both olive and lemon peel.

"How's it going?" Jimmy placed the stemmed glass on a little cardboard mat advertising an Eighth Avenue massage parlor.

"It's all shit," I said pleasantly.

"Oh, you discovered that, did you?" the bartender showed his gold tooth in a grin and moved away. I took a small sip of my drink, looking about casually as I waited for it to go down and warm. Some people I knew waved to me; I flipped a hand to them. Cops and actors: losers all.

Singles were at the bar, hunched over their drinks or staring at their crackled reflections in the back mirror. Two barstools to the left of me was something: a woman, standing, in a dark mink coat down to her ankles and a matching sombrero. I wondered how many little animals had been executed to provide that outfit.

I watched her in the mirror. Alligator handbag, gold Dunhill lighter, gold-tipped cigarettes. Gold rings, bracelets, heavy chain choker. Fingernails that didn't end. Hands that didn't look young. The face was shadowed by the brim of the mink sombrero, and she wore outsize sunglasses.

I was still trying to figure her age when she slid a bill onto the bar, snapped her handbag shut, and strode directly to me.

"Fifty," she said in a husky voice.

"What?" I said, startled.

"Fifty," she repeated patiently. "Fifty dollars."

I was amused, wondering what a Park Avenue hooker was doing on Eighth Avenue.

"I'm flattered," I said, smiling. "Do I really look like a man who can afford fifty dollars?"

"Dummy," she said. "Do I look like a woman who *needs* fifty dollars?"

We stared.

"You'll *pay* fifty?" I asked in a low voice.

She nodded. "Yes or no?"

For the rest of my life I was to wonder why I had never hesitated.

"Where?" I said.

"Your place," she said.

"I'll have to make a call."

"Do that," she said. "I'll finish your drink. I love olives."

I used the telephone near the greasy kitchen. Someone had written on the wall: "I suck," followed by a phone number. I dialed my own apartment. My roommate, Arthur Enders, picked up on the fifth ring.

"Art?" I said. "Peter. Can you clear out right now?"

"What?" Enders said in his wispy voice. "Peter, I don't understand."

"I need the place for an hour," I said. "Alone. Right now. It's very important."

"What's it all about?"

"Art, will you do this for me? I'm supposed to meet Jenny at Blotto's at six. Will you please leave now and wait for her there? Okay?"

"Well . . . if it's important."

"It is. I'll explain later. I'll join you and Jenny at Blotto's at about six-thirty. I'm buying dinner."

"You got the job?" Enders said excitedly.

"I got *a* job," I said. "You'll leave immediately? Promise?"

"Can I take a crap first?"

"A fast crap," I said, and hung up.

Back at the bar, she had finished my drink, eaten the olive, and was nibbling on the lemon peel. I paid the tab with Sol Hoffheimer's sawbuck and we left. People looked at us curiously. I didn't care.

In the cab going uptown, we spoke twice. At 61st Street I said, "What were you doing in the Losers'?"

She said: "Slumming."

At 72nd Street I said, "Why me?"

She said: "You look reasonably clean."

4

It was a six-story converted brownstone on West 75th Street. Entrance three steps down from the sidewalk. Green plastic garbage cans in the paved front areaway. Twelve apartments; north windows faced the street, south windows faced a scabrous courtyard with one valiant ailanthus tree.

Arthur Enders and I shared the back one-bedroom apartment on the first floor. It had been broken into only twice. Now we had three locks and a chain on the front door. Bars on the ground-level windows, of course.

Each month we alternated. One slept in the bedroom, one on the convertible in the living room, and then we switched. The kitchen was minuscule, the bathroom (shower stall, no tub) even smaller. We paid $450 a month for this gem and counted ourselves lucky.

For almost five years we had considered it a temporary habitation—

until I landed a juicy role and Arthur completed The Great American Play. The cast-off furniture had been donated by friends, purchased at the Salvation Army warehouse, or retrieved from the gutter.

Orange crates served as bookcases. A Con Ed cable spool, lying on its side, was a cocktail table. Lamps were clamp-on photographers' reflectors, and the dining table was a flush door supported on cinder blocks. The place reeked of roach spray and cremated hamburgers. Clothing hung from curtain rods and doorjambs. Shredded rugs, contributed by a cat-lover, covered patches of a linoleum floor so worn that the brown backing showed through.

When I managed the three locks and ushered the woman into this shambles, she took one look around and said, "Jesus!"

"It's not much," I admitted.

"*Much?*" she said. "It's not *anything.*"

But she took off her fur and sombrero, placing them gingerly on the back of an armchair that had a spring poking from the seat cushion. Then she took off her sunglasses. It was the first time I had a good look at her.

Upper forties, I guessed. Not much natural beauty, but hairdressers and makeup experts had made the most of what she had. I hoped aerobic dancing and a good masseuse had done the same for the body, hidden under a loose shift of champagne-colored wool.

The face certainly had strength. Maybe too much. Hard eyes, boxy jaw. Thin lips extended with rouge and gloss. Madder-dyed hair teased to soften the high brow. The neck was firm. Wide shoulders. A deep bosom. She endured my scrutiny with aplomb.

"Okay?" she asked.

"Choice," I said.

"You're a dear," she said, touching my cheek. "Got anything to drink?"

"Red wine."

"Any port in a storm."

"Actually," I said in my best British accent ("Eckshully"), "it's Chianti."

She laughed at that. When I brought her the wine, she was coming out of the bedroom.

"Men's clothes," she noted. "Not all your size or style. I gather your roommate is a male."

"Right."

"You're not gay, are you?"

"Mournful," I said. "Most of the time. What do you want me to call you?"

"Martha," she said. "It happens to be my name. What's yours?"

"Peter."

She didn't make a joke out of that, for which I was thankful.

She finished the wine in two gulps and I led her back into the bedroom, which luckily was mine that month.

Her body turned out to be rich and sturdy. Nipples like red gumdrops. A heavy thatch, but that didn't turn me off. A blocky torso, but she did have a waist, and the thighs of a linebacker. It was a big, strong carcass, but it didn't daunt me.

"You're beautiful," she said, inspecting me.

"Thank you."

"Nothing kinky," she ordered. "Just a good, hard bang."

I delivered.

After, when our breathing returned to normal, I said, "It's none of my goddamned business, Martha, and you can certainly tell me to go to hell, but do you do this often?"

"Fuck?" she said. "All the time."

"You know what I mean—picking up strangers in bars."

"When the mood is on me," she said blithely. "It offends you?"

"Of course not. But isn't it dangerous?"

"That's half the fun—the risk. Listen, buster, it's a whole new ball game out there. Every year there are more and more women like me. Independent, with enough money to choose their pleasures. How many women in the past could do that?"

"You're right," I said thoughtfully. "I'm glad you chose me."

She kissed my cheek, then gathered up her clothes and handbag and headed for the bathroom.

"After you flush," I called after her, "you've got to jiggle the handle."

"Of course," she said. "In a place like this, naturally."

I dressed swiftly, made for the living room, and went through her coat. A book of matches from the Four Seasons in one of the pockets. In the lining, embroidered initials: M.T. The label was from the Barcarole Boutique. I knew the place. Hellishly expensive.

She came out of the bathroom and handed me some bills, folded. I slid them into my jacket pocket without even glancing at them.

"How can I get in touch with you, Peter?" she asked as I helped her on with her mink.

I jotted down the number of my answering service and told her my last name. She tucked the paper into her handbag.

"I'll get you a cab," I said, and she kissed my cheek again.

I went out with her, not bothering to put on hat or coat. In the dim lobby we met old Mrs. Fultz who lived in the ground-floor front. She looked at us sharply.

I got Martha a taxi going uptown on Amsterdam. We smiled and nodded goodbye. Then, the cold beginning to get to me, I jogged back to the apartment. My watch, a Hong Kong ripoff of a Cartier, told me I had about twenty minutes to meet Arthur and Jenny Tolliver at Blotto's.

It wasn't the first time I had been unfaithful to a woman who loved me; I knew the drill. You brushed your teeth. Twice. You showered. Twice. Most important, you washed your hair. Perfumes clung. And the smell of sex.

Freshly dressed, I urinated in the bathroom sink, not bothering to jiggle that damned handle. Then I slapped cologne along my jaw and neck and hoped for the best.

I looked at the bills in my jacket pocket. Three twenties. She had given me a ten-buck tip. Nice. Just before I sallied forth, I glanced at my reflection in the bathroom mirror. I hadn't changed.

5

The renaissance of the West Side that had brought antique shops, boutiques, and unisex beauty salons to Columbus Avenue had also brought Blotto's, a restaurant catering to those who equated the quantity of garlic with the quality of Italian cuisine.

When I entered, the noise in the crowded ristorante had already reached demonic levels. The humid air was redolent with a fine mist of aglio, olio d'oliva, and Blotto's special pomodora sauce, acid enough to remove plaque. A banner over the bar read: MERRY XMAS AND HAPPY 1986!

Sweating waiters rushed about, trays balanced overhead. A distraught maître d' screamed at standees to wait at the bar. The ancient Wurlitzer was wheezing "Arrivederci Roma." Somewhere a platter went down with a crash, a woman screamed, a bartender clanged the bell that signified a generous tip.

I searched about, saw Jenny Tolliver, Arthur Enders, and King Hayes, a black model, holding down a corner table for four. I squeezed my way through the mob, shaking the maître d's hand, patting waiters' shoulders, waving to a few people I knew.

I bent over Jenny, kissed her upturned brow.

"And how is my consenting adult tonight?" I said.

"You smell nice," she said. "Where have you been?"

"Arthur," I said, smiling. "King." I slid onto the vacant chair, poured myself a glass of wine from the carafe they had already ordered. "This is on me," I announced to them all.

"What happened?" Arthur Enders asked, pale eyes blinking.

"A rich uncle died," I said, then changed the subject.

We studied the menus, but knew we'd all have the cheapest dinner available: spaghetti and meatballs, a mixed green salad, and another carafe of the house wine which, I claimed, was used by Blotto's proprietor in the early-morning hours to etch counterfeit plates.

We finally persuaded a waiter to take our order, then began to trade stories of the day's activities.

I told them I had struck out at the audition, but had been promised a voice-over and that Sol Hoffheimer had advanced me enough to pay for the dinner.

Arthur Enders announced in high Nebraskan that he was starting work the next day as a Christmas temp at Macy's, selling men's gloves three days a week.

King Hayes was still on his exhilarating holiday job at the Post Office, turning first-class letters right-side up so they would feed into the canceling machine.

Jenny Tolliver, a fabric designer, was the only one with a full-time job. She described her efforts to rip off a Burlington Mills floral pattern for bed linens, on her employer's orders.

"It has to be the same," she said, giggling, "but not so same that we get sued."

Then our food was slammed down on the table, and we busily passed salt and pepper, oil and vinegar, grated cheese, wineglasses and carafe.

We ate heartily, with laughter, chivying, and a third carafe of wine. I was thirty-five. Arthur Enders and King Hayes were thirty-two. Jenny Tolliver was twenty-eight. It all waited for us; we still were convinced of that. Whatever we wanted, whatever we dreamed—it was all possible.

In that crowded, smoky, odorous place, we pushed back from the littered table and were content with the harsh wine, crude food, good talk, and companionship.

We thought life was ours for the taking; occasional setbacks, of course, but in the end we could not fail. As we rose, I tossed money onto the table with the careless gesture of a grand seigneur, lord of the universe.

6

Jenny Tolliver wanted to walk over to Central Park West and get a bus. But I hated waiting, for anything, and insisted on cabbing to her place on West 95th Street.

She was, I thought, a curious woman. Periods of cool, thoughtful, sometimes despondent deliberation alternated with fits of bright, antic activity when she was all laughs and bustle. We had been intimate for four years, and it was her mysterious contradictions that held me.

In the cab going uptown, she leaned close to me. "You're going to hate me," she said.

"Probably," I said. "What for?"

"It's that time of the month."

I thought: Thank you, God. "Ah," I said sorrowfully, "a disappointment."

She leaned closer. "But we can do other things. At least I can. To you."

"Oh, no," I said. "What kind of a man would I be if I accepted pleasure without being able to respond in kind?"

She pulled away to look at me admiringly.

"You're so full of shit," she said, "it's coming out your ears."

I laughed and hugged her to me. "But I will accept a noggin of that lousy brandy you keep for medicinal purposes. Then I'll take off. I'm working all day tomorrow."

She lived in a high-ceilinged studio in an old elephant of an apartment house with an art deco lobby and Watteau-like murals in the elevators.

On her door was pasted a hopeful warning: THESE PREMISES GUARDED BY ATTACK DOGS.

The apartment reflected the dichotomy in her character: light, breezy Swedish modern furniture and dark green and blue drapes and upholstery. Abstract graphics on the walls, a Snoopy doll on the couch. A crystal decanter next to a tin ashtray bearing the legend SOUVENIR OF ATLANTIC CITY.

She poured a dollop of brandy for me and went into the bathroom to change. I took a cigarette from the enameled box on the cocktail table. I sat relaxed, knees crossed. I sipped and smoked, and reflected what a fortunate man I was. (I was an actor; I could do humble.)

She came out, hair down, barefoot, wearing her scruffy old flannel bathrobe with a frayed cord. She curled up on the couch close to me. I put an arm about her shoulders and we snuggled.

"Brandy?" I asked.

"A little," she said.

I took a sip of brandy, held it in my mouth, kissed her firmly, passed the liquor into her mouth. She pulled away, swallowed, coughed.

"My kisses are intoxicating," I declaimed, a French lover pleading his grand passion in an accent more Minsky than Molière.

"And they burn going down," she said.

Jenny Tolliver was a willowy woman with thick chestnut hair. I was so enamored of that hair I made her promise that if I died, she would weave it into a shroud for me.

No single feature dominated her face, but all blended in a lovely serenity. It was a long face, limpid as her body. Everything about her appeared smooth and untroubled.

What I admired most about her was her physical completeness. She was total and absolute. Not a false hue or line awry. That perfection precluded beauty.

"Class," was the word I used when I thought of her, and wondered if my admiration sprang from a fear that it might be a quality I lacked.

"Cuddling is nice," she said, wriggling closer to me.

"They don't call me the Mad Cuddler of Manhattan for nothing."

"What's going to happen to us, Peter?" she asked suddenly, and I took a hasty sip of brandy. "What's going to happen to you and me?"

I looked down at her. "Getting bored with me, Jenny?" I said softly.

"No."

"So why the soul-searching?"

"I don't know. It seems so—so casual."

"I thought that's the way you wanted it," I protested.

"Maybe I did—once. Now I'm not so sure. Peter, could we live together?"

"Where?" I asked. "Not in my place; I need Arthur to help pay the rent. Here, in one room? We'd be at each other's throats in a week."

"You could—" she started, and stopped. I took my arm from about her shoulders.

"Get a steady job?" I said with a tinny laugh. "Nine to five? Doing what? And even if I could, I wouldn't want to. Jenny, do you want me to give up acting?"

"Nooo," she said slowly, "not if you don't want to. But . . ."

I was silent a moment. I didn't want to lose her. Then: "I told Sol today that I was near the breaking point, and I am. I'll make you a deal. Okay? Give me another year. All right? I've put in twelve; another one isn't going to kill me. If I haven't landed something in a year, I'll chuck the whole damned thing. Join the bourgeois. Get a regular job. Will you give me the year?"

She reached up to pull my face down. We kissed. Her lips were soft and yielding and sweet.

"All right," she said. "Next year at Christmastime. Promise?"

"Of course," I said. "Have I ever lied to you?"

"Probably," she said, sighing. "But as long as I don't know . . ."

At the door, I snaked a hand into the flannel bathrobe and touched one of her gentle breasts. She closed her eyes.

"Peter," she said faintly.

"When does the flood recede?" I asked her.

"By Saturday."

"I get paid on Saturday. We'll have a marvelous dinner somewhere and then come back here and have an orgy. Can two people have an orgy?"

"We can try," she said.

In the taxi going home, I reflected on the plight of the actor. A novelist can write books, even if they're never published. An artist can create flights of fancy on canvas and stack it all away. A poet can write the world's greatest sonnets and flush them down the toilet if he likes. But a player has to have an audience to be a player.

I wondered if my relationship with Jenny Tolliver—with all my friends, for that matter—was based on the need for an audience more than the need for love and understanding.

I leaned forward to speak to the cabdriver through the perforated screen. "I yam what I yam," I said, imitating the cartoon Popeye.

"Whatever you say, buddy," the driver said.

7

Like most of out-of-work actors, I had taken a temporary job during the Christmas season. I worked as a salesclerk, Thursdays and Saturdays, 10:00 A.M. to 8:00 P.M., at a fashionable men's boutique on East 57th Street, the King's Arms. ("Where is the King's Arms?" "Around the queen's arse, you silly twerp.")

I found my duties depressing. Mostly, I supposed, because of the marvelously beautiful and expensive items I sold: wallets of buttery pigskin, waistcoats of silky suede with pearl buttons, ascots of gossamer paisley. Things I couldn't afford.

And, because of a sharp-eyed manager, things I couldn't steal.

To endure, I made my contacts with customers a series of theatrical shticks. I would be a fawning homosexual, a sniffy London clark, an excitable green immigrant, even a defecting Russian ballet dancer.

The customers were intrigued and convinced. I survived by not being myself.

On Thursday, I volunteered to take an early lunch hour, at noon. I shrugged the Burberry over my shoulders like an open cape, leaving sleeves and skirt to swing free. I tossed my scarf about my throat, tilted my Irish hat. Driven by an impulse I could not understand, I set forth, walking rapidly north on Madison Avenue.

It was a muffled kind of day, gray and wrinkled as an old hide. The air smelled of ash, and people scurried.

The Barcarole Boutique was in the middle of the block between 67th and 68th streets. A handsome limestone townhouse had been vandalized into a four-story luxury shop offering women's coats, suits, dresses, sportswear, accessories, jewelry. Mostly from Milan and Rome. No sales or discounts at the Barcarole.

The knife-eyed guard at the door allowed me to enter. I strolled about the first floor, perhaps hoping to bump into the mysterious M.T.? I could not have said. I played the bemused shopper, and saw immediately there was little I could afford to buy Jenny Tolliver for Christmas.

I realized with a shock that the money I made in one ten-hour day at the King's Arms was less than the money Martha had given me for her "good, hard bang." It was an unsettling comparison.

I left the store and spent a few moments gazing longingly at the window display. It was a New Year's Eve scene: confetti, streamers, tin horns—and two exquisite sequined gowns, one black, one white, with feathered boas and elbow-length gloves of kid glacé. Even the plaster mannequins were disdainful of my stares.

I crossed Madison Avenue and stood at the curb, watching the parade of chic, well-groomed East Side women in and out of the Barcarole.

They all, young and old, had the erect, heads-up haughtiness of the wealthy. I noted their strut with envy and a kind of awe, wondering how money conferred its own beauty.

I stood there for almost ten minutes, unable to give up the sight of that affluent procession. Finally I turned away. I had a hot dog and a caustic orange drink at a fast-food joint. Before I headed back to the King's Arms, I called my answering service. More from habit than any hope of a life-changing message.

The operator told me a woman named Martha had left a number and wanted me to call back.

I dialed her.

She said she'd like to see me tomorrow.

I said I thought I could manage it.

8

Martha really made me put out. She bucked and reared like a demented mustang. I hung on, gave it my best shot and hoped her fingernails wouldn't leave scratches on my ass that Jenny Tolliver might notice.

After a while, of course, little worries like that evaporated. I got caught up in my own drive and wanted to punish her for using me. So I slammed into her, and she, grunting, loved it.

Spent, I collapsed and put lips to her impressive breasts. She would not release me, but held me close, panting.

"Ah, Jesus," she said.

"Peter," I reminded her.

"Listen," she said. "I've got to go make wee-wee. But don't get out of bed. There's something I want to talk to you about and this is the best place for it."

When she headed for the bathroom, she didn't take her handbag. The moment the door closed behind her, I was out of bed and fumbling through the bag. Wallet, driver's license, credit cards, makeup, condoms, tissues, keys, this and that.

Her name was Martha Twombly. More important, a sterling silver case of business cards identified her as the manager of the Barcarole Boutique. The *manager,* for God's sake! I was back in bed, smoking a cigarette, when she rejoined me.

She lay on her hip and dug a forefinger gently into my navel.

"That was a good one," she said.

"Satisfaction guaranteed or your money back."

"Yeah," she said, smiling. "Well . . . Peter, have you got any friends?"

I turned my head to look at her. "Of course I have friends."

"Could you get a guy for me?"

I stared, then understood. "Ahh, Chollie," I said sorrowfully in a passable imitation of Marlon Brando in *On the Waterfront,* "I coulda been a contendah."

She laughed. "Nothing personal, Peter. You're great, and that's the truth. But I like variety—you know?"

"You told me. The new woman. Choosing your pleasures."

"That's right."

"Sure," I said. "I can get you a guy. Reasonably clean."

"Fine," she said briskly. "You set it up. Then give me a call. Twenty for your trouble."

"Fair enough," I said.

She looked at me shrewdly. "But not as good as sixty—right? Not to worry, Peter. A friend of mine would like to meet you. Fifty. Interested?"

"Sure," I said, without hesitating.

"Monday, okay? Three o'clock? Her husband's going on a business trip."

"Perfect."

"That's it then," she said, slapping my hip. "Now I've got to run."

"I'll see you to a cab."

"You've got manners," she said.

9

Arthur Enders was so pale that I had once referred to him as "a slightly flushed albino." His skin was pallid, hair flaxen, eyes a washed-out blue. The would-be playwright usually wore suits in beige or off-white hues, making him look like a shambling wraith.

We had been roommates for two years when, without warning, Enders announced that he had decided to become a homosexual.

"Not from any physical or emotional need," he had explained earnestly. "This is purely an intellectual decision on my part. If I'm going to write plays, I've got to know how all kinds of people think and feel and react. I've got to experience *everything.*"

"Beautiful," I said. "Like murdering your mother, screwing your sister, and buggering a wild turkey?"

Enders turned out to be the most inept homosexual in Manhattan's gay community, where he soon earned the sobriquet of "Señor Klutz." He had a one-night stand with an S&M fancier, lost the key to the handcuffs, and a locksmith had to be called to release the poor fellow from the bedpost.

Another time, it was reported, he showed up for an assignation carrying a tube of Krazy Glue instead of K-Y Jelly. Homosexuals pleaded with him to go back in the closet.

This phase of Enders' life lasted almost a year, and he claimed he had learned much that would be of value in his writing.

"That's fine," I said. "Now will you get rid of that disgusting underwear with 'Home of the Whopper' printed on the fly?"

On Friday night I treated my roommate to dinner. We went to a steak joint on West 72nd Street, but settled for the "Jumbo Steakburger."

We had vodka gimlets and demolished half a loaf of garlic bread before our food was served.

"How's the play coming?" I asked. It was a four-hour epic of sensitivity about a boy coming of age in Nebraska.

"I really think I've got it now," Enders said hopefully. "I'm on the fifth rewrite. The only thing that bothers me is that the boy's childhood might be too downbeat."

"If people had happy childhoods, America wouldn't have any playwrights."

"Gee, I suppose so," Arthur said. "Peter, you never talk about your childhood."

"About average," I said, shrugging. "Not so good, not so bad."

"Do you have any family?"

"Of course I have family. My parents are dead, but I have a married sister in Spokane. She's married to a guy who owns a car wash, and they've got eight kids. Every year she sends me a birthday card, a month late. It's a good relationship."

"I've got a big family," Enders said, sighing. "Golly, no one *ever* dies. I wish they wouldn't send me money. I know they can't afford it."

"If they can't afford it, they wouldn't send it. Besides, when your play is a big success on Broadway, you'll pay them back."

"Yes," Enders said, brightening, "that's true."

Then our rare steakburgers arrived, with French fries and a side order of sliced tomatoes and Bermuda onions. Arthur asked for more garlic bread, and we split a bottle of Heineken between us.

"Hey," I said, "I had a weird one at the boutique yesterday. This woman who's been in at least three times. Reeks of money. Buys expensive stuff. Nothing but the best. But all in different sizes. So I figure she's buying gifts for several guys—right?"

"Her sons?" Arthur Enders asked guilelessly.

"She's not *that* old," I said, busy with my food.

"Is she good-looking?"

"She takes good care of herself. Anyway, I got the idea that she's coming on to me. Everytime she comes in, she wants me to wait on her. So yesterday she buys a cashmere sweater, and while I'm writing up the sale, she says, would I like to jump her?"

"You're joking!"

"I swear," I said, holding up my palm. "I couldn't believe it either, but that's what she wanted. And here's the kicker: She was willing to pay."

"Good gravy! How much?"

"Fifty."

"Wow."

"I was tempted," I said. "Fifty bucks for a quick toss in the hay."

Enders, who was madly in love with Jenny Tolliver, said indignantly, "You couldn't do that to Jenny."

"Of course not. So I told this woman I loved my wife. She laughed and asked me if I knew anyone else who might be interested."

"Peter, she sounds like a flake."

"No," I said seriously. "Just a well-heeled woman getting a little long in the tooth who knows what she wants and is willing to pay for it."

"My gosh, what's the world coming to," Enders said wonderingly. "How about coffee and a brandy?"

Arthur had recently taken to smoking a pipe. Now he packed it carefully, used three matches, couldn't get it lighted, and set it aside. He took a gulp of brandy and clenched his teeth.

"Fifty dollars?" he asked.

I was amazed, not for the first time, at how easily the innocent can be manipulated.

"Interested?" I said casually.

"Gee, I don't know," Enders said, frowning. "Where would we do it?"

"Oh hell—take her to our place. I'm out all day. Listen, you're the guy who said you want to experience everything."

"Golly," Enders said, laughing nervously. "You think she'll come by the store again?"

"I'm sure of it," I said. "Want me to set it up for you?"

"Uh . . . How long would I have to, uh, be with her?"

"That's up to you, but don't give her over an hour."

10

I didn't know if there was any word for a male prostitute. "Gigolo" came close, I supposed, but that conjured up the image of a swish with patent-leather hair and a toothbrush mustache who was always dancing the tango.

There was really no one word that defined what I had done with
Martha Twombly. But there was a word for what I was doing with Arthur
Enders. Pimp. One who took money for supplying the body of another.

The thought occurred to me that if I was procuring, so was Martha
Twombly. I was providing the man, she the woman. The world turned
upside down. I wondered if she was being paid for her services just as I was.

I pondered these matters while waiting for Jenny Tolliver at the bar
of a French bistro on 51st Street, just west of Eighth Avenue.

I had come directly from the King's Arms, and still wore my "boutique uniform": a navy blue blazer with brass buttons, gray flannel slacks,
black tasseled loafers, a white shirt (button-down collar), and a tie with the
stripe of a British regiment to which, obviously, I did not belong.

In the bar mirror, my image seemed to me that of a darkly handsome
man with a sardonic smile. Something of the devil in that smile, I decided.
Something of the eternal tempter. And on my hip, the comforting pressure
of a relatively plump wallet: my pay from the King's Arms and what was
left of Martha's fee.

Jenny Tolliver came rushing in a little after 8:30, breathless and
glowing. The theater crowd had departed; we were ushered to a corner table
where we sat at right angles to each other. We ordered gin Gibsons, held
hands, and beamed.

Jenny looked smashing in black silk slacks and a tunic of honey-
colored challis. Her makeup was minimal. That marvelous mane of chestnut hair swung free. She was the loveliest creature in the restaurant, and I
told her so.

"Peter," she said, laughing, "there are only three other women
here."

"I know," I said, "but a few of the busboys aren't bad. What did you
do today?"

She had cleaned her apartment, taken in her laundry and dry-clean-
ing, gone shopping, and then had spent the remainder of the day working on
fabric designs at home. She was fiercely determined to have her own studio
one day.

"My portfolio is getting fatter," she reported happily. "Some really
good things. Much better work than I do on my job. Is that awful?"

"What's awful about it?" I demanded. "You want to be an entrepre-
neur. Your own boss. It's the great American dream. And any way you can
swing that is justified."

"You think the end justifies the means?"

I grinned. "As someone said: If the end doesn't justify the means,
what the hell does? Let's order."

We both had frogs' legs, so garlicky that when we finished, we shared a saucer of chopped parsley to sweeten our breath. We finished the dinner with espresso and Strega.

"That was scrumptious," Jenny said and kissed the back of my hand. "Thank you."

"What would you like to do now?" I asked benignly.

She considered, eyes half-closed. Her elbow was on the table, cheek on palm. Her hair fell glinting over one shoulder. In the dim, soft light, she seemed so desirable that I was weak with longing.

"What I'd like to do," she said slowly, "is—Peter, are you listening?"

"Of course I'm listening."

"Well, the first thing I'd like us to do is buy a bottle of chilled white wine."

"And then?"

"Buy a Sunday *Times.*"

"And then?"

"Go to my apartment, make ourselves comfortable, drink wine, and read the *Times.* You can have the magazine first."

"And then?"

"Then, when the wine is finished, go to bed."

"I see nothing to object to there," I said gravely. "Let's do it."

And so we did.

She had bought me a bathrobe for my birthday: a tent of a robe in creamy wool flannel with a monk's cowl, belted with a thick rope. I kept it at her apartment for occasions like this. She wore a yellow nylon nightgown and matching peignoir.

By 1:00 A.M. the wine was finished; but not the *Times.* I tossed the sports section aside. "Let's go to bed," I said.

She nodded.

"Are you all right?" I asked her. "The monthly madness is finished?"

"I think so," she said cautiously. "But maybe we better wait for tomorrow. Peter? Do you mind?"

"Of course not."

"I adore it in the morning," she said dreamily. "It seems so much more intimate and—and loving. It's so nice to wake up and be in bed with someone."

"Someone!"

"With you," she said hastily. "You know what I mean. Peter, are you sure you don't mind?"

"I may get carried away and nibble on your elbow."

"You've been so sweet and considerate tonight," she said, sighing. "You even buttered my breadstick for me. You've never done *that* before." Suddenly she looked at me narrowly. "Peter, you haven't done something *awful* and are being nice to me out of guilt?"

I groaned. "That's what I get for being the tender, attentive lover. No, I have not done anything *awful.*"

"Cross your heart and hope to die?"

I laughed, and kissed her.

We opened the convertible couch, turned out the lamps, disrobed. I adjusted the venetian blind on the front window so the glow of a streetlight streamed through. I lay down beside her. I pulled sheet and blanket away.

I never tired of looking at her. Small breasts. A wand of a waist. Legs that went on forever. Her flesh flowed smoothly, curves artfully joined. There was no part of her that did not enchant my eye and woo my touch.

For one mordant moment I thought that this woman deserved better than Peter Scuro. But that mood passed, and we fell asleep in each other's arms, murmuring.

And in the morning, we came together in languorous passion, moving like somnambulists. There was a smear of kisses, throaty gasps, a hot and crude grappling. Fevered flesh awoke; we used each other mightily, entwined in her hair and crying out.

Ten minutes later she was asleep again. I disengaged myself as gently as I could, dressed, took her keys from her purse, and slipped out the door. Double-locking it behind me, I went down in the elevator and headed west to Broadway. The cold air stung. The whole city seemed to be hibernating.

On Broadway, I bought fresh bagels, cream cheese, lox, two smoked chubs, a big Bermuda onion, and a container of orange juice. Jenny was still sleeping when I returned. I put the coffee on, set the little dining table, and started making bagel, cheese, lox, and onion sandwiches.

I was unwrapping the chubs when I glanced up and saw she was watching me from the bed.

"You dirty dog," I called. "You've been awake all the time, letting me do the work."

She held her bare arms out to me. "Come here," she said.

I sat on the edge of the bed, embraced her, stroked her boneless back. She pulled away to hold my face between her palms, look deep into my eyes.

"Lovely, lovely, lovely," she said.

"I took advantage of you," I said. "While you were sound asleep."

"Hah!" she said.

She dashed into the bathroom, and came out, robed, just as I was pouring coffee. Her face looked clear and scrubbed. I held the chair for her, leaned over to nuzzle her neck. She reached up to pull me closer.

"Darling," she breathed.

"Who's Herbert?" I asked.

"Who?"

"Herbert. This morning, when we were having it off, you kept moaning, 'Herbert, Herbert, oh, Herbert.' "

"You bastard!" she said, "I've never been unfaithful to you and you know it."

I did know it.

I left the cleanup to her, went back into the bathroom, and took a hot shower. I used her electric shaver to diminish the blue shadow on my jaw. Then I dressed again.

While Jenny went in to shower and dress, I sat comfortably in what she called "Peter's chair." Scanning the *Times'* employment ads, I was bemused by the number of jobs for which I was not qualified. I tossed the paper aside and looked about this pleasant place.

Safe, warm domesticity. To savor and enjoy, like those garlicky frogs' legs last night. But as a steady diet?

Jenny came out of the bathroom, dressed, booted, and ready to go.

"Bundle up," I said. "It's nippy out there."

But when we went down to the street, the sun had warmed and the wind had softened; men and women strolled with their coats opened.

On our way to Central Park, we passed a church that had just ended a service.

Jenny Tolliver said: "Will you attend midnight mass with me on Christmas Eve?"

"No, thanks," I said. "I've caught that show. Great tunes; lousy lyrics."

"I thought you were brought up Catholic."

"I was," I said. "But I quit when I realized that saints are just as dead as sinners."

11

On Monday morning I had a "cattle call": preliminary interviews for a series of TV commercials featuring a cowboy wearing Bronco jeans.

"Do I look like the Western type?" I had asked Jenny Tolliver.

"Western Italy maybe," she said.

Arthur Enders was working that day, so we shared a cab to Seventh Avenue and 36th Street. Enders walked down to Macy's and I walked over to Madison Avenue.

The office of the production company was thronged with would-be cowboys, some already wearing faded jeans, fringed buckskin jackets, and Stetsons. One even had spurs buckled to his high boots.

Ages ranged from eighteen to forty. They were handsome, rugged, or craggy. Most of them were tanned (naturally or artificially), and hard and lanky in build. I imagined the field day Martha Twombly would have with that gang.

I waited two hours, standing most of the time, before I was called into the inner office. There was one woman in there, a tall, frosty blonde. She took one look at me and didn't return my smile.

"Sorry," she said tonelessly, "we're looking for a younger type. If you'd care to leave your comp with the girl in the outer office . . ." Her voice trailed away.

I refused to give her the satisfaction of telling her "Up yours!"

Out on the street, I finally found a public phone that was working and called Martha Twombly at the number she'd left with my answering service (which wasn't hers—she wasn't in the phone book—and wasn't the Barcarole Boutique).

Either her home number was unlisted or she had a private line at the Barcarole that didn't go through their switchboard.

She picked up on the third ring.

"This is Peter," I said.

"I hope," she said tartly, "you are not going to disappoint my friend."

She was all business.

"I'll be there," I said. "Three o'clock?"

"Right."

"What's her name?"

There was a short pause. Then: "Glenda."

"Glenda," I repeated. "Now about that young man you wanted to interview . . ."

I didn't know exactly why I was speaking in such circumlocutions, but it seemed smart.

". . . will tomorrow be all right?" I finished.

"Let me take a look at my schedule," she said crisply. "Yes, to-morrow will do nicely. At noon."

"Good," I said. "Let's keep—"

But she had already hung up.

It was cold in that kiosk, so I went into a nearby luncheonette for a cup of black coffee and a toasted English muffin. As I ate, I reflected that in the past week I had made $120 from Twombly, with the promise of twenty more for setting up her meeting with Arthur Enders, and fifty (plus a possible tip) from Glenda.

Not only was that more than I had made in the last three months from my acting career, but it was cash income that the IRS would never see. A sweet deal. I didn't want it to end.

I went back to the phone and called Sol Hoffheimer to tell him I'd bombed out on the Bronco jeans interview.

"I'm too old," I said. "They're looking for a boy of nine."

"Yeah," Hoffheimer said mournfully. "I know what you mean."

"Sol, do you know anyone in the rag business?"

"I got a cousin on Seventh Avenue."

"There's a favor I'd like to ask you . . ."

I told him that a friend of mine, a female model, had done some work for the Barcarole Boutique, couldn't collect her fee, and wanted to sic her lawyer on the owners.

"Sol, could you find out who owns the Barcarole?"

"I'll ask my cousin," Hoffheimer promised. "If he doesn't know, he can find out. Call me in a day or so."

Since I was in the neighborhood, I worked my way up Madison Avenue, lugging my portfolio and leaving my new composite at three adver-tising agencies, two TV film production companies, and an outfit that specialized in commercial shows for large corporations.

I had done this kind of donkey work a hundred times before. I knew the chances of someone looking at the comp and calling me for a job were practically nil.

But today it didn't depress me. I knew where my next buck was coming from.

12

Glenda was almost twenty minutes late. She was a petite brunette with a helmet of shiny black hair. Not ugly, but plain. Undeniably plain. Expensively dressed. A trim little figure.

She looked at everything except me. I gestured at the dilapidated apartment.

"We call it the Taj Mahal," I said.

"I think," she said in a choked voice, "it's—it's very, uh, quaint."

Suddenly she was weeping.

"Hey," I said. "It's not *that* bad."

She shook her head side to side, short hair fanning.

"Would you like something?" I asked solicitously.

"Water," she said in a low voice. "Please."

When I brought the glass, she was seated on the couch, head in her hands. I had to tap her on the shoulder to make her look up. She drank in frantic gulps, then let me put the empty glass aside and sit next to her.

"What's wrong?" I asked gently.

She rummaged through her purse for a tissue.

"I've never done anything like this before," she said, sniffling.

"Look," I said, smiling at her, "if you like, you can put on your hat and coat and walk out of here right now. It's not worth your getting so upset."

"No," she said defiantly. "I'm going through with it."

"Sure?"

"Yes."

"All right. But remember that you can change your mind anytime you like."

I took her by the hand and led her to the bedroom. When she saw the rumpled bed, she began weeping again. I sat her next to me on the bed and put an arm about her shoulders.

"Why are you going through with this, Glenda?" I asked softly.

"It's my husband. He cheats on me all the time. I know he does. What am I—chopped liver?"

"No," I said solemnly, "you are not chopped liver."

She took a deep breath and looked at me timidly with brimming eyes.

"I don't know, uh, what to do," she confessed in a quavery voice. "I mean, do we get undressed—or what?"

"It's up to you," I said.

She considered. "I think we should get undressed. I don't want to wrinkle my dress."

Her fingers were trembling so much that I had to help her. When she was naked, she scuttled into bed and pulled the sheet up to her chin. When I undressed, she turned her head away.

I got into bed alongside her, my body not touching hers. I began to stroke her bare shoulder and arm.

"You're so lovely," I murmured. "So lovely."

She whirled around to face me.

"Am I?" she said eagerly. "Am I *really?*"

It took me almost a half-hour of kissing and whispering how beautiful she was before she came alive beneath my hands. Nipples turgid, flesh blood-flushed, she was gripping me, gasping, nails digging in.

"Oh my God!" she kept saying. "Oh my God!"

When we were done (she before, during, and after me), she would not release me, but clung desperately. When I looked down, I saw she was crying again.

"Now what?" I asked.

"I'm so happy," she said tearfully.

While we dressed, she asked if she might see me again. I told her I'd be delighted, and jotted down the number of my answering service. I wondered if I should have business cards printed. Vice president might be a fitting title.

She gave me my fee in a sealed white envelope which, I thought, showed a nice delicacy.

I took her to a cab. ("You're a real gentleman," she said.) Mrs. Fultz was putting out her garbage in the areaway and looked at us queerly as we passed. I didn't even glance at the old biddy.

That night, Arthur Enders, King Hayes, and I went to Blotto's for dinner. They had spaghetti and meatballs. I had steak tartare.

13

At one time I believed I had the makings of a great tragedian, but an acting coach had a different idea:

"Scuro," he said, "you have a natural talent for farce. Onstage and off. It's farce all the way for you."

I had to admit that judgment was not completely inaccurate. Too many incidents in my life could be considered farcical.

Item: My teetotal parents had died in a nightclub fire. It was the first (and last) time they had visited such a place.

Item: I had been expelled from Notre Dame in my sophomore year following a complaint by parents of a fifteen-year-old girl. I could have sworn she was eighteen, but had neglected to ask.

Item: During the summer I'd toured as a clown with a small circus. I'd been a tremendous success with children.

Item: I'd delighted audiences in a small Chicago cabaret with my impersonation of a drunken actor trying to recite speeches from *Lear* and *Macbeth.*

Item: A year after I came to New York, I met and married Sally Lee Soorby, an ex-pompon girl and baton twirler from Macon, Georgia.

I married her because I was infatuated with her fresh blond pretti- ness and her enthusiasm in bed. We were divorced about a year later. She returned to Macon and married a man who owned a fish hatchery.

I had long since given up questioning why my life seemed a succes- sion of haphazard encounters, ridiculous coincidences and bizarre acci- dents.

No man was master of his fate. It was purely a matter of luck. You paid your money and took your chances.

"Go with the flow," I was fond of remarking. "Go with the flow!"

The unplanned meeting with Martha Twombly and all that ensued were, I told myself, merely another drama in this theater of the absurd. But I was more than curious to know what role fate had chosen me to play.

14

I called Hoffheimer on Tuesday morning. Sol took a deep breath and started:

"The Barcarole Boutique is owned by Roman Enterprises. They're in the Empire State Building. Until a year ago, it was owned by a big Italian conglomerate that's in fabrics, fashion, leather goods, book publishing, and olive oil. When they sold it to Roman Enterprises, everyone was surprised because the place is a gold mine. Roman isn't the real owner. It's a company that's owned by a company that's owned by a company. Anyway, my cousin says when you get to the top—except no one knows if it *is* the top—there's mob money involved."

"Mob money?" I said, dazed.

"Sure. You know the three biggest moneymakers in the world, don't you? General Motors, the Mafia, and the Vatican. The mob has the smallest gross income of the three, but when it comes to net profit—*mamma mia!*"

"Yeah, Sol," I said. "Thanks. You've been a big help."

I hung up, not knowing exactly why I had asked in the first place. Still, such a stray piece of information could come in handy.

I stayed out of the apartment all day, leaving Arthur Enders a clear field with Martha Twombly. I made the rounds of theatrical producers in Times Square, dropping off my new comp and shmoozing with the secretaries.

On Tuesday night I had a date with Jenny Tolliver.

I didn't sleep over, but got back to my own place a little after midnight. Enders was awake, working on his play. He looked up and grinned as I walked in.

"I bought a bottle of vodka," he said. "It's in the kitchen. Make yourself a drink."

"Screw the drink," I said. "How did you make out with Martha?"

"I made out okay," Enders said, still grinning. "She gave me a ten-buck tip. Gee, she's a nice lady."

"Seems to be."

"She said she might want to see me again, and if she does, she'll call. Did you give her our number, Peter?"

"My answering service number. So she was, ah, satisfied?"

"I guess so; she kept laughing. Gosh, Peter, she's strong. I really worked."

"No hangups about taking money from a woman?"

Enders frowned and blinked a few times. "I thought there would be, but I can honestly say I didn't feel funny about it at all. Martha says a lot of financially independent women are career-oriented and don't want all the hassle of an emotional relationship. They're not interested in a husband and children, or even a steady boyfriend—at least not at this stage in their lives —so there's a real need for guys who can provide sexual servicing on a professional level at a reasonable price. Golly, that's interesting—don't you think so, Peter? It would make a great play."

"What would you call it? *As You Like It* has already been used."

Arthur stood and pulled his wallet from his hip pocket. "Look, you set this thing up. I want to give you ten of what I made."

"Oh no," I said. "I couldn't."

"It's just the tip she gave me. You said fifty, and I got fifty. So you should get something for arranging it."

"Okay," I said, plucking the bill from Enders' fingers. "Thanks."

I called my answering service on Wednesday morning. There was a message from Martha asking me to call. She picked up on the first ring and was brusque.

"I want to see you at ten o'clock tonight at the place we met."

"The Losers'? I'll be there. What is—"

"Ten o'clock," she repeated sharply and hung up.

I spent all day wondering if her meeting with Enders hadn't been as satisfactory as described. If she complained, well, I'd tell her she couldn't expect to win them all.

I got to the Losers' Place a few minutes before ten. Martha Twombly was already there, sitting in a back booth, hunched over a drink. There were a few people at the bar and tables, but thankfully no one I knew.

I slid onto the seat opposite her and, when the waitress slouched over, asked for a vodka gimlet. Martha drained her glass and ordered another straight scotch. As usual, she was expertly groomed, wearing a classic suit of dark, chalk-striped flannel with a ruffled jabot.

"Good evening," I said pleasantly. "You're looking well."

She didn't answer.

"What's this—" I started.

"You listen," she said, her voice crackling. "When I fix you up with a friend of mine, I don't want you giving her your number or making dates I don't know about."

Then I was certain she was getting a cut off the top.

"Glenda?" I said mildly. "She asked if she could see me again, so I gave her my number. What's the harm?"

She leaned across the table, thrusting her angry face at me. "I don't want you doing it."

"Look," I said. "I'm new to this game. If there are ground rules, you should have told me before. But don't come on hard because I was polite to your friend."

She gradually calmed, pulling out a cigarette and waiting for me to light it.

"I guess you're right," she said grudgingly. "But now you know."

"Now I know," I agreed.

"I'm new to this game, too," she confessed, though neither of us had named the "game." "We'll take it slow and figure out the angles as we go along."

I nodded. "Glenda was satisfied with the service?"

"I think she's in love with you."

I laughed. "God forbid. I've got a lady at the moment and she's all I want."

She looked at me curiously. "I don't know much about you, Peter. Do you work?"

"Unemployed actor."

"I figured. You have the look."

"Hungry, you mean? During the Christmas season, I'm working two days a week at the King's Arms, a men's boutique. You know it?"

"Nice stuff," she said. "What happens after Christmas?"

"Nothing. And I mean *nothing.*"

"Good," she said unexpectedly. "That'll make things easier. Let's have another round."

I decided that if I tried to match this woman drink for drink, I'd end up in Intensive Care at Roosevelt Hospital. I switched to vodka and water, determined to nurse it.

"Are you free on Friday night?" she asked.

"Only for my friends," I said, grinning. "If you want to know if I'm busy, no, I am not busy on Friday night."

"Fine. An old friend of mine flew in from the Coast on Monday. For shopping and to see some shows. She's staying at the Bedlington on Park. She's been going every night. Dinner at friends' homes. The theater. New discos. She's flying out early Saturday morning, so she didn't schedule anything for Friday night. Just wants a quiet dinner, a few drinks."

"Sounds reasonable."

"She wants an escort. She'll pay you a hundred and for everything else: cabs, dinner, and so forth. She just wants company for the evening. Interested?"

"Sure. She doesn't want anything more than company?"

Martha Twombly shrugged. "That's up to you. I should warn you, she's pushing sixty. But very regal looking. She's been divorced twice. Very smart and very wealthy. She's an investment counselor and does well at it."

"What's her name?"

"Grace Stewart. Pick her up at the Bedlington at eight o'clock on Friday. Don't disappoint me, Peter."

"Have I ever? Which reminds me—how did you and Arthur get along?"

She laughed and drained her glass. "He's sweet, but a little ineffectual. Not my type. But I know some women who'll love him. Let's have another drink."

"You go ahead. I'm fine with this."

She was slugging scotch like there was no tomorrow, but I couldn't see that it was having much effect. Her face might have been slightly flushed, but she sat erect and there was no slurring in her speech.

"You don't know any blacks, do you?" she asked suddenly.

"Sure," I said promptly, "I know a black. Big guy. Part-time actor, part-time model, part-time this and that."

"Think he'd be interested?"

"I can try."

"Will he take thirty?"

I looked at her stonily. "Sorry. I'm an Equal Opportunity Employer."

"Okay," she said, laughing. "Fifty for him and twenty for you for setting it up."

She finished her drink and fumbled in her purse.

"Reach under the table," she said.

I reached and she slipped bills into my hand.

"Fifty," she said. "Twenty for Arthur, twenty for the black, and the rest for these lousy drinks."

"They don't call it the Losers' Place for nothing. I'll call you about the black. His name is King."

"King?" she said. "And I shall be Queen of the May. I like you, Peter."

"I like you, too."

"My life hasn't exactly been a bed of roses," she said casually. "A lot of hard knocks. But I've gradually developed an instinct for the main chance. I think we've got something good going here. Let's play it slow and cagey. You can make a few bucks and have a few laughs."

I smiled wanly, with the familiar sensation of being pushed into a future over which I had no control.

15

Martha was taking a cab to the Upper East Side and offered to drop me. We went north on Eighth, into Broadway, into Amsterdam, and I got out a block from Blotto's.

King Hayes wasn't there. The bartender said he had been in earlier but had called it a night. I picked up a bottle of Manischewitz Concord wine, which King preferred to Dom Perignon, and headed west.

Hayes lived in a superannuated Single Resident Only hotel off Broadway. He had a cramped one-room apartment he shared with a colony of energetic roaches. The bathroom down the hall could only be improved by a wrecker's ball. Graffiti was everywhere, and visitors breathed through their mouths because the odor made your knees buckle.

"Who's that?"

"Peter Scuro."

There was the sound of locks, bolts, chains being opened. King peered out, then grinned. When I was inside, he went through the routine of barricading us in.

I looked around. "Be it ever so humble . . ." I said.

It was a hundred times worse than my pad. A scarred metal cot for a bed. Stained sink in the corner. One window painted shut and covered with a torn green shade. A crusted hot plate. A rickety table and two wobbly chairs. A chest of drawers tattooed with cigarette burns.

On the walls were taped 8 × 10 glossies of King Hayes' modeling assignments. In sports clothes, swimming trunks, lifting a glass of beer. And many nudes. He was built like Michelangelo's *David,* but hung somewhat better.

I handed him the brown paper bag. "Greeks bearing gifts," I said.

King looked inside, then cast his eyes upward. "I thank thee, Lord," he said. "Let me rinse out a couple of glasses."

"Not for me," I said. "You go ahead."

I sat down gingerly on one of the teetering wooden chairs, watching as he shook the dust from an empty peanut butter jar and filled it with wine. He raised the jar to me.

"God bless you, massa," he said, drained the wine, refilled the jar.

He was big, big, big. And black, black, black. Clients who felt they had to include a Negro in their magazine ads or TV commercials usually preferred blacks who looked like heavily tanned Caucasians. Hayes was undeniably African, with a splayed nose and thick lips. So modeling jobs were few, and as for acting . . . How many times can they do *Othello?*

He had been a longshoreman, truck driver, cabbie, wrestler, bodyguard, short order cook, waiter, masseur, seaman, and had sold Bibles.

He sat opposite me, sipped wine, and smiled genially. I didn't waste time. "I know a woman who wants to get laid," I said.

"Lucky you."

"She wants a black."

"Oh-ho," Hayes said, his smile still in place. "Is this a charity case?"

"No. She'll pay fifty."

The smile faded. "I didn't know you were in that line of work, Peter."

"I just started," I said. "A whole new career."

"Yeah," Hayes said. "Where could we go?"

"My place. On Friday, when Arthur works all day; I'll make myself scarce. Okay?"

"For fifty? I guess."

"Meet me at Blotto's tomorrow night about ten and I'll give you the details."

"You get a cut of my fifty?"

"No. The lady's taking care of me."

"Jesus," he said, shaking his head. "If my mother ever finds out, she'll kill me."

16

The Bedlington was a mossy hotel with a staff that tiptoed and whispered. Faded Oriental rugs covered parquet floors. In its one accommodation to the modern world, the Bedlington had converted its billiard room to a cocktail lounge. Ladies served only at tables.

I arrived promptly at eight o'clock. I was charmed by the single house phone, a contraption of gilt and mother-of-pearl that looked like a survivor of La Belle Epoque. I asked for Miss Grace Stewart.

"Peter Scuro here," I said.

"Ah yes," a musical voice said. "You're very prompt. Please wait for me in the cocktail lounge. Order what you like and a gin and bitters for me. Tell the bartender—his name is Harry—that it's for me; he knows how I like it."

The lounge, dark as a cave, was empty except for the bartender. I asked for a kir for myself and a gin and bitters for Miss Stewart. I watched, fascinated, as Harry measured precisely three drops of bitters into an Old-Fashioned glass, swirled them about, coating the inside of the glass, and dumped the residue.

He then added two ice cubes, no more, no less, and filled the glass to the brim with Tanqueray gin. He stirred gently with a long-handled spoon and, finally, added an olive stuffed with a pepper.

"Interesting," I said. "I must try that someday."

"Within walking distance of your bed, sir," Harry respectfully advised.

I took the two drinks to a corner table. I was halfway through the kir when a woman entered the lounge, peered about in the gloom, started toward me. I stood up, smiling.

"Miss Stewart?" I said.

"Grace," she said. "And you're Peter. How nice."

Her handshake was firm. She was carrying a sealskin coat over her arm. I took it from her and got her seated. She moved nimbly, but Martha had been honest; sixty was about right.

She was elegantly dressed in a sheath that glittered. But what caught my attention was a skullcap of silver paillettes.

"I love your yarmulke," I said.

She laughed and squeezed my hand. "I think you and I are going to get along just fine."

We did.

She had hired a stretch limousine for the evening. TV set, bar, and calfskin upholstery. I lolled back.

"I wonder what the poor folks are doing," I said.

"Do you care?" she said.

"Not really."

We had dinner downtown at Windows on the World. When the sommelier presented the list, Grace Stewart asked me, "Are you a wine maven?"

"Only if the bottles have handles," I said.

She ordered knowledgeably. I drank what she drank, ate what she ate. I was a long way from the Losers' Place and, looking around, decided this was where I belonged.

I had come prepared to entertain her with theatrical shticks, impersonations, dialect jokes, raffish anecdotes about my stage career. She didn't give me a chance. "You don't have to be on with me," she said.

She regaled me with scandalous stories about life on the Coast: Beverly Hills, Bel Air, the movie and television crowd. She knew everyone and had been everywhere. She had a taste for gossip and a cruel wit.

"You're wicked," I told her.

"Am I not?" she said happily.

Another woman I could not match drink for drink. After dinner, we sat at the bar and she had two vodka stingers while I had one. We looked north over the island of Manhattan: necklaces of lights, a rich, rosy glow.

"You're sweet," she said, stroking my cheek. "And handsome in a dirty kind of way."

"Dirty?"

"Sinister," she said. "I like that."

When we went down to the limousine, she told the chauffeur to take us to Eleventh Avenue between 47th and 48th streets.

"Charming neighborhood," I said.

"I want you to see this place," she said. "If it's still there and I can find it."

She had a sharp, hard face, unlined, with a nose like a scimitar. A slender, twisty body. The hands were young. Hair a shiny gray beneath that skullcap. Her legs were bare, which bemused me. She caught me looking. She laughed, took my hand, put it on her bare calf.

"Shaved," she said.

We found the place she was looking for: a scabrous seamen's bar with sawdust on the floor and a smell of disinfectant so strong it watered the eyes. Everyone drinking boilermakers. A drunk snoring in a corner.

"I hope you brought your shoulder holster," I said nervously, looking around.

She ordered gin from the bearded bartender.

"Bring a fresh bottle," she commanded. "I want to see you break the seal."

"Whatever you say, lady," he said.

She turned to me. "What do you think of me?" she asked, blue eyes suddenly cold.

"Very nice, very good company."

"Cut the crap. You'll get your fee. What do you really think?"

"All right," I said. "I think you're a bright, successful and lonely woman. All those Hollywood stories you told me—I think the life out there amuses you, but you're not really part of it. You're an observer. You've obviously got class. But maybe once or twice a year you've got to cut loose and come to a place like this. Just to remind yourself what the real world is all about."

"Close," she said, "but no cigar. I've got class, have I? Forty years ago I was a waitress in this dump. I was born and brought up in Hell's Kitchen. Now let's get out of here and get back to my four-hundred-dollars-a-day suite on Park Avenue."

It was all velvet and gladioli in crystal vases. A sitting room, bedroom, and bathroom with a tub on clawed feet. Quiet opulence. Nothing shouted.

"I may move in," I said.

"I wish I had met you on Monday," she said. "I would have invited you. May I see you again the next time I come to New York?"

I thought Martha Twombly might have set that up to test me.

"Of course," I said. "Martha will be able to get in touch with me."

She nodded. "Shall I order something from the bar?"

"Thank you," I said, "but I think I've had enough to drink for one night."

"I know I have," she said, "but I have something better."

She went into the bedroom, came out with a small, filigreed silver box. She opened the lid and displayed the contents.

"Poppers?" I said. "I'm afraid they're wasted on me. You go ahead."

She cracked a vial and inhaled deeply.

"Women have fantasies, too, you know," she said.

"I never doubted it for a minute," I said. "What are yours?"

"Oh," she said vaguely, "this and that. Would you like to get undressed?"

I began disrobing. I was stepping out of my trousers when I looked up and saw she was still sitting there, fully clothed.

"Not you?" I asked.

"I think not," she said.

She had me lie naked on a chaise longue in the sitting room. She pulled her brocaded armchair alongside and stared down at me through half-closed eyes.

"Lovely," she said.

"Thank you. Is there anything you'd like me to do?"

"Not at the moment."

She touched me lightly with cool fingers. I became aroused.

"It's good for your complexion," she said.

Later, she gave me the hundred-dollar fee and a hundred-dollar tip. I wished her a safe flight back to the Coast. We shook hands and parted.

17

Jenny Tolliver said she was going home for Christmas week. Home was Rutland, Vermont, where her father, a retired locomotive engineer, and her mother lived in a house that looked like a stale wedding cake. Jenny would leave the morning of December 24 and return at noon on New Year's Eve.

"We won't spend Christmas together?" I said. "Is that because I refused to go to midnight mass with you?"

"No," Jenny said. "Mother and Dad are getting old and want me back for the holiday, and I think I should go. Peter, you're welcome to come up for the week if you'd like."

"I don't think so," I said. "They'd be curious about me, and ask you questions, and it would ruin your visit. But you'll be back for New Year's Eve. I'll talk to Arthur. Maybe we'll have a party. Nothing fancy. Beer and baked ham. How does that sound?"

"Like fun. Peter, will you behave yourself while I'm gone?"

"Don't I always?"

"Liar," she said sadly.

The Saturday before Christmas was my last day at the King's Arms. I was paid off, nodded coldly to the surly manager, and decided to walk up Madison Avenue to the Barcarole Boutique. I wanted to see if there was anything I could afford to buy Jenny for Christmas.

As before, I was impressed by the chic and obvious wealth of the patrons. I had never seen so much mink in my life.

I found a gorgeous Hermes scarf for Jenny. It cost more than I had intended to spend, but I comforted myself with the thought that she might be able to steal the pattern for her own fabrics.

I was on my way out when, in a showcase, I saw a glittering skullcap of silver paillettes. Exactly like the one Grace Stewart had worn. Too much of a coincidence to be a coincidence.

Martha Twombly wasn't getting her "friends" laid; those women were good customers who deserved a little extra service. I was intrigued. The demand was there. It was the supply that might prove a problem.

I had dinner with Jenny on Tuesday night and gave her the scarf. She was delighted. She gave me gold Tiffany cufflinks in a love knot design. We kissed and wished each other a Merry Christmas.

We had a steak at the Old Homestead, went back to her apartment, and rushed into bed. She was frantic, cleaving to me, biting.

"Hey," I said, "take it easy. You'll only be gone a week."

"I want to drain you," she told me. "Wring you out. So there's nothing left for any other woman while I'm gone."

I groaned and took her into my arms.

It would have been nice if there had been a blizzard outside—wind howling, snow driving. But it was just a clear, cold night—still, we had the sense of a warm, safe sanctuary, a world of two.

When we were both sated, she began to talk about love. I agreed with everything she said, not wanting to spoil that splendid night.

18

It was fortunate Jenny was away that week; it turned out to be a busy one for me, Arthur Enders, and King Hayes. On Saturday, we were running clients in and out of the apartment on a split-second schedule.

We called them "scenes." "How was your scene?" "I've got a scene scheduled for noon." "That was some wild scene." During that week, Hayes had three scenes and Enders and I had two each, so we decided to have champagne instead of beer at our New Year's Eve party.

On Tuesday, at 3:00 P.M., I had a scene with a woman named Joan. She was short and more than plump. She said that since she had gained weight, her husband wouldn't touch her. He told her that her obesity turned him off.

It didn't turn me off. Joan asked me to spank her before sex, and I did. She paid me the usual fifty-dollar fee plus a ten-dollar tip—all in crumpled fives and singles—probably saved from her household allowance.

By then I knew I had a good thing going, but pondered how it might be made better. The essential problem was a physical one.

An experienced whore, I supposed, could easily turn ten tricks a night. No male prostitute could even come close.

Even if Enders and Hayes and I managed three scenes a week, it only came to $150 each, plus tips. Easy, tax-free money, but hardly a fortune. If business was to grow, the difficulty, as I had suspected, would be recruiting new talent.

I thought of all my male friends and acquaintances. There were at least three I guessed would be amenable: two actors and a model, all desperate for a buck. The model was pushing fifty, a gray-haired executive type, but he was reputed to be a ferocious cocksman.

I devised a way to set up an organization to maximize my income without increasing my personal labor. I worked out details to present to Martha Twombly. I was confident she'd go along.

19

It was such a grand party that shortly before midnight a cop showed up and asked us to hold down the noise; there had been complaints.

"That'll be Mrs. Fultz," I said. "Our dear next-door neighbor."

We promised to lower the decibel count, gave the cop a glass of champagne, and sent him on his way. The moment the door closed, the joints came out again.

Jenny Tolliver was there, and Enders and Hayes with their dates. I had invited the three possible recruits, who showed up with ladies. There were three other couples, and five singles, male and female.

Some of the men had brought bottles, and two of the women had brought a giant pepperoni pizza. So, with the baked ham and potato salad and Syrian bread and champagne, there was plenty to eat and drink. There *was* a shortage—of places to sit.

The executive-type male model, raffishly dressed, escorting someone else's wife, had arrived half-smashed. His name was Wolcott Sands, and he had appeared in print ads and TV commercials as an attorney, chairman of the board, admiral, and proctologist.

"How's it going, Sandy?" I asked him.

"Surviving."

We were crammed into the tiny kitchen where Sands had gone for ice cubes to add to his tumbler of straight scotch.

"You available?"

The model looked at me. "For anything short of murder. And maybe even *that* if the price is right. You hear of anything?"

"A woman I know," I said vaguely. "Her husband's away for a while. She's looking for a quick bang. In and out and no entanglements. She'll pay fifty to someone she can trust."

"Fifty?" Sands cried. "Just tell me where and when."

I smiled, patted his shoulder, and went back into the living room.

The party became rowdier. One of the women threw up on her date,

Arthur Enders wanted to Indian wrestle with Jenny Tolliver, and King Hayes' lady had to be restrained from disrobing. But there were no fights and no bloodshed.

I spoke briefly with the two unemployed actors I had selected as potential recruits, making the same pitch I'd used with Wolcott Sands. Not only did both respond eagerly, but one even had a sublet on West 68th Street, which he volunteered for his scene.

Guests began straggling away around 2:00 A.M., and within an hour the place had emptied out. Jenny stayed, and Enders passed out on the couch.

Jenny and I made halfhearted efforts to put food away, throw out garbage, and clean up the worst of the mess. Then we went into the bedroom and closed the door on the snoring Enders.

"What were you and Sandy talking about?" she asked idly, beginning to undress.

"Sandy?" I said. "When?"

"You were in the kitchen. The two of you had your heads together."

"Oh," I said. "That. He was telling me a funny story about a woman paying him to have sex with her."

"I don't think that's funny. I think it's disgusting."

"And when a man pays a woman—is that disgusting, too?"

"Of course. No matter who does it, it's selling your body."

My reaction was mild. "Maybe they have nothing else to sell."

"Peter, have you ever paid a woman?"

"No."

"I should hope not. It's—it's—"

"I know," I said. "Disgusting. Jenny, it's not all that simple. I've known men—real macho types—who claim they don't have to pay for sex. But these same guys will buy a woman gifts, take her to the theater and expensive restaurants, or maybe spring for a week in St. Croix. And all the time they swear indignantly that they don't pay for sex. That's hypocrisy, isn't it?"

"Not if they love each other."

"I'm talking about sex, not love. If a man is turned on by a woman, or a woman by a man, what's wrong with paying for your pleasure?"

"It's reducing sex to 'Should we have another martini or should we screw?' It trivializes something marvelous into something casual and insignificant."

"You're a romantic," I said, laughing.

"I wish you were," she said sorrowfully.

"I am," I told her. "But we want different things."

"What do you want?"

"At the moment? You."

Later, I started again on the same subject. It was suddenly important to convince her.

"Look," I said. "Suppose a woman marries a man she doesn't love. For whatever reason. Maybe he's rich or maybe he's just a good, solid, hardworking, faithful guy. The woman is thinking about her future. But if she doesn't really love him, she's selling her body?"

"Well . . ." Jenny said cautiously, "not exactly."

"She doesn't love him, but she's going to bed with him because he's supporting her. That makes her a whore, doesn't it?"

"Not if she's working hard to make a nice home for him and taking care of the kids. Whores don't do that."

I was silent.

"And besides," she went on, "maybe over the years she'll come to love him."

"Maybe," I said. "But don't bet on it. It could just as easily go the other way. All I'm saying is that one way or another we all sell ourselves. Look at you; you're selling your artistic talent, aren't you?"

"Of course. But that's my job. It's got nothing to do with my personal life. You don't think I'm selling myself to you, do you?"

"Sure," I said. "For the use of this luxurious apartment and all those diamonds I give you."

"Pig," she said, punching my arm. "Now let's go to sleep."

I held her until her breathing deepened. Then I gently withdrew my arm and stroked the long hair back from her face. She murmured happily.

I lay awake a long time, thinking we had not arrived at the truth of the matter. She *was* selling something: her love. And I was providing an object for that love. So I was selling something, too—was I not?

I despaired of that complexity and fell asleep reflecting how wonderfully a fifty-dollar fee simplified existence.

20

Sol Hoffheimer said his wife was having trouble with her plumbing and might need an operation. His younger daughter had been to an orthodontist who wanted $3000 for the job. ("Probably platinum braces," the agent said mournfully.) And two days ago the transmission of his '78 clunker had dropped out on the Long Island Expressway.

"Sol," I said, "maybe the man upstairs doesn't like you."

"I'm beginning to wonder. Last week I grossed a grand total of five bucks. You know how? I found a five-dollar bill on the floor of a cab. I was so happy."

I had brought lunch to the agent's office: two black coffees, two hot pastramis on rye, and two apple Danish, purchased at the deli in the lobby of Hoffheimer's office building. We ate in our overcoats; something had happened to the boiler and there was no heat.

"So business is lousy?" I asked.

"No, not lousy. Nonexistent."

I took out my wallet, put three ten-dollar bills on the desk. "Part of what I owe you. Many thanks."

Sol looked at the money. "You're sure you can manage?"

"I'm sure. Drink your coffee before it freezes."

"I've got a couple of little things you should look at," Sol said. He shoved two slips of paper across the desk. "One is for 'Emergency Ward,' the soaper. There's a rumor they're looking for an intern-type feller. The other one's for a voice-over on some cockamamie documentary about the South Bronx. Watch out for that one; the director's a real momser."

"Sounds swell," I said, putting the slips of paper into my trenchcoat pocket. "Thanks, Sol; I'll give them the old college try. Tell me, am I the only client you've got who keeps striking out?"

"Nah," the agent said disgustedly. "It's not you; it's the business. Six million people for every job."

"How many clients do you have?" I asked casually, glancing at the wooden filing cabinet.

"Who counts?" Hoffheimer said. "They're calling me every day and then they're gone. Maybe they go home to Iowa or wherever. I'd say that right now I got maybe forty regulars, half boys, half girls. Around there."

"Any of them making a good living?"

"Would I be sitting in an ice-cold office worrying about my wife's tubes if my people were making a good living?"

"Twenty guys?" I said thoughtfully. "Mostly young?"

"Mostly. Why?"

"Just curious."

Twenty minutes later, down on the street, I took the two slips of paper from my trenchcoat pocket. Without even looking at them, I tore them into small squares and let the pieces drift away on the winter wind.

21

King Hayes was scheduled for a scene, but when the woman showed up, she had a compact full of coke and wanted him to snort with her. When he refused, she spit in his face, called him a "nigger turd," and stalked out.

I had a scene with a woman who, when the bang ended triumphantly, said, "That was lovely. Let's do it again." I had to explain, as diplomatically as possible, that the fifty-dollar fee did not include seconds. She was not a satisfied customer.

I decided the time had come for that meeting with Martha Twombly.

I called and said I had to see her. She asked if it was important. I said it was. She suggested I come to her place at nine o'clock that night.

"I can give you a drink," she said, "but no dinner."

"Fine," I assured her. "Where?"

She gave me her address and added lightly, "By the way, my name is Twombly."

She lived on East 83rd Street near York. It was a converted

townhouse, and her one-bedroom apartment was high-ceilinged and comfortable, but not as splendid as I imagined it would be. She collected elephant figurines in enamel, brass, wood, tin, etc. The tuskers were everywhere, most of them trumpeting.

"You've got to keep all the trunks turned to the front door," she explained. "For good luck."

"I'd like to hear what Dr. Freud thinks about that," I said.

She was wearing lounging pajamas of orange velour, an odd choice for a red-haired woman. Her feet were bare, and I was charmed to see that her toenails were painted black.

"In mourning?" I asked her, pointing.

"Yeah," she said. "For my fallen arches. I have a nice Armagnac. Would you like to try it?"

I said I would, and she served it in little Baccarat snifters, so fragile I was afraid of crushing the glass in my fingers. When we were settled at opposite ends of a black leather chesterfield, she asked what was on my mind.

"We've got problems," I said. I told her what had happened to King Hayes, and how the black had been insulted.

"God *damn* it!" she said wrathfully. "That sweet boy. The best lay I've had in years."

"Present company excepted?" I said wryly.

"What? Oh, yes, sure."

"The point is, we've got to keep drugs out of this. We're teetering on the edge of legality as it is."

"I couldn't agree more," she said warmly, "and I apologize for that stupid twat. You'll never see her again. And I'll make sure all the friends I send you from now on know the rules: no drugs."

"Good," I said. "Now there's another thing . . ."

I described my scene with the woman who wanted seconds for her fifty-dollar fee.

"Can't be done," I said firmly. "No way. We start that and they'll be wanting to stay all day. It's got to be a one-shot deal, Martha."

"I see your point," she said slowly. "I'll go along with that. But let's look at something else: What if the guy can't cut the mustard?"

"Well, that hasn't happened yet, and I don't think it will. But if it does, the woman pays nothing."

"Fair enough," she said, nodding. "Peter, this is why I wanted to go slow. I knew we'd have problems as we went along. Anything else?"

At this point I had intended to tell her that I knew her name was Twombly before she told me, and I was aware she was manager of the

Barcarole Boutique, and guessed the women she was providing were probably her customers rather than her "friends."

But now it occurred to me that it would be foolish to reveal all that. I thought her secrecy might have something to do with self-esteem. Providing an hour of pleasure for friends was one thing. Pimping for customers was another. She didn't want to face reality.

"This is great brandy," I said. "Could I have a nip more?"

"Help yourself, and give me a drop while you're at it."

I spoke as I rose to pour more of the Armagnac.

"I'm finished at the King's Arms and there's not much doing acting-wise right now. The money I've been making from your friends is great—don't get me wrong; I really appreciate it—but a couple of yards a week, and that includes tips, isn't all that much. Do you think your friends might spring for a hundred?"

"They might," she said. "God knows they've got the loot."

"Here's what I've been figuring . . ." I said.

Clients would pay a hundred dollars in advance directly to Martha. Of that amount, she would keep twenty-five for herself, twenty-five would go to me, and fifty to the man. There would be a weekly settlement.

"That way," I explained, "the woman doesn't have to hand cash to the guy, which isn't exactly conducive to romance. If she wants to give him a tip, that's her business."

"In fact," Martha said shrewdly, "tips might be more if she hasn't already paid the guy fifty in cash."

"Exactly."

"You think your boys will go along with a weekly settlement?"

"Arthur and King will; they trust me. Which brings me to another thing . . ."

I described the three possible recruits I had lined up. "The model," I told Martha, "is a mature-type guy. Silvery-haired but handsome. He's about fifty, but he's supposed to be a terror in the sack."

"That's all right," she said. "I have some young friends who might go for the father image."

"Also," I said, "one of the actors has offered us his studio sublet on West Sixty-eighth Street. I'll have to check it out first, but if it's okay, it would keep my place from becoming too congested. Anyway, taking on the three new studs would double our work force and, hopefully, our income. With the new money-split, we should do all right—providing you have enough friends."

"No problem there," she said after a pause. "I have a lot of friends, and my friends have friends. I can keep your crew busy. All right, let's try your plan. Just one thing: I want to try those three new guys before we take them on."

, "What's that," I said, laughing, "the feminist version of droit du seigneur?"

"No," she said seriously. "I just want to be sure we're not hiring any slobs or weirdos."

"The new boys will get fifty for their auditions?"

"Of course."

"Then I'll set it up for next week. Meanwhile I'll check out that pad on West Sixty-eighth and see if it's suitable. Martha, if this works out, I think we'll both make a nice piece of change. God knows I can use it."

"I can, too," she admitted. "I've got a boy in a military academy down in Virginia, and it's costing me an arm and a leg."

"Oh? I didn't know you were married."

"Was. He took off for parts unknown years and years ago. Good riddance."

"Well . . ." I said, "our partnership should help your cash flow problem."

She jerked her head toward the bedroom door. "Want to seal the deal, partner?"

"Why not?" I said.

22

I discovered with surprise that I had a talent for administration. During the next few weeks, I accomplished the following:

Set up successful auditions for the three recruits with Martha Twombly. She was especially enthusiastic about Wolcott Sands, the mature model.

"A killer," she reported.

Inspected the studio on West 68th Street. I found it suitable, but insisted the *Playboy* centerfolds be removed from the walls.

Phoned Martha daily for assignments, set up schedules for myself and my five cohorts, and used both apartments to avoid too much traffic in either.

Visited Martha's apartment every Thursday night at 9:00 P.M. to go over accounts, get paid my share, and collect the money for the studs. All dealings were in cash.

Remunerated my crew every Friday night in businesslike pay envelopes purchased from an office supply store.

I watched, fascinated, as my income steadily increased. During the first week of February, my crew and I had sixteen scenes. My gross was over $400, with tips. I bought a new raincoat at Burberry's and a suede sports jacket at Paul Stuart.

I also took Jenny Tolliver to dinner at the Four Seasons. She was amazed.

"Peter, where *are* you getting the money?"

"Didn't I tell you?" I said glibly. "I did the voice-over for a cockamamie documentary they made on the South Bronx. The damned thing will probably never be screened, but the producer wants to keep me in mind for more jobs."

"Oh, Peter—how wonderful."

I thought that with the addition of fresh bodies I wouldn't have to make any scenes. Then I could devote myself solely to management, make a good income, and be faithful to Jenny.

If I wished . . .

23

The woman's name was Betsy, and the moment she was inside my place, she began:

"I hope you don't think I make a habit of this sort of thing because I certainly don't. I wouldn't be here at all if a certain friend of mine hadn't nagged at me. But I certainly don't have to pay a man to go to bed with me, I assure you. Not only am I happily married and very well satisfied in the sex department, but in addition to my husband there are other men who, shall we say, do not find me unattractive."

"Would you like to take off your hat and coat?" I asked.

She had the shortest hair I had ever seen on a woman. It was a wheat-colored crewcut; a pink scalp showed. Her eyebrows had been shaved, then penciled into thin arches.

"But then everyone seems to be doing it, so I thought, well, why not? All my friends say, 'Betsy isn't afraid to try anything,' and it's true. If I told you some of the things I've done, you'd just scream. But I feel it's all part of living, and if you—"

"Would you care for a drink?" I said. "White wine? Vodka?"

"No, thank you. And, you must admit, it *is* a new experience. With a perfect stranger. I'm never afraid to seek out new experiences, even though there may be some more dangerous than—"

My eyeballs beginning to glaze over, I led her gently to the bedroom, hoping the sight of the bed might halt or at least slow her verbal diarrhea. But it did not.

"I think the most important thing is absolute, complete self-honesty —don't you? To recognize exactly what space you inhabit and your own reality. One must come to terms with one's own ego, mustn't one, if full self-awareness is to be achieved. The answer is in inwardness, not outwardness, and only by searching the interior cosmos that is within each of us can some measure of oneness be achieved."

In desperation, I began to undress her, unbuttoning, unhooking, unzipping. She was a mannequin and let me do as I liked.

"The one," she went on. "We all seek the one that is within us—is that not true? That's what life is all about, I feel, and only in the search can we—could I have a glass of water, please? With ice. A lot of ice with very little water."

When I returned with the tumbler, she was lying on the bed atop the blanket. Her arms were raised, hands clasped behind her head.

I had never seen such a *naked* woman. Armpits, legs, and pubic hair shaved. She was as smooth as an icicle.

"Drink?" I said, proffering the glass.

I undressed swiftly. When I turned back to her, she had taken an ice cube from the glass and was rubbing it across her forehead, back and forth.

"Are you all right?" I said anxiously. "Not feeling faint, are you?"

"You do it," she said, holding the glass out to me.

I took the tumbler, fished out another ice cube, began to move it over her brow.

"Lower," she said.

Then I caught on. I did what she asked. Her hairless skin became slick with a film of melted ice. She closed her eyes.

"Everywhere," she said in a breathy voice.

That's what she wanted. That's *all* she wanted. Her skin flushed, her respiration became more rapid. I used up all the ice cubes and went back to the kitchen for more. I had to empty the trays.

Later, I brought her a towel so she could dry herself. I dressed, wondering why I had taken my clothes off in the first place.

"I do think," she said, stepping into her skirt, "that only by exploring one's innermost feelings and desires that a certain measure of soul-serenity may be attained. For we must go down, down, down to the essential ego, explore the darkness and by self-knowledge bring it to the shining light."

She was still talking when I put her in a cab. She didn't give me a tip, but I supposed *that* experience had nothing to do with the cosmic oneness.

Laughing ruefully, I returned to my place. A well-dressed man stood in the lobby, examining the names on the mailboxes. He looked up as I entered and smiled.

"Mr. Peter Scuro?" he asked.

"Yes. Who are you?"

The man took a wallet from his inside jacket pocket and flipped it open to show a gold shield and an ID card.

"Detective Luke Futter," he said, still smiling. "May I talk to you for a moment?"

24

I took his hat and coat, then gestured toward the best chair. But the detective perched on the edge of the couch.

"Mind if I smoke?" he asked.

"Not at all. Go right ahead."

He was a tall man with a whippy body and a loose-limbed, floppy way of moving. I noted the manicured fingernails and the blond hair that lay in precise waves almost as if it had been marcelled. His complexion was a startling pink, his eyes hard denim blue. He would have been handsome except for those thin lips and a quirky smile. The shoulders were broad enough, the stomach flat. He was not a soft man.

"You're the first detective I've seen in Italian tailoring," I said.

The visitor looked down, smoothed wrinkles from one knee. "Giorgio Armani," he said. "You like?"

"Very much. With your height, you should try a double-breasted with the lapel rolled to the bottom button. Would you like something to drink?"

"No, nothing, thank you." The detective looked around the littered apartment. "Doesn't look much like a den of iniquity."

I laughed. "Is that what you were expecting?"

Futter waved a hand. "You know how it is. We get a complaint; we've got to check it out."

"That would be Mrs. Fultz, the sweet old lady who lives next door."

"Whoever," the detective said. "Anyway, I caught it—this was a couple of weeks ago—and dropped around to take a look. To tell you the truth, I didn't think it would be anything."

"Glad to hear it."

Futter's smile widened mirthlessly. "But I have to admit," he went on, "I got interested. I'm not going to tell you I parked across the street eight hours a day; I didn't. But whenever I got some free time, I'd stop by and watch. I couldn't figure it."

"Couldn't figure what?"

"Well, there was you and the other guy who lives here. Arthur Enders—right? But then there was also a smoke using the place, and two other guys at least, coming and going. And then of course there were the women. Most of them good-looking, well-dressed. Mink coats and so forth. They'd stay for like an hour and then the guy who was in the apartment would come out with them and put them in a cab."

"It's simple," I said. "Those other men are personal friends of mine or of Enders'. We lend them the apartment occasionally so they can meet their girlfriends in private."

"Sure. But only for an hour, huh?"

I shrugged. "As long as they want. I don't keep track."

"You know what I thought it was?" the detective said, lighting another cigarette from the butt of the first. "You'll get a laugh out of this; I thought it was drugs. I thought those ladies were dropping by to get a fix, or snort a little. I thought you and your friends were pushing. But then I said to myself, what pusher sees his customers to a cab? And the women walked straight and steady after their hour was up. And you don't look like a doper."

"Thank you," I said sardonically.

"So I knew it wasn't drugs. There was only one other thing it could be, unless you guys were giving bridge lessons."

"Are you accusing me of something?" I said stonily.

The detective held up his palms. "Whoa! I'm not accusing anyone of anything. We're just having a friendly chat—right?"

"If you say so."

"You got a nice thing going here," Futter said, examining the tip of his burning cigarette. "Clean, quiet, polite. In and out within an hour and no hassle. I figure you guys are each dragging down a couple of yards a week. Maybe more. Tax-free. Last Thursday it was like Grand Central Station in here. Beautiful."

"Look," I said, beginning to steam, "I'm not doing anything illegal."

"Don't get your balls in an uproar, sonny," the detective said mildly. *"Everything* is illegal if I say it is. Like keeping what they call a disorderly house. Loitering for the purpose of prostitution. Stuff like that. It's a laugh, I know, but it's on the books, waiting for me if I want to use it."

"Go ahead."

The detective looked at me narrowly. "Pretty snotty, aren't you? Let's you and me take a little walk, shall we?"

"Am I under arrest?"

Luke Futter laughed. "No. I like to talk in the open air and it's hard as hell to bug Central Park."

We put on our hats and coats.

"I like your trenchcoat," the detective said. "A Burberry, isn't it?"

"That's right."

"I'd get one like it, but if I wore a trenchcoat to work I'd get laughed out of the squad room."

We sat on a bench on Central Park West and watched the bananas shamble by, mumbling to themselves.

"There are ways of handling it," Futter said casually. "I can report the matter is under investigation, and if the old woman calls in again, I can tell her the same thing. Or I can say I investigated and there's not enough hard evidence to make a case. What I mean is that I can fuzz the whole thing, bury it, lose it. And I can work it so that no one else comes poking around."

I sighed. "How much?" I asked.

"I thought you'd never ask," Luke Futter said, grinning. "Only a hundred. A month."

I was silent for a long moment. "And if not?" I said finally. "What then? Arrest?"

"Possible," the detective said, nodding. "A garbage arrest. It would never hold up. But it would be, ah, an inconvenience. You know, like mugging, fingerprinting, lawyers, bail, publicity, and all that shit. We'd probably raid while some woman was in the place."

"That's nice," I said.

"Actually," Futter said, "we could probably take you out a lot easier. Just park a manned squad car outside your place twenty-four hours a day. I don't think your customers would be overjoyed by that."

"No, they wouldn't."

"Well," the detective said, "it seems to me your choices are limited. You can take a collar and hope for the best. You can go out of business voluntarily. You can move to a new location. I'd find you, of course. Or you can move to another city and set up shop."

"Or I can pay you a hundred a month."

"Right."

"Guaranteed protection?"

"No guarantees. But I'll do my best."

"I can't give you an answer right now," I said. "There are other people involved."

"Of course. Take your time. Suppose I drop by your place on Friday?"

"That'll be okay. I'll have an answer for you by then."

The detective stood up, straightening his black, velvet-collared chesterfield. "Listen," he said. "Where did you get that knitted hat? It's really got class."

25

"Son of a bitch!" Martha Twombly said bitterly.

She stalked back and forth, smacking her mouth with a cigarette and blowing the smoke out in angry puffs, doing the Bette Davis bit.

"Are you sure he's a detective?" she demanded.

"I saw his shield and ID. They looked real."

"Did he come on hard?"

"Not really," I admitted. "Rather polite, as a matter of fact. But he's a cold bastard. Martha, up to now, this has all been a gas. But this guy made me feel like garbage."

"I know the type," she said grimly. "I'm going to make a phone call. Help yourself to a drink."

She went into the bedroom and closed the door. I looked at the Armagnac bottle but didn't feel like drinking. That meeting with Futter had depressed me. It left me feeling unclean.

Martha came out of the bedroom about five minutes later.

"I called a lawyer friend of mine who's experienced in things like this. He's going to check some sources and call me back within an hour. Meanwhile let's do our bookkeeping."

We went over the week's accounts. Gross income was up again. My take was almost $600, and Martha had made $450. Our best worker was, surprisingly, fifty-year-old Wolcott Sands, who had handled five scenes.

"I told you he was a killer," Martha said. "The girls love him. Peter, if we stay in business, can you find some more boys?"

"Any preferences?"

"Maybe another black. And—oh, I don't know—something different. An Oriental? A rough truck-driver type?"

"You think your friends are looking for something different?" Then I laughed. "That was a stupid question; I know they are." I told her about Betsy and the ice cubes.

Martha gave me a queer smile. "Peter, I like you, and I trust you. I know that whatever I tell you stops with you. Well, when I was half as old as I am now, I spent three years in a Chicago house. You understand? And if you think women have some kinky ideas, you should see what men come up with. They make women look like Goody Two-shoes."

"I believe it," I said.

"Sex is a crazy thing. There are the instruction manuals and the how-to books, and then there's what really goes on. Ask any whore; she'll tell you."

"It's all dreams."

"Most of it," Martha agreed. "I remember one guy who came in every week and hired four girls who would . . ."

She hadn't finished the story when the phone rang and she dashed into the bedroom, closing the door behind her. She came out a few minutes later.

"Futter is legit," she reported. "He works out of a precinct house, but he's a member of a special squad. Vice, mostly, or whatever they call it now. Anyway, my friend says the best thing to do at the moment is pay him off, but that he'll probably up the ante as we expand."

"All right," I said, sighing. "Futter's hundred will come half from me and half from you. Is that okay?"

"Sure."

"But maybe we should switch more of the scenes to the West Sixty-eighth Street pad. I don't think Futter knows about that yet. If he sees my apartment getting busier, he'll want a bigger cut."

"Good thinking," Martha said. "Talk to the boy who sublets the place. Maybe we let him live there rent-free if we have the use of it during the day."

"He says the super has been asking questions."

"So slip the super twenty a month."

"Right. I'll take care of it. Anything else?"

"Yes," she said. "I have a friend who wants two boys in one scene. She'll pay three hundred."

"All white?" I asked. "Or chocolate and vanilla?"

26

The meeting with Detective Luke Futter made me aware of how casually I had been conducting my enterprise. Now I saw that it was more than a profitable diversion; it was a *business* and deserved to be handled with serious respect.

I had been recording my accounts in a small daily diary and appointment book. A single page, for instance, might note: "Arthur, noon, 75th St., Jean" or "King, 3:00 P.M., 68th St., Harriet." I now saw that such a ledger might conceivably, in the future, prove dangerous.

So I devised a simple code: A for myself, B for Enders, C for Hayes, and so forth. My apartment was 1, the 68th Street pad was 2. Women's names were never noted, and appointments recorded cryptically as B-12-1 or C-3-2. At the end of each week, after the settlement, all written evidence was destroyed.

Another problem was what to do with my money. I spent freely of course. Mostly to replenish my wardrobe. And Arthur and I now had a cleaning woman who came twice a week to make our apartment a little more presentable.

Still, my cash accumulated. I had a minuscule savings account in a Columbus Avenue bank, but had no desire to make deposits I might later have to explain to the IRS. The same held true for opening a checking account or making investments. I wanted nothing on paper.

I finally rented a safe deposit box and began to store my excess funds there. It was not, I acknowledged, a perfect solution, but better than keeping large amounts of cash on my person or hidden in the apartment.

A third problem arose from explaining my unexpected wealth to Jenny Tolliver. The obvious answer, of course, was to continue playing the poor, unemployed actor.

But it seemed chintzy not to allow her to share my good fortune. So I simply lied, counting on charm and good humor to convince her that my prosperity was legitimately earned.

27

I insisted on taking a cab to the restaurant.

"Oh, Peter," Jenny said reproachfully, "with you it's easy come, easy go."

I laughed immoderately, but of course she didn't grasp the double entendre.

I had made a reservation at Gian Marino, a comfortable Italian restaurant on East 58th Street. I ordered briskly and authoritatively: a glass of Soave to start, a plate of pasta al'olio to share, an enormous lobster in a diablo sauce, sticks of french fried zucchini, a salad of arugula. A big bottle of Valpolicella with that, and a Galliano with espresso to finish.

"My God," Jenny said nervously. "Can you afford all this?"

"No," I said, touching her cheek tenderly. "We're going to have to wash dishes."

Then back into a cab and over to Times Square where we were seated in eighth row center just as the curtain was rising on a revival of *The Iceman Cometh.*

I had been frolicsome during dinner, laughing and joking, breaking up the waiter with my rendition of Italian double-talk. And in the taxi to the theater, I had rattled off verses from Gilbert and Sullivan with a brio that even had the cabbie cheering.

But as *The Iceman Cometh* unfolded on the stage, my mood soured and darkened. The actor playing Hickey was not much older than I, and brought to the role a sweet vulnerability and, at the end, an intensity that left the audience shaken and silent, and then on their feet, applauding madly.

"Let's get out of here," I said thickly.

I refused to go home, but demanded we stop at Blotto's for a nightcap. No one we knew was present, so we sat at the bar and I ordered brandy stingers.

I drank like a madman: one, two, three—just like that. Jenny, a hand on my arm, tried to slow me, but I was now in a manic mood and would not be tempered.

I roared, shouted, sang bits of nonsense, insisted on buying drinks for strangers, and only agreed to leave after I toppled from my barstool and sprawled on the littered floor.

She wanted to take me back to my place, only a block away. But I insisted on seeing her home and we finally got a cab to stop for us.

At her apartment house, I threw money at the cabdriver and went staggering into the lobby ahead of her. Upstairs, I asked for more brandy and drank wildly without removing my hat or coat.

Jenny watched me, her face wrenched with concern.

"Peter," she said. "What *is* it?"

"The theater tonight," I said in a whispery voice. "The guy who played Hickey. I could . . . I might . . ."

And then I fell to weeping.

28

King Hayes recruited another black, a young café au lait dancer from a Harlem troupe. He was built like a basketball forward and wore his hair corn-rowed. Martha Twombly auditioned him and gave her approval.

She wasn't so enthusiastic about the Oriental, an Off-Broadway set designer who, she reported, had displayed a distressing tendency to giggle during his tryout.

Then, through Wolcott Sands, I was put in touch with an Indian Indian. He was small, energetic, and the color of old meerschaum. Martha commended his sinuosity.

"Only one bone in his body," she said, "and that's a good one."

The truck-driver type proved the most difficult to find. I interviewed a few weight lifters and karate experts, but they all lacked the correct mixture of couth and raw physical power.

Finally I called my agent, told him I'd joined a weekly play-reading workshop on the West Side, and that we were looking for someone to do Stanley Kowalski in *A Streetcar Named Desire.*

"I got a kid named Seth Hawkins," Hoffheimer said. "He's from Amarillo, and with that accent, no way is he ever going to play Hamlet. But he's big and brawny and pretty. He might make a Kowalski. He's stage-struck enough to try anything."

"Give him a call, will you, Sol? If he's interested, give him my number and have him call me and I'll set up a meet."

I recognized Seth Hawkins the moment he walked into the Losers' Place. I waved him over to my booth and discovered the kid had the thickest West Texas accent I had ever heard.

"Whoo!" Seth said. "Ah'm tarred."

We drank beer as Hawkins told me he'd attended an A & M college, figuring to help out on his pappy's spread after he graduated. But during his sophomore year a girlfriend had talked him into joining a little theater group. He had played one small role and become totally stagestruck. Pappy had staked him to two years in New York, but he had only five more months to go.

"Everything costs so much," Hawkins complained. "I been going to a voice teacher to get rid of this cornpone accent. Now you know how many bucks I been spending on *that?*"

"You think it's done any good?"

"Sheeit, no!" the boy said explosively. "You think it has?"

"Sheeit, no!"

Hawkins grinned. "Well, anyway you talk straight. Listen, what's this Kowalski thing you told Sol about? I know that play six ways from the middle. I seen the movie three times."

"Seth, I don't want to insult you, but I've got to be honest; I don't think you're right for the part. It's the accent."

"Yeah," the boy said, sighing. "I've heard that before. Many, many times."

"Have you thought about modeling?"

"Naw, not really. Acting is all I want to do. You model?"

"Not exactly," I said.

"You got a job then? Look, I don't want to be nosy, but I can't figure out how so many out-of-work actors in New York can keep their heads above water."

"I found a way," I said earnestly. "It's not nice and I'm not particularly proud of it. But it only takes three or four hours a week and pays enough for me to get by."

"Yeah?" Hawkins said, interested. "How do you do that?"

So I told him.

"Naw," he said, staring at me. "I could never do nothing like that."

"Depends on how much you want to be an actor," I told him sternly. "Your big chance may be just around the corner. It's a question of time. If you can hang on, your break has got to come."

"I guess."

"Acting has got to be the biggest thing in your life. The *only* thing. If you won't sacrifice to succeed, then you shouldn't be here in the first place."

"I suppose."

"If you'd like to try it," I said, "I could fix you up with one of those women. Fifty bucks for an hour. Easy money."

"Well . . . I reckon I could try it. Once."

Martha said Seth Hawkins would do just fine.

29

I ordered all my boys to escort customers to a cab after the scene, stressing that it cost nothing and created goodwill.

I also insisted that every client be offered one drink. Preferably white wine.

"It relaxes them," I said. "Makes them think that you're interested in their comfort. It'll pay off in higher tips; you'll see. But absolutely no drugs. Not even a joint."

As the business expanded and prospered, other rules were put in force. No scenes before noon or after midnight. If a woman wanted a "double" (two boys), the price was raised to $400, but three hours were allowed.

One woman paid a grand for a "multiple": four men in a scene that lasted all afternoon. She departed much refreshed. The four guys were exhausted.

Certain women became regulars, and although most of them accepted whomever was available, some always insisted on the same boy. These clients were called "wives."

Most of the men had at least one wife. King Hayes had two and Wolcott Sands had three. The way Seth Hawkins was going, he'd soon have nothing *but* wives, and clients would have to reserve his services days in advance.

Counting myself, I now had nine active studs. During the last week of March, my take-home pay was $855 and Martha Twombly drew $675. She said she was beginning to get a lot of referred customers. "Off-the-street trade" she called them.

"We're going to need more boys, Peter," she warned. "And another thing—be sure your guys stay clean."

"VD, you mean?" I said. "God forbid one of our customers should get the clap. Ask that lawyer friend of yours: Could we be sued for malpractice?"

30

My personal income had grown large enough so I could easily have devoted all my time to scheduling and management. But I continued taking two or three scenes a week. I told myself the money was so easy I would be a fool to give it up.

The woman's name was Amy. At first I thought she was in her early thirties, with golden hair halfway down her back. Then I saw the gold was streaked with silvery gray, and there were fine lines at the corners of her eyes and mouth. She was, I guessed, at least forty. Perhaps more. She wore a wedding band.

I helped her off with her old-fashioned Persian lamb coat. Beneath it, she was wearing a dress of calico flannel, floral patterned, with tiers of ruffled lace at neckline and hem. Awful. Much too girlish for her.

I brought her a glass of white wine. She held it to her eye and surveyed the apartment through the liquid.

"It makes all the world glow," she said.

"You're a poet," I told her.

She gave me a small smile. "I am," she said. "A poet. Two books published."

"Wonderful. Is it a living?"

"It is for me. The only way I want to live."

In the bedroom, she asked me to undress first. I did, and lay naked atop the sheet. She sat alongside, put one palm on my bare chest, stared down at me.

"How wonderful," she said.

"Aren't you going to undress?"

She bent over me, so close that her long hair drifted across my face.

"There is something I must tell you," she said. "I have only one breast. Will that disgust you?"

"Nothing about you could disgust me."

She touched my lips lightly with a forefinger. "You are a dear, dear man."

Her body was pale, soft: a white shadow. I kissed the scar where her breast had been. She caught her breath in a sound that was half-sob, half-laugh.

"Sweet," she said. "So sweet."

She did not want me to enter her, but devoured me instead, with little mews of delight. She was slow and adroit, and I wondered where she had learned such expertise.

Later, I asked her to recite one of her poems, and she readily agreed. I couldn't understand it, but I liked the sound: The words were all chimes and tinkles.

"That was lovely," I told her.

She swooped to kiss me fiercely, pressing me to her wounded breast, smelling faintly of lavender.

After she was dressed, she began working the wedding band from her finger. When it was free, she handed it to me.

"Here," she said. "Take it."

I was horrified. "I can't—"

"Please. I want you to have it. I was a fool to keep it."

I didn't understand what she meant, and told her so. But she wouldn't answer my questions.

"You don't have to wear it of course," she said with her small smile. "Just keep it. A souvenir."

I escorted her to a cab on Columbus Avenue. When I returned to my place, I found Luke Futter leaning against the fender of a parked car.

31

The detective was wearing a knee-length coat of green loden, closed with wooden toggles. Perched on his head was a fuzzy white Tyrolean hat with what appeared to be a shaving brush stuck in the band.

"And are you wearing lederhosen?" I asked.

Futter looked at me, not comprehending.

"Let's take a walk," he said.

I turned my face to the steely sky. A drizzle was falling, straight as ruled lines. The air was sharp enough to bite, and even the detective's pink face looked gray in that oysterish light.

"There's a nice little bar on Columbus," I said. "Blotto's. Warm and dry."

"A little walk," Futter insisted. "It won't take long."

I sighed and we headed for Central Park West, heads bowed.

"You got another place on West Sixty-eighth," the detective said. "You didn't tell me."

"That's right; I didn't. How did you find out?"

"I like to drop around occasionally. Just to keep an eye on my investment, you understand. Your roomy, that guy Enders, comes running out like a scalded cat. He's in a hurry to get someplace. So I tailed him. Just for the fun of it, you know. He ends up at this Sixty-eighth Street place, waltzes right in, and a few minutes later, lo and behold, this bimbo in a fur coat shows up. What the hell, you got a chain of places like Colonel Sanders?"

"No. Just the two of them."

"If you say so. I'd hate to discover you were holding out on me. Let's say a hundred a month for each place."

"All right," I said equably. "I'm in no position to argue."

"Right you are," Futter said, looking sideways with his dodgy smile.

We walked slowly around the block, trudging. Our shoulders were hunched, fists dug deep in coat pockets. Beads of wet gathered on our hats and shoulders.

"Now for the bad news," Futter said.

"Oh-oh," I said.

"That old bitch, your neighbor. She's still at it. She's gone to my lieutenant, and now she's threatening to call the mayor's office."

"Shit!" I said angrily.

"Yeah. She says she belongs to one of these citizens' groups, or whatever, and she's going to sic their lawyer on you."

"Beautiful. That's all I need."

"Well . . ." Luke Futter said, raising his head, "I figured a scam to take her out. No guarantee, but I think it'll work."

I was silent.

"Don't you want to hear about it?" the detective asked.

"No."

"That's smart," Futter said. "It'll cost you an extra fifty."

"She's not going to get hurt, is she?"

"What do you think," the detective said indignantly, "I'm some kind of a bad guy? No one's going to get hurt."

32

And there were personnel problems . . .

One of the actors was habitually late for appointments. Regretfully, I was forced to terminate his employment. It took me almost a week to find a replacement.

When the café-au-lait dancer departed to tour with his troupe, King Hayes recruited another amenable soul brother, a jazz musician. But he fell asleep during his audition with Martha Twombly. The search for a suitable black continued.

King Hayes himself was a problem. He told me that one of his "wives" wanted to set him up in his own apartment, buy his clothes, and pay him $200 a week for a monopoly of his services. The deal sounded good to King.

I said it might sound good, but King would be foolish to trust his income and future to the whim of one woman. He could earn more and enjoy his freedom in his present career.

Hayes acknowledged the truth of that, but complained that he was being forced to have scenes with some women he found physically unappetizing.

I said I was aware of that complaint; it was one repeated, frequently, by most of the studs. I was making every effort to arrange the scheduling so no guy would be assigned a customer he considered, for whatever reason, to be distasteful.

I urged King to consider carefully before opting to become a kept man. He promised to think it over. During the next few weeks I made certain his scenes were with only the youngest, prettiest clients. I heard no more of the matter.

Arthur Enders' case was more complex. When he said he wanted out, and I asked why, he replied simply, "It's not right."

I asked him if that was a moral judgment. He finally said it wasn't *exactly* the morality of their work that disturbed him, it was—uh—ah—its sleaziness.

That infuriated me. Wasn't the whole thing set up so that no money actually changed hands between client and stud unless the woman proffered a gift? What about the glass of wine and the escort to a cab?

"This is a class operation," I declared. "The whole thing is done with taste." Besides, I persevered, what crime was being committed? Who was the victim? Who was getting hurt? And wasn't he finding inspiration for his writing in this new endeavor? And weren't the hours and income well-nigh perfect for a man of his artistic ambitions?

When Arthur seemed impervious to these arguments, I pointed out that without his present employment, he would again be dependent on the monthly checks sent by his impoverished family.

"How long are you going to live off them?" I demanded cruelly.

Enders flinched. After dithering a few moments, he agreed to continue as one of my crew, only until he found a "decent" job.

Then Arthur, who thought Jenny Tolliver the finest and loveliest woman in the whole wide world, asked me if I had told Jenny the kind of work I was doing. I replied shortly that I had not.

"I don't know how you can live with yourself," Enders said sadly.

"I don't," I said, laughing. "I live with you."

33

Reflecting that all liars are actors and all actors are liars, I told Jenny that I had been rehired by the King's Arms.

"Not full-time," I said casually. "Just to fill in on the regular guys' days off and vacations, and so forth. And I'll be working on Thursday nights when they're open late."

The last falsehood, of course, was to account for my whereabouts during the weekly meetings with Martha Twombly. Jenny accepted my lies without question, and I thought our relationship had never been sweeter or more intimate.

I sensed that the scenes with other women might be related to my increased tenderness toward her, but I couldn't understand how or why. Certainly, it had nothing to do with physical pleasure.

Were the sexual delights I shared with Jenny more intense than those with paying customers? To be honest, hardly at all. So, I reasoned, what attracted me to Jenny must be something more: an affinity beyond the flesh.

But why, since embarking on my new career, had I become more loving toward her?

We had a marvelous evening together. Dinner at Café des Artistes, during which I assured her that she was more beautiful than any of the women in the murals, though perhaps not quite as hippy.

"And not quite as young," she reminded me.

"To me," I vowed, "you will always be in a middy blouse and gym bloomers."

"Nut," she said, laughing. "You should be writing lines for Arthur. By the way, how is he?"

"Madly in love with you. As usual."

"I know," she said, looking down. "I must find a nice girl for Arthur."

"Oh . . ." I said lightly, "Arthur does all right."

We went to the ballet at Lincoln Center, for since that night at *The Iceman Cometh,* I had refused to attend the theater. We saw a set of short dances intended to be comedic.

"The only thing more embarrassing than ballet humor," I pronounced, "is opera humor."

We didn't stay to the end, but pushed our way out and walked down to Top of the Park. There we sat at a window, drank white wine, and winked at each other.

Then home to Jenny's apartment, holding hands and feeling no need to talk.

In bed, she raised the sheet, looked down, and said, "What are you doing under there?"

"Hiding," I said.

She laughed, tucked the sheet beneath her arms, and let me do as I would.

I *was* hiding. In that cotton tent, breathing her hot, musky scent. Enveloped all around. I wanted never to emerge. I could live out my days in that dark, secret place.

"Come up here," she called.

But I couldn't, and why my eyes should sting, I would never know. I curled about her, hanging on desperately.

"What are you doing?" she said. Then: "Oh. Oh, my."

I nuzzled, seeking wet warmth and safety. It was difficult to breathe, difficult to live.

"Lover," she said.

So I was. Seeking to make myself indispensable, to hold her forever by abjectness, to become an infection from which she might never recover.

"Monster," she said.

I would not, could not stop. It was expiation and salvation. And if I did not win her, I might cease to exist.

34

A "Mr. Burberry" had called my service and left a number where he could be reached. Burberry? Luke Futter. I returned the call.

"Where are you?" he demanded.

"At home."

"You got another number so I don't have to go through that service?"

I gave him the private unlisted number.

"Stay right there," Futter ordered. "I'll call you in exactly five minutes."

He did. "Now I'm calling from a public phone," he said.

"Getting paranoiac?"

"No. Just careful. Tomorrow, Wednesday, be out of your place between noon and three o'clock. That goes for Enders, too, and anyone else. Your place has got to be vacant from noon to three. Got that?"

"What's this all about?"

"I thought you didn't want to know."

"I don't," I said hastily.

I had Enders scheduled for a scene at noon on Wednesday. I moved it to the 68th Street studio and told him not to come back to the 75th Street apartment until three o'clock. Arthur wasn't happy about it, but he complied. He always complied.

I knew I couldn't handle Sol Hoffheimer as easily. Before I went down to his office on Wednesday morning, I had decided to tell him the truth—*almost;* Sol was too street-smart to con.

Hoffheimer and his office were both dingier than ever. He had looked up hopefully when I entered, then seeing it was me, had sagged and busied himself cutting the frayed end from a dried cigar butt with a pair of scissors. When I asked about his wife's health, he changed the subject.

"I see you're doing okay," he said sourly. "Nice raincoat. Nice sports jacket."

"I'm doing fine," I said cheerfully.

I took out my new pigskin wallet and counted a hundred and ten dollars onto Hoffheimer's desk.

"That clears me," I said. "Thanks very much, Sol. It was a big help when I needed it."

Hoffheimer stared at the money. He reached out and poked at the bills with a stubby forefinger.

"Beautiful," he breathed. "You can spare it?"

"Sure."

"Honest money?" Sol said, looking at me closely.

"I earned it."

"And how did you earn it?"

"A woman gave it to me," I said, returning the other man's stare. "For services rendered."

Hoffheimer drew a deep breath and blew it out, heavy lips burbling. He lighted his short cigar butt, tilting his head so he wouldn't burn his nose.

"I'm not going to tell you how to live," he said. "I'm doing such a great job of it myself? But, Peter . . ."

"I'm making enough money to support myself. To eat in good restaurants and buy new clothes."

"There's a Yiddish saying," Sol said: " 'No one sees his own hunchback.' Maybe if I was you, I'd be doing the same. Did you go to those two places I gave you?"

"No," I said. "Forget it, Sol. I've given up."

"I'm sorry to hear it," the agent said, sighing. "You've got talent."

"Talent?" I said hotly. "What the hell is talent? Everyone's got talent. The world reeks of talent. But if it doesn't pay off, what good is it? Screw talent. It never did a thing for me."

"I'm not going to argue with you," Hoffheimer said sadly. "I know the disappointments you've had. All I can do, from the bottom of my heart, is wish you luck. So this is so-long and farewell?"

"That's up to you," I said.

The agent put the little cigar butt into a discolored steel ashtray. "Soggy," he said. "A smoked-out nothing. What do you mean it's up to me?"

"It's more than one woman I've been getting money from. She's got friends, and the friends have friends. Sol, there are a lot of women in this town with enough money to pay for their pleasure."

"So?"

"So I get fifty for an hour's work—if you can call it work. I manage three, maybe four scenes a week. Tax-free."

"Why are you telling me all this?"

"These women, they're always looking for new men. Young, good-looking, reasonably clean. I thought some of the guys on your list . . ."

"No," Sol Hoffheimer said instantly.

I sat back, crossed my knees, looked at the other man intently.

"You say no damned fast."

"A pimp I'm not."

"No one's asking you to be a pimp. You send the men to me. It's a possible job you heard about; you don't know what it is. Then I make the pitch. If they go for it, fine; the decision is theirs. If they won't play, that's the end of it. But you're not pimping; I am."

"Peter, Peter," Hoffheimer said, groaning. "What are you doing?"

"Making money. *Living.* And you can, too. For every acceptable guy who's willing, you get a one-time fee of a hundred bucks. And I can use all the men you send me."

"Gott im Himmel!" Hoffheimer cried. "What are you running—a mail-order business?"

"Is that supposed to be a pun? Well, these women friends of mine go mostly for actors and models. And they complain that the guys are always leaving town on jobs or getting married or turning gay or whatever. So there's always a demand for new talent. You could make yourself a nice piece of change."

"I want no part of it," the agent said firmly. "And you should be ashamed of yourself for asking."

"Whatever you say," I said, shrugging. I rose, began to pull on my new raincoat. "But think it over, Sol. All you'd do is refer the men to me."

Sol Hoffheimer said indignantly, "Get the hell out of my office!"

I walked smiling up Fifth Avenue. I was not disappointed at Hoffheimer's immediate rejection. Later, when he had time to consider the proposition, he might see the advantages. And if not Sol, then some other theatrical agent. It was the answer to the supply problem. Martha Twombly would provide the demand.

It had rained during the morning, but now it was clearing; a fresh April sun shone through. The streets were flushed clean; the air had the sharp sparkle of early spring.

I walked with a lift, a prance. I was employed and generously rewarded. My future, if not secure, was at least promising. I belonged on this avenue. At last I was winning a place in this affluent society.

On impulse, I went into the gourmet food shop I had cruised in poorer times. I bought a small container of Beluga caviar, a jar of black truffles, a tin of pâté de foie gras. The cost was a shock, but how can you put a value on a whim? I took a cab home, laughing.

There was a police car parked in front of my brownstone. A knot of neighbors and passersby had gathered on the sidewalk, looking down into the areaway. Sammy, the building's super, was leaning against the fender of the squad car.

"What happened, Sammy?" I asked.

"Old Mrs. Fultz got ripped off," the super said.

"Jesus! Was she hurt?"

"Nah. She wasn't home, thank God. You know how she goes shopping every day around noon, and that's when they got in. Crowbarred her door open and really trashed the place. Broke every dish and glass, slit open her couch and chairs. Stuff like that. They even tore open the mattress. Maybe they figured she had some money hidden away."

"Maybe. What did they get—did she say?"

"Just some old jewelry. Her radio. All junk. I guess they were sore; they shit on her living room rug. The old lady's hysterical."

I went down to my own place. I took a look through the open door of Mrs. Fultz's apartment, but turned quickly from the desolation. I went into my kitchen and put away the gourmet foods.

35

We sauntered down Central Park West, opened coats flapping in the breeze, faces turned to the sweet sun.

"She's a stubborn old bitch," I said. "Won't move. Has all new locks on her door."

"Patience," Detective Luke Futter counseled. "Rome wasn't built in a day."

"And now she's got a watchdog," I went on. "A scruffy little fox terrier. Yapping all the time."

"Oh?" Futter said. "Well, we'll try again."

"You really think this is going to work?" I asked.

The detective gave me one of his smarmy grins. "It always has," he said.

And it did. Mrs. Fultz's apartment was broken into again, a week after the first burglary. Nothing was stolen or destroyed, but the little fox terrier was found lying on the kitchen linoleum, disemboweled.

That did it. Mrs. Fultz tearfully announced her intention of leaving and moving in with her daughter and son-in-law in Bensonhurst.

The moment I heard of her decision, I went to Sammy, the super. Enders' reproachful mien was getting more than I could bear, and this opportunity seemed the solution.

"Sammy," I said, "Enders and I decided we want separate pads. How's about your renting Mrs. Fultz's place to Arthur? He's good for the rent. Quiet."

"I don't know . . ." Sammy said, looking over my head. "Some people came by, they promised me fifty if I could find them an apartment."

"You can't eat promises," I said, taking out my wallet. "Here's fifty cash—win, lose, or draw. If we get the apartment, there's another fifty for you."

We got the apartment. Arthur accepted the new arrangement happily and moved his things next door. He agreed his pad could be used for scenes if he could approve the schedule in advance. I promised him ten dollars a scene for use of the premises.

I did not tell Detective Luke Futter that I had added a third bagnio to my chain.

36

Martha Twombly approved of the decisions I had made, but she was concerned about a possible cash flow problem.

"Aren't we expanding too fast?" she asked.

We were having our regular Thursday-night business meeting in her apartment. We were seated side by side at a leather-topped desk, going over accounts and drinking black coffee. The trumpeting elephants watched us.

"We may have a temporary shortfall," I acknowledged, "but only until we can increase production. We've been averaging twenty-five scenes a week. Call it a hundred a month, minimum. That's a gross of ten thousand dollars. Half of that for labor costs. That leaves you and me five thousand a month, or twenty-five hundred each."

"Sure," she agreed. "But the overhead is beginning to murder us. Two hundred a month to Futter, the rent on the Sixty-eighth Street place, the fees to Enders for using his apartment, tips to the supers, and so forth. You and I will be lucky to clear four hundred a week each, not counting your personal scenes. Maybe we should cut the studs' share."

"Absolutely not," I declared, throwing down my pencil. "Martha, this is a labor-intensive business and we've got to attract qualified employees. The only answer to increased income is increased production."

We both sat back, sipped our coffee, and reflected.

She was wearing black silk harem pants and a man's broadcloth shirt, neckline open, sleeves rolled up. Her face was scrubbed free of makeup and, oddly, her hard features were softened. She seemed younger, more vulnerable.

"Increased production means more boys," she reminded me.

I told her about my meeting with my theatrical agent without naming Sol.

"I think eventually he'll cooperate," I said. "But if he doesn't, I'll find an agent who will. It'll give us a dependable source of fresh talent. Can you supply more clients?"

"I don't anticipate any problem there," Martha said. "Seventy percent of last month's list was repeat customers."

"We must be doing something right," I said.

"Sure, but I'd like to increase the first-timers. They tell friends, and their friends tell friends. The only way this business will really take off is by word of mouth. Now, there are two more things. One: Most of our clients will be going away for June, July, and August. That will probably cut into our score."

"Mmm," I said. "Is there some way we could contact the tourists—all the women who'll be coming to New York for a summer vacation?"

Martha made no reply.

"What's the other thing?" I asked her.

"Most of my friends live on the East Side, and a lot of them are turned off when I suggest a scene on the West Side. Either they're scared of the street crime over there or they're just snobbish. I think we should keep in mind the possibility of opening an East Side place."

"No doubt about it," I said, nodding. "But we'll need big money for that. Meanwhile let's concentrate on building up our clientele."

"Which means more studs."

"Right. Well, that takes care of everything. Want me to split?"

"I've got no plans," she said lazily. "Kick off your shoes and have a brandy."

We moved to the black leather chesterfield. It seemed natural that she should curl up close to me and that I should put an arm about her shoulders.

"You got a guy?" I asked her.

"Occasionally," she said. "When he can make it."

"He's married?"

"Is he ever! With a couple of kids. He's a big shot. Politics, business, charities—you name it. So he can't get away too often."

"Does he know what you're doing? Your business with me?"

"No."

"If he found out, would he leave you?"

She looked up at me. "He can't do that. I know how to pull his trigger. His wife doesn't."

"Wow," I said. "Sounds dangerous."

"I can handle it," she said, shrugging.

"There's no chance of his showing up while I'm here?"

"Not to worry. He always calls ahead."

I bent, lifted her chin, kissed her.

"That's the first time you ever kissed me on the lips," she said. "Does that mean we're engaged?"

"No," I said, laughing. "It just means I like you."

She craned up to kiss me again. "I like you, too," she said.

I unbuttoned her shirt and found she wasn't wearing a bra. I cupped one of her meaty breasts in my palm.

"Are you just inspecting the merchandise," she asked, "or do you have some evil purpose in mind?"

"Oh . . ." I said, "why don't we let nature take its course. You're in no hurry, are you?"

"I've got all night."

37

Of course it wasn't all trouble-free. There were crises that sorely tested my managerial skills.

I was in my own apartment one afternoon, working on the next week's schedule, when I received a frantic phone call from Seth Hawkins. Seth was in the 68th Street place, supposedly servicing a woman named Lois. In the background I could hear screams, heavy thumping, and the sound of glass shattering.

I rushed over to 68th Street and found a policeman already there, summoned by neighbors. Seth, stripped to the waist, was looking simultaneously furious and frightened while another man was trying to stanch a bleeding nose. Lois, fully clothed, cowered on the bed. The cop was trying not to appear amused.

As I got the story, Lois had appeared on schedule. Five minutes later, a man claiming to be her husband showed up, threatening to kick the door down if he wasn't allowed in. When Hawkins unlocked the door, a short, roly-poly man rushed in, slapped Lois, and allegedly assaulted Seth, who was forty pounds heavier and thirty years younger.

So far, the cop told me, the husband wanted to sue Seth for "illicit fornication" ("Whatever the hell that is," the cop said). Hawkins wanted to charge the husband with assault and battery, and Lois was accusing everyone of personal humiliation and grievous emotional injury.

I drew the cop over to a corner and stood with my back to the combatants, as I persuaded him to get Mr. and Mrs. Lois not to press charges. A bargain for the three folded twenties I passed to him.

"I'll see what I can do," he said.

A half hour later, the studio cleaned up and put in order, I took Seth Hawkins over to Blotto's for a drink.

"Gawd dayam!" the Texan said. "What a foofaraw over shit-all. I swear that good woman just wanted a little loving. Ain't nothin' wrong with that—am I right?"

"Absolutely," I assured him.

The second incident wasn't exactly a crisis, but it left me feeling disturbed and apprehensive.

I had a scene with a woman named Lucille. She had crusty blond hair and a stringy body. Her breath smelled faintly of licorice, and her eyes roamed.

"Not much of a joint," she said, looking around.

"No, it isn't," I agreed.

When I brought her a glass of white wine, she tasted it and said, "Haven't you got anything better than this junk?"

"I'm afraid not," I said equably.

"How did you get in this business?" she asked.

"You mean," I said, trying to keep it light, "what's a nice boy like me doing in a place like this?"

"How much do you get out of what I paid?" she demanded.

"You'll have to ask Martha."

"How many studs is she running?"

It went on like that: question after question. How many tricks did I turn a week? Was this the only place or were there others? Any trouble with the cops? I was evasively polite.

Her prying turned me off and I didn't perform very well. But she didn't complain.

"Do you do gays?" she asked as she was dressing. "Are you into S and M? Any interest in making films? Are you available for mob scenes?"

I was glad to get rid of her. I saw her to a cab ("Nice touch," she said) and, walking back, wondered if she might be an undercover police-woman.

I called Martha Twombly and related what had happened. She said she didn't know Lucille personally; she was a friend of a friend.

"Did she have a douche in her purse?" she asked.

"I don't know. She went into the bathroom. Why do you ask?"

"Just wondering. She sounds like she's in the game."

38

Sol Hoffheimer called and said he wanted to see me. I cabbed down to the agent's office. He sat turned away, staring at the dirt encrusted window. I saw him in profile: slack features, sagging jowls, the whole face worn and defeated. All strength and elegance fled.

"Tell me again how we're going to work this," Hoffheimer said tonelessly.

Patiently, I went through it once more. We agreed that for every suitable guy he directed to me, Sol would receive a hundred dollars in cash.

"How many guys can you send me?"

The agent pondered a moment. "Five or six right off. But I'm always getting new ones. And with summer coming up and colleges closing, there'll be more."

"Fine," I said. "I can use all you recommend."

I rose to leave.

"I used to like you," Hoffheimer said heavily. "But I don't like you anymore."

I nodded and left. I walked west toward Eighth Avenue, figuring it would be easier to get a cab there.

I was saddened by Sol's last words, but not shamed. He had made his own decision, just like Arthur Enders, King Hayes, Seth Hawkins, and all the other studs. No one *made* them do anything; the choice was theirs.

But I acknowledged I had played the devil in all this. It had been the free choice of the others, true, but I had offered the temptation. Without my sly enticement, they might never have succumbed. I had exploited their need and wagered on their weakness.

I saw my role in theatrical terms. Like most actors, I found it difficult to distinguish illusion from reality, so I was playing in an opera bouffe, lurking in the shadows, red cloak held up to mask my face, energizing all the action.

The other actors blithely played their roles, not recognizing that the man in the dark who fed them their cues and determined their destiny was the devil. That was the fun.

It was, I decided, the juiciest part I'd ever had, and it might even make me a star.

39

Early in June I rented a car, and Jenny Tolliver and I packed a picnic lunch and drove out to Jacob Riis Beach. The sea was still too cold for swimming, but the sun was a delight.

We took our picnic basket down to the beach. Fried chicken, potato salad in a plastic container, pickles and radishes (we hadn't forgotten the salt), and two bottles of wine with elegant stemmed glasses.

We sat in the lee of the boardwalk and spread our lunch on a paper tablecloth, weighted down at the corners with handfuls of sand. The wind whirled above our heads, but the sunshine, reflected from the concrete wall, was beamy enough so we could remove our sweaters.

It was a chiseled day, so keen and clear that I swore I could see Portugal. A cerulean sky stretched forever, with thin plumes of clouds that looked like chalk marks. Light glinted on the wings of descending airliners, and we watched a black freighter plunging toward Ambrose Channel.

We ate chicken and drank wine. Then we leaned back against the concrete and smoked a cigarette. We turned pale faces to the sun, sipped away at the second bottle of wine, and sighed contentedly.

"Stick with me, kid," I said, "and you could be doing this every day in the year."

"I'd love it in January," she mocked.

"In January? The Caribbean. Or the Greek islands."

"Dreamer," she said, smiling.

"It's possible," I said thoughtfully. "I've never been abroad. There's a lot of the world I'd like to see before I'm too old to enjoy it. All it takes is money."

She poured us more wine. "Maybe," she said. "Someday."

Her placidity annoyed me. "Aren't there things you want? Right now? I know there are. You want a larger apartment, a studio of your own, designer clothes, a car—right?"

"Yes, but I'm not as impatient as you are. If I work, and I'm lucky, those things will come. And if they don't, it won't kill me."

"The thought of just going along, day after day, year after year, with nothing dramatic happening or likely to happen . . ." I said, shaking my head. "I just can't wallow in ordinariness."

"Do you think I wallow?" she asked quietly.

"Of course not. But you know me. If I win, I want to win *big*. And if I lose, I want to go down with a world-shaking crash."

"Peter, sometimes you scare me. You're so wild."

"I think I'm not wild enough. I've got to learn to really gamble. Not money; I haven't got that to gamble. I mean my future. My life. I've got to be willing to risk it."

"For what?"

"Oh . . . travel, clothes, a home, expensive restaurants, antiques, art—all that."

"In other words money," she said.

"Money," I agreed. "Plus a sense of accomplishment. There's a place waiting for me somewhere in this world. I've just got to find it."

"By the end of this year," she reminded me.

"What?" I said, remembering only after a moment my promise to quit the stage if I hadn't made it by Christmas. "That still goes."

"You'll stick to it?"

"Of course. I have six months, don't I?"

I laughed, grabbed her, kissed her cold lips. We stretched out on the sand and held each other tightly. I stroked her beautiful hair, looked deep into her beautiful eyes.

"What if I robbed a bank?" I said suddenly. "Would that count?"

"No," she said firmly. "You have to succeed on the stage, where you belong."

"No one else—particularly producers and directors—thinks I belong there."

"Well," she declared, "I think it's the only place you'll be happy."

"If I did rob a bank," I said, "or something just as stupid, would you still love me?"

She thought about it for a long time. "I would still love you, but it would be the end of us."

"You'd leave me?"

"If you did something stupid to get money? Yes, I would."

"But you'd go on loving me?"

"I could live with it."

"I wish I had your strength," I told her. "Oh God, how I wish it!"

"Why, Peter," she said. "Your eyes are glistening."

"The wind," I said.

I rose and stalked away from her. My back turned, I stood with legs spread, hands thrust into my pockets. I stared out at the heaving ocean.

Now the beauty of this day offended me. I wanted a lowering sky, gusting gale, the hammer of sleet. I wanted the excitement of menace.

Similarly, the simple goodness of Jenny Tolliver discomfited me. Her nobility! That quiet surety was a reproach, reducing everything to yea or nay, a simplism that mocked my dreams and brought my ambitions low.

I turned back to her. She was on her knees, gathering up the remnants of our lunch. I saw the fine arch of her back, the strands of chestnut hair flickering like flame in the sunlight. Breath caught in my throat. I wondered what I might sacrifice for this woman.

40

The summer turned out to be busier and more profitable than Martha Twombly and I had dared hope. By August we were each netting about a thousand dollars a week—thanks to the men recruited by Sol Hoffheimer. I now had between fifteen and twenty studs in my stable, though some were occasionally unavailable because of jobs or travel, and others dropped out for various reasons, to be replaced by newcomers.

"We're going to have to live with the turnover," I said. "Most of my boys look at this job as temporary."

"That may be a good thing. Most of the women are interested in new talent."

As she had predicted, many of our customers left the city for summer homes in the Hamptons, Fire Island, Montauk, the Berkshires, Catskills, and even as far afield as the Poconos, Cape May, Kennebunkport, and Nantucket.

What Martha and I had not anticipated was that in many cases married clients were alone and lonely all week in their country homes. There was a steady demand for services from Monday through Thursday.

Fees were not raised for sending studs out of the city, but customers were charged travel expenses. In two cases this included air fare—to Bar Harbor, Maine, and to Hyannis. I wondered about the legality of sending male prostitutes across state lines.

"I happen to know," Martha told me, "that the Mann Act makes illegal the interstate transportation of women for immoral purposes. I don't think it mentions anything about men. Should I ask my lawyer friend?"

"Forget it," I said. "In for a penny, in for a pound."

41

On Fridays at midnight, when all the studs met at Blotto's for a few drinks and some shop talk (during these informal gatherings I surreptitiously distributed pay envelopes), the conversation invariably got around to on-the-job oddities.

Wolcott Sands had a regular who insisted he wear a false mustache and beard during their scene.

Seth Hawkins serviced a client who requested he wear his cowboy boots in bed.

King Hayes had a "wife" who wanted only to slather his naked body with Johnson's Baby Oil. Once he was slippery and glistening, she put on her clothes and went home.

Such harmless eccentricities could easily be accommodated, but as business increased that summer, there were several cases of more deviant client behavior. So much so that Martha and I had to consider expanding the rules to protect our reputation.

The no-drugs edict was to be rigidly enforced. Obvious drunkenness, of client or stud, was taboo, as was excessive noise (shouts, cries) and the use of obscenities, unless specifically requested by the customer. Making a date with a client independently was grounds for instant dismissal.

The following relations were allowed, to be specified by the client: intercourse, fellatio, sodomy, cunnilingus, and anilingus. Since not all studs were willing to provide the full range of services, the problem became merely one of scheduling.

Sadism and masochism gave us the most trouble, since it was difficult in this area to frame approved standards of behavior. Generally, studs were instructed to accede to their clients' wishes as long as neither party's health or safety was threatened.

Physical violence was to be avoided, particularly if it left marks. "Water games" were permissible if proper care was exercised, and mouth-to-mouth kissing had to be initiated by the client. Condoms were to be issued and used on request of the customer, as were mechanical devices such as vibrators.

We had hoped this Code of Conduct would cover all eventualities, but it soon became apparent that no set of regulations could encompass the full range of ingenuity in human sexual vagaries. For instance:

When Martha said she had a request for a scene between two women and one boy, I was intrigued and volunteered. We both guessed that one woman would be participant, the other spectator.

They turned out to be an oddly matched pair. The younger, Janet, was petite, dark, with a full figure and skin that could not have been creamier without curdling. The older, Gertrude, was tall, raw-boned, with horsey features and hair cut short. Her voice was deep, with a masculine rasp.

Both women chatted easily about the summer theater season on Broadway as they sipped their white wine. Gertrude smoked a brown cigarillo. Janet, with flashing eyes and pouty lips, begged a second glass of wine.

Then the three of us went into the bedroom to undress. I believed a woman's underthings were an infallible tipoff to her personality. I was not surprised to note Janet's bra and bikini of buttery silk trimmed with Alençon lace. Gertrude's lingerie hardly deserved the name: coarse white cotton with panties almost long enough to be Bermuda shorts.

When we were all naked in bed together, Janet said, "Do her first."

Gertrude lay on her back, arms stiff at her sides. The body was a challenge: heavy, muscular, with broad shoulders and hips.

I used all my wiles and she came alive. My palms slid lightly over ponderous breasts, thick waist, pillared thighs. I could feel her flesh enkindle.

Janet, lying on her side, chin propped on one hand, watched intently.

Gertrude's breathing quickened. Fingers rose to my neck to pull me down. I bent to kiss one of her erect nipples—and bumped heads with Janet, who was setting to work on Gertrude's other aroused breast.

I looked up in astonishment. Janet was frantic, mouth and hands moving avidly over the older woman's body.

"Darling, darling, darling," she was murmuring. "At last, at last . . . Why did you make me wait so long?"

Janet glanced up, saw me staring at her.

"We won't need you anymore," she said crisply.

I went into the living room, had a glass of wine, and reflected mournfully that I didn't know a goddamned thing about women.

42

During that summer of our content, Martha was able to provide vacation fun for a surprising number of visitors, all of whom apparently wanted to take home a lasting memory of their stay in New York.

Many of the Americans were schoolteachers, eager to explore the cultural amenities of the Big Apple. Others were career women en route to or returning from European tours and eager for a final fling before going back to the daily grind.

There was also a liberal sprinkling of moneyed women from England, France, Germany, Italy, Saudi Arabia, Argentina, and especially Japan. Almost invariably they were poor tippers, but their patronage was welcomed by studs jaded with the regular clientele.

Seth Hawkins had flaxen-haired Swedish twins in a wild scene he talked about for weeks.

Arthur Enders happily serviced a doll-like Korean matron who, he insisted, smelled of camphor wood.

A French lady, Claire, worked her acrobatic way through almost the entire lineup of studs during her two-week stay, earning the sobriquet "Claire de Loony."

One of the black studs, not King Hayes, fell in love with a six-foot-tall ebony beauty and had to be restrained from following her home to Senegal.

As the summer progressed, many of the tourists insisted that the studs come to their hotel rooms. Martha was initially leery about this, fearing possible interference by security personnel. But as more and more rendezvous safely took place in hotels, motels, and motor inns, she began to see new possibilities for us.

"I think we should try to build up the escort end of the business," she said. "Most of your boys are well-dressed and presentable. A lot of women might want a date just for dinner, the theater, a party, or whatever. The money is good, and it's legal. In fact," she added, "remember my telling you about friends who won't go over to the West Side for a scene? Well, how about sending studs to their apartments?"

"A call boy service?"

"Exactly. What do you think?"

I reflected a moment. "I don't see why not. But only for single women, and preferably in the evening. A handsome stud arrives at a married woman's apartment in the middle of the afternoon, and neighbors are going to talk."

"I guess you're right. We've got to protect the client."

I snapped my fingers. "Got it!" I said excitedly. "I'll buy some of those big books of wallpaper samples. If a woman wants a scene in her apartment, the stud goes with a couple of those books. If anyone stops him or asks questions, he's an interior decorator."

"Peter," Martha Twombly said, gazing at me admiringly, "you were made for this business."

43

The call boy service was initiated after Labor Day. Although it never approached the trade volume of the three bordellos, it made a significant contribution to gross income. It also necessitated increasing our labor force, so Sol Hoffheimer had to double his efforts.

Early in October, I met with one of Sol's "possibles" in a back booth at the Losers' Place. The boy was as handsome as a young Tyrone Power, and I tried to be especially persuasive in making my pitch. All I got for my pains was indignant scorn.

After threatening to punch me out, he jerked to his feet and stalked away. I took my rejection—not the first—philosophically. I had a grudging admiration for starving actors who turned down the opportunity for easy money so immediately and instinctively.

I picked up my stein of beer and carried it to the bar. At once there was a man at my elbow, saying in a jeering voice, "Well, you can't expect to win them all."

I turned to look at the interloper. A very short, slight man wearing a soiled raincoat. Cavernous face with pitted cheeks. Small, squinched eyes and a black mustache no larger than a toothbrush. Bluish lips and ears like flaps of veal.

"I beg your pardon," I said stiffly.

"Go ahead and beg," the stranger said with a wolfish grin. "I love it. I saw you strike out with the pretty boy in the booth."

"I don't know what you're talking about."

"Sure you do," the other man said. "Your name is Peter Scuro and you were just trying to recruit a new stud for your cathouse on Seventy-fifth Street. I think we ought to talk. Come on . . ."

He turned his back and limped over to the booth I had just vacated. Then I saw the built-up black shoe, the sole three inches thick.

My first panicky reaction was to walk, if not run. But that would avail nothing; the man knew my name and where to find me. Reluctantly I carried my drink back to the booth.

"The name is Quink," the man said. "Sidney Quink. I won't offer to shake hands."

"Thank you," I said ironically.

"I guess you're wondering how much I know," Quink said with his fierce grin. "About everything, I figure. You're running twenty studs or more in two hot-pillow joints on Seventy-fifth and Sixty-eighth streets. The customers come from that woman in the dress shop on Madison. She collects a yard a lay. Have I got it right?"

"Where did you hear all this?" I demanded.

"A little bird told me."

I recalled the scrawny woman who had asked all the questions. "The little bird's name wouldn't be Lucille?"

"Ask me no questions and I tell you no lies. You got a nice thing going and all I want is a little piece of it."

I decided that if I showed weakness, I was doomed. "You're too short and ugly to be a cop," I said.

Quink grimaced. "Now, now," he said. "Let's not get personal. I prefer to keep things on a business basis. I figure about five grand would be fair."

"You're crazy!" I burst out.

"It would still leave you with a nice score," the other man said calmly.

"And what am I supposed to get for the five grand?" I said.

Sidney Quink leaned across the table and blew his fetid breath directly into my face. "Silence!" he said.

"Silence?"

"That's right," Quink said, sitting back and showing those tarnished teeth again. "And if you don't come up with the kale, I won't have to go to the cops. I go to the tabloids and maybe the local TV news shows. Think of what they could do with the story: 'East Side Socialites Pay for West Side Cock.' A real grabber."

I drew a deep breath. This wasn't just a sleazy crook, this was a menace, endangering everything I had worked so hard to achieve. Threatening my safety and future as well.

Cool, I cautioned myself. Play it cool.

"So?" Quink said.

"There's no way I can give you an answer right now," I said earnestly. "There are other people involved."

"Sure," the blackmailer said. "I appreciate that. I'll meet you right here a week from today. Bring the money in unmarked used bills, nothing larger than a twenty, no consecutive serial numbers."

"Sounds like you've done this before," I said scornfully.

"I been around," Sidney Quink acknowledged. "Remember, you only got a week or I sing my heart out." He began to drag himself from the booth, then stopped. "Say, maybe you should add me to your string. Some of those hoity-toity customers of yours might go for a gimp with a ten-inch schlong."

I looked at him with loathing.

44

Martha Twombly listened to my story intently. When I finished, she rose and began to pace about her living room.

"He sounds like a real crud," she said.

"Oh, he's a sweetheart," I said. "He uses dated slang like 'kale' and 'hoity-toity,' and he's got a breath that could peel paint. Martha, what are we going to do?"

She didn't answer but poured Armagnac into two snifters, handing one to me before resuming her pacing.

"Did he mention my name?" she asked.

"No. He just said the customers come from a woman in a dress shop on Madison. Is that true?"

"Dress shop?" Martha repeated with a bleak smile. "It happens to be one of the most exclusive boutiques on the Avenue. The Barcarole. You know it?"

"I've heard of it," I said casually. "You work there?"

"I manage the joint," she said harshly. "Where do you think I find all those loaded ladies?"

Finally she fell into an armchair, crossed her legs, drew a deep breath. She was wearing a black velvet hostess gown with a front zipper from neckline to hem. As usual, her feet were bare.

Sitting there, brooding, with the lamplight cutting cruel shadows, she seemed suddenly old and worn. Raising her glass, she tossed back the brandy, then shuddered.

"Son of a bitch," she said bitterly. "The guys I work for are a couple of tough nuts. So far they don't know what I've been doing."

"What would happen if they found out? Fire you?"

She gave a loud bark of laughter and rose to pour more Armagnac.

"Fire me?" she said. "Not bloody likely. They'd cut themselves in, and before we knew what was happening, we'd be working for them at a weekly salary you could stick in your ear."

"They sound like hard men," I said.

"Hard enough. I've been planning to break loose. We don't really need my Barcarole connection anymore. Most of our new customers are referred by old clients. I was figuring on working out of my apartment here, and looking around for that East Side place. Now that's all shot."

"Wait a minute," I said. "Could the men you work for take care of Quink?"

"With one phone call."

"But you don't want to ask them?"

"It would mean chopping down the money tree."

"So what do you want to do—pay Quink?"

She came over to pat my cheek and gaze down at me fondly.

"You are a dear, sweet boy," she said, "and I love you madly. But you don't, honey, really think a scuz like Quink is going to take the five grand, thank us politely, and quietly fade away? Never! He'll be back. He'll bleed us dry."

"Then I'll have to take care of him," I said grimly.

She looked at me with astonishment. "*You'll* take care of him?"

"Yeah. I'll just bounce him around a little. I can do it. I must outweigh him by fifty pounds. And he's a cripple."

She drew a deep breath. "Have you ever done anything like that before?"

"No," I said, "but I could."

"No," she said, "but you couldn't."

"Hey," I said, "wait a minute!"

"No," she said, resuming her pacing, "you wait. You couldn't muscle anyone, Peter. You're a softy. Come on, admit it. Look at the way you feel about our business. You got this romantic idea that we're running some kind of dating service to bring wealthy ladies and poor, deserving young men together. We're pimps, Peter. Can't you get that through your head? We're running illegal whorehouses. We're selling flesh."

I could feel my face flushing. I was holding up both hands, palms outward, as if she were pummeling me.

"I told you I was in the game in Chicago," she went on. "It's a dirty business. It attracts crooked cops and blackmailers like horseshit attracts flies. There's nothing romantic about it. The only thing it offers is lots and lots of money. That's the only reason I'm in it, and that's the only reason you're in it."

"God *damn* you!" I said in a choked voice.

She stopped to face me. "You want out?" she challenged.

I hung my head. "No, I don't want out."

"Then use your brain. You're not the type to lean on Quink."

"Well," I said defensively, looking up at her, "if you don't think I can do it, and you don't want to pay him off, and you don't want to ask your bosses to take care of him, what the hell *do* you want?"

"There's only one way. The cop. Futter."

"No," I said immediately. "Not him."

"Why not?"

"Because he took care of Mrs. Fultz. And now we're running to him again. Once he figures we can't operate without him, he'll jack up his price and we'll never get rid of him."

"That's a danger," she agreed. "But we've got no choice. Anyway, Futter's got too nice a thing going with us to let us go down the drain. And he's got the experience and know-how to handle a creep like Quink. Sure, it'll cost us, but not as much as Quink would."

"What do you expect Futter to do?"

"Oh . . ." she said vaguely, turning away from me, "just take care of Quink. So he'll never bother us again."

I helped myself to more brandy. "I don't like it, but I can't come up with anything better."

Martha arranged herself on the leather couch and held out an arm to me. Obediently I sat beside her. She began to fondle the back of my neck.

"Tell me about this Futter," she said. "Everything: what he looks like, how he dresses, how he talks. Is he married? How old is he? Has he got any kinks?"

I described the detective's quirky smile, his hopeless efforts to dress elegantly, his insistence that all conversations and payoffs take place out-doors.

"Uh-huh," she said. "Now here's what I want you to do. . . . Contact him as soon as possible. Tell him exactly what happened. Don't leave anything out. Tell him we want a report on this Quink and we've only got a week before the payoff."

"There's not much to go on," I said doubtfully.

"Don't worry about it," Martha advised. "If this Futter is any kind of detective, he'll find him. Works out of Vice, doesn't he? I'll bet Quink has a record. And tell him that Quink is probably running a whore named Lucille. That might help."

"How much should we pay?" I asked.

"Not more than five hundred for a rundown. But hint there may be more to get rid of Quink. Think you can handle it?"

"Of course," I said, offended. "After all, I *am* an actor."

"That you are, sweetie. One more thing: When Futter is ready to report, get him here. Tell him your partner wants to meet him."

"I'm not sure I can," I said. "He's a very suspicious guy. He's got this thing about bugs and tape recorders. I told you we always deal outside."

"He'll go for it," she said confidently. "Tell him your partner is a sexy lady who supplies all the customers. His curiosity will get the better of his good judgment. And he'll figure the more he learns about the operation and the people involved, the stronger his clout will be."

"All right," I said. "I'll do as you say."

She pressed her palm against my cheek, turned my head so we were facing. I could feel her warm breath on my lips.

"You're not sore at me, are you, Peter?" she said softly. "For all those nasty things I said about you."

"Not so nasty," I said. "And probably true."

"We're still friends?"

"Of course."

"Good," she said. "I've got a sweetheart. I need a friend."

45

When I had a scene with a woman, a stranger, I rarely had any desire to know her longer than the allotted hour. Sex had become theater, and those "scenes" were really one-act plays.

But with Jenny Tolliver, the curtain never came down. I thought it might be her mystery that attracted me; I simply could not get to the end of her.

She could be a wanton in bed, as lubricious as any of the clients I serviced. But at other times she offered nothing but calm flesh and silent acquiescence. Her manic moods were frenzied; her periods of quiet deliberation disturbing, because then she looked at me thoughtfully, as if she might be summing me up.

I found myself resenting her inconstancy. I wanted her of a piece, so I might grasp her. But she slid away from me.

"You're never the same woman twice," I told her, vexed.

And all I got for that was a secret smile.

I wondered if I loved her, and then wondered what love might be. I thought it could be a special kind of attunement. I saw her the night after my meeting with Martha when we had discussed the problem of Sidney Quink, and Jenny caught my mood instantly.

"What's wrong, Peter?" she asked.

"Nothing's wrong."

"Something must be. You're strung as tight as a fiddle."

"I'm fine," I told her.

"No, you're not. You're all dark and broody. I can tell."

She was that perceptive of my humors.

"If you don't want to screw," I said crossly, "just tell me. I won't be insulted. My ego is monumental."

"You keep saying that," she said, "but it's not true. Your ego is a poor, fragile thing. I want to screw whenever you want to; you know that. Although," she added reflectively, "it's been rather infrequent lately, has it not?"

I envied her completeness, her certainty. She had none of the illusions of the actor. She played a single role—herself—and had no need for cues or audience. I could not believe she ever questioned her own motivation. It was maddening.

"You're dressing very well these days," she observed.

"I get a discount on things at the King's Arms," I lied smoothly.

"Anything new on acting jobs?"

"Maybe," I said shortly. "Let's go to Blotto's and see if Arthur and Hayes are there."

I was tempted occasionally to confess all and beg her forgiveness. But I knew I could expect no mercy. Not because I had lied to her; not because she was holier than thou; not because of what I had done to her by my commercialized unfaithfulness. Her horror would spring from what I had done to myself. She would see me as a feckless man bent on self-destruction.

She would never understand my temptations. She would think me as diseased as an alcoholic who recognizes his fatal affliction but has neither the desire nor strength to stop.

She might pity me, but she would never forgive me.

So I made love to her desperately, did my Russian commissar shtick, played the fool, and wondered how much longer I could go on betraying her.

46

"My God, Martha!" I staggered back in an exaggerated Bert Lahr bit. "Let me look at you. What's with the getup?"

She was wearing a shiny black silk dress, cut so tightly that horizontal wrinkles crossed her ungirdled hips. Cut so low that breasts bulged; her cleavage looked like the valley of the damned. Spike heels and ankle straps. Too much makeup, too much perfume.

"You never bought that outfit at the Barcarole," I said.

"I never did," she agreed. "But trust me; I know what I'm doing."

I looked around her living room. "Something's changed."

"Nothing much," she said offhandedly. "I rearranged the elephants, that's all." She patted the rump of a Korean ceramic tusker at the end of the leather couch. "I decided to use this beauty as a cocktail table. You like?"

"Very handsome," I said, looking at her curiously. "But you haven't explained the clown's costume."

"I'm a tart," she said. "You knew that, didn't you?"

"A tart at heart?"

"That's it," she said, smiling tightly. "When is this cop going to show?"

"He said nine o'clock. Listen, Martha, I had the devil's own time talking him into coming up here."

"Did you tell him I was a sexy lady?"

"That line went over like a lead balloon. Finally I persuaded him it was time he met my partner and got to know the operation. He agreed, but he wasn't happy about it."

"His happiness is pretty low on my priorities," Martha said. "Look, Peter, when he shows up, let me do the talking. Okay?"

I threw up my hands in an Italianate gesture. "You're the boss."

"Only for tonight. I've handled guys like this before, believe me."

"I do," I said. "Now how about a drink?"

"No," she said. "Not until he comes. Then we drink what he drinks."

"Oh-ho," I said. "You're going to psych him out?"

"Something like that. I'll bet he drinks bourbon. You want to bet something else?"

"He's trying to be elegant. I'll bet he drinks scotch. Five bucks?"

"You're on."

We sat, chatting easily, until the bell rang.

"You buzz him in," Martha said. "Then put him in that armchair facing me."

I went to the door to press the button. When I turned back, I saw Martha sitting at one end of the couch. She was leaning forward slightly, bosom overflowing. Her legs were crossed, tight skirt hiked above bare knees.

"Whistler's Mother," I said, grinning. "Wish us luck, Mom."

I ushered Futter into the room, introduced them, and got him into the chair Martha had indicated. She leaned toward him.

"I want to thank you," she said sincerely, "for your help on the Mrs. Fultz matter. You handled it like an expert."

Futter shrugged and flipped a palm back and forth.

"May I call you Luke?" she asked brightly. And then, not waiting for an answer: "How about a drink before we get started. What's your pleasure?"

"Not booze," Futter said with a sniggering laugh, staring at her neckline. "But if that's all that's available, I'll take a bourbon."

"Bourbon!" Martha cried. "My favorite. Peter, will you do the honors? Everything's in the kitchen."

While I was going through cupboards to find the bottle and glasses, I heard them laughing together in the living room. Martha was one sharp lady. Suddenly I knew everything was going to turn out all right.

When we all had our bourbons, the detective took out a small pocket notebook and began to flip the pages. He had a problem dragging his eyes from Martha Twombly.

"Sidney Quink," he said. "He wasn't hard to find. Real name: Samuel Quillan. Funny how these cheapies always keep their initials when they take an alias. Maybe he's got a monogrammed jockstrap or something."

"Luke," Martha said, giggling, "you're just *awful!*"

"Yeah," he said. "Well, this Quink or Quillan has a sheet as long as your arm. Nasty stuff, like kiddie porn. At the moment he's living in a fleabag hotel in the East Village. Running three overaged hookers. One of them is that Lucille you mentioned. The guy's done time in Florida and California for this and that. No outstanding warrants. He's not on parole or probation."

He snapped the notebook shut, took a swallow of bourbon, looked from Martha to me and back to Martha again.

"That's all I got," he said.

"Luke," Martha said earnestly, "Peter and I are babes in the wood when it comes to a shakedown like this. We're depending on your experience and know-how. You tell us: What do we do?"

Luke Futter rose and, drink in hand, began to wander about the living room. As he talked, he ran his fingers along the bottom edges of tables, the back edges of a bookcase, and the frames of paintings.

He even picked up a lamp to take a swift glance at the bottom of the base. He flipped up the cushion of the chair he had been seated in. He kicked back the edges of the Persian carpet. He felt the tops of the doorjambs. He pulled back the drapes briefly to peek behind them.

He did all these things so casually, it hardly constituted a search—more like standard paranoid operating procedure.

"You can pay him off," the detective said. "But once he gets his hooks into you, you'll never see the end of him. You can try scaring him off, but he can close you down with one phone call or one anonymous letter. Just out of meanness—you know? You could frame him, but you've only got two days left to set it up and he could still scream his guts out."

"All right," Martha said. "You've told us what we can't do. Now tell us what we can."

Futter handed his empty glass to me. "Refill?" he asked. "Please."

I took all three glasses to the kitchen and returned with fresh drinks. The detective was sitting negligently in the armchair again, legs crossed. He was smoking a cigarette slowly and staring at Martha's bare knees with his loppy smile.

"I could handle it," he said quietly. "But it'll cost you five grand. The same amount you'd have to pay Quink. The only difference is that this would be a one-shot. My word on that."

"Five thousand dollars, Luke?" Martha repeated.

"In cash. The same way he wanted it. Small, used bills. No consecutive serial numbers. It isn't all for me. I'll need to bring in a couple of buddies. So split three ways, it's not so much."

"What will you do?" I asked.

The detective stared at me blankly.

"You'll never see him again," he said. "That's all you need to know."

"What about his whores?" Martha asked. "Will we be hearing from them?"

"No problem there," Futter said. "Well? Is it go or no-go?"

"Go," Martha said firmly. "Peter?"

"Go," I said in a low voice, troubled. "I don't see we have a choice."

"That's right," Luke Futter said. "No choice at all."

"Five thousand to you in cash, Luke?" Martha repeated again. "A one-time payment?"

"Right."

"And we'll never be bothered by this guy again?"

"You've got it."

"All right," she said. "Do it."

The detective turned toward me. "Here's how we handle it. . . ."

47

Following Luke Futter's instructions, I arrived at the Losers' Place a half-hour early. I sat at the bar, where I could watch the entrance in the back mirror. I ordered a stein of beer, paid, and sipped it slowly.

I was carrying a shoebox stuffed with cut newspaper, wrapped in brown paper and tied securely with twine.

Futter had explained that I was to get Sidney Quink outside; he couldn't be taken in the bar. Too many cops hung out in the Losers' Place.

Quink was right on time. I saw him enter, look around, then limp to the bar. He stared at the brown paper parcel. He said he was happy to see that I had decided to play it smart.

I said there were too many people I knew in the Losers' Place; I didn't want to be seen handing over the package. I turned and started for the door. Quink had no choice but to follow.

Outside, still following Futter's orders, I walked toward Eighth Avenue. I slowed, giving the blackmailer a chance to catch up. Then I thrust the wrapped box into Quink's hands. The cripple looked down at it, turning it over and over.

Two burly men got out of a dusty-blue Plymouth double-parked on West 54th Street. Their approach was perfectly timed: not too fast, not too slow. The few passersby paid no attention.

I stopped. The big men moved in. They took Quink by the upper arms and half-carried, half-dragged him toward the double-parked Plymouth. I saw Futter sitting behind the wheel.

Just before he disappeared, Sidney Quink turned a twisted face to me.

"You prick," he said bitterly.

48

"Sit down," Martha Twombly said. "Have a brandy. You look shook."

I held my drink in a hand that trembled slightly. I told her what had happened.

"It went down just the way Futter said it would," I finished. "It was all over in seconds. No one noticed a thing. Martha, what's going to happen to Quink?"

"Do you really want to know?" she asked him.

"No. Do you?"

"No."

"Do you think Futter will keep his part of the bargain?"

"Do you mean will we ever hear from Quink again? I don't think so."

"That wasn't what I meant," I said. "Futter won't come back for another five grand, will he? We haven't traded one blackmailer for another, have we?"

She looked at me with a sardonic smile. "I've got something for you," she said.

She went into the bedroom, came back with a small portable tape recorder, and pressed the play button. I heard the final part of our conversation with Detective Luke Futter.

Martha: "Five thousand to you in cash, Luke? A one-time payment?"

Futter: "Right."

Martha: "And we'll never be bothered by this guy again?"

Futter: "You've got it."

Martha: "All right. Do it."

Futter: "Here's how we handle it . . ."

Martha switched off the recorder.

"Jesus Christ!" I burst out. "Where was it?"

She stroked the trunk of the ceramic Korean elephant at the end of the couch. "In here. It's hollow but heavy enough so he couldn't take a look without making a big deal."

I took a deep breath. "If he had found it, I don't know what he would have done."

"I figured he wouldn't make a thorough search. Not with me making like Sadie Thompson. Peter, a man can be the smartest guy in the world, but he sees a couple of tits and an ass, and his brains go out the window. That cop was so busy trying to see up my skirt, he wasn't thinking straight. If you remember, I had him repeat everything twice. If he ever tries to shake us down, we've got enough on this tape to break him. I'm going to make two copies. One for you. Keep it in your safe deposit box."

I said, "You're so smart it scares me."

"Not so smart," she said, smiling. "I think I may still have a problem with Detective Luke Futter. Not us, but me. I've got a feeling he's going to come sniffing around, looking for a freebie."

"And how will you handle that?"

"Tell him I have herpes," she said promptly, "and fix him up with a beautiful young call girl I know who'll fuck his brains out. I'll pay for it."

I laughed and drank my brandy. I was feeling a lot better.

"And talking about beautiful young girls," Martha said, "we've got a new client who's absolutely smashing. Her name is Coral, and she was referred by a regular customer. Peter, this Coral is something special. Tall, willowy, skin like satin, a fantastic figure, and the loveliest face I've seen in years. You better take her yourself."

"I will," I said. "She sounds great."

Martha stood up. "Sorry to give you the bum's rush, dear, but my boyfriend's coming over in about an hour."

"Which boyfriend—the lawyer or the big-shot politician?"

"I only have one boyfriend. The lawyer is strictly for business, but the politician is for fun and games."

At the door, she said firmly, "You owe me five. Futter drank bourbon."

I handed over the money gratefully.

49

Several of the other studs had regular customers—their "wives"—but I had none. All the clients I serviced assured me of their complete satisfaction, but few booked a second scene with me, and none a third.

One woman offered a clue on why this was so.

"You're just too perfect, dear," she told me. "You know all the moves and all the buttons to press. You act a great lover. The only thing missing is passion. Can't you manage to sweat a little?"

I couldn't believe any of that. It wounded my pride as a player.

When Coral entered my 75th Street apartment, I decided instantly that I wanted her for a "wife." She was everything Martha had said—and more. I resolved to give the performance of my life.

Fine, wheaten hair cascaded halfway down her supple back. Her complexion was a matte porcelain and her blue eyes danced merrily. I thought her nose divine, her pouty lips adorable. I wanted to consume those delicate ears.

She wore a black cashmere turtleneck sweater, wide belt of crushed leather, a skirt of mushroom-colored wool. The sweater revealed a flawless bosom, the belt cinched the waist of an emaciated wasp, and the tight skirt delineated hips and rump of luscious proportions.

She spoke in Tallulah Bankhead tones and laughed throatily at my jokes. She was, I decided, without fault—except possibly that gold slave bracelet supporting a small diamond. And her hands and feet were a mite largish.

But only a churl would be disenchanted by those minor defects.

"You're an actor, darling," she said. "Are you not?"

"I was," I said. "How did you know?"

"You have the presence," she said. "I love actors."

She had a trick of smiling naughtily as she briefly stuck out her tongue. I thought it a heavenly habit.

"Have you ever been on the stage?" I asked her. "You're beautiful enough."

"Thank you, darling. Yes, I had theatrical ambitions. I wanted to be a singer. I had a few engagements in small clubs, but then my husband made me give it up."

"What a shame," I commiserated. "I think you would have been a smash. What sort of things did you sing?"

"Oh . . ." Coral said with that roguish smile and quick tongue-dart, "love songs mostly."

I couldn't wait to see that pliant body uncovered, but it was not to be. In the bedroom, she asked me to disrobe, but she made no effort to remove her clothes.

"I'm disappointed," I said.

"You won't be, darling," she said. "I promise."

When I was naked, I reached for her, but she drew back.

"Now, now," she said. "You just lie there quietly and let me make love to you."

"If that's what you want," I said somewhat grumpily.

She sat on the edge of the bed and drifted her feathery hair back and forth over my body. Her pouty lips fastened on my nipples. Teeth pinched. Then she looked up at me through half-closed eyes.

"Do you like that?" she asked in her deep voice.

"I like everything you do. But I wish you'd let me—"

"Shh," Coral said. "Just lie still. I'll do everything."

And so she did, with her cool fingers and warm mouth. Her expertise was amazing, and I thought, not for the first time, what a marvelous profession I was in.

"I love your body," she said thickly. "Such a lovely man's body."

I endured her practiced lovemaking as long as I could. But then I yelped and lurched upward. She held me imprisoned. I felt the sharp edges of her teeth, and I sobbed.

Demented, I thrust a hand roughly beneath her skirt. I grabbed frantically. And there, within silken panties, I felt the unmistakable shapes of penis and testicles.

"Surprise!" Coral cried.

50

Business was brisk that November. In addition to the three brothels on West 75th and 68th streets, we were running a small but growing call boy service. And our escort branch seemed to have a potential.

The problem was personnel. I had a work force of perhaps forty studs. But of these, only half were "steadies" who could be depended upon. They included whites, blacks, Hispanics, Orientals, and one full-blooded Cherokee Indian.

The remainder were "floaters," in New York between acting jobs, or drifting away to be married, or leaving hopefully for television auditions on the Coast. They usually checked in with me when they were available, but there was a constant demand for "new talent."

I went to Sol Hoffheimer.

I tossed a manila envelope onto the agent's desk.

"Four hundred," I said. "Cash. Small bills. Count it."

Hoffheimer didn't touch the envelope. He stared at it.

"What am I doing?" he said wonderingly.

"Making money," I said. "Money has no conscience. It's just green paper. A dirty twenty buys as much as a clean twenty."

"You say."

"We've got a problem," I said briskly. "We need more boys. Too many are temporaries. I've got to build up my hard-core permanents."

"Hard-core," Sol said. "Ho-ho. That's rich."

"So what I'd like," I went on, ignoring him, "is for you to take out a small, discreet ad in the trade papers. I'll pay for it."

"Studs wanted? Willing to put out on demand?"

"Come on. 'Young men wanted for rewarding career.' Something like that. I'll even write it for you."

The agent was silent.

"Sol," I said softly, "you can walk away from this anytime you like.

According to my records, you've made close to two grand already. If you have a terminal attack of the guilts, I'll find someone else."

Hoffheimer didn't answer.

"Give me a piece of paper," I said. "I'll write the ad copy right now."

Another problem was that of scheduling. It had become so complex and time-consuming that I seriously considered the purchase of a small, desk-top computer.

Many of our clients demanded a specific time. Others asked for a specific boy. There were several regulars who reserved the same time, same stud, once a week, or twice, or thrice.

I discussed the scheduling difficulties with Martha, and we agreed that at last it was time for the East Side apartment.

"Three bedrooms," I said, jotting notes, "available twelve hours a day. That gives us a daily maximum of thirty-six scenes. I don't think we can handle that with our present personnel, but I think twenty scenes a day is possible, don't you?"

"Of course," Martha said. "That gives us a gross of sixty thousand a month. Half to the studs. That leaves thirty grand for rent, expenses, and our cut. I think we could go as high as five thousand a month rent."

"Heavy," I said, shaking my head. "But I suppose an elegant place would help business."

"Sure it would," she said. "We'll try to get something suitable for less, but we better be prepared to spend. The trouble is, neither of us has time to go apartment-hunting. I know how busy you are, and I'm not leaving the Barcarole until the first of the year. Peter, my lawyer friend does a lot of wheeling and dealing in real estate. Suppose I ask him to keep an eye out for us."

"We'll have to pay him if he finds something, won't we?"

"Not necessarily. There aren't many people looking for five-thousand-a-month apartments, and he might be able to get his cut from the owner or real estate agent."

"Fine. Three or four bedrooms. And the place has to be furnished."

"I'll tell him."

"One more thing . . ." I said. "Detective Luke Futter would like to see you. Socially."

"Shit," Martha said.

51

When Arthur Enders asked me to have dinner, I suspected what was coming but readily agreed. We ate at that steak joint on West 72nd Street, in the same booth where Enders had been recruited. But this time we had oysters, rare sirloins, and a forty-dollar bottle of Pommard.

Arthur was his usual pale, bewildered self. Twice he dropped his fork, and once he choked so violently on a hunk of steak that I had to pound his back.

He calmed down with coffee and Rémy Martin, but he still couldn't bring himself to do it. So I said it for him.

"You want out."

Enders nodded dumbly.

"Mind telling me why? The money's good."

"It's got nothing to do with money," Enders said. "I can't even give you any sensible reasons. It just doesn't *feel* right."

"Guilt? Morality? All that bullshit."

"I suppose so," Arthur said miserably. "Partly at least. But mostly it's the way it makes me see myself. Crawly."

"Crawly? What the hell does that mean? That I'm a creep?"

"Look," Enders said earnestly. "It's got nothing to do with you. This just concerns me and how I want to live."

"How *are* you going to live? Off your family?"

"I'll make out."

"Sure," I said. "Spaghetti and meatballs at Blotto's while you hack away at a play you'll never finish. And even if you do, your chances of selling it are one in a zillion."

"Then I'll write another one," Arthur said stoutly. "I'm getting better; I know I am."

I stared at him. "You're a pisser, you are. You think you have talent? I thought I had talent and look where it got me."

"You should have hung on."

"For how long?" I said hotly. "Until I could play the ghost in *Hamlet* without makeup? Jesus, Arthur, sooner or later—and probably sooner—we're going to be fucking dead. Me, you, everyone. Life is short and precious. Do you really want to waste it?"

"I think I'm wasting it humping strange women for money. If life is precious, shouldn't you try to give it value by doing something meaningful with your days?"

I couldn't agree, but Arthur's defection rankled. When everyone was a coward, no one was a coward. A single hero was a danger.

"What are we doing that's so terrible?" I demanded. "Who's getting hurt?"

"I am," Enders said sadly. "In a way I can't even understand. I just know I'll feel, uh, more comfortable if I get out."

"I suppose that means you don't want your pad used for scenes anymore."

"That's right. The whole place smells of sex."

"It smells of money, is what it smells of. Well, it'll be a problem, but we'll manage."

We sipped our cognac slowly. I looked across the table at that pallid, twitching bunny, feeling a sudden surge of affection and admiration for a man I considered one of life's great losers.

"Arthur," I said, "this doesn't mean we have to stop being friends, does it?"

"Oh my God," Enders said. "Of course we can still be friends. I want to be. I really do. Besides, I want to see what happens to you."

"Yeah," I said with a sourish grin. "Me, too."

52

Oscar Gotwold was a Kewpie doll of a man with a large, round head you expected to start bobbing at any moment and never stop. A comfortable corporation bulged the vest of his pin-striped suit. His hair had thinned to a horseshoe of silver around a polished pate.

The attorney had delicate hands, fingernails beautifully manicured, and tiny feet shod in gleaming wingtips. Shrewd little eyes looked out with some amusement at a corrupt world. There was a burble of laughter in his sonorous voice, mocking his own solemnity.

"In my opinion . . ." he said, looking back and forth from Martha to me.

He told us that the nature of our business, with its high traffic flow, dictated an East Side apartment with a private entrance.

"You want to maintain a low profile," he said, "and minimize the neighbors' curiosity, the attention of doormen, elevator operators, and so forth."

Gotwold conceded such apartments were rare, especially in the size and neighborhood we desired. A townhouse would be the ideal solution, but the cost would be prohibitive.

"Did you find anything at all, Oscar?" Martha said.

But he would not be hurried. After torturing us with a couple of unlikely candidates, he finally told us his assistant had located a penthouse on the top floor of a modern, twenty-nine story apartment house on East 81st Street near Third Avenue. Three bedrooms and a den that could easily be converted to a fourth. Completely furnished, including linens and kitchenware.

"You could move in tomorrow with nothing but a toothbrush," he assured us.

The penthouse was presently rented under a three-year lease by a man who had moved to Rome until his problems with the IRS could be resolved. Meanwhile, he was subletting his apartment on a monthly basis, mostly to large corporations for the use of out-of-town executives or foreign visitors.

There were three hundred apartments in the building, which made for a busy lobby. Two doormen were on duty during the day, one at night. Security arrangements included alarm systems in all apartments and closed-circuit TV cameras on all floors, with monitors at the doorman's desk.

"Best of all," he said, "the penthouse has its own self-service elevator, so there's your private entrance. You can't go up until the resident of the penthouse identifies you on an intercom and presses a button activating the elevator."

"Oscar," Martha said, "did you actually see this place yourself?"

"I saw it," he said. "It's handsomely furnished, in my opinion. Very modern. Lots of glass and stainless steel. The living room is enormous, done in shades of beige and sand. Good rugs. The three bedrooms are done in different colors: rose, blue, and green. Three bathrooms and one lavatory. Terrace, den, pantry, kitchen, dining room."

"My God," I said. "How much for this palace?"

Oscar Gotwold looked at us with his impish smile.

"Seventy-five hundred a month."

We were silent.

"They won't give more than a year's lease," the attorney said. "In case the owner settles his tax problems and wants to move back. If you take it for a year, I think they'll come down to seven thousand. Two months' security."

"It's more than we wanted to spend," I said in a faint voice.

"I am aware of that," Gotwold said. "But in my opinion you should at least look at the place."

"All right," Martha said firmly.

"Good. And now may I offer a little unsolicited advice?"

"Of course."

"Because of the, ah, peculiar nature of your business, in my opinion you should take steps to disguise your activities if you decide to rent the penthouse. The manager and doormen will have to be paid off, of course. But even with the private elevator, other residents of the building are bound to notice the unusual traffic."

"What do you suggest?" I asked.

"Oh . . ." the attorney said with his elfin smile, "some sort of nonobjectionable business or association that could provide a façade of respectability and justify all the comings and goings of your, ah, employees and customers."

"A boutique?" Martha suggested.

"Oh, no," Gotwold said. "The building isn't zoned for anything like that. In my opinion, some kind of a service would be best. I was thinking along the lines of a school that provides instruction in yoga or an esoteric Eastern religion."

"A school?" I said. "I could teach acting."

"Could you?" the lawyer said. "An acting school? That might do very well. It would account for that busy private elevator. You might even put up a modest brass plate."

"Peter's Academy of Dramatic Arts," I said.

"Splendid!" Oscar Gotwold said, beaming.

53

Jenny Tolliver had gone home for Thanksgiving. Arthur Enders had a date. Martha Twombly had a miserable cold. King Hayes, Wolcott Sands, and some of the other studs were planning a drunken dinner at Blotto's. I was invited, but begged off. I wanted to spend the evening alone.

Which was odd, because I was not a man who cherished solitude. But of late I had found myself smothered by people. I needed quiet, peace, a moment to reflect.

I had a late lunch and then, with no scenes scheduled for the holiday, went home and took a long nap. I spent the evening watching television and sipping vodka gimlets from one of my new Swedish glasses that were all bubbles and swirls.

At about ten o'clock, feeling no pain, I showered, shaved, and donned my new dinner jacket. Patting my pockets to make certain I had my new gold Dupont lighter and packet of Gauloises Bleues (very *in* that year), I sallied forth into a dark night riven with gusts of freezing rain.

I took a cab to an East Side piano bar I knew, but found the place shuttered for Thanksgiving Day. So I ordered the cabdriver to continue south to the Hotel Parker Meridien on West 57th Street.

The elegant cocktail bar was crowded, all tables and banquettes filled, but I found a place at the corner of the bar and ordered a half-bottle of champagne. I lighted a cigarette, took an experimental sip of the wine, and looked grandly about.

I was the only single in the room. There were a few groups of men and fewer of women, but all the others were couples, male and female leaning toward each other eagerly. I felt neither loneliness nor envy. I looked on these lovers kindly, wishing them well.

When Martha had accused me of being a "softy," of believing in the romance of my new career, she had been correct, and her scorn had forced me to take a harder look at my activities.

But I saw her realism as cynicism. Drinking my champagne and looking around at all the smiling couples, I suddenly realized that I was no mere flesh peddler.

What I was selling was dreams.

Those women who paid a hundred dollars for a scene—weren't they trying to concretize a fantasy? What about that client who insisted her favorite stud, a clever mimic, imitate Clark Gable in bed? And what of the customer who brought along pressurized cans of whipped cream, or the one who couldn't get it off unless she was listening to a Mario Lanza recording?

I told myself I was providing all those women the opportunity of realizing their wildest dreams and most enigmatic wants.

In that sense, I told myself, I was not far from playing the role of a psychotherapist. I was enabling women to fulfill themselves.

Satisfied with this conception of myself, I ordered another half-bottle of champagne and stroked the silken lapel of my dinner jacket with gratification.

54

When I told Martha about my scene with Coral, I expected her to fall laughing to the floor. But she was goggle-eyed.

"I can't believe it! Peter, I've seen a lot of beautiful transvestites, but I would have sworn that Coral was a woman."

"Well, she, he, *it* isn't," I said crossly. "I *know.*"

"I'm sorry," Martha said humbly. "But you've got to admit she, he, it looked like a foxy chick."

"Forget it," I said. "It wasn't your fault."

She sighed. "I've got another problem. There's this woman—her name is Becky—who wants a scene. She's a widow, riddled with loot, with a lot of rich friends she could send us."

"So? What's the problem?"

"Becky is eighty-four."

"Holy moly!"

"Listen, have you got any flaky studs who might like to brag they banged an octogenarian?"

"Come on," I said. "There are no guys like that."

"Oh, I don't know," Martha said reminiscently. "When I was in that house in Chicago, we had a customer who claimed he had shtupped a hundred-year-old woman in Peru."

"That's gross."

"Sure it is," she said cheerfully. "And so is life. Peter, will you take her?"

I groaned. "If she goes into cardiac arrest, it's your fault."

Becky was a small, plumpish, chirpy woman with a mop of white hair rinsed with blue. Her complexion was peachy velvet. She had snappy brown eyes and a devilish smile. Chunky rings on all fingers, including thumbs.

I helped her off with her chinchilla.

"A beautiful, beautiful coat," I said.

"You like it?" she said, pleased. "Sonny, you got good taste. I bought it last year, and would you believe it, one of my daughters-in-law said, 'Ma, what do you need a new coat for at your age?' Can you imagine? She was saying I wouldn't live long enough to enjoy it."

"Well, don't worry about it," I told her. "You'll live forever. How many children do you have?"

"Five children, fourteen grandchildren, and three great-grandchildren. All living and in good health, thank God."

"That's marvelous," I said, smiling. "You must have quite a Christmas list."

"I give money," Becky said. "It always fits and nobody ever takes it back. Are you married, sonny?"

"Divorced. And I really don't want to meet a nice girl."

"If you say so," she said, shrugging. "But you'll be sorry. My marriage was so happy, I want everyone to be happy like that. I had fifty-eight wonderful years."

"How did your husband die?"

"He choked to death on a fishbone," Becky said. "At a private party. The funny thing is that Morris never did like fish. He was just eating it to be polite."

In the bedroom, I admired the teddy she was wearing. It was ecru silk trimmed with white lace.

"From Paris, France," she said proudly. "I like nice things." She checked out my naked body. "Sonny, you've got a nice figure there, but you're awfully thin. I don't think you eat right."

"Sure I do," I protested. "Lots of rich, nourishing food."

"So how come your ribs show?" She took my face between her palms. "Listen, sonny, don't be afraid of hurting me. You won't break anything. I'm a tough old bird."

She was more than tough; she was a rowdy, driving lover, and for a few moments I had to hang on to the headboard to keep from being bucked out of bed.

Her body was firm and plushy. Small, pink breasts, smooth thighs, a pillowy ass. I hoped I'd be in as good condition when I was eighty-four.

She led me a merry chase, and after a while her passion became a challenge and I forgot her age. She knew tricks that were new to me, and I was hard put to keep up with her.

When we finally blasted off, I was sobbing, hooting, sneezing, wheezing like a geezer. Becky patted my shoulder comfortingly, and I decided Morris hadn't choked to death on a fishbone; he had died of exhaustion.

Becky became a regular customer, working her way through all the studs in my stable. The boys called her "Grandma Moses" and loved her for her zest, good humor, and for her willingness to listen to their personal problems and offer wise advice.

Also, every time she showed up for a scene, she brought the stud a nice box of homemade cookies.

55

Oscar Gotwold called the real estate agent who called the manager of the Delacroix who instructed one of the doormen to allow Martha Twombly and me to inspect the penthouse apartment.

The doorman, who said his name was Max, took us up in the private elevator. On the twenty-ninth floor, he unlocked the door of the penthouse, told us to take our time, to close the door behind us, and to check with him before we left.

We moved slowly through the apartment. The living room was

indeed enormous, the other chambers as generously proportioned, and the decoration not quite glitzy.

The bedrooms, bathrooms, and kitchen were completely furnished with linens and accessories. Television sets in the living room and master bedroom. A hi-fi set and tape deck in the den with individually controlled loudspeakers in the other rooms.

The view from the L-shaped terrace was south and west. We could see a slice of Central Park, the skyline of lower Manhattan, the West Side, and New Jersey in the hazy distance.

Back inside, we planned how we might use the spacious foyer as a reception room and the den as an office.

"The other day," Martha said, "a client asked about having a party for her girlfriends, with studs serving as waiters. Then, after lunch, everyone would get it off. I had to tell her we didn't have the facilities. With this place, we could easily cater parties. Did you see the size of the kitchen?"

We went downstairs, checked out with Max, then walked back to Martha's apartment. It had snowed, then sleeted the night before, and the sidewalks were treacherous. Martha took my arm. We didn't speak until we were back in her place.

Then we set to work figuring out the finances. The big initial bite would be the $21,000 for one month's rent and two months' security. After that, we'd be laying out $7000 a month, plus telephone, electricity, laundry, bribes to manager and doormen, Sol Hoffheimer's fee, etc.

I said, "Futter will probably raise his price to five hundred a month when he sees that layout."

Martha added, "We'll need a maid at least eight hours a day. And a cleaning crew. Call it another three hundred a week."

We'd be saving something by giving up the West 68th Street studio and my apartment on 75th. But the penthouse would require a tremendous investment—no doubt about that.

If we stayed open six days a week, twelve hours a day, from noon to midnight, we might average twenty-five customers daily. That would give us a gross income of about $65,000 a month, but only $32,500 after the studs were paid.

Even subtracting rent and overhead, the bottom line still looked good. I thought we could net $22,000 a month. Martha's estimate was $20,000.

"Ten grand a month for each of us isn't bad," she said. "Let's do it."

"Let's," I agreed.

56

My one big problem with the move was Jenny Tolliver. What lie could I possibly tell her to explain relocating to an East Side penthouse? My febrile imagination concocted a dozen explanations, all outlandish. I could, of course, tell her the truth, but I didn't dare.

As it turned out, I needn't have bothered.

We had planned to spend a festive Christmas Eve together. We would dress up, have a late dinner at the Four Seasons, then go on to a Greek nightclub to dance and throw dishes.

I bought Jenny a choker of cultured pearls, nestled on white satin in a long black velvet box. A thousand dollars, but I didn't care. I was in a manic mood, wearing my dinner jacket with a new set of onyx studs from Tiffany, and a miniature orchid on my lapel.

But when she opened the door, she was wearing her scruffy old flannel bathrobe with the frayed cord and no makeup.

"What's wrong?" I said anxiously. "Sick?"

"Come in," she said coldly. "I want to talk to you."

Oh-oh, I thought.

"Since I was near the King's Arms yesterday," she said, staring at me, "I thought I'd just pop in and say hi."

"Ah . . ." I said, "I didn't work there yesterday."

"The manager told me you didn't work there at all. You haven't worked there since last year. Peter, why have you been lying to me?"

"Not lying," I said. "Not exactly. Could I have a drink?"

"No," she said. "What have you been *doing?* All your new clothes and the expensive restaurants we're going to—where is all that money coming from?"

"An inheritance," I said suddenly. "A rich uncle."

"*Another* rich uncle? You seem to have an inexhaustible supply. Peter, please tell me the truth. What have you been up to?"

"Well . . . ah . . . it's a long story."

"I have all the time in the world."

I began to pace about the room, away from her clear, direct gaze, my coat thrown open, hat tilted to the back of my head.

"Peter," she said quietly, "have you been acting in porn movies?"

"What?" I said, laughing. "Of course not. Besides, they don't pay anything."

I gave up. I would tell her something close to the truth.

"It's this woman," I said in a low voice, scuffing at the carpet. "An old, lonely woman. She gives me money."

"You're a gigolo?"

"Sort of."

"Do you have sex with her?"

"Oh no," I said hastily. "Nothing like that. I told you she's an *old* woman. Seventy at least. I just escort her to restaurants. And hockey games. She loves hockey games. But no sex. Nothing like that. She's just lonely."

"What's her name?"

"Uh . . . Martha Twombly."

"Where does she live?"

"On the East Side."

"How often do you see her?"

"Twice, maybe three times a week."

"And she pays you?"

"Yes."

"How much?"

"Oh . . . fifty, a hundred a night. Like that."

"So you've been making a few hundred a week from her?"

"Well . . . about," I said cautiously. "Sometimes more."

"And out of this you've been buying new coats, suits, shirts, shoes, jewelry?"

"Well, ah, sometimes she gives me gifts."

"Goddamn you!" she screamed at me. "Can't you *ever* stop lying to me? Don't you realize how you insult my intelligence? Don't you realize how it makes me feel? There's more than one woman, isn't there?"

"Yes," I said, sighing.

"Yes," she said. "There are many women. Many. You're fucking for money, aren't you?"

"It's not like that," I protested.

"No?" she said. "What are you doing—taking them all to hockey games?"

"You don't understand," I said, and eloquently began to explain my role in relieving these poor, troubled women of their inhibitions and frustrations.

While I was orating, Jenny Tolliver rose and went into the kitchen. She came back with a tumbler of brandy for herself but nothing for me. She sat in the armchair that had once been mine—and listened to my rhetoric.

Finally, when I ran down, she said quietly:

"The worst thing, the absolutely *worst* thing, is that you believe all that—don't you? You've always been able to delude yourself. *Always!*"

"That's not fair," I said. "And not true at all. I have to earn a living, don't I? I'm a realist. There *are* no acting jobs, so I—"

"Did you ever consider," she interrupted, "that it may be because you're a lousy actor?"

"That's your opinion," I said lamely.

She took a gulp of brandy, then drew a deep breath. "I think you better go." Her lips trembled. I thought her eyes were glistening, but I couldn't be sure.

I looked at her with longing. What a woman! I would never find another like her. Now, at parting, I could recognize what I was losing: the completeness of her, the elegance of her body, and the glory of her lovemaking.

I tried the charm bit that had worked so successfully with Arthur Enders.

"We can still be friends," I said, smiling winsomely. "Can't we?"

Her eyes weren't glistening at all. She looked at me keenly.

"No," she said. "I don't think so."

57

I walked over to Broadway, finally found a working street phone, and called Martha.

"Busy tonight?" I asked her.

Her voice sounded slurred. "What's the matter?" she jeered. "Get stood up?"

"Something like that."

"Me, too. Come on over."

It took twenty minutes to find a cab. And all the way across Central Park, the driver complained bitterly about the paucity of tips on the eve of the celebration of Christ's birth.

"What kind of shit is this?" he demanded.

"We all got troubles," I told him.

Martha was gussied up in a strapless sheath of silver lamé. Her red hair had been coiffed and her makeup professionally applied. She had kicked off silver silk evening slippers.

Looking at my dinner jacket, she smiled wryly.

"We're a pair, we are," she said. "All dressed up and no place to go."

"Want to party?" I offered. "I'm game."

"Too late now," she said. "I'm half in the bag. Here . . . help yourself."

She was eating smoked eels and drinking slivovitz. The tin and bottle were on the floor alongside her.

"I'll pass," I said, making a face. "May I have Armagnac?"

"Help yourself. What happened with your old lady?"

"She found out what I've been doing. So that's the end of that."

"I'm sorry, Peter," she said.

"It had to happen sooner or later. Still, it feels like a kick in the groin. I'll miss her. What happened to you?"

She took a slug of the plum brandy. "My old man's wife and kids went down to Tobago for the holiday week. He's supposed to join them in a couple of days, but he promised to spend Christmas Eve with me. We were going to have dinner at some small, discreet place—it would have been the first time I've been out in public with him—then back here for a night of fun and games. But he called at the last minute and canceled. Some political big shot asked him over for dinner and he couldn't say no. He felt bad, but so what?"

"I'm sorry, Martha."

She shrugged. "He'll pay for it one way or another."

"Mind if I take off my tie and jacket?"

"Make yourself at home. Put the chain on the door and then come over here and sit beside me."

I put an arm about her bare shoulders and she leaned her weight into me. She was an odd mixture of scents: the musk of her flesh, a light, fruity perfume, smoked eels, and slivovitz.

"Tell me about your guy," I said. "Rich?"

"His wife has the money. She's high society and very ambitious. I think she'd like to be the First Lady."

"Are you joking?"

"Nope. And it's not impossible. The man he's having dinner with tonight pulls a lot of political strings. If he decides to go with my friend, the machine will move him up fast. He could be our next governor."

"Wow."

"He's the perfect candidate: tall, handsome in a rugged way, married, with photogenic kids. He comes across great on TV, and his wife's family has enough loot to kick off a campaign in style."

"You're not going to tell me who he is, are you?"

"No. Knock me a kiss."

Her mouth tasted of eels.

"That's enough foreplay," she said. "Let's forget our troubles in the sack."

In the bedroom, we undressed slowly, talking about all the things that had to be done the following week: sign the lease on the Delacroix penthouse, transfer funds, hire a maid, buy a small desk and chair for the reception foyer, get the phones connected, call Con Ed, etc.

I was naked, about to get into bed alongside her, when I stopped and said, "Wait a minute."

I went back into the living room, took the black velvet box from my coat pocket. I brought it to Martha, leaned over to kiss her cheek.

"Merry Christmas, dear," I said.

She gave me a wisenheimer grin, opened the box, and drew a sharp breath.

"Beautiful," she said. "Just beautiful. Thank you. Your gift is hanging in the closet. In front. Go look."

I looked, and found a maroon cashmere dressing gown. I smiled at that. My ex-wife, a few other women I had known, Jenny, and now Martha —all gave me dressing gowns or bathrobes.

I slipped it on.

"Perfect fit," I announced. "Thank you. I'm glad I'm the same size as your boyfriend."

"Bigger," she told me. "Where it counts. And I'm glad your old lady kicked you out before she got the pearls. Merry Christmas, darling."

I was hanging the dressing gown away when something clattered to the floor of the closet. I bent to pick it up.

"What's this for?" I asked her, holding up a braided leather riding crop. "I didn't know you rode to the hounds."

"Fun and games," she said casually. "Put it away and come to bed."

She insisted on wearing the pearls, and I helped her with the clasp. Then we made love. Our coupling was physical combat tinged with hysteria. There was no tenderness. Only desperation. We called each other obscene names.

Then, drained, we drew apart and stared, defeated, into each other's eyes.

"Jesus," Martha said, suddenly weeping. "Just hold me."

So I held her.

58

On New Year's Eve, I was still packing last-minute stuff. My apartment had been sublet to Wolcott Sands, and personal effects like clothing, LPs, books, cassettes, and playscripts had been transferred to the East Side place.

But on the last day of the year, I was busily filling two new Mark Cross suitcases with shirts, ties, jewelry, toilet articles, my liquor supply, and the almost three thousand in cash that remained after paying my share of the rent and security for the penthouse.

When I heard the shouts and firecrackers at midnight, I drank a split of champagne, finished packing, and went to bed. I awoke refreshed and polished off another split mixed with orange juice.

Having decided to depart the West Side in style, I'd hired a huge Cadillac limousine, which arrived promptly at 3:00 P.M. The chauffeur carried out my luggage and I closed the door of the apartment behind me without looking back. I felt released and buoyant.

It was an icy day, steely and bright. Patches of snow sparkled in Central Park, and the sun danced from windows of East Side high-rises. Inside the limousine it was warm, the air redolent of rich leather. It was, I decided, class.

At the Delacroix, Max, the doorman, helped me up with the luggage. I gave him a sawbuck. He was impressed and appreciative. Inside the penthouse, on the kitchen counter, I found a bottle of Armagnac with a note from Martha: "Welcome to our new place."

I went out to a Third Avenue chophouse for a steak sandwich, homefries, and a bottle of dark Löwenbräu. Then I returned to the penthouse and began stowing away my belongings in the den and master bedroom.

I finished a little before midnight, opened Martha's brandy, and poured myself a dram. I took it out onto the terrace and stood at the railing, the city at my feet.

Beneath me glittered flashing lights and necklaces of diamonds, rubies, emeralds. The city seemed richer in the dark, winking and twinkling, infinitely promising.

I stared at this wonder a long time, marveling at how far I had come and yearning for what lay ahead.

But it was bitterly cold. I shivered and went back inside.

59

January came close to being a disaster. The unexpected that almost did us in was the weather.

The cold that had driven me from the penthouse terrace was a harbinger of a mass of frigid air, pouring down from Canada, deep-freezing the Eastern Seaboard, bringing gale-force winds, snow, driving sleet. The city was closed down for almost two weeks.

On one horrendous day, when the windchill factor was minus 20 degrees, only four horny women fought their way through the drifts to my place.

The thing that saved us was our call boy service. With the first heavy snowfall, the phone began to ring as clients felt the first symptoms of cabin fever.

Loyal studs, books of wallpaper samples clutched tightly under their arms, slogged through slush to bring succor to anxiously waiting customers. Tips were high and business active enough to see us through our cash flow crisis.

Toward the middle of the month, as the weather brightened, so did our prospects. We threw a Sunday-afternoon cocktail party for all the studs, to introduce them to their new workshop and explain the improved compensation system.

Martha Twombly served as hostess, since she knew all the men present intimately, if briefly, and they listened attentively to her welcoming speech.

She told them that she would be working as receptionist at the desk in the foyer. Customers would pay her in cash prior to the scene. After the client—presumably satisfied—had departed, the stud would be paid his fifty dollars.

This announcement was greeted with cheers.

Studs were urged to split as soon as possible after their scene so the bedroom could be freshened up. If questioned by residents of the Delacroix, they were to reply they were students at Peter's Academy of Dramatic Arts.

This announcement was greeted with some merriment.

Promptness, Martha stressed, was of the utmost importance; clients didn't like to be kept waiting. As an added incentive, a monthly prize of one hundred dollars would be awarded to the stud with the best record of satisfactory productivity.

This announcement was greeted with applause, and Wolcott Sands proposed a toast to the success of the new establishment.

60

During that first dreadful week, Martha Twombly struggled daily through garbage-clotted snowbanks to the penthouse. She brought with her a photocopy of the Barcarole Boutique customer list which she had thoughtfully snitched during her last day as manager.

She also brought Nicole Radburn, whom she introduced as "the lady who got Luke Futter off my ass." I was surprised. Martha had described the call girl as young and beautiful, but I didn't find her particularly either. Twenty-six at least, I guessed, and more striking than pretty.

I made a fresh pot of coffee and we sat in the cavernous living room, grousing about the weather and talking shop. I could tell there was a genuine bond between the two women, despite their cheerful contempt for each other. Nikki called Martha "Madame Defarge," and Martha referred to the call girl as "Miss Nipples."

It was early evening and the snow had started again. They were predicting six to ten inches. The ladies had planned to have dinner out, but I urged them to stay for canned soup, barbecued chicken, and salad.

They promptly agreed to the indoor picnic, kicked off their shoes, and settled in while I stirred up a pitcher of vodka martinis. As the women began comparing the merits and problems of their professions, I listened, smiling, and took a good look at Nicole Radburn.

She was almost as tall as I, built like an Eberhard Faber No. 2. Long black hair with one white flash. A triangular face tapering to a sharp chin. The mouth was wide and quirky; her laughs were roars. The eyes were tremendous; you could swim in them.

She was so swaddled in sweaters I couldn't assess her figure, but guessed it was thin, hard, and whippy. She had none of Jenny Tolliver's soft fullness, but I sensed a kinetic strength that Jenny never had.

When Martha explained we were using Peter's Academy of Dramatic Arts as a front, Nicole suggested we list the Academy in the telephone directory rather than use my name. I asked her if she used a front.

"Only for tax reasons," she said seriously. "I'm a schoolteacher. It's legitimate; I'm licensed. I fill in as a temporary at private schools in Manhattan when I want to. I'm really a very good teacher, and it gives me a legal cover. I declare that income to the penny."

"What do you teach?"

"Grade school English and composition. I have a master's in English Lit. I used to teach full-time. I've only been in the game two years."

"Two wonderful years," Martha said, grinning.

"Two profitable years," Nicole said, not grinning.

We adjourned to the kitchen, and as we prepared dinner, I put a good dent in a jug of California chablis.

Afterward, we drank Armagnac in the den and watched the ominous weather bulletins on TV. Buses had stopped running and most taxis were off the streets.

"Shit," Martha said. "Nikki, we better start moving if we're going to get home."

"Look," I said. "We've got three bedrooms here. Why don't you stay the night? I can loan you pajamas."

"Martha?" Nikki said.

"Suits me," the older woman said. "But screw the pajamas; I sleep raw."

"I'll take a jacket," Nicole said. "Thank you, Peter."

We watched a lousy movie on the tube as we finished the brandy, adjourned to the kitchen for canned chocolate pudding, then retired to our separate bedrooms.

Shortly after midnight I was lying in bed reading the tattered script of an unproduced play, *Places, Everyone!* It was terrible but had a wonderful part for me. Reading the script for the umpteenth time, I dreamed of what I might have done with that role.

My bedroom door opened and Nicole Radburn stuck her head in.

"Hi," she said.

"Hi," I said.

"May I come in?"

"Sure."

She closed the door behind her. She was wearing one of my pajama jackets. Her bare legs were long and well-muscled. A runner's legs. Her skin was olive. There was a small mole on her right thigh: a disk of velvet.

"Just a visit," she said. "No sex. Okay?"

"Okay," I said, "if you'll tell me why Martha calls you Miss Nipples."

She unbuttoned the jacket and showed me.

"Incredible," I said. "How many men have you blinded with those things?"

"I've made a lot of them happy. Do you have a nail file?"

"Some emery boards in the bathroom cabinet," I said.

She came out of the bathroom, examining the package. "Eighty-nine cents!" she exclaimed. "Highway robbery. I pay fifty-nine for the same thing at a discount drugstore."

I laughed. "Is saving thirty cents so important to you?"

"You better believe it. I watch those pennies like a hawk."

She sat on the edge of my bed, one leg up and bent. The pajama jacket was open, but she was wearing white bikini panties. Her body was tough and bony. Ribs showed. And hipbones.

"You look great," I said. "How do you keep in shape?"

"I work out at a health club three times a week."

"That's what I should be doing."

She lifted the blanket and sheet and looked down at my naked body.

"You do all right," she said. "Nice dork."

She covered me up and, still filing at her nails, glanced about the master bedroom.

"You've got a beautiful place here, Peter."

"It should be, for what we pay."

"Martha told me," she said. "Don't worry; you'll make out."

"If it ever stops snowing. How are you doing?"

"Can't complain," she said. "Last year I grossed almost fifty grand. That's not counting what I made teaching."

"What do you charge?"

"A hundred minimum. More for kinks."

"Got a daddy?"

She looked at me. "No," she said. "I did when I started. But it didn't make financial sense, so I got rid of him."

"How did you manage that?"

"One of my regulars is a hard case, and he took care of it for me. He gave the pimp a turban."

"A turban?"

"You know," she said, gesturing. "A bandage. He broke the pimp's head. The guy never bothered me after that. I'm strictly on my own."

"How do you line up new clients?"

"Referrals, mostly. I'm listed with a lot of public relations guys, so I do well at conventions. I very rarely have to hustle. I figure I'm good for maybe another ten years. But even with fifty grand a year, it's hard to accumulate investment capital."

"Ten years should give you half a million."

"Not enough," she said, shaking her head. "I'm into tax-exempt municipal bonds, but at a ten percent average return, that'll bring in only fifty grand a year when I retire."

"*Only* fifty grand! It sounds like a lot to me."

"Not if inflation averages ten percent per annum. Fifty grand a year ten years from now won't mean shit-all if bread costs ten dollars a loaf."

I sighed. "I don't understand all that high finance."

"You mean you're not providing for your future?"

"I never give it a thought."

"You should. Do you know anything about incorporation, a personal holding company, the Keogh Plan, IRA, annuities?"

"Nothing," I confessed. "But I'd like to start learning. Willing to teach me?"

"Sure. I'm no financial whiz, but I can explain the basics."

"Great," I said. "Can we have dinner?"

"Why not? Martha will give you my number. I'd like to see you again. But no sex. Okay? I don't give away what I can sell. You understand, don't you?"

"Sure," I said. "No sex. But that doesn't mean we can't be friends."

"I can use another friend. Martha's my one and only."

"How did you meet her?"

"She used to work in my mother's place in Chicago years ago. In fact, Madame Defarge is my godmother."

Nicole went into the bathroom to replace the emery boards. When she came back, she bent over me and kissed my cheek. She smelled tangy.

She stood beside the bed, held open the pajama jacket, postured.

"Not bad for an old lady," she said. "Right?"

Her body was springy and tight, with a nervy, barracuda quality. I guessed that in bed she could make men sob.

"They'd have to peel me off the ceiling," I told her. "How old are you, Nikki?"

"Twenty-four," she said promptly. "Going on thirty. Thanks for the hospitality, Peter. You're nice people. Ta-ta."

With a wave of her hand, she was gone. I turned off the bedside lamp, pulled up the covers, closed my eyes. But I kept seeing that dark, tendoned body, the smooth hollows at her waist, those unbelievably sharp nipples.

I dozed, but the room grew colder and I tossed about restlessly. But then, about an hour later, Martha slipped into my room, into my bed, and warmed me.

61

In addition to the weather, unexpected expenses depleted our reserve that January.

For instance, our supply of bed linen and towels was hopelessly inadequate, and we had to buy dozens of sheets, pillow cases, hand towels, and bath towels. Linen was, after all, changed after every scene. "This is a class operation," I insisted.

When business picked up, we hired a full-time maid from an employment agency. She was a basalt-skinned Haitian called Patsy, who claimed to be fifty-eight.

"And I'm twenty-three," Martha said.

We figured Patsy was an illegal and would be delighted to work a forty-eight-hour week for two hundred clear.

At the end of the hour it took her to figure out what was going on, she demanded three hundred.

We surrendered. She was a demon worker and also turned out to be a stupendous cook. We even paid her extra to stay late on Fridays and prepare her special bouillabaisse.

The next financial shock came via Detective Luke Futter: He now wanted a thousand a month.

"Look," he said with his smirky grin. "On the East Side *everything* costs more. Also, on the West Side I was working on my own territory. But over here I've got to shmear three or four other guys. I mean, it's *their* turf. You're lucky to get away with a grand a month."

Grumbling, we paid, hoping it would insure protection from street cops, etc.

We also had to budget bribes to the employees of the Delacroix. The manager, an offensive twit who wore Chanel 5, demanded three hundred a month, non-negotiable. Since we didn't know how to handle the three doormen, we finally decided to ask Max, the senior day guy, for advice.

We called him upstairs, gave him a beer, and told him what we were doing. He was a street-smart Brooklynite with an unpronounceable Greek name and a bushy black mustache that went from here to there. He listened closely, then asked, "No loud parties?"

"Absolutely not," I assured him.

"No drunks in the lobby?"

"No way," Martha said. "And no drugs either. Our clients are ladies and the boys all behave themselves."

"It'll cost you two hundred a month," Max said, twisting his mustache. "I keep one. Seventy-five goes to the other day guy and twenty-five to that yutz on nights."

"They'll go for that?" I asked.

"They better," Max said ferociously.

Then there was the cleaning crew twice a week, the enormous laundry bill, the high Con Ed and New York Telephone deposits and charges, and that heavy February rent of $7000, looming closer and closer.

But as the weather improved, customers began drifting back and our daily income rose steadily. Seven clients on January 14, twelve on the 20th, sixteen on the 23rd, twenty-one on the 29th. On the last day of the month, we hit the magic number: Twenty-five students attended Peter's Academy of Dramatic Arts.

"We're going to make it!" Martha said triumphantly.

62

After moving to the penthouse, I had decided to eliminate my own scenes and devote myself full-time to management. Even with Martha on duty from noon to eight, problems arose that necessitated my personal attention.

For instance, it soon became evident that we needed a fallback for boys who were late or pulled a no-show. Since this happened two or three times a week, I had no choice but to sub for the missing stud—or lose the customer.

But, late in the month, I had a scene that was unscheduled—and unprecedented.

I was in the den, working on the next week's schedule, when Martha came in and perched on the edge of my desk.

"A problem," she said. "There's a woman in the foyer who wants a scene. I've never seen her before, never heard of her. She says we've been recommended by a friend. I know the woman she named—she's a regular—and called her. She said yes, she had recommended us. I told this woman who's waiting—her name is Connie—that it's customary to call first and set up an appointment. She almost burst into tears. She's very nervous, Peter. What do you want to do?"

"What does she look like?"

"Presentable enough. She could be attractive if she'd do something with her hair and wear makeup. You want to take her? The Blue Room's available."

I thought a moment. "All right," I said finally. "I don't like off-the-street trade, but right now we can't afford to turn anyone away. Send her in."

Connie was more than nervous; she was close to hysteria. Her face was chalky and her hands fluttered uncontrollably. Her eyes flickered and she had an occasional facial tic that pulled down one corner of her mouth.

As Martha had said, a hairdo and makeup would have improved her appearance immeasurably. And, I wanted to tell her, a visit to the Barcarole would help, too; she was wearing a shapeless gunnysack of a dress that hid her body.

I joined her in the Blue Room, bringing two glasses of white wine. I introduced myself, smiling, then turned to lock the bedroom door.

"Don't do that!" she said in a voice that came perilously close to a scream.

"All right," I said equably. "No lock—see? Now why don't you sit down, have a glass of wine, and we'll get acquainted."

I did most of the talking. It was hard to pry a reaction from her. She sat there like a stick, gripping her hands to stop the flutter. Teeth kept biting her lower lip. I was afraid that at any moment she might shatter into a million bits.

"Look, Connie," I said as gently as I could. "If you want to call this whole thing off, the lady at the front desk will refund your money."

She was silent a long time.

Then she said: "No. I want to go through with it."

"I can draw the drapes if you like."

"Leave them open," she said in a cracked voice. "I want to see everything."

"Would you like to take off your clothes?"

"Turn your back."

Obediently, I turned away and disrobed swiftly. When I got into bed alongside her, she was lying flat on her back, arms crossed over her breasts, eyes closed. Now she wasn't a stick; she was a stone, so rigid that she trembled.

"Connie," I said softly, "you're not a virgin, are you?"

Her head whipped wildly, side to side.

"All right," I said. "I'm not going to hurt you. Anytime you want me to stop, tell me and I'll stop. Trust me. Will you trust me?"

One nod.

I smoothed her tangled hair. I touched her lightly. It was a sympathetic role, and I played it. Fingertips. Brush of lips. Murmured endearments. I got her crossed arms moved away. Stroked her. Told her how beautiful she was. Whispering.

Her eyes remained closed.

"Look at me," I urged. "You said you wanted to see everything."

Lids quivered, opened halfway. She stared into my eyes.

I smiled. "Just me," I said. "A guy as scared as you are."

It took a while. A long while. But I finally got into her. She lay flaccid, staring over my head at the ceiling.

"Does it hurt?" I kept asking. "Do you want me to stop?"

She said nothing, and I began to feel my energy ebb. But then, as if she sensed it, she responded. Her body thawed, came alive. Legs rose, curled. She grasped me to her. She started panting.

"Do you like me?" she gasped. "Really like me?"

"I love you. You're a desirable woman. So lovely. Fantastic."

Her body became silk. I plunged happily and she heaved to meet me. Her eyes were wet, and at the end we were both crying out, singing a weird song. And then she would not let me go, but grappled me tighter.

"Connie," I said. "What *is* it?"

"I was raped," she said.

I pulled away to stare at her.

"Oh my God," I said. "When?"

"Two years, three months, and fourteen days ago."

"And this is the first . . . ?"

"Yes," she said.

63

I picked up the chipped coffee cup on Sol Hoffheimer's desk and smelled it.

"Since when have you been hitting the sauce at ten in the morning?"

"Since I've been working for you."

"You're not working for me; you're working for yourself."

"Whatever," the agent said wearily, waving a hand. "What are you selling today—cancer?"

"I'm not selling anything. I'm giving." I tossed an envelope onto the desk. "Eight hundred. Ain't dot nize?"

"It makes me proud," Hoffheimer said.

"Sol, listen. The ads are pulling okay and I'm getting some good boys from you. But those preliminary interviews are wasting a lot of my time. More than half the guys turn me down."

"So?"

"So it would be a great help if you did the preliminary interviews." The agent was silent.

"You'll increase your take," I went on briskly. "A hundred and fifty for every stud we accept. Maybe a grand a month."

"And maybe a year for procuring," Hoffheimer said.

I shrugged. "There's risk in every business. And the higher the profit, the greater the risk."

The agent drained his coffee cup. Then he took a pint bottle of cheap whiskey from his desk drawer and poured more into the cup with a hand that shook.

"And what's my next promotion?" he said. "Towel boy?"

"You're treating this like some kind of a seedy, hole-in-the-wall business," I said angrily. "It's not like that at all. We've got this beautiful penthouse apartment. Our clients are wealthy, well-dressed women. A lot of them are on the society pages. Some are executives in big corporations. Women like that wouldn't touch anything that isn't top drawer. Sol, we're providing a professional service in a clean, attractive atmosphere."

Hoffheimer looked at me curiously. "You really believe all that bullshit?"

"I believe it because it's true. I wouldn't have anything to do with it if it wasn't a class operation."

Before I returned to the penthouse, I stopped at a Times Square drugstore and bought a gross of Fourex condoms.

64

Having researched laws applicable to establishing a private school in New York State, Oscar Gotwold advised us to consider incorporation. He further suggested we start a checking account for Peter's Academy of Dramatic Arts from which we would pay all the legitimate expenses—telephone, Con

Ed, rent, and so forth. He thoughtfully offered the services of his wife's cousin, a young, clever CPA, to help us organize a set of books.

"You'll want to operate at a loss, of course," the attorney went on. "But that should be easy to finagle with your overhead. The important thing is to have some paper to show the IRS next year. We'll have plenty of time to rig a dummy operation."

Gotwold advised against Martha and me taking a monthly split by check from the Academy. His reasoning was that the Academy wouldn't show enough income to justify enormous salaries. He suggested, instead, that we draw a token salary of a hundred a week by check on which we'd pay personal income taxes. His wife's cousin would work out how much we should bank monthly to cover legitimate expenses.

So we set up a checking account for Peter's Academy of Dramatic Arts. At the same time we began accepting "cash" checks from regular customers.

Another innovation, which began as a joke, proved so profitable that we continued it.

When a valued client purchased a scene for a friend as a birthday present, I jokingly suggested that we issue hundred-dollar gift certificates.

The concept amused us, so we had a limited number of certificates printed on fake parchment, entitling the bearer to "One Lesson at Peter's Academy of Dramatic Arts." The idea became so popular that we had to print more.

"Our next step is accepting credit cards," Martha said.

The establishment of the Academy did have one unwanted result: Several kids showed up inquiring about curriculum, faculty, and tuition.

Martha got rid of most of them by explaining we only accepted students with five years of professional experience. When that didn't work, she quoted a tuition of a hundred dollars an hour, enough to discourage the most eager would-be thespian.

Meanwhile, business continued to improve and, during the first week in February, we frequently had all three bedrooms going simultaneously. We considered converting the den to workspace, but decided to postpone it until we could build up our cash reserve.

65

I discussed all these financial developments with Nicole Radburn, who was savvy about money and shrewd in solving problems unique to our business.

"It's a service industry," she told me. "And anytime you deal with the public, you're going to have problems."

She usually dropped by the penthouse several times a week, in the late morning or sometimes at night after she had turned a trick. She always called first.

Occasionally she and I had dinner together in the penthouse after the last client and stud had departed. She always brought a steak, a bottle of wine, and pastries.

When she slept over, we shared the big bed in the master bedroom, but we abided by her "no sex" edict. As we became more intimate, it seemed of less and less importance.

I was in bed, reading *Variety,* when Nicole came out of the bathroom naked. She had just showered and her hair was wrapped in a towel. I looked up as she went to the full-length mirror on the closet door and examined herself critically.

"Looks good to me," I called across the room.

"Getting old scares me," she said, staring at her reflection. "You ever think about it?"

"Only twenty-four hours a day."

I told her about the jobs I had lost because producers and directors were looking for "a younger type," and that every year countless stage-struck youngsters with beauty and talent flocked to Broadway.

"My business isn't so different," she said.

She perched cross-legged on the bed and began to paint her toenails a bright vermilion.

"Every year there are more young hookers in town," she said. "You read the papers; you know. Fourteen- and fifteen-year-olds. Maybe younger. That's tough competition."

"Only a freak would take a chance on a fourteen-year-old."

"The trouble is," she said, "that with makeup and the right clothes, they look legal. All the johns can see is a young, plump chick. So the guy takes a chance. A cock has no conscience."

"You keep yourself in great shape," I assured her.

"Sure, but a teenager I'm not. That's why I'm hoping for just another ten years."

I watched her work on her toes, lips pursed, expression intent. She painted with a steady hand.

"I've got a kink who loves to do this for me," she remarked. "But he's out of town."

"Nikki, does it bother you at all? The business you're in."

"Not a bit," she said. "Maybe because my mother was in the game. She tried to keep me away from it, but I knew what was going on. As I told you, I was straight until two years ago. I went into this deliberately, with my eyes open."

I admired her surety. She was as certain in her way as Jenny Tolliver was in hers.

"It wasn't easy at first," she admitted. "I've known a lot of girls who became alkies or went the drug route. A few suicides. It takes a lot of self-discipline to keep your head together."

"I believe it," I said. "All those weirdos."

"That's not the big problem. The big problem is the initial one: deciding to sell, or rent, your body. That can be a big ego-downer."

"But you did it."

"I did it. I've got a good brain; I approached the problem logically. I even made out lists of advantages and disadvantages."

She finished her toenails, capped the bottle of polish tightly, and put it aside. She lay on her back and waved her feet in the air.

"The advantages," she went on, "were big money, independence, no nine-to-five shit, and a feeling of power I won't go into right now. The disadvantages were the legal risks, the danger of a customer turning homicidal, and the problem of what happens when I'm old and gray. I finally decided to do it, and I've never regretted it. Shove over and give me some room."

She slid into bed alongside me. She had taken off the towel, and wisps of her long black hair tickled my lips. She smelled of soap and her own tangy scent. Her thigh felt silky on mine.

"Nikki, we get a lot of our studs from a guy who used to be my theatrical agent. He gets paid, of course, and I know he needs the money.

That's the only reason he does it. But I also know it's eating at him. The, uh, morality of it. Does that ever bother you?"

"Never," she said promptly. "What the hell is morality? It's no absolute. I've read a lot of history, and some of the most famous statesmen and artists and philosophers owned slaves. It wasn't considered immoral when they lived. Whores have been respected and honored in several periods. Soldiers drank the blood of their enemies, royal brothers married royal sisters, and harems still exist. So what *is* morality? Shame, guilt, sin—those are foreign words I don't understand."

"But," I argued, "you still have to live in a society where those words have meaning."

"Don't be so sure. Morality is just like fashion: a new style every year. And right now a lot of people feel that morality is superfluous in a world where money and power are what count. Virtue is a luxury only the poor can afford."

I laughed. "What a cynic you are!"

"No. I just see things clearly. Maybe fifty years from now I'd be burned at the stake. But right now I *belong.* Let's go to sleep."

I turned off the bedside lamp and settled down, turning onto my side away from her. She came close, pressing her hard body into mine, spoon-fashion.

"Peter," she said in the darkness, "you won't believe this, but you're the first man I've ever slept with. I mean *slept.* All night."

"And how do you like it?" I asked.

"I like it," she said. "It's comfy."

66

We had a wonderful day: twenty-nine scenes and no problems. There were two "doubles," so our gross for the day was $3300.

By 11:00 P.M. the place had cleared out. I was in the den, putting the day's take away. There was a knock on the door. Wolcott Sands peeked in. He had serviced the last customer.

"Hi, Sandy," I said. "Come on in."

As usual, the stud was dressed like an English country gentleman. Fawn-colored whipcord slacks. Blanket-plaid hacking jacket with leather patches on the elbows. Suede waistcoat with pearly buttons. Foulard ascot at his throat. Tasseled cordovan loafers.

"You should be carrying a shotgun," I said. "For grouse, you know."

"I guess," Sands said. "Got a minute, Peter?"

"Sure. You drink scotch—right? I've got some Chivas."

"Two thick fingers, please."

I went to the cellarette and poured us each a hefty tot. I raised my glass.

"Here's to our schlongs," I said. "Long may they wave."

"I'll drink to that," Sands said. He took a sip, then slid into the club chair at my desk.

"It was a sensational day," I said. "Not a crisis in the lot. Everybody happy."

"Uh-huh," he said. "At a hundred a shot, you must be doing all right."

"Can't complain," I said, beginning to feel a vague unease. "Of course, we're carrying a fierce overhead."

"Sure. But you still must be grossing about fifteen thousand a week."

"It depends," I said tersely. "But you're not doing too bad. Two hundred a week plus tips for four hours' work."

Wolcott Sands stared at the ceiling. "I'm not complaining. It's a good deal; I admit it. But I've decided to split, Peter. I know you've already made out next week's schedule, so I'll put out through then."

"Jesus," I said, jerking forward in my swivel chair. "That *is* bad news. How come, Sandy?"

"Well . . ." the stud said, looking at the far wall, "I've got this woman. Not a customer; she doesn't know what I've been doing. A rich widow lady. She wants to marry me. It's a good deal, Peter; I'd be a fool to pass it up."

"Sandy, have you thought this through? The money may be good, but do you think you can be satisfied with one woman?"

Then Wolcott Sands looked directly at me and I knew he was lying.

"Who says it has to be one woman?" he asked. "But I'll have a wife paying the nut. What she doesn't know won't hurt her."

"Well, if you feel that way, why not keep working?"

Sands shook his head. "Too risky. She might have friends who come up here. My God, she might even drop by herself. No, Peter, I better cut loose."

"You've made up your mind about this?"

"Absolutely."

"Then what can I say except good luck. We'll be sorry to lose you, Sandy."

We sipped our drinks thoughtfully.

"I appreciate all you've done for me, Peter," Sandy said sincerely. "I couldn't have survived without it."

I shrugged. "You earned it. I just hope everything turns out right for you."

"I'm sure it will," Sands said, smiling.

67

Oscar Gotwold's wife's cousin, the "young, clever CPA," was named Ignatz Samuelson, but he told us to call him "Iggy."

He was a whippet of a man, bone-thin and staccato. His sunken cheeks seemed blue with beard. He jerked his long hands about: pointing, stabbing, slashing. He sucked on a porcelain cigarette, puffing, blowing out nonexistent smoke, tapping the cleverly designed ash. He even had a fake cough.

He went over our current accounts, telling us what to pay by checks drawn on Peter's Academy of Dramatic Arts and what to keep in cash.

"The trick is to keep the paper to a minimum," he told us on his way out. "Now about current income. You figure the rest of the year will equal the first two months' take?"

"We hope so," Martha said.

Iggy punched rapidly at a thin pocket calculator.

"What you're talking about," he said, "is three-quarters of a mil min. And a mil max. Take out salaries, overhead, this and that, and you'll each net a hundred grand at the end of the year."

"You're kidding!" Martha said. "A hundred thousand each?"

"Probably more," the accountant said. "So what are you going to do with it?"

"Spend it!" I said.

"On what?" Iggy said. "You're earning ninety-five Gs more than you're declaring. You buy real estate or a Rolls Corniche, the IRS comes in and says, 'Hey, wait a minute.' If your life-style is way beyond your declared income, you're in trouble."

"Shit," Martha said. "So what do we do—keep it under the mattress?"

The CPA told us there were ways and means. A friendly stockbroker he knew could help us with investments. We could "lend" funds to a front: a restaurateur, a theatrical producer, any businessman who needed cash and was willing to conceal our contribution.

"It can be done," Iggy said. "Right now your cash is not a problem. By July it will be. My advice to you at the moment is what you said before: spend, spend, spend. But not on big-ticket items. Clothes, jewelry, cruises—like that. Stuff you can pay cash for and no one will ask where it came from. You want me to come in every month?"

We both nodded.

"Okay," he said. "It'll cost you a grand a month." He gave us a wolfish grin. "That'll help reduce your cash balance."

After Iggy had left, we sat in the den and stared at each other.

"Martha," I said, "it's getting to be big business."

"Scared?" she asked.

"A little. It's happened so fast."

"Hang in there, kiddo. It's not all that big. My God, Nikki turns fifty grand a year by herself."

"Where do we go from here?" I wondered. "We're getting awfully close to our maximum take. Three bedrooms for twelve hours a day. We can't do any better than that."

"Concentrate on the call boy service," she said. "Build up that division."

So we discussed how to increase income from our escort business. Neither of us suggested it might be wise to be satisfied with what we had.

68

Since moving into the Delacroix, my social life had dwindled to zilch. But late in February, with the business running smoothly, I invited Arthur Enders to the penthouse for dinner.

He arrived promptly, awed and blinking, bearing a bottle of New York State champagne. I hadn't the heart to tell him there was a case of Krug in the kitchen cupboard.

The would-be playwright was properly impressed with the size of the living room, the spacious terrace, the luxury of the three bedrooms. But it was the walnut-paneled den that really aroused his admiration.

"Golly," he said. "Would I love to have a place like this. You've come a long way, Peter."

"Yeah," I said, laughing. "Across the Park. Let's go eat—and drink."

We pan-fried a couple of sirloins and had baked potatoes and a salad of arugula and ruby lettuce. We drank negronis before dinner, a '78 Margaux with dinner, and poured Cointreau on fresh pineapple after dinner.

"Remember Blotto's?" Enders said. "Remember spaghetti and meatballs?"

"I'm trying to forget," I said. "Let's adjourn to the den. We'll drink your champagne in there—okay?"

We settled down in our chairs, feet up on my desk.

"Doesn't it take a while to get accustomed to this life?" Arthur asked.

"About two minutes," I said. "Want to come back to work?"

Enders shook his head. "Thanks anyway."

"If you say so. But it's easy money, Arthur. Say, how is your play coming?"

"My gosh, I'm really excited about it. I'm on the seventh rewrite. I met a guy who runs a workshop in the Village. It's associated with an Off Off-Broadway theater. He promised to take a look at the script when it's finished. They have informal readings and it gives the playwright a chance to hear his words and make changes."

"I know how it works," I said somewhat crossly. "Has this Village guy got any money?"

"Gee, no. He's operating on a shoestring. But it's a chance to have my play read. Money isn't important."

I wagged my head dolefully. "Arthur, that's the most un-American thing I've ever heard."

"I guess," Enders said. "I meant it's just not important to me."

He leaned forward to refill our glasses. As he was pouring, he said, blushing:

"By the way, I have a confession to make."

"Confess away," I said blithely, not expecting what was coming.

"I've been seeing Jenny Tolliver. I bumped into her on Columbus Avenue one night and invited her to Blotto's for a beer. Honest, Peter, that's the way it happened. I mean, I didn't call her or anything like that."

"I believe you," I said, stung, but not showing it.

"She told me you two had broken up. Is that right?"

"Yes."

"Well, I've seen her a couple of times. I hope you're not sore."

"Why should I be sore? Jenny has every right to date anyone she pleases."

Enders looked at me. "She found out what you're doing, didn't she?"

"Yes."

"She didn't tell me, but I figured it out. I told her I was in it, too, for a while. She said that was all right as long as I was out. Peter, she's a marvelous woman."

"I know."

"And so beautiful! I've never dated such a beautiful woman. I'm just proud to be seen with her."

"I know."

"And intelligent! She really thinks about things and has some very original ideas. She's very—"

"You finish the champagne, Arthur," I said. "I think I'll switch to brandy."

69

The money was good—no denying that—but it wasn't the sole attraction of the "game." I saw my profession as theater. It gratified my taste for drama.

The legal risk involved—that provided the suspense and excitement. And the cast! Martha Twombly, Luke Futter, Nicole Radburn, Oscar Gotwold, Sol Hoffheimer—a great roster of supporting players. And for a chorus, the studs and customers.

And the penthouse—what a set!

The best thing about it, of course, was that there was no script. It was all impromptu. I winged it, improvising my role as circumstances changed. It demanded a fast wit and a hundred guises. But sometimes, I admitted, the minor players took over.

It was late; Martha had already left, and I was seated at the reception desk. One more customer was expected: a woman named Bertha, referred by a regular client.

The assigned stud, waiting in the Green Room, was a Latvian contortionist whose name was such a mess of consonants that we called him Mike. I knew he'd be gone when the carnival season started, but meanwhile he was pulling down a couple of bills a week from a faithful clientele who, after a scene with him, departed with their eyeballs whirling.

The intercom clicked on, an authoritative woman's voice stated, "This is Bertha," and I pushed the button activating the elevator. When the foyer door opened, not one but two women entered. I rose to greet them.

They were wearing matching mink coats of a rather old-fashioned cut, too long and too full. They were both tall, but the older was also broad in the shoulder and hip: a massive woman with a hard, doggish face.

This commanding matron was wearing a Minnie Pearl hat. The younger woman was hatless, her mousy hair, obviously long, up in a tight bun. She was, I estimated, about thirty, with fine, pale features. She wore glasses with wire rims.

"Good evening, ladies," I said. "My name is Peter. Are you together? Which of you is Bertha?"

"*I* am Bertha," the gorgon declared loudly. "*I* made the appointment. But it's for my daughter. *This* is Annie. Stand up straight, Annie."

"Yes, Mama," the daughter said, but couldn't raise her eyes to look at me.

"Bertha, will you be waiting for your daughter?" I asked casually, as if we had mother-daughter customers every day in the week.

"Of course," she snapped. "Go with the man, Annie."

"Yes, Mama," the daughter said in a faint voice.

I conducted Annie to the Green Room. She plodded behind me, a prisoner heading for the gibbet. I returned to the foyer to find Bertha seated next to the desk. She had removed her coat. She was wearing something awful in brown.

"Would you care for a glass of wine while you wait?" I asked politely.

"I do not drink alcohol," she announced.

I nodded.

"And I don't smoke either," she added.

I had a topper for that, but I didn't say it.

"That will be one hundred dollars, please," I said.

She paid with two fifties. New bills. She crumpled them to make certain a third wasn't sticking.

"How long will this take?" she demanded.

"The appointment is for an hour," I said as mildly as I could.

She made a noise. It sounded like "Hump!"

"The silly girl," she said. "She has as much personality as a tadpole. And totally inexperienced, if you know what I mean."

She looked at me challengingly and I could only nod.

"I only hope," Bertha said, "that your man knows what he's doing."

"All our employees are thoroughly experienced, ma'am," I assured her.

"I've tried everything else," she said. "The child is so shy, so withdrawn. I've arranged dates for her with many fine young men from the best families, but they never call a second time. Can you blame them?"

I didn't reply. I knew whose side I was on.

"I want her to learn something about life," she went on. "She sits all day in that room of hers reading books. It's ruining her eyes and her complexion. She's only twenty-five and looks ten years older. She simply cannot talk, to me or to men or to anyone else. She doesn't dance. She takes no interest in *anything*. Sometimes I believe the child may be—well, you know, just a wee bit retarded. She simply has nothing to say."

I wondered if poor Annie ever got a chance.

"She seems so listless," she continued almost angrily. "I've had her to a dozen doctors, but they all say there's nothing physically wrong with her. The last doctor suggested long walks, outdoor exercise, but the one time I forced her to go out, I found her two hours later sitting on a park bench, reading a book. I ask you! I do hope this experience may help bring her out of her shell. She is *so* wishy-washy."

Her complaints went on and on, and I got the picture: Annie was infuriating her mother by obeying commands in silence, never volunteering, and pulling back into a world of books. Probably to preserve her sanity, I thought.

That was surely one of the longest hours I have ever endured, listening to the indignation of that frumpy harridan. But finally I heard, within the apartment, a burst of laughter and then the slam of the Green Room door.

Annie came sailing into the foyer, wearing her mink coat like a cape. Her head was up, spine stiff. Her wire-rimmed glasses were gone and her long hair splayed about her shoulders.

"Annie!" her mother wailed. "What have you done to your hair? And where are your glasses?"

"Mama," Annie said, flaming with happiness, "you go straight to hell!"

70

Early in March there was a development that was to have an important effect on our future.

A few clients, having finished their scenes, asked if they might kill a little time in the penthouse before departing for their next engagement. We put these loungers in the dining room with the door closed to ensure other customers' privacy. Since they often asked for a drink while waiting, we felt a serious drain on our liquor supply and began charging two dollars per drink. No one objected. I acted as bartender and Patsy served, happy with the tips.

When several women asked us to arrange small luncheons, we started accommodating groups of no more than four. Patsy served simple meals, usually salads. We charged five dollars per person, desserts and wine extra.

Eventually, Patsy's cousin, Maria, got the sheet-changing job while Patsy claimed the food and liquor concession. She would buy all the supplies, do all the cooking, all the serving, and pay us 25 percent of her profits.

We didn't see how she could possibly do better than the three hundred a week she was already making, but we had underestimated her ambition and energy. She put leaves in the dining room table to seat twelve, enlarged her menu, and raised her prices. The succulence of her cuisine delighted customers who lunched before or after their scenes.

Patsy brought in another cousin, Luis, to work as waiter and busboy. Before long she was providing dinners as well. Within a month she had established her own profitable business and we had a new source of income.

Late in March, two regulars asked us if they might rent the penthouse one evening for a bridal shower for a third friend. It would include dinner, drinks, and studs for fifteen guests.

We estimated costs and finally charged $3000, including decorations. We barely broke even, but garnered valuable experience in planning and managing a large affair.

The pièce de résistance of this riotous evening was Seth Hawkins popping naked from a gigantic (cardboard) cake, pelting the bride-to-be with confetti and streamers, and presenting her with several ribald gifts to ease the pangs of her wedding night.

The studs did very well with tips, and the guests assured us it was the best party they had ever attended. In the following weeks we booked luncheons, dinners, bridal showers, birthday parties, and a wake.

71

After Wolcott Sands resigned, I asked Sol Hoffheimer for an older, silver-haired "executive type." He sent two applicants to the penthouse. Martha rejected both of them.

"They haven't the fatherly approach Sands had," she complained. "All the daddy-lovers went for that guy. He made incest fun."

But a replacement for Sands wasn't my only problem with the studs.

Harry Bellinger, an aspiring stand-up comic who had given us almost a year of yeoman service, announced he had an offer from Las Vegas. I couldn't believe it. I had seen Harry's professional routine, and Vegas caliber it wasn't. Punxsutawney maybe.

Then one of our black stars said he was splitting to get married. I happened to know he was already married.

And then, worst of all, Seth Hawkins came to me, stammering and blushing, and said he had decided to go home to Amarillo and become a television newscaster.

Three of our most dependable and popular studs were leaving, and if the exodus continued, we'd be in serious trouble.

When King Hayes showed up in the den, I feared the worst. I gave him a drink of Manischewitz Concord from a bottle I kept just for him, and prepared to argue him out of leaving. But I didn't have to.

"Desertion in the ranks, Peter?" he said, grinning. "I hear you've lost some good boys."

"You heard right," I said. "You, too?"

"Nah. I'm sticking. But I'm here to tell you that you're going to lose more."

I shook my head, bewildered. "What's happening, King? No one has been complaining; they just come in and quit."

"You've always treated me straight, Peter, so I might as well tell you. You'll hear it sooner or later anyway. Wolcott Sands is setting up his own place. He's offering a seventy-thirty split, and he's giving all your boys a hard sell."

"That bastard!" I cried indignantly. "He's going to pay the studs seventy?"

"That's it."

"Where is his place?"

"I don't rightly know. I guess I could find out if it's important."

"Would you do that, King? It *is* important."

I sat there, seething. Wolcott Sands' infamy enraged me.

"King, did he pitch you?"

"He sure did."

"So how come you're not switching?"

"Like I told you, Peter, you always treated me right. Also, you run a tight ship here. Nice and clean. Everyone behaves. But Sandy, I got the feeling he's going to run a wide-open joint."

"Drugs?"

"Maybe. He didn't come right out and say it. Also, he's going to do gays."

"Jesus," I said. "Maybe he can do one or the other, but not *both*."

"That's what I figure."

I went to our concealed safe, took out a hundred dollars, handed it to him.

"For your loyalty," I said.

He looked down at the money. "Peter, you don't have to do that."

"I know, but I *want* to do it."

He ran his fingers over the bills, stroking them. "This is what it's all about, isn't it? Money."

"You know Rain Water?"

"That crazy Cherokee? Sure, I know him."

"He calls it wampum. That's the way to think about it, King. It's just beads."

72

I called Martha at home and asked if I could come over.

"Is it important?" she said.

"Hell, yes, it's important."

She was silent a moment. "Make it around midnight, will you, Peter? The boyfriend's coming up, but he'll be gone by then."

When I got there, she was wearing a bathrobe and looked like something the cat dragged in. She was cradling a snifter of brandy in hands that trembled.

"That must have been some session," I said.

Martha didn't want to talk about it. "What's the big emergency?" she demanded.

I repeated what King Hayes had told me.

"That son of a bitch Sands," she said angrily. "Well, I guess it had to happen sooner or later. We better find out what kind of a crib he's running."

"And how do we do that—bring him a big wreath with a 'Success' ribbon?"

She thought a moment. "We'll send Nikki Radburn. Sands doesn't know her."

"You think she'll do it?"

"Nikki? She'll do anything for a buck."

I could have left then, but I had the feeling she wanted company. I helped myself to some of her Armagnac and sat in an armchair where I could look at her.

"Come on," I said. "Tell Daddy. What's got you?"

"Ah, shit," she said. "Every time I try to act noble and self-sacrificing, I end up with my ass in a sling. You'd think I'd know better by now."

"What happened?"

"It's the boyfriend. He wants to run for governor."

"Governor? Good God!" I said.

"He's got a lot of competition. But most of them are lightweights and none of them has the money he's got."

"You think he has a chance?"

She nodded. "A good chance. Except for one thing. Me."

"He must know that."

"Oh, he knows it all right. That's what we argued about tonight. Old big-hearted me, I told him to forget about me. I told him I understand completely and won't blame him a bit for giving me the brush. He's got too much riding on his Mr. Clean image."

"What did he say to that?"

"He started to cry. Can you believe it? He said he couldn't give me up. He carried on like a maniac."

I shrugged. "Maybe the guy's in love with you."

She looked down into her brandy glass. "No, it's not love. Remember what I told you about Luke Futter? The smartest man in the world gets the hots, and his brains go right out the window. That's what's happened to my guy. The power of the puss."

"Well, Martha, he's a grown man; it's his decision. Unless you decide to cut him off."

"Nooo," she said slowly, "I don't want to do that."

It was hard to believe, but she was in love. I kept thinking she knew too much about men and about life to get deeply involved with a married guy who'd never desert wife, family, and career.

But maybe she was as screwed-up as all the rest of us. And just maybe this guy had gotten to her. Maybe she loved him.

And, loving him, she was willing to give him up because she knew it had to be if he was going to achieve his ambitions. If that's not pure soap opera, I don't know what is. All it lacks is the final scene where she presses her nose against the window of the governor's mansion and watches the inaugural ball, tears streaming down her cheeks.

"So you're going to keep seeing him?" I asked.

"I guess," she said, sighing. "It's his funeral."

I remembered that later.

73

We had a bad few weeks following King Hayes' revelation of Wolcott Sands' perfidy. Four more studs left and our income fell as we were forced to turn customers away.

We took steps to minimize our loss. Just because we had an X-rated business didn't mean we couldn't operate on sound and prudent managerial principles.

In a labor-intensive profession such as ours, a stable and dependable work force was the key to success. But, driven by necessity, we began accepting inferior studs provided by Sol Hoffheimer. I don't mean they were slobs or crazies, but they weren't up to our usual high standard. We vowed this would be only a temporary expedient.

We also called in Oscar Gotwold and Iggy for a long conference on restructuring our pay scale.

We rejected meeting Sands' wage policy by raising our studs' fee to seventy dollars per scene, fearing it might lead to a price war.

Iggy suggested a salary plus commission system that would guarantee the studs a fixed minimum, with additional compensation depending on the number of clients they serviced each month.

Martha pointed out that such a system might tempt the studs to overextend themselves, which could produce dissatisfied clients.

Oscar then said we might consider incorporating Peter's Academy of Dramatic Arts and hiring the studs as "instructors" at a fixed weekly wage.

Iggy nixed that. Employing studs in such a manner, he reminded us, would necessitate such things as withholding tax and deductions for Social Security, unemployment insurance, workmen's disability, etc.

Oscar claimed this might prove advantageous in the long run. He suggested we could obtain a net tax saving by setting up a retirement and/or pension fund for the studs. Profit sharing was another option worth exploring.

The meeting was adjourned with all firm decisions postponed until we could evaluate Nicole Radburn's report on Wolcott Sands' operation.

74

It was after midnight. We were sitting around one end of the long dining room table. The two women and I were drinking marc. Luke Futter was drinking bourbon. I had put out a bowl of salted almonds, and the detective was tossing them into the air and catching them in his mouth. He didn't miss once.

"It's on the south side of East Fifty-eighth Street," Nicole Radburn told us. "Near Sutton Place. The whole first floor of a converted townhouse. The other tenants are commercial, and most of them are gone by five o'clock."

"What's the layout?" Martha asked.

"A dozen cubicles with wallboard partitions. No doors, but curtains that slide on rods. Strictly sleaze. I mean, you can hear *everything.*"

"Who takes the money?" I said.

"I guess it was Sands. Anyway it was a guy like you described. He asked me what I wanted: white, black, Chink, or whatever. I hadn't made an appointment, so he must keep a crew on hand. I paid for a white stud. When we were alone, I asked him if he could get me some grass. He said sure, no problem. Five bucks a joint. Good stuff, he claimed. Then he said if I wanted something stronger, that was available, too."

Luke Futter was interested. "Did he say exactly what was available?"

"No, but when I asked him if I could get a snort, he nodded."

"Did you see any gays in there?" I asked.

"When I was leaving, I saw an old queer coming in. He sure as hell wasn't a stud. That's a grungy operation Sands is running. But from what I saw, it's as busy as Times Square."

Luke Futter popped a final salted almond and dusted his fingers. "Sounds good," he said. "I'll have to do some digging to see if he's got any clout. If he has, it'll cost you to close him down. If he's just shmearing the locals, we can bust him easy."

"And what will that cost?" I said.

"Nothing," Futter said with his sloping grin. "On the house. I can always use a clean arrest. I'll send a couple of undercover policewomen in. Maybe they can make a coke buy. If it looks as good as you say, we might even mike the place or put a tap on the phone."

"How long will all this take?" Martha demanded.

"Weeks," he said. "Maybe a month. If you want this guy out of business for good, it's got to be done right."

He looked at Nicole. We had told her we'd pay her to keep the detective happy.

"You don't have to leave right this minute," she said, "do you, Luke?"

"I guess not," he said slowly.

"Let's go tell each other the stories of our lives," she said, rising.

"Suits me," he said.

We waited until we heard the door of the Blue Room close. I poured Martha another marc.

"He doesn't think she's doing it for love, does he?" I asked.

"Probably," Martha said, shrugging. "He ranks pretty high in the conceit department."

I nodded.

"What's with you?" she said, looking at me closely. "Jealous?"

"I like Nikki," I said.

"I do, too. So what? Peter, this is *business*. You know how the girl makes her living. Futter means nothing to her."

"I know all that," I said. "Still . . ."

She put a hand over mine. "You *are* a softy," she said gently. "Want to go to your room and make nice-nice?"

"I think I'll pass," I said. "Thanks anyway."

So we sat there, sipping our brandy slowly. After a while, Nikki and Futter came back in, we all had a final drink, and the three of them left. I was alone.

I wandered through the apartment, turning off the lights. Then I went out onto the terrace. It was early April, but still nippy. I paced up and down for a few minutes, came back inside, and did something incredibly stupid: I called Jenny Tolliver.

Her phone rang seven times. Her sleepy voice said, "H'lo?" I hung up.

I should have made nice-nice with Martha.

75

I'll tell you something about money: Unless you're as ingenuous as Arthur Enders, it's only important when you haven't got it. After you have it, it loses its importance *as money*. But it does take on new significance.

For instance, as I've already mentioned, money enables you to act on whim. Buy silk underwear, hire a limo, fly to Paris for lunch. Cash gives you the ability to indulge a caprice. That's joy.

Something else happens when you have money. (At least it happened to me.) You can act exactly as you please, with not a thought of what other people might think.

After I had money, I was perfectly capable of putting ketchup on ice cream or snapping my fingers at a waiter. *I just didn't care.* I came to the conclusion that snobbery is a refuge of the poor.

Money also releases you from bondage to fools. I would guess that 90 percent of people who work for a living must take orders from someone they don't respect. I know I did.

In effect, wealth gives you freedom, and for the first time in my life I had it.

When Arthur Enders invited me to dinner at Blotto's, I accepted gladly. Not only did I like Arthur, but continuing our friendship proved I was devoid of snobbery. I was even capable of eating spaghetti and meatballs again and drinking that corrosive red wine.

Only later it occurred to me I might have been a modern male equivalent of Marie Antoinette playing shepherdess.

We met for dinner on Sunday night when the penthouse was closed.

Blotto's hadn't changed a bit: The maître d', waiters, and bartender remembered me, but no one asked where I had been.

"What's with your play?" I asked Arthur.

He replied with his usual enthusiasm that the most recent version had been submitted to the Off Off-Broadway theater in Greenwich Village and he was waiting to hear if they'd accept it for a workshop reading. I said nothing to daunt his hopes.

I let him splutter on, smiling and nodding as he recounted the latest changes in the script. When he paused to pour us house wine from a chipped carafe, I asked casually:

"Have you seen Jenny lately?"

"My gosh, yes," he said, blinking. "I see her two or three times a week and call her almost every day."

"Oh?" I said, twirling my spaghetti. "And how is she?"

"Fine. She's opening her own studio after Labor Day and she's very excited."

"Good for her," I said. "She always dreamed about that. I'm glad she's going out on her own. She's talented."

"She sure is," he said fervently. "You should see some of her fabric designs."

"I have," I said.

"Oh," he said, blushing. "Yes. Of course. I—umm—I told her I had dinner with you. I described your penthouse. She was happy you were doing so well."

"Uh-huh. Tell me, Art, where do you go with her? What do you do?"

"Well, ah, I don't have much money, as you know, and Jenny's saving for her studio. So mostly we eat at her place or mine. We eat a lot of hamburgers and tunafish. We're both poverty-stricken."

He laughed happily and I could have killed him.

"But don't you ever go out?" I asked.

"Oh gosh, yes. Last week we went to a movie. And we've been to the Bronx Zoo, and to the Metropolitan Museum to see the Turner exhibit. And once we took a ferryboat ride to Staten Island. We walk around a lot. In the Village and SoHo. Last Sunday we walked all around the Lower East Side. We just like to walk around the city. And we talk a lot."

I wanted to but couldn't ask if they then went home and fucked.

"Well . . ." I said, as lightly as I could, "give her my best. And if she needs money for her studio . . ." I stopped there.

"Gee, Peter," he said, troubled and blinking furiously. "I really don't think she'd take it from you."

"No," I said, "she wouldn't. It was a stupid suggestion. Don't mention it to her."

I wasn't having a particularly enjoyable evening, but for reasons I couldn't understand, I didn't want to leave. So after we finished eating, we moved to the bar and I persuaded Arthur to let me buy us vodka stingers.

I think I got smashed. I remember I kept bringing the conversation back to Jenny Tolliver. How did she look? Had she bought any new clothes? How were her parents? Had she lost any weight?

After a while I realized Arthur was looking at me with sad sympathy, and I couldn't stand that. I told him I expected a busy Monday and had to split.

"Thanks for the dinner," I said.

"Thanks for the drinks," he said. "Let's do this again real soon."

"You bet," I said. But I knew we wouldn't.

76

Losing our best studs to Wolcott Sands hurt us, no doubt about that, but we survived. I filled in more and we accepted almost every boy Sol Hoffheimer sent us. There were a few customer complaints; even a refund when an overworked stud just couldn't cut the mustard.

I kept calling Luke Futter about how his investigation was going, but all he'd say was, "These things take time."

About the middle of April, I scheduled myself for a scene with a woman named Sally who, her sponsor told us, was from out of town, in Manhattan for a week on a shopping trip.

I waited for her in the Rose Room, the master bedroom where I slept. I had glasses of white wine ready and I checked the bathroom to make certain Maria had supplied fresh towels.

There was a knock on the bedroom door. I opened it, smiling. There stood Sally Lee Soorby, my ex-wife.

I saw her jaw drop, as I suppose mine did. Then we both shouted with laughter. I dragged her inside, slammed the door, and embraced her. She smelled of Estée Lauder and Jim Beam.

She pulled away to look at me, holding my arms.

"Honey," she said, "what in the world are you doing here?"

"I own the joint," I said. "What are *you* doing here?"

"I was figuring to sample some Yankee cockadoodledoo," she said.

"Sally, if you'd rather sample someone else, I'll line up another stud for you."

"Wouldn't dream of it, honey," she said. "It'll be like old times."

While we were undressing, she told me she had divorced the man who ran the fish hatchery in Georgia.

"Honey, even his private parts smelled of flounder."

Her name was now Sally Lee Randolph, and her present husband owned a string of laundromats, a Cadillac dealership, and the local franchise for Gobble Burgers, patties of ground turkey meat served on salted buns.

"We're rich, rich, rich," she said.

"Glad to hear it," I said. And then, when I saw her naked, I added, "Sally, you've been eating too many Gobble Burgers."

"I guess," she said, patting her plump hips. "But Hank—he's my hubby—likes me this way."

"You still look great," I assured her. "No sag, no sink, no flop. Hank is a lucky man."

"His brother is, too," she said, giggling. She fell into bed and held her arms out to me.

She was as crazy and as acrobatic in bed as she had been when we were married. To her, sex was a romp, a loving tussle. If it wasn't a laugh, it wasn't anything.

She was delighted because I remembered how she liked to be tickled. It drove her wild. Blowing on her breasts drove her wild. Licking her palms drove her wild. Gnawing on her earlobes drove her wild. She was 130 lbs. of raw nerve ends.

We had a funny scene together, very sweet and affectionate. We could play with each other, remembering the buttons to press and the triggers to pull. I had almost forgotten how dear total physical intimacy can be. Bodies are nice.

We went over the allotted hour, but finally I had to call a halt, hyperventilating like I had just run the 440. I knew she could go on and on and on, until the paramedics came for me. She had always been like that, but never ill-tempered when I collapsed. A very good-natured woman.

I hoped Hank—and his brother—appreciated what they had.

"No children, Sally?" I asked her while we were dressing.

"Naw," she said. "Something's wrong with my plumbing. Hank and I were talking about adopting. What do you think?"

"To be absolutely honest, I can't really see you as a mother."

"I guess you're right, honey," she said, sighing. "I'll just go through life screwing up a storm."

I walked her to the foyer door, my arm about her waist. Martha looked at us strangely.

"Sally," I said, "it was good to see you. Come back again."

"How many boys you got here?" she asked.

"Oh, I don't know exactly. Thirty or forty, I guess."

I could see visions of sugarplums dance through her head.

"Honey," she said, "I do wish you'd open a branch in Atlanta."

77

We worked hard to make our business a success. All our studs were clean. We served good meals and honest drinks at reasonable prices. We supplied fresh bed linen and towels to every customer. We even had flowers in the bedrooms and foyer. In every way, it was a class operation.

And then the roof fell in. I remember the day very well: April 22. On that date we received a registered letter from the real estate agent who had rented us the penthouse. We were informed that the original lessee planned to return to the U.S. at the end of the year and that we would have to vacate by December 31.

"Look," Martha said. "This is too sweet a deal to let go down the drain. We've got eight more months here. That'll give us time to find a new crib. Meanwhile we'll build up our cash reserve so we can finance a move."

"But I love this place," I wailed.

"I know, Peter," she said. "I do, too. But we've got to face facts. We started in your West Side fleabag and ended up in this palace. We can do the same thing again."

She went on, talking me out of my depression. I admit it: She was the stronger partner, and after a while I began to regain my confidence. It wasn't the end of the world. It might even be the beginning of something truly grand.

78

A few days after we received the bad news about the penthouse, something odd happened.

Martha came to me a little after twelve noon and in an offhand way said she had a request for call boy service at three o'clock that afternoon. I told her I'd make some phone calls and line up a stud.

"I wish you'd take it, Peter," she said, not looking at me.

"Why me?" I protested. "I'm right in the middle of next week's schedule."

"Well, uh, it's a new customer. Supposed to be very wealthy. Influential. I think we should try to make a good impression."

She seemed—well, not nervous perhaps, but disturbed. Something was obviously bothering her.

"All right," I said. "What's her name?"

Her name was Mrs. Wilson Bowker. Her address was on East 82nd Street, in the block between Fifth and Madison avenues. In the space for comments on the job order slip, Martha had jotted: "Discreet."

"What's with this 'Discreet'?" I asked her.

"She was very anxious," Martha said, "that the man we send her be discreet."

"Too bad," I said, sighing. "I was going to wear a big sign around my neck that said STUD."

I arrived at the address a few minutes before 3:00 P.M., carrying a book of wallpaper samples under my arm. It was a small, sleek, modern apartment house. (I learned later it had only ten duplexes.) In the marble-lined lobby, a uniformed attendant sat in a glass booth labeled CONCIERGE.

"For Mrs. Bowker," I told him. "From the interior decorator. I have her wallpaper samples."

He spoke into a white French phone in a respectful voice. Then he motioned toward the single elevator.

"Mrs. Bowker is expecting you, sir. Apartment Five-B."

The apartment made my penthouse look like a littered closet. There was enough room on the first floor for the Knicks to play the Nets. A gracefully curved staircase led to a second-floor balcony and, presumably, the bedrooms.

The white was so dazzling it stunned the eye. White walls, ceiling, rug, furniture. Even a white grand piano. Oh, there were a few monochromatic touches, but generally the apartment looked like it had just been through a blizzard.

The woman who greeted me was also white, white, white. Silvery-blond hair pulled back in a tight chignon. White robe zipped to the neck. White pom-pons on white slippers. Her skin was pallid, with a glossy translucence. The features were fined to the point of fragility.

I guessed her age at about forty-five.

"Mrs. Bowker?" I said.

"Yes," she said in a low voice. "What is your name?"

"Peter."

She nodded as if her worst fears were confirmed.

"You have a lovely home," I said.

She looked around, almost surprised, seeing it for the first time. "Thank you," she said faintly. She saw me looking at the white piano. "Do you play?" she asked.

"Not the piano, no," I said, trying a small joke. But she didn't pick up on it.

Actually, I wasn't staring at the piano so much as what was on it: a number of what were obviously silver-framed photographs, all turned facedown.

"This is a new experience for me," she said hesitantly. "What do we do now?"

"We're alone in the apartment, Mrs. Bowker?"

She nodded.

"Then shall we go to the bedroom?"

She stood a moment without speaking. A slender, erect woman. Her face was composed. She seemed self-possessed. The only tipoff I had to an inner turmoil was that quavery, almost creaky voice. I thought she might be desperately hanging on to herself.

"Very well," she said finally, turned and marched up the staircase. I followed her.

The blizzard had struck in the bedroom as well. An enormous chamber, all brilliant white with one mirrored wall. And on the dresser, bureau, and bedside table, more silver-framed photographs tipped down.

She turned to face me. "And now?" she said tensely.

"Shall we undress?"

Again she stood without speaking. This was like pulling teeth. I paused a moment, then began to take off my jacket.

"Wait," she said, holding out a palm.

I waited.

She drew a deep breath. "I'm sorry," she said huskily, "but this isn't going to work. You'll receive your fee, but now I wish you'd leave."

She turned away, took a few steps toward the mirrored wall, stood gazing at her image.

"It's not you," she said in a dead voice. "You're quite attractive. It's me."

She stopped with that and said no more. It didn't give me much of a clue, but I thought I'd take a chance . . .

"Mrs. Bowker, there are many ways of obtaining sexual release. I know several, ah, techniques, if you'd like me to try."

"I think it's disgusting," she said in a dull voice, staring at her reflection. "I know I shouldn't feel that way, but I do. I thought this would . . . But I can't. I'm sorry. Please go."

So we went back downstairs, and she gave me the fee and a hundred-dollar tip.

"If you should change your mind . . ." I said.

"No," she said, "I don't believe I shall. Ever. Please forget all of this. Promise?"

"Of course," I said, and that was that.

The moment I got back to the penthouse, Martha wanted to know what the apartment was like and all about Mrs. Bowker: What kind of a woman was she, did I think her beautiful, was she a good lay?

I told her what happened.

Martha was silent and thoughtful.

"Why all the questions?" I demanded. "What's your interest in this?"

But she just shook her head and turned away. A month later I guessed what it was all about.

79

When we met at Martha's apartment, Luke Futter was in a jaunty mood.

"It's all set," he said. "Two undercover policewomen made buys at Sands' crib. We'll bust the joint on Wednesday. He's got a lot of rich, influential customers; it'll be strictly a drug thing."

"Who gets charged?" Martha asked.

"Just Wolcott Sands. We'll have a warrant. The others will probably be taken in, questioned, and released. And the place will be sealed, of course."

We were silent. I knew it had to be done, but I wasn't particularly happy about it. It was true that Sandy had betrayed us, but it seemed a harsh reprisal.

"What do you think he'll get?" I said.

"Depends on how smart a lawyer he gets and how much money he's willing to spread around. If he plays it right, he can plea-bargain a felony down to a misdemeanor and get off with a fine and probation. He's got no prior record. But if he gets a snotty lawyer, he's liable to end up doing time."

"How much?"

Futter shrugged. "A year maybe. Eighteen months. You don't much care, do you?"

"Let the son of a bitch rot," Martha said wrathfully.

"Yeah," the detective said, laughing. "He's giving prostitution a bad name. But there's something I better warn you about. If he guesses who tipped the cops to his operation, he may blow the whistle on you out of spite or hand you to the DA as a bargaining chip. Either way your business is in danger."

"So what do we do?" I asked anxiously.

"Take my advice," Futter said, "and close down for a week. We're raiding on Wednesday. Shutter yur place on Tuesday night. Take a week's vacation, preferably out of town. If things look clear after a week, you can open up again."

"Jesus," Martha said. "That's a week's revenue lost."

"It should all blow over in a week," the detective urged. "Look, this is no big deal. Just another drug bust. Because of the rich people involved, we're not looking for publicity. It may not even make the papers. But play it safe. Then, if Sands shoots his mouth off, the guys sent to investigate will report a locked apartment, nobody in residence, and that'll be the end of that."

We saw the logic of what Futter said and agreed to shutter the penthouse for a week. Although he hadn't asked an additional fee for putting Sands out, we'd decided on a bonus of five hundred.

"Thanks," the detective said, slipping the money into his pocket without glancing at it. He drained his drink and rose to go. "What made it easy," he said, "was that this Wolcott Sands wasn't paying off *anyone*. Can you imagine? The guy was a fucking outlaw!"

80

After Futter left, Martha and I kicked off our shoes and settled down on her leather couch.

"I don't like that man," I said.

"But he does what he's paid to do," Martha said. "We don't have to like him."

"It's a whole new world to me," I said, shaking my head.

"What is?"

"Bribing people. Paying off cops. Getting rid of Sidney Quink. Putting Sandy out of business. And what you told me about your boyfriend—how a few men decide who may be our next governor. I guessed a world like that existed but I've never been a part of it."

"It exists all right," Martha said grimly. "And believe me, it's better to be in it than out of it. I call it the overworld. The underworld is all cheap crime and senseless violence. But the overworld is wealth and power. The crimes are big ones, and if violence is used, there's a reason for it."

"The movers and shakers," I said.

"You better believe it. Most of whom you've never heard of. But they have more influence on the way you live than you can imagine. Power is the goal, and money is the way to get it. Mostly through genteel corruption. The first law of the overworld is: Everyone has his price. The only things money can't buy aren't worth having."

"I didn't know you were a philosopher."

"I have a brain," she said, "and occasionally I use it. I see what's going on. Be a dear and pour us a brandy."

When I brought the drinks, she patted the cushion alongside her. I sat close and put an arm across her shoulders. She snuggled into me.

"Maybe I'll go down to Virginia and see my boy," she said. "For three or four days. Then I'll come back here and check with Futter. Where will you go when we close?"

"I haven't thought about it. I've never had a real vacation. I've never been able to afford it."

"Why don't you try Florida?" she suggested. "It shouldn't be too crowded this time of year. They've got horse tracks, dog tracks, jai alai. If you want a casino, you can always fly over to Freeport."

"I'm not much for gambling with chips."

"Then just lie on the beach, relax, and soak up the sun. We've both been working hard. A few days off will do us good."

We sat quietly, sipping our Armagnac.

"What you said," I remarked reflectively, "that the only things money can't buy aren't worth having . . . what about love?"

"What about it?" she said, looking up at me. "You can buy love, one way or another."

"I can't," I said, and told her about Jenny Tolliver.

"Shit," she said disgustedly. "If you really loved her, you'd have given up the business to keep her. And if she loved you, she'd have hung on to you no matter what you did."

I sighed. "I guess you're right. But I do miss her."

"Not really," Martha said. "She fascinates you because she's probably the first woman in your life who's given you the brush."

I laughed and hugged her. "Stop using your brain," I told her. "You're killing me."

It was nice being with her. Everyone's got to have someone to whom they can claw their chest open and say, "Look at that." Despite our sexless relationship, I was more physically intimate with Nicole Radburn than with Martha, but Martha was the woman I could tell about the darkness.

"Do you love your boyfriend?" I asked her suddenly.

She didn't answer. I saw her staring into the middle distance and realized it wasn't that she didn't want to tell me; she just didn't know.

"Before we leave," I said, "why don't you give Oscar Gotwold a call and start him looking for a new place for us."

"I already have," she said. "He wasn't very optimistic."

We had another drink and then went into the bedroom without speaking. I don't know why, but the business with Futter and the raid on Wolcott Sands' crib had soured the evening. We weren't depressed exactly, but thoughtful.

"Look at that," Martha said, peering down at her naked body. "I'm going to rack and ruin."

"Don't feel sorry for yourself," I said. "You're in great shape for—" I stopped.

"For a woman my age," she finished with a sour grin. "Peter, will you do me a favor?"

"Of course. Anything."

"I just want to lie quietly and let you make love to me. All right?"

"A pleasure," I said manfully, and she never knew that I had been about to ask her the same thing.

81

I took a Wednesday-morning flight to Palm Beach. I rented a snazzy Pontiac Grand Prix (which the attendant insisted on calling Grand Pricks. Had my fame spread?) and drove south on A1A, following a map I had purchased at the airport.

I found the kind of place I was looking for about a mile north of Boynton Beach: a motel so close to the ocean it was almost under water.

A half-hour later I was in my new Eminence nylon briefs, daring the warm surf.

After my swim, I pulled on espadrilles, white duck slacks, a pink Izod shirt, and found a big liquor store that not only sold booze, but offered glassware, wine racks, corkscrews, and anything else a drinking man might need.

Also, I discovered, many large Florida liquor stores have a connecting cocktail lounge. After stowing my purchases (vodka, gin, brandy, tonic water, lemons and limes) in the trunk of the Grand Prix, I went back into the dim cocktail lounge and swung aboard a stool at the bar.

The barmaid wore short-shorts, a thin halter top (without bra), and looked like a high school cheerleader. She also looked dumbfounded when I ordered a negroni, the most lethal drink known to living man. But she had all the ingredients, and I taught her how to mix one. I even gave her a sip.

"Yuck!" she said, making a face. "Tastes like medicine."

"That's exactly what it is," I said. "For whatever ails you."

"I like apricot brandy," she said.

So I bought her an apricot brandy and told her what I was looking for: a typical Florida restaurant where I could get fresh seafood. She recommended a place called the Crab Palace on Federal Highway, casual and reasonable.

I had two negronis and left her a heavy tip.

"You have a nice day now, y'hear?" she called after me.

That Crab Palace was something. The wooden kitchen tables were spread with newspapers in lieu of cloths, and beer was served in cans, the tabs popped at the table by the waitress with all the aplomb of a Manhattan sommelier removing the cork from a bottle of d'Yquem.

But there were some sophisticated touches. Each table had a bottle of sherry, to be added to shrimp or lobster bisque. And the selection of condiments included, by my count, seven different kinds of pepper, pepper flakes, ground pepper, pickled peppers, and one container marked simply: X-RATED PEPPER.

I had conch chowder and an enormous platter of Alaskan king crab legs, which I cracked with the length of broomstick attached to the table with a long chain. I also had french fries, a salad with the garlicky house dressing, and two cans of Rolling Rock beer. I finished with a wedge of Key Lime pie. It was a memorable meal.

On the way out, as I was paying my bill, I saw they were selling T-shirts that had, printed on the front, the legend: I HAD CRABS. I bought two of them, one for Martha and one for Nikki.

Around midnight, I strolled out onto the beach in front of my motel. I carried a small brandy, a nightcap.

A bloated moon cut a silver swath across the softly heaving sea. The air was bland and smelled of salt. I heard the rustle of palm fronds and saw, far out, the twinkling lights of passing boats.

It was beautiful, but after five minutes I went back inside and went to bed. I'm a city boy, and enough's enough.

On Thursday morning I found a drugstore that sold the national edition of *The New York Times*. I bought a copy and took it to the local McDonald's, where I leafed through it while eating my Egg McMuffin and drinking two cups of black coffee.

I found the story hidden away at the bottom of page seventeen. It was a short paragraph and said only that New York police had raided an "establishment" on East 58th Street where, it was alleged, illicit drugs were being sold. One individual, Wolcott Sands, home address unknown, had been taken into custody.

I spent the morning on the beach, swimming and sunning. Then I took a nap. Around four o'clock I dressed and went back to the cocktail lounge I had visited the day before.

The cheerleader barmaid was on duty again. This time she was wearing a tight sweater with PAT embroidered over one breast.

"Is that your name or an invitation?" I asked her.

"Oh *you!*" she said, giggling. "You want one of them niggeronis?"

"Negroni," I said. "And yes, I'd like one."

She was young and fresh-skinned. Long blond hair, bleached almost white, feathered around her shoulders.

When she brought my drink, I asked her, "Are you working tonight?"

"I get off at eight."

"How about having dinner with me at the Crab Palace?"

"Okay," she said promptly. "I'm driving this little old Pinto. I'll meet you there at eight-thirty."

"Fine," I said.

"What's your name?"

"Peter."

"Oh wow," she said. "That's heavy."

I tried catfish that night, for the first time in my life. It was all right, but not something I'd want for a steady diet. Pat had two portions of broiled dolphin.

"I just love it," she said, "and it costs the same no matter how much you eat."

"How about more fries and another beer?" I suggested.

"Okay," she said.

As we were leaving the Crab Palace, I said, "How about going back to my place for a drink?"

"Okay," she said. "You go ahead and I'll follow in my Pinto."

In my motel room I started mixing gin and tonics. She wandered about, looking into cupboards and closets, testing the softness of the twin beds, peering into the efficiency oven.

"I'd just love a cozy little place like this all my own," she said. "Where I live it's like a crazy house—you know? I got five brothers and sisters, all younger than me, and I got no privacy."

"How come you're not married, Pat?"

"I'm going to be," she said. "My boyfriend—he works in a garage—well, him and me are saving our money, and we figure by next year we'll have enough to get our own place."

"That's wonderful," I said. "I wish you the very best of everything."

"I thank you," she said formally. Then: "Would you like to have some fun?"

There is no substitute for youth. She was firm, sun-warmed, juicy with life. Her inexperience was a delight.

"Oh wow," she gasped at one point. "You sure know about loving."

"I make it my business to know," I said.

She was enthusiastic, agreeable to anything, eager to learn.

"I'll have to remember that," she said several times.

Later, we showered together, which pleased her mightily. After we were dressed, I gave her a hundred dollars, which made her eyes round.

"So much!" she said, but took it without demur. "You're a doll," she said. "A living doll. You come back and see me again, y'hear?"

I spent a few hours swimming on Friday morning. But my skin was beginning to tingle, and I didn't want to stay in the sun. I dressed in madras jacket and light flannel slacks and drove up to Palm Beach.

It was a revelation. I had a typical New York provincial attitude that wealth and elegance exist only in Manhattan. Worth Avenue disabused me of that notion. The Via Mizner made Madison Avenue look like Orchard Street.

It wasn't so much the stores and boutiques with their eye-popping displays of dazzling items. What impressed me most were the fashionably dressed women strolling from shop to shop with apparently no desire except to spend money.

I found an outdoor café where I could sit at an umbrella table, sip a Campari and soda, and watch the glittering parade.

These Florida women were, perhaps, a trifle older than the Barcarole clientele. But they were just as haughty, splendidly dressed and coiffed, and appeared to me to be a more athletic group, with deep tans, sturdy strides, and the look of women who took their golf and tennis seriously.

I won't say my Great Idea came to me at that precise moment in a flash of light. I did not leap to my feet shouting, "Eureka!" But a concept was born.

My Great Idea was this: a private club in a townhouse for moneyed women. It would require a hefty membership fee and annual dues. It would be as lush and elegant as the famed Everleigh Sisters' bordello in Chicago. It would offer food, drinks, and perhaps a trio in the bar.

It would have several upstairs bedrooms. In addition to supplying studs, the club would rent these bedchambers to members (for a fee, of course) for discreet assignations with their lovers.

My imagination ran wild. I could foresee a beauty salon on the premises. And a small health club with sauna and masseur.

That evening, I dined in Palm Beach in a restaurant where there was candlelight on the tables and the red snapper was served almondine. Out of a full bottle of excellent muscadet, I left only a glass, and hoped the busboy would have sense enough to finish it.

I drove back to my motel and spent hours striding the beach barefoot, my brain still churning with my Great Idea. I decided "Peter's Place" would be a logical and easily remembered name. I saw it occupying a splendid East Side townhouse, the interior decorated in restrained good taste.

But if the Manhattan Peter's Place proved successful, was there any reason why it couldn't go national? I saw a chain of Peter's Places, wholly owned or franchised. A Peter's Place in New York, Palm Beach, Atlanta, Los Angeles, Chicago, etc.—any city that provided an ample supply of affluent women. Maybe even London, Paris, Rome!

On Saturday morning I bought a legal size yellow pad and began making notes. When I had filled pages with ideas on how an opulent cathouse should be organized and maintained, I finally—and with reluctance—turned to the problem of how such an establishment could be financed.

I figured that by the end of the year, Martha and I might be able to come up with a quarter of a million cash. If we could persuade, say, a thousand clients to pay a $500 membership fee—or five hundred customers to pay $1000 each—it would yield an additional half-million. That was, I knew, far short of the investment needed to open this kind of private club. I faced the sobering realization that Peter's Place would require outside financing.

On Sunday, around noon, I called Martha Twombly, who had just returned from Virginia. She had been in touch with Detective Luke Futter and brought me up to date on what had happened.

Wolcott Sands had been released on $10,000 bail. He had, indeed, told the police about us. Detectives sent to investigate found a locked and unoccupied apartment. Max the doorman—God bless him!—had assured them that we were a legitimate acting school. So that was that.

Futter thought we could reopen for business on Tuesday, barring unexpected developments. I told Martha that I was having a marvelous time, would come back as soon as possible, and had something to discuss with her.

I made a first-class reservation on the Monday-noon flight out of Palm Beach, then went to the ocean for a final swim and walk along the strand.

Around five o'clock, I went back to the cocktail lounge, thinking I might take Pat to dinner on my last evening in Florida. The bearded man behind the bar told me she didn't work on Sundays, but that she'd left a note for "Peter."

The note had only "Pat" written in a childish scrawl and a telephone number.

So I called her from the Gents, standing next to the urinals and staring at a wall-mounted vending machine that dispensed rainbow-colored French ticklers.

The man who answered sounded drunk.

"Is Pat there?" I asked.

"Who's this?" he demanded.

"My name is Peter. Is Pat there?"

"Who the—" he started.

Then I heard a thump, what sounded like a scuffle, and in the background the sounds of children yelling and crying.

"Hello?" Pat said breathlessly.

"This is Peter. I was—"

"Oh, Peter," she wailed. "Pa is soused, and Ma's sick, and I've got to make supper for this gang of morons, and I swear I'm going right up the wall."

"I'm sorry, Pat. I was hoping we might have dinner, but—"

"Listen, honey," she said in a conspiratorial whisper, "I can't get away right now—you know? But how's about I come over to your place around eight, eight-thirty, like that. Okay?"

"Sure," I said faintly. "Fine." All I had in mind was dinner.

"You go ahead and eat," she said swiftly. "See you later." She hung up.

Before I left the Gents, I bought two packages of rainbow-colored French ticklers for Martha and Nikki.

I went to the Crab Palace again and had a platter of sautéed soft-shell crabs with wild rice and a plate of sliced tomatoes and Bermuda onions. Also a carafe of the house wine.

Then I drove back to my motel, sat outside on a metal lounge chair, and watched the moon come up while I sipped a Tanqueray on the rocks.

Pat arrived like a hurricane a little after nine o'clock, hair flying, T-shirt and short-shorts stained, her expression tense and twisted.

"That fucking family!" she said wrathfully.

"Hey," I said. "Calm down."

"Give me a drink," she said. "Please. Anything will do fine."

I mixed her a strong gin and tonic. She drank it off without stopping. I mixed her another. She held that one and took a deep breath.

"Shit, shit, shit," she said. "Excuse my language. Peter, I smell like a goat. Can I take a shower?"

"Help yourself," I said.

Fifteen minutes later she came out of the bathroom sleek and dripping, all creamy and rose-tinted. She was toweling her hair.

"Clean, dry towels," she said happily. "Lord, it's a blessing. Ma hasn't been able to do any laundry for a week, and Pa's no help."

I watched her dry her body. It was stirring without being sexy. I can't explain it. I fixed myself a weak gin and tonic and freshened her drink.

"Oh wow," she said. "I'm just beginning to feel human again. You're a doll to let me come over."

She dropped the damp towels on the floor. She sat cross-legged on one of the beds, unsnarling her hair with an enormous coarse-toothed comb.

"Where you from, Peter?"

"New York."

"I guessed. When you going back?"

"Tomorrow morning."

She looked at me, lifting her arms to comb that long, sun-bleached hair. Then: "Take me with you?"

I shook my head slowly.

"You married?"

"No, but I've got a regular lady friend and I don't think she'd understand. Besides, you're getting married next year—remember?"

"You know what's going to happen to me?" she demanded. "I'll have five brats in five years and get as fat and sick as my ma. My man will drink as much as my pa, my tits will sag to my knees, and my hair will thin out, and I'll never get to go nowhere."

What could I say? She was right.

"Ah, the hell with it," she said, smiling brightly. "That's all tomorrow, and tonight's tonight." She held her arms wide, offering. "Peter, give me some more lessons."

I really didn't want to, but I owed her.

The next morning I flew back to New York, carrying my plans for Peter's Place.

82

Before Martha and I fled New York, we had left a message on our answering machine telling clients we would be closed temporarily and to try us again in a week's time. We had hardly reopened when the phone began to ring off the hook, and we booked our best week's business so far.

We never would have been able to accommodate our eager customers if it hadn't been for the return of the stud defectors. When they came crawling back, we welcomed them without rancor and put them immediately to work.

I was especially happy to have Seth Hawkins with us again. The cowboy was enormously popular, so profitable an addition to our staff that Martha called him the Man with the Golden Whang.

One other incident of significance occurred during that frantic week . . .

I was flipping through *The New York Times* one Friday when I came across a photograph that caught my eye.

It was of an attractive blond woman and a tall, handsome man, their linked hands raised, smiling down from a dais at a presumably applauding audience. The caption identified them as Mr. and Mrs. Wilson Bowker.

There was absolutely no doubt that the Mrs. Bowker in the photo was the frigid lady from the white duplex on East 82nd Street. I read the entire article.

It stated that Wilson Bowker, a prominent Manhattan businessman, had delivered a speech in which he said that crime was the Number One problem, and that until law and order were restored, the city, state, and nation had no future.

The speech had been greeted with enthusiastic approval, and Mr. Bowker had been joined on the podium by his wife, Alice, to acknowledge the plaudits of the audience. When questioned if he had any ambitions for political office, Mr. Wilson Bowker had smiled and said, "Who knows?"

I put the paper aside thoughtfully, finally understanding Martha's interest in Alice Bowker. Wilson Bowker was Martha's fun-and-games boyfriend, and he *was* being groomed to run for governor—and on a law-and-order platform.

It was all very interesting.

83

When our business was running smoothly again, I arranged a conference with Martha, Oscar Gotwold, and Ignatz Samuelson. We met on Sunday evening in the penthouse den.

I had planned this initial presentation of Peter's Place with some care. If these people didn't go for my Great Idea, it was dead in its tracks. I needed their enthusiasm.

I had decided to pitch Peter's Place as a one-shot deal, a single private club in Manhattan. If I mentioned a nationwide chain or a franchise arrangement, they'd think I was completely demented: The concept of an exclusive New York cathouse for women was novel enough.

For almost a half-hour I gave what I thought was an effective performance. I am, after all, an actor, and a damned good one. Serious, sincere, persuasive, I brought up all possible objections and answered them before they could be voiced.

I threw numbers at them, based on our most recent daily gross at the penthouse. I showed them what our income would be from ten or twelve bedrooms plus food and beverage, membership fees, and annual dues.

I mentioned concessions such as a beauty parlor, health club, gift shop, boutique, etc. They listened closely, and I could tell they were beginning to grasp my vision and see the potential profits.

When I finished, there was dead silence. I freshened my drink and, as lightly as I could, said, "Well?"

Martha was the first to respond. She said admiringly, "Peter, I told you that you were made for this business."

Iggy Samuelson said slowly, "The numbers sound good."

"Let's not get carried away," Oscar Gotwold said. "You're talking about buying or leasing a five- or six-story East Side townhouse, converting all the upper floors to bedrooms, installing a big kitchen, dining room, bar, and so forth. Iggy, what's your estimate on the investment?"

The accountant pondered a moment. "At least three or four million."

"It wouldn't have to be that lavish," I protested. "Not at first. And if Martha is willing, the two of us could put in a quarter-million plus another half from membership fees before we open."

"Not enough," Iggy said, shaking his head. "You'd need at least another two mil to launch this. Peter, between construction and renovation costs and closings, licenses, shmears, and so forth, you'd be bled white before you could open."

"And if you didn't open," Gotwold said, "the customers who paid membership fees would come down on you hard."

"All right," I said. "That means we have to raise, say, two million—am I correct?"

"Yes, but it's a gamble," Oscar warned. "A big gamble."

"I don't think so," I said sternly. "I don't think it's a gamble at all. Not if it's run right. If I had two million, I wouldn't hesitate a minute in sinking every cent into this thing."

"But you haven't got it," Iggy pointed out. "Where are you going to get it?"

I looked at Martha. Her boyfriend, Wilson Bowker, had access to that kind of money. Maybe Martha could work a deal. But she didn't volunteer.

It was Oscar Gotwold who saved Peter's Place. "Honey," he said to Martha, "those two ex-bosses of yours at the Barcarole. They've got two million—or know where to get it."

She didn't answer immediately. Then she sighed. Then she said, "They're hard men, Oscar. As you well know. If they came into this thing, they'd want to pull the strings, and Peter and I would end up working for bupkes."

"No way," I said determinedly. "This is our baby. We do the work and we have majority control. That has to be understood."

"All right," Gotwold said equably. "With that in mind, let me talk to them and see if there's any interest. If there is, Peter can give them his spiel."

"Yes," Martha said, nodding, "that's the best way to handle it. But remember, Peter and I are the owners."

"Absolutely," Oscar said.

84

I was on the phone to Sol Hoffheimer at least once a week, and my message was always the same: Send us more warm bods. I delivered Sol's cash fee once a month, and realized his drinking was rapidly becoming a problem. But at the time, I had more pressing vexations.

I kept nagging him for a reasonable facsimile of Wolcott Sands—an older executive-type, a father figure. Early in June he delivered. The stud's name was Yancy Burnett (we called him Yance), and he had played a psychiatrist in a soap opera for seven years until he was written out of the script.

He was a squarish man who admitted to being fifty-two, and if you had called Central Casting, you couldn't have done better. Fine, silvery hair topped a warm, rubicund face with the sparkiest blue eyes I've ever seen. Martha auditioned him and was impressed.

"As good as Sands," she reported. "Maybe better. He's not as breezy, but he's more sympathetic and tender."

As it turned out, he proved tremendously popular with our younger customers. And even our octogenarian, Becky, pronounced him "A real mensch."

Yance was slyly sardonic, mordantly witty, and always ready to volunteer when needed. For instance, he filled in at the reception desk when Martha was out, and he began helping me with scheduling and other day-to-day tasks. He was paid extra for these duties, of course.

Early on, he said to me, "Peter, I better tell you something. You'll find out sooner or later anyway. I swing both ways. But I promise you, I won't come on to any of the studs."

"Okay then," I said. "What you do on your own time is your business. You married, Yance?"

"Was," he said. "Twice. Two mistakes."

"What happened?" I asked curiously.

"It was my fault," he said. "I made the mistake of not realizing that women can have soft bodies and iron wills. I couldn't take that emotional obligation. So now I just cruise."

"In other words," I said, "this is the perfect job for you."

"Perfect," he agreed.

85

I called Jenny Tolliver again. This time I was sober.

"Hello?" she said.

"It's Peter," I said. "Please don't hang up."

Silence.

"I just wanted to ask how you are," I said.

"Fine, thank you," she said coldly. "And you?"

"Surviving. I had dinner with Arthur and he told me that you're opening your own studio."

"Yes. After Labor Day."

"Where is it?" I asked. The insurance salesman's pitch: Get the customer talking about himself.

"In the Garment District," she said. "Just a small loft. I'll have one assistant to help out with the mechanical stuff."

"I wish you the very best," I said. "You know that."

"Thank you," she said faintly.

That voice did things to me. Voices can have the effect of old popular songs. In themselves they're nothing. Cheap, tinny tunes. But you wrap them in memories and give them meaning.

"Your parents are well?" I asked.

"Yes. Mother has trouble with her arthritis, but she lives with it."

"Have you been up to see them?"

"Not since Easter."

I searched desperately for something else to keep her talking. Then I decided to take the plunge and get it over with.

"Jenny," I said, "I was hoping I might see you again." I swallowed. "Just a lunch or dinner," I added hastily. "Whenever and wherever you say. Just to talk."

Silence again.

"Enough time has passed," I said. "Surely we can have a friendly dinner."

Pause. About three beats.

"I'll think about it," she said.

"Then I can call you again?" I said eagerly.

"If you like."

86

Nicole Radburn sat on a small, cretonne-covered armchair in the Rose Room, giving herself a pedicure. She lavished as much loving attention on herself as a man might give his Mercedes.

She was wearing only the I HAD CRABS T-shirt I'd brought her from Florida. Her body was sensuous and she moved with a fluid grace. I was puzzled as to why I wasn't aroused by her.

I finally decided I was like a man who works in a bakery all day. In his hours off, he can't endure the sight of a charlotte russe.

I had just showered and was wearing a towel wrapped around my hips. Nikki looked up.

"I mixed us a couple of wine spritzers with your white burgundy," she said. "Is that all right?"

"You know you can help yourself to anything in the house," I said.

"Terrific dinner tonight," she said. "I like the idea of sautéeing veal with scallion greens. You're a good cook."

"You could have left a small tip under your plate," I told her.

I sat on the bed, sipped my drink, watched her work carefully on her feet. I thought a sculptor would be delighted with her musculature. Maybe not a painter.

"How's business?" I asked her.

"Good," she said, not looking up. "Last week I added six new names to my file. By now, I've got almost a thousand. Can you believe it? When I bow out, I can sell the file to a beginner for a good price."

"You mean in ten years?"

She put all her scissors and files away, brought her drink over, and sat alongside me. She put an arm across my bare shoulders.

"Maybe sooner," she said. "Did I tell you a couple of my customers want to marry me?"

"No," I said. "You didn't tell me that."

"They're nice guys, but they can't come up with the funds. But if a john with real loot asks me, I might be tempted."

I turned to look at her. "Would you be faithful to him?"

She was astonished at my question. "Of course. Peter, sex isn't all that important to me. As you well know."

"That I do," I said mournfully. But she was not fooled by my pretended chagrin at our chaste relationship.

She went into the bathroom, put the toilet seat down, and began to pee. I could hear it. She kept talking to me through the open door. The first time she had done that, I was shocked. Now it seemed perfectly natural.

"Actually," she called, "I'd probably make a good wife. I've got a head for business and I know the value of a buck. And my husband would be able to tomcat around as long as it didn't endanger my income."

She flushed the toilet and came back to the bed.

"I'm in a game now, Peter," she said. "And so are you. But money's the biggest game of all. And the most fun. One of my regulars is a shrink, and he says all my sexual passion goes into acquisitiveness."

"You have a psychiatrist for a customer?" I said. "That's wild. What do you do for him?"

She laughed. "Spank him with a Ping-Pong paddle."

"I'm ready for a refill," I said, holding up my empty glass. "How about you?"

"All right," she said, draining her drink. "But not a spritzer or I'll be running all night."

"Frangelico?"

"I'll buy that," she said.

When I came back with the drinks, she was lying flat, hands clasped behind her head, staring at the ceiling. She had taken off the T-shirt. Those crazy nipples jutted. She took the drink from me.

"Thank you, nurse," she said. "You're very good to me."

"Damned right," I said.

I unwound my towel and got into bed alongside her. Our thighs touched.

"Anything doing on the new crib?" she asked.

"We're meeting with the moneymen next week."

"They'll come in," she said. "It can't miss."

"Bless you," I said.

"If you get the go-ahead, what are you going to call it?"

I hesitated a moment. "I haven't told anyone this, not even Martha, but I want to call it Peter's Place."

She didn't laugh. "Good name," she said, nodding. "A natural."

We finished our small drinks and put the glasses aside. Turned off the bedside lamps. As usual, I moved onto my side, away from her. As usual, she bent her supple body to mine, cleaving to me.

"We're like an old married couple," I said in the darkness.

"Whatever," she said, sighing with content.

87

Their names were Michael Gelesco and Anthony Cannis. They looked like former weight lifters who had gone to suet. They both wore suits with padded shoulders, sharp creases, and sleeves precisely cut to show a half-inch of shirt cuff.

They were groomed in a fashion I detest: blow-dried hair, complexions flushed by facials, manicures with clear polish. Gucci loafers had mirror shines, and pinkie rings were set with square diamonds. Gold Piaget watches, of course. And they both smoked cigars only slightly smaller than Louisville Sluggers.

We all sat around a long rosewood table in a conference room on the top floor of the Barcarole Boutique. Martha made the introductions. Gelesco and Cannis knew Oscar Gotwold, of course—he had arranged the meeting—but they nodded to Ignatz Samuelson and me.

We chatted a few minutes before Gelesco glanced at the wall clock and said, "Well, what's on your mind?"

I stood up and began my performance.

I started by describing the exact nature of our business. How much we were grossing. The numbers of clients and the studs' take. Overhead and expenses.

"It's a gold mine," I said.

Then I described what we wanted: an exclusive private club for well-fixed women who were willing to pay for their pleasure in discreet surroundings.

Using ten bedrooms as a minimum, I estimated an average take of $10,000 a day in the townhouse. With half going to the studs, it still meant a monthly gross of $130,000. Not counting food and beverage income, membership fees, and annual dues.

I watched Gelesco and Cannis as I spoke. Their only obvious reaction came when I mentioned our present profits and the anticipated net of the new club. Then they blinked.

I finished with a grand oratorical flourish. Then I sat down. The four of us looked at the two Barcarole owners. For a moment they were silent.

"How long you been in the business?" Cannis finally asked.

Martha told them we'd been operating for about eighteen months and detailed exactly how we worked.

"Drugs?" Gelesco said.

Martha said absolutely not, and went over our code of behavior for studs and customers alike. She also described the call boy and escort services which could, of course, continue as adjuncts of the new club.

"You pay protection," Cannis said, more of a statement than a question.

Then Oscar Gotwold jumped in with a list including current penthouse income, bribes, expenses, profits, and a set of numbers projecting the same factors for the new establishment.

"Are we talking partnership, corporation or what?" Gelesco said.

Iggy said we felt a corporate structure would be best, with majority control shared by Martha and me.

"It has to be," Martha said stonily. "Or no deal."

"We're willing to put in our own money," I added.

Iggy went on to explain that the investors would get paid off the top in mutually agreeable monthly or annual increments, depending on income. Oscar Gotwold pointed out that the restaurant, bar, and beauty parlor would serve as a legal front for what would go on upstairs.

"Who runs the place?" Cannis asked.

"Martha and I manage it," I said, "with three-year employment contracts. We know the, ah, desires of our clients and how to accommodate them. We have a class reputation and a very loyal following. We're bringing you a great deal of goodwill."

The two owners glanced at each other.

"Look," Cannis said. "You're asking for heavy money. We got to think this over."

"Of course," Oscar Gotwold said smoothly. "We understand that. And if you gentlemen feel that you are not in a position to make the entire investment, perhaps some of your friends and associates might be willing to come in."

"With a corporate setup," Iggy said, "blocks of stock can be sold at X dollars per share. Or we might consider a limited partnership at X dollars per minimum unit. There are several ways we can structure this."

"Look," Gelesco said to Gotwold and Iggy. "Why don't you two stick around and go over these numbers with us. We need a closer look." Then he turned to Martha and me. "No use you two hanging around. We're not going to say yes or no today. So you might as well take off."

I should have followed my instincts and insisted on staying. But I didn't. I shook hands with both of them. Their pinkie rings hurt. They both kissed Martha on the cheek.

"Good to see you again, babe," Cannis said.

"Don't be such a stranger," Gelesco said.

In the small self-service elevator, on our way down, I said to Martha, "What do you think?"

"They're interested," she said.

"How do you know?"

"They let their cigars go out."

88

Martha wanted to talk to some old friends at the Barcarole, so I walked back to the penthouse alone.

It was a gorgeous June afternoon, one of those rare days when the city seems polished and perfumed. Colors were back on the street, and everyone appeared younger and more attractive.

There's something sexually arousing about giving a good performance. You're so up and charged that humping is the only way to relieve your excess energy.

After that presentation to Cannis and Gelesco, I was high as a kite. As luck would have it, there was a woman waiting in the penthouse foyer when I got back. I took a quick glance at her. Tall. Raw-boned. Almost gaunt.

Yancy Burnett was manning the reception desk. He motioned me close.

"Off-the-street trade," he said in a low voice. "But I checked the sponsor, and she's legit. I can't get hold of a stud. My spirit is willing, but . . . Would you take her, Peter?"

"All right," I said. "Give me five minutes, then send her in."

Her name was Hetty and she had a farm woman's body: all knobs and cords. Her smoke-colored hair had been permed into a million tight curls. She had a long, horse face, but not without dignity. Give her a wart and you'd have a female Lincoln.

When she saw me naked, she raised her eyes and cried, "Oh lord!" I didn't know if it was an expression of dismay or a prayer of thanksgiving.

I was to hear that "Oh lord!" several times in the next hour, along with "Forgive me, sweet Jesus!" and "Good God Almighty!" I finally understood what was going on: She thought she was committing a mortal sin.

But she didn't give the devil much of a fight. She was all over that bed like a catch-as-catch-can wrestler, bouncing and flinging and twisting about, singing "Onward, Christian Soldiers."

She guided my hands, my mouth, legs, even toes. She grappled my body. Now the hymn was "What a Friend We Have in Jesus."

She segued into "Brighten the Corner Where You Are," sat on my face, hopped off, rolled me over, licked my coccyx, whirled me about, bit my nipples, stuck a thumb in my mouth, pulled my hair, explored my navel with her tongue.

Then she flung herself around, lurched to her knees, put her forearms flat on the bed. She glared at me over her shoulder.

"Do it like hounds," she gasped. "Just like hounds."

And away we went, with me hanging on desperately while she sang "Rock of Ages." How I survived I'll never know.

I do remember that when I erupted with a howl, she collapsed facedown, reached behind her to pull me closer, and asked if I'd like to join her in a chorus of "Amazing Grace."

89

I had known women more beautiful than Jenny Tolliver. More passionate. More intelligent. So why couldn't I get her out of my mind?

I didn't think Martha was correct—that I was fascinated with Jenny because she was the first woman to reject me. I was hardly a stranger to rejection; it had been the motif of my stage career. I could endure rebuffs.

So what brought me back to Jenny, slinking like a whipped cur? Romantic love? I didn't think so. Maybe I just liked being with her. I liked being with Martha and Nikki, too. And a dozen customers I serviced. I liked them all.

Perhaps it came back to my obsession with "class." It wasn't only Jenny's elegance; it was a *fineness* that attracted me. I think that secretly I was in awe of her, or envious.

I called her again early in July, acting reserved and sincere.

"Have you thought about it?" I asked her earnestly. "About having dinner with me some night?"

"Well . . ." she said slowly, "all right."

"Wonderful," I said. "Thank you. I figured I'd hire a limo and we could go over to Peter Luger's in Brooklyn, and—"

"No," she interrupted, "nothing like that. Just a hamburger in the neighborhood will be fine."

So we made a date for later that month. I was to call her early in the evening and she'd decide where we were to eat. We would meet there; she didn't want me coming to her place. I agreed to everything.

I hung up, feeling like a kid who's wangled a date with the prom queen. I told myself to play it cool and never once allude to my success. If it took humility to win her back, I could do a Uriah Heep she wouldn't be able to resist.

90

After July 4, our summer rush began. We had increased penthouse business, mostly from out-of-town visitors, and our call boy and escort services were straining to accommodate all the tourist requests.

Without Yancy Burnett I wouldn't have been able to cope with the scheduling problems. Since I handled the penthouse scenes and he arranged appointments for the call boys and escorts, we worked together to prevent superhuman exertions from individual studs.

Yance hated coarse language, and if he thought someone was about to tell a dirty joke, he'd quietly leave the room. Other than that minor idiosyncrasy, he was the perfect assistant: dependable and cheerful.

One afternoon we were scheduling at my desk in the den when Martha entered.

"We've got a problem," she said. "I had a call from a woman named Louella who wants a scene. I told her I'd call her back. Then I checked her reference, and the woman who recommended us said yes, she was okay. But then she added, 'By the way, Louella is black.' How do you like that?"

Yance and I looked at each other.

"Have you ever had a black customer before?" Yance asked quietly.

"One African lady," I said. "A tourist. A black stud fell in love with her."

"Well, this Louella's a local," Martha said. "The question is, do we want to start servicing blacks? Won't it scare away some of our white regulars?"

"I don't think we have a choice," Yance said in his thoughtful way. "If we turn her down, she could bring a race discrimination suit against Peter's Academy of Dramatic Arts."

"I guess you're right," Martha said. "Can you find a stud willing to take her on?"

"I'll take her," Yance and I said simultaneously, and Martha laughed.

"Trying to change your luck?" she said. "All right, I'll make the appointment."

"How about a beer?" Yance asked me after she left.

"Splendid idea."

He went into the kitchen and came back with two cold bottles of Kalback lager and two frosted pilsner glasses. We put our feet up on the desk and sipped the brew slowly.

"I don't get it," I said. "Why would a black woman want to come to a white male cathouse?"

"Perhaps she's a feminist," Yance said. "Some black women are."

"All right, then tell me, professor, why would a feminist want to come to a male cathouse?"

"Why should women want to be policemen or test pilots or deep-sea divers? To prove to the world that there's no male job that can't be just as competently performed by a woman."

"Come on, Yance," I said.

"The principle is the same," he argued. "Paying for a one-hour scene with a strange man is a symbol of true equality. Men have been buying women's bodies for centuries. Now it's women's turn. Peter, this place is giving liberated women the opportunity to achieve a kind of equality that's always been denied them. I think a lot of our clients are feminists whether they know it or not. A scene here does wonders for their independence and female pride."

I laughed. "You make it sound like we're performing a public service."

He looked at me without smiling. "You're not far wrong. Perhaps not a public service, but we are advancing the sexual revolution."

"And you think Louella's coming to us because she's a feminist?"

But before he had a chance to answer, Martha came back into the den. She was grinning.

"You two hard-ons can relax," she said. "Louella specifically asked for a black stud."

Yance and I gulped our lagers.

"I'll fix her up with King Hayes," I said. "He's the best. And I'll ask him to try to find out why she came here. Martha, Yance thinks most of our customers are feminists. What do you think?"

"Who cares?" she said, shrugging. "As long as they come up with the bucks."

"There you are," Yance said to me. "The final equality—the dollar."

91

While Martha was away getting her son settled in at summer camp, Oscar Gotwold phoned me. Michael Gelesco had called to arrange another meeting with Martha and me, this time at Roman Enterprises in the Empire State Building. I remembered what Sol Hoffheimer had told me a year ago.

"Is Roman Enterprises the real owner of the Barcarole?" I asked Oscar.

"Could be," he said cautiously. "The chief executive, Octavius Caesar, is the power man. He's the one who says yes or no. He wants to meet you two personally."

I explained that Martha was out of town and asked if the meeting could be postponed until she returned.

"Maybe it could be," Gotwold said, "but I don't think it would be wise to ask. Postponements are a bad way to begin a business relationship. Could you meet with them yourself?"

"Will you and Iggy be there?"

"No. Octavius Caesar said specifically that he wanted to meet only with the principals."

"All right," I said. "I'll talk to him."

"Don't make any commitments," Oscar warned. "Don't talk money at all if you can help it. They have the numbers. If they want more details, refer them to Iggy or me. They just want to get acquainted with you."

To my surprise, the reception room of Roman Enterprises, bare of chairs, was not much larger than a phone booth. The receptionist, a prim lady ready for Medicare, slid back a glass panel and said coldly, "Yes?"

When I gave her my name, she pressed a button on her desk phone and spoke in a low voice. Then she turned to me.

"Through that door," she said, pointing. "Then down the corridor to the oak door at the end."

"Thank you," I said. I added: "Your cameo brooch is lovely. Is it an antique?"

"Eighteenth-century Italian," she said, thawing. "It's shell, not ivory."

"It's beautiful," I assured her, and got a warm smile. It costs nothing to make friends.

She must have pressed a button because the electric lock on the inner door buzzed and I entered. The door clanged shut behind me and I realized it was steel.

The hallway was long, narrow, and carpeted. It was also under surveillance by a small TV camera suspended from the ceiling. The single door at the end appeared to be heavy oak planks fastened with hammered iron straps.

I knocked twice, bruising my knuckles, and twisted the ornate knob. It was like pushing open the door of a bank vault. But I stepped into the library of a Victorian gentleman.

Slate floor. A buttery Oriental rug. Walnut bookcases. Thick velvet drapes. Dark oil paintings in gilt frames. Crystal and silver on a marble-topped sideboard. A tiled fireplace with a timbered mantel. All the books on display were in leather-bound sets.

There was a baroque partners' desk that could have been inherited from President Rutherford B. Hayes. The couch and two armchairs were upholstered in maroon calfskin with brass studs. The only illumination came from a student lamp with two arms and green glass shades on the desk.

Michael Gelesco and Anthony Cannis were seated side by side on the couch. They nodded to me when I came into the room but made no effort to stand. The old gentleman behind the desk rose slowly from a high-backed swivel chair and held out a palsied flipper to me.

"Mr. Caesar?" I said, pressing that soft, white hand gently. "A pleasure to meet you, sir."

"Mr. Scuro," he said with a wintry smile. "Thank you for taking

time off from your busy schedule to . . . I believe you have already met Mr.
Gelesco and Mr. Cannis. Please sit here. I think you will find that
chair . . ."

I waited while he eased himself back into his swivel chair. It took a
while.

"I apologize for my associate not being present, Mr. Caesar," I said.
"Miss Twombly was unavoidably detained by family business."

He made a vague gesture. "I understand completely, Mr. Scuro.
One's family must always come . . . Always. Now let me tell you a little
about Roman Enterprises. Although I am the chief executive officer . . .
Our organization is an association of several gentlemen who wish to diver-
sify their interests . . . We have a great deal of venture capital available and
are constantly looking for . . . One thing I should make clear is that we are
an investing entity, and the actual managing of our various endeavors is left
to . . . The Barcarole Boutique is a good . . . We make it a point never to
interfere in the day-to-day . . . Are you following me, young man?"

I was not only following him, but I had, in my mind, been finishing
his uncompleted sentences. Which was probably what he expected.

"Now then," he went on, swinging gently back and forth in his
swivel chair, "I have reviewed the proposal you presented to Mr. Gelesco
and Mr. Cannis, and I find it of absorbing . . ."

As he spoke slowly in a thin, creaking voice, I looked at him attentively. He was, I guessed, in his late seventies or early eighties. A thick sheaf
of pure white hair was plastered sideways across his big skull. His complexion was ruddy and there was a road map of capillaries in his fleshy cheeks
and bulbous nose.

Hang a white beard on him, I thought, and put him in a red suit, and
next Christmas he could star at Macy's, going "Ho-ho-ho!"

But the suit he was wearing was a rust-colored cheviot, vested and
double-breasted with four buttons in a vertical row. I had once worn a suit
like that in a revival of *The Importance of Being Earnest.* His white shirt had
a stiffly starched collar, and he wore a wide tie of purple jacquard.

He was an extremely clean, almost luminous old man. He held
himself stiffly erect. He had, as we say in the theater, *presence.* And, glancing at Gelesco and Cannis, I saw suddenly that, compared to Octavius
Caesar, they were nothing but thugs.

" . . . have always found it best," he was saying, "before a decision is
. . . I like to meet personally with those with whom . . . Please forgive me
if I ask questions you may believe inconsequential or impertinent but . . .
Tell me, young man, what do you want out of life?"

The question came so abruptly that I wasn't prepared for it. I replied automatically, without giving the matter any thought.

"I want money," I said.

He regarded me gravely. "An honest . . . I understand you were previously in the theater."

I didn't know where he had obtained that information, but I gave him a précis of my stage career. It didn't take long.

"I see," Octavius Caesar said. "I would imagine your training and experience have proved valuable in your present . . ."

"Yes, sir," I said. "There is a strong theatrical element in our business. In a sense, we are selling illusion."

"Selling illusion," he repeated, smacking his lips delicately. He swung around to face Gelesco and Cannis. "Did you gentlemen hear that? Selling illusion. Isn't that grand?" They both nodded madly. Then he swung back to me. "But I hope, Mr. Scuro, you are under no illusion as to the amount of work necessary to make your concept . . ."

"No, sir," I said, "none. Miss Twombly and I are not afraid of work. With luck, we can—"

He held up a white hand to interrupt me. "Please, do not prate to me of luck, young man. Luck is the alibi of losers. If your ambition is powerful enough, you don't need . . . Well, Mr. Scuro, thank you for coming by and indulging the curiosity of an old man. You will be informed of our decision . . . Either way . . ."

He climbed laboriously to his feet and I reached across the desk to press that soft hand again. I was at the door when he called, "Young man," and I turned back.

"A question," he said. "What do you propose to call this . . . ?"

I hesitated a second, then said, "Peter's Place."

"Fitting," he said, and I left.

92

I was supposed to meet Jenny Tolliver at a hamburger joint called The Dirty Shame on Amsterdam near 84th Street. I cabbed over an hour early and killed time by walking around the neighborhood.

I couldn't believe the West Side was changing so rapidly. It was beginning to look like Greenwich Village, rampant with antique shops, art galleries, boutiques, and gourmet food stores. The people on the streets were younger, and prices were skyrocketing.

I remembered the hole-in-the-wall candy store where I bought my *Variety*, the mom-and-pop bodega where I could get Mexican beer, the old Italian who resoled shoes, and a Gypsy place where you could get your fortune told and your wallet lifted. All that was gone now. Progress. Ah, what the hell . . .

I took a back table at The Dirty Shame and had a vodka gimlet while I waited for Jenny. It was an artsy-craftsy kind of place. All the waitresses wore denim skirts, and I bet they stocked carrot juice.

I saw her coming through the door, and something caught in my throat. What a *complete* woman; she just sailed. Memories came flooding, and I almost wept.

She was wearing something great that flowed. Her hair was down and her chin was up. She looked around, spotted me, and came winding through the tables. I climbed to my feet. I wanted to grab her, but I shook hands.

"Peter," she said, looking at me critically. "You've gained weight."

"I've gained what you've lost," I said. "You look marvelous, Jenny."

"Thank you," she said faintly.

She wanted white wine and I had another vodka. We both ordered cheeseburgers, french fries, and a mixed salad. The business of ordering covered our initial unease. But then we were alone. Together.

"Tell me about your new studio," I said. "It sounds great."

She talked about what she wanted to design and how she hoped eventually to merchandise her own high-fashion fabrics. Maybe get into bed linens. Draperies. Everything.

As she spoke, I stared at her across the table. It was the way I remembered: thick chestnut hair falling about a long face. The still, clear features composed in an untroubled expression. All smooth, all serene.

"Don't you agree?" she said.

"What? Oh. Absolutely."

She laughed. "You haven't been listening, Peter."

"I haven't," I confessed. "Just admiring."

She looked down, played with a crust of bread. "Arthur sends his regards."

"You told him you were seeing me?"

"Yes."

"How is he?"

She lifted her eyes for a direct look. "Arthur is a darling," she said.

"Yes, he is."

Our food came then, thank God, and we were busy for a few minutes.

"And how is your business, Peter?" she asked, nibbling on a french fry.

"Oh, let's not talk about that."

"Let's," she said. "Are you doing well?"

"Very well."

She shook her head. "I just can't believe it."

I felt the stirring of Iago's hatred of Othello's innocence.

"What can't you believe?" I said, showing my teeth. "That women are willing to pay for pleasure? Is that so outrageous? Why should women want to join the police force or be test pilots? To prove to the world they're equal to men."

"What has that got to do with paying to go to bed with a man?"

"The principle is the same," I said. "Paying for sex with a strange man is a step toward true equality. Men have been buying women for centuries. Now it's women's turn. They can achieve a new kind of equality. It gives them a sense of independence and female pride."

Jenny chomped on her cheeseburger.

"It's advancing the sexual revolution," I said earnestly. "Like a public service."

She finished her food, patted her lips with the paper napkin. Then she looked at me.

"Peter," she said quietly, "I honestly don't know who you are, *really,* and I don't think you know either. You're always playing a role."

"Shakespeare said it better," I said, as lightly as I could. " 'All the world's a stage.' "

"There's a difference," she said. "An actor plays the same role for weeks, months, years. Another actor may take over, but the role remains essentially the same. When we go to see *Hamlet,* we know we're going to see Hamlet. But I never know who I'm going to see when I see you."

"Are you saying I'm insincere?"

"Of course not. It's just that I'd like to see you someday without the greasepaint and fright wig."

I tried not to reveal how crushed I was. "Even if that were so, Jenny —and I'm not admitting it is—isn't it more intriguing not to know who I am? You *know* Arthur is a darling, but who am I? If I'm the Man of a Thousand Faces, aren't you curious to find the man behind the mask?"

She was silent a long moment, staring at me.

"Yes," she said finally, "I am intrigued. Unless . . ."

She didn't finish. She didn't have to. I knew what she meant: Unless the last mask came off and there was nothing there.

93

I was coming out of the kitchen when I saw a customer going toward the Blue Room. I did a double take. She didn't look like a woman; she looked like a *girl.*

"Hey," I said to Martha. "That client going to the Blue Room—is she a Girl Scout? Or maybe a Brownie?"

"I thought the same thing," Martha said. "I checked her reference and she says the kid's okay. Just to make sure, I asked to see her driver's license. It says she's nineteen, Peter."

"Going on twelve," I said. "What's her name?"

"Susan Forgrove. Interested?"

"A child molester I'm not," I said, and we laughed.

We saw a lot of Susan in the next few weeks. She booked frequently, always asking for a stud she hadn't had before. We had no problems with her, except the studs said she didn't smell so great.

She was chubby, with long, stringy, orangish hair that could have used a good shampoo. She wore granny glasses and giggled a lot. Her clothes were expensive but too elegant for her. She looked like a young frump.

We took her money, of course, and were glad to add her to the roster of clients we called "rovers": women who seemed determined to work their way through our entire stable of studs.

"Why do they do it?" I asked Martha.

"For the same reason men climb mountains," she said. "Because they're *there.*"

94

That summer was hot with promise. We didn't hear from Octavius Caesar, but took that as a good sign; surely a rejection would have come immediately. Meanwhile, the money poured in.

Yancy Burnett proved so efficient that Martha and I were each able to take a day off. She chose Tuesdays; I took Thursdays. I spent my first holiday replenishing my summer wardrobe at men's boutiques on Third Avenue and on East 57th Street.

I learned with a pang that I now had a 36-inch waist; one pair of white sharkskin slacks had to be let out in the seat. I knew I had been living well, but not *that* well. I resolved to go on a diet and consult Nikki Radburn about an exercise regimen.

I lunched by myself at Le Perigord on medallions of lobster in a peppercorn sauce (magnificent), an oiled spinach salad (divine) and, for dessert, strawberry mousse over whole berries (super). I dawdled over a full bottle of beaujolais primeur, and decided to start my diet on Monday morning.

As I strolled back to the penthouse, I twice passed regulars of Peter's School of Dramatic Arts. I was certain they recognized me, but they gave no sign and, of course, I didn't so much as smile. That was a house rule. I could understand the need for this discretion, but I must admit to a small rankle.

I did not consider that what I was doing, my job, my profession, automatically made me a pariah. I was simply involved in a financial transaction.

I knew how Jenny Tolliver felt about it, and I suppose there were other people who would judge my way of life reprehensible. But I swear that never once did I feel I was sinning, harming anyone, or defying some universal law.

Despite what Jenny might think, it had nothing to do with good or evil; it was just business. That's why it rankled when I couldn't tip my boater to good customers I passed on the street.

95

I rolled off and lay panting and slobbering like an overheated bulldog.

"What was *that* all about?" I asked.

Martha turned her face away from me. "A stiff cock is the thinking woman's Valium," she said.

It was a Tuesday night early in August; the air conditioning was going full blast. Martha had been gone all day. The last customer and stud departed around 10:00 P.M. Then Yance and I shared a seafood casserole Patsy had left for us. He took off a little after eleven.

I wanted to do some bookkeeping, but Martha called right after Yance left and told me she was coming over. She arrived about a half-hour later, dragged me into the Rose Room, and we got it off. It was practically rape; she was in a murderous mood.

When I asked her what it was all about, she said furiously, "The boyfriend!"

"Again?" I said. I hadn't told her I knew his name. "What is it now?"

"Same thing," she said. "Buy me a drink? Something powerful."

"Brandy stinger?"

"A double," she ordered.

But when I mixed the drinks in the kitchen, I took it easy on hers. She was so hyper, I didn't want to push her over the edge.

We took our drinks out onto the terrace, sitting naked in the darkness.

"So?" I asked idly.

"I don't want to talk about it," she said angrily.

And I didn't want to hear about it. Martha's close relationship with a rich politico made me uneasy. The guy had too much clout. He could close us up with one phone call.

So we sat silently, sipping our stingers and staring at the night sky. The air was velvety. A sprinkle of stars. The glow of the city softened everything.

"Nice night," I offered.

She didn't answer, and I turned to look at her. She was white and massive in the gloom. Heavy legs thrust out. Thick bush bristling. The big breasts sagged. If I had put on weight, so had she. But her body had gone slack and lumpy.

"I told him to get lost," she said finally.

"And . . . ?"

"He started crying again."

"So you're going to keep seeing him?"

"I don't know. If I really give him the boot, I'm afraid he'll do something stupid. Like leaving his— Peter, the phone is ringing."

I hadn't heard it, but I went inside, closing the sliding glass door to keep the cool air locked in. It was Nicole Radburn. She had just finished a trick and wanted to visit. I cleared it with Martha and told Nikki to come right over.

Martha and I moved back to the Rose Room and left the door open so we could hear the buzzer when Nikki arrived. I brought a new round of drinks from the kitchen. Martha wanted straight brandy and I switched to light beer.

Nikki brought an anchovy pizza. We took it into the master bedroom. Martha was still naked, but sitting up in bed with the sheet pulled to her waist. I was wearing a robe.

"I need a shower," Nikki said. "That last john grossed me out."

She came out of the bathroom naked, rubbing Vaseline into red marks around her wrists.

"A bondage freak," she reported. "The poor slob's dentures kept slipping."

I brought her a white wine and we sat on the bed near Martha, all of us gobbling wedges of anchovy pizza.

"What's with you, Madame Defarge?" Nikki said. "Your tits are drooping."

"Go to hell, Miss Nipples," Martha said. "That guy I'm saddled with . . . I can't cut him loose."

"Hang on to him," Nikki advised. "The day may come when you'll need someone who swings a lot of weight."

I hadn't thought of it, but Wilson Bowker might turn out to be a valuable friend if we ever got into bad trouble.

"It makes sense," I told Martha.

"I guess so," she said grumpily.

We finished the pizza and I took the garbage into the kitchen to dump it. When I got back to the Rose Room, Nikki was in bed alongside Martha.

"What do I do?" I said. "Sleep on the floor?"

"Plenty of room," Nikki said, holding up her edge of the sheet. "Climb in."

The two women moved over to give me room.

"I think you're in love with the guy," Nikki said. "But you won't even admit it to yourself."

"Could be," Martha admitted. "But he's married and he's going to stay married."

"Impossible loves are the best kind," Nikki said. "They never sour."

"Have you ever been in love?" I asked her.

"Not me," she said. "I'm too self-centered. If a guy ever fell in love with me, it would be like a triangle."

"You'll get hooked one of these days," Martha said.

"No way," Nikki said. "Look, when you're lousy at arithmetic, you don't try to become an accountant. If I settle down someday, it'll be with a richnik, and love will have nothing to do with it."

"You're a hard woman," Martha said.

"And you're running to flab," Nikki said.

She grabbed under the sheet and Martha said, "Jesus! Take it easy!"

"The two of you are getting obese," Nikki told us.

"And you bring us a pizza," I said. "Thanks a lot."

"Everyone shut up," Martha said, "and let's go to sleep."

So we did.

96

King Hayes came into the den and slumped into one of the armchairs.

"Drink?" I said.

The big black shook his head. He seemed broody.

"What's eating you?" I asked him. "Besides the customers."

"You know that black chick? Louella?"

Of course I knew her. She'd been coming in at least twice a week, always for King, so I figured she was one of his "wives."

Louella was a small, dapper, bronzy-brown woman with a modified Afro. She usually wore tailored suits of men's-wear flannel with a ruffled jabot. Very cool, very self-possessed. I guessed her around thirty.

Hayes sighed. "You remember asking me to find out what she's doing in a place like this?"

"I remember. Yance thought she might be a feminist."

"Naw, nothing like that. She's got other reasons. She is one smart lady. Got a master's in business administration. Good job at some downtown bank. Well, first of all, she has trouble finding black guys who are as educated as she is, and when she does, all they're interested in is a one-night stand or else they're looking for a white chick. And most white guys don't want the hassle of taking out a black woman."

"You're kidding."

"I'm not kidding," Hayes said, shaking his head. "She's got her own pad, a car, plenty of clothes and all that, and she's so lonely she could cry."

"My God," I said. "That's what brought her here—just loneliness?"

"That's it," he said, nodding. "I guess she figures it's better than nothing. Peter, a lot of these educated black women have a rough time of it."

I looked at him closely. "King, it sounds to me like she's getting to you."

"I guess I feel sorry for her," he admitted. "Which is a laugh because I never got out of the eighth grade, and no way am I in her class. I mean, she uses long words I never even *heard* of. And she's so clean and dainty, she makes me feel like King Kong."

"She must like you," I pointed out. "She keeps asking for you."

"Yeah . . . well . . ." he said, shifting his big carcass uneasily, "there's a reason for that. I'll tell you if you promise not to repeat it."

"You know I don't talk."

"Yeah . . . well . . . the first time she showed up here, she was a virgin."

I made a whistling sound. "You're sure?"

"Man, I *know*. First of all, she told me. Second of all, she was tight as a fist. Third of all, she made a mess of the sheet. I rinsed it out before I gave it to Maria. Oh, it was her first bang, no doubt about that. Well, you know a woman always has a soft spot in her heart for the man who copped her cherry. Till the day she dies. That's why Louella keeps asking for me."

"Uh-huh," I said, staring at him. "King, if this is bothering you, the next time she calls I can have Martha tell her you're all booked up and try to sell her another stud."

"No," he said quickly. "That's all right. I'll take her."

97

Hoffheimer's office was as dreary as ever. Drearier. Dust was as furry as an army blanket, and the air smelled of cheap cigars and sour mash.

Sol was sitting slack-jawed behind his battered desk. It was about 11:00 A.M., but it was obvious he had been at the crock he kept in his desk drawer. His eyes were blank and gummy and his face looked like a punched pillow.

"Payday," I sang out and scaled an envelope across the desk. He didn't look at it.

"I saw Maurice Evans in *Hamlet*," he said dully. "Did you see that?"

"No."

"And I saw Gielgud in—in something," he maundered on. "Did you see that?"

"Sol, for God's sake, make sense, will you? Count your money."

He looked up at me with a leer. "Is it all there?"

"Of course it's all there."

"Then why should I count it?"

He cackled like a maniac, and I thought suddenly that we'd have to dump him. But still, he was functioning; he was providing a steady supply of studs, fronting our procuring operation. In a way, I owed him. I couldn't decide.

"What's with the booze?" I said as sympathetically as I could. "You never hit it so hard before. And you were hurting then; now you've got a steady income."

"For snakebite," he said, pulling his lips back in what he thought was a grin. "Never know when a snake might bite you."

I wasn't particularly enjoying this tête-à-tête and rose to leave. But then the office door flung open and a woman swept in. She glanced at me and batted eyelashes that looked like feather dusters.

"Oops," she said. "Sorry. Am I interrupting?"

"Clara," he said. "My love. Meet Peter Scuro, a very, very, very valuable client. Peter, meet Clara, my faithful spouse."

She held a talon out to me with twenty-three rings and nails that had been dipped in blood.

"Sooo nice," she said. "Sol speaks of you frequently."

"A pleasure to meet you, Mrs. Hoffheimer," I said.

"Clara," she said.

"Clara," I said.

"Clara," Sol said.

We ignored him.

"I've got to run," I said. "It's been—"

"Oh, now you make me feel just awful," she said, pouting. "I bet I did interrupt something important."

She was a walking Christmas tree. Bangles, beads, bracelets, rings, baubles, necklaces, pins. I mean, she *dangled.* Her purpled hair was piled high, whipped, like frozen custard.

She was so *brassy.* Big lungs and a ripe ass. Perfume that filled the room. Poor Sol. Married to her and married to me.

"Daddy," she said brightly, "I've got some shopping to do and—"

"Take," he said, shoving my envelope across the desk to her.

"Nice to have met you, Clara," I said, smiling determinedly. "Hope to see you again."

"Peter," she said, flashing her caps, "don't be a stranger."

"He is," Sol said. "A stranger."

I got out of there.

98

Finally, inevitably, it came my turn to service Susan Forgrove. She was the juvenile-looking nineteen-year-old with stringy hair and steel-rimmed granny glasses who was going through the studs at an astonishing rate. Yancy Burnett wouldn't take her because she was reputed to have a gamy aroma. Since all our studs had the right of refusal, Yance declined and I took the case.

She turned out to be more pitiable than offensive. There was a desperation. She was trying so hard to be cynical that she came across as a caricature. I could have told her that you've got to underplay sophistication; it's more of an absence than a come-on. You play it dolcemente, not vigoroso.

I figured any woman flitting from stud to stud would be amenable to something different, so I suggested that we might start by taking a shower together, thinking that would take care of the fragrance problem. Susan readily agreed, giggling, but wouldn't take off her glasses.

"I'm blind without them," she confessed.

She might have been nineteen, but she had a chubby child's body. Baby fat on waist, hips, thighs. Her breasts were large and bleary for such a small woman. She just looked *used*, with bruises on shoulders and back. There were fading welts across her plump buttocks.

Susan soaped me, then soaped herself. She scrubbed us both with the long-handled bath brush. She worked frantically, water streaming through her long, orangy hair and splashing off her spectacles. And all the time, she had this half-ass grin, mouth open and twisted, and every so often a high-pitched whinny came out of her.

She wasn't hurting me, so I let her do as she pleased. But I was ready to grab her if she went violent. I think she was close to it. I realized she wasn't just kooky; she was *nuts*. We ended up with me sitting on the tiled floor of the shower stall with her impaled on my dink.

What a sight she was, with that empty, open-mouthed grin. Her sodden hair streamed about her shoulders, and her glasses were opaque behind running water. It looked like she was weeping quarts.

She leaned forward to yell in my ear. "Do me!" she screamed. *"Do me!"*

I thought I *was* doing her, but sometimes I'm slow on the uptake. Then I remembered those bruises and welts and figured out what she wanted. I don't go for the rough stuff but I can play the role. It was a mechanical performance, but it seemed to please her. She kept nodding her head like a Chinese doll.

Later, while we were dressing, I saw the track marks on her arms.

After she left, I went into the foyer and told Martha to take Susan Forgrove off our list. Martha agreed but, as we were soon to learn, it was too late.

99

I called Arthur Enders and got the address of Jenny Tolliver's new fabric design studio on West 36th Street. Right after Labor Day I sent her a hundred bucks' worth of flowers with a card wishing her success. She sent back a cool thank-you note. I wasn't discouraged.

Then, on Wednesday, we got a call from Octavius Caesar's secretary, saying the great man wished to see us at 3:00 P.M. on the following day. I was elated.

"I've got good vibes about this," I told Martha. "I think he's going to go for it."

"What should I wear?" she asked anxiously.

"Martha," I said, "calm down. Dress conservatively."

She wore a black crepe dress, long-sleeved, buttoned to the neck, with a necklace of small pearls. No nail polish and minimal makeup. But the dress was snug, and if you got close enough, you caught a slight whiff of Opium.

"You'll knock him dead," I assured her.

Octavius Caesar's office looked exactly the same as it had during our first meeting, except for the absence of Cannis and Gelesco. It was just the three of us, for which I was thankful.

I introduced Martha, and the old man took her proffered hand in one of his white flippers and patted it with the other.

"A true pleasure, my dear," he said, beaming. "I have been looking forward to . . ."

He dragged one of the armchairs around to the side of his desk and seated Martha there with a courtly little bow. He motioned me to the chair across the desk from him.

I knew this maneuver would not be wasted on Martha, and it wasn't. She crossed her knees slowly. She was wearing sheer gunmetal pantyhose and black patent leather pumps. Martha's legs were weighty but shapely. Succulent calves. Octavius Caesar noticed.

"You know," he said in his creaky voice, "we should all be thankful for living in . . . Where else but in America could we hope to . . . The free enterprise system . . . It has certainly served me well. I do believe it is the best economic system the mind of man has . . . Could Godless Communism offer such a . . . How fortunate I was that my parents sought a new life in this . . ."

He had started this speech by looking back and forth from Martha to me. Then gradually his gaze drifted downward to her crossed knees. She was aware of his interest.

"There is no limit," the geezer rattled on and on, finally raising his gaze to Martha's. "But I am boring you with the wanderings of an old man."

"Not at all, Mr. Caesar," Martha said warmly. "I find them fascinating."

"Do you, dearie?" he said with his wintry smile. "How kind of you to . . . Well, enough of this. My dear friends, I am happy to announce to you that my associates agree your proposal is worthy of encouragement. And financial backing, of course. We feel you have devised an imaginative and pioneering concept that . . ."

"Thank you, sir," I said fervently.

"Thank you, Mr. Caesar," Martha said.

He smiled benignly as he stared at Martha's legs.

"Mr. Cannis and Mr. Gelesco . . . who you, Peter, have . . . will be in touch with your attorney and accountant," he went on. "There will be, as always, minor disagreements as to the precise financial structure this . . . But with goodwill and patience on both sides, I'm convinced that . . . And, I assure you, the day-to-day management will be in your . . ."

"And will we have majority control, Mr. Caesar?" Martha asked eagerly.

"I wouldn't have it any other way. The original concept is yours, and you have the experience to . . . But now, regretfully, I must bring this extremely pleasant meeting to a close . . . Thank you for taking time from your busy schedule to . . ."

In the elevator going down, I enthused, "We did it! Isn't that great, Martha? We've got to celebrate!"

"That guy scares me," she said.

100

Detective Luke Futter stalked into the penthouse, minus his smirk. We took him into the den. He didn't want a drink and he wouldn't sit down.

"You got a customer named Susan Forgrove?" he demanded.

Martha and I looked at each other.

"We did have," I said cautiously, "but we got rid of her."

"She's fifteen," Futter said.

"Jesus Christ," I said.

"Bull*shit!*" Martha said angrily. "She said she was nineteen. She showed me her driver's license."

The detective's smirk returned. "Give me fifty bucks," he said. "I'll go out on the street and be back in half an hour with a driver's license in any name you like. They're as easy to buy as food stamps. Anyway, you got what you might call a crisis. Her old man says you're running a white slavery ring up here or something, recruiting underage girls. Apparently the mother caught the kid clipping money from her purse, and the kid said she was spending it here. The father's ready to bring charges."

"Come on!" I said. "You think we'd have let her in if we knew how old she was?"

Futter shrugged. "I'm just telling you what her father is claiming. His name is Lester Forgrove, and he's a big, big Wall Street broker with plenty of clout."

"Luke, honey," Martha said, almost purring, "you can do something, can't you?"

"Nothing," he said. "Zero. Zip. Zilch. This guy's involved in East Side politics, he's got muscle, and he's steaming. I don't want to get involved."

"Thanks a lot," I said bitterly.

"Look," he said. "I only know about this because my buddy caught the squeal and tipped me. If you're willing to grease him, I can have him try to stall until you figure something out. But I warn you, he can't lose this thing, and Forgrove isn't going to drop it. Buying a little time is the best I can do."

"We'll pay whatever your friend wants," I said promptly. "Ask him to stall as long as he can."

My brain was clicking; I was acting decisively. It was a new role for me and I enjoyed it.

After Futter left, Martha and I had a brandy.

"That dirty little bimbo," she said wrathfully. "Peter—what are we going to do?"

"Let me think," I said, pacing around the den. "I know one thing: No one's going to close us up now that we've got that commitment from Caesar. There's too much riding on this."

I paced to the desk, pulled a telephone book out of the bottom drawer, and began to flip the pages.

"Lester Forgrove," I said. "East Seventy-ninth Street. Near Madison."

"So?" she said.

I stared at her thoughtfully. "Martha, does your boyfriend live on the East Side?"

She looked at me queerly. "Yes."

"Well, if he's in East Side politics, and Susan's father is in East Side politics, they must know each other."

"You want me to get my boyfriend to go to bat for us on this?" Martha said harshly. "No way. He doesn't even know what business I'm in, for God's sake."

"No no," I said. "Nothing like that. Just try to get a line on the

Forgroves. If we're going to fight this, we've got to know more about the people we're dealing with."

"I could ask," Martha said hesitantly, "but what reason can I give him for wanting to know?"

"Does he know you've got a son?"

"Sure."

"And your kid's about sixteen—right? Okay, that's it. Tell your boyfriend that your son met this Susan Forgrove the last time he was in New York, and he's hung up on her. So you're trying to find out about this girl to make sure she's okay for your boy."

"Peter," she said admiringly, "you've got the makings of a first-class con man."

101

I convinced Jenny Tolliver to have dinner at a slightly more elegant place than The Dirty Shame. She wouldn't consent to any of the restaurants we used to go to, so we settled on The Kerry House, a pub-type joint on East 44th Street where the Tiffany lamps were fake but the roast beef was real enough.

I arrived first and picked a secluded booth with smoke-darkened paneling and worn leather upholstery. I was on my second kir when Jenny came in. I stood and waved to her. I was hoping for a friendly peck on the cheek, but no luck.

She apologized for being late and said she had come directly from finishing a twelve-hour stint at her studio. She gulped a gin and tonic thirstily as she told me about her day.

I interrupted just long enough to order rare roast beef (on the bone) for both of us, with baked potatoes and a mixed salad. Then I signaled for another round of drinks and got her talking again.

She was flushed with the excitement of owning a business and having to make important decisions every day.

When the food was served, she attacked it ferociously, then stopped, laughed, and confessed she had been too busy to have lunch. I watched her as she ate.

In the soft ruby light, she positively glowed. Her beauty had taken on a new dimension. She seemed more confident, forceful even. It was hard to remember her moods of quiet deliberation.

"Ooh, that was good," she said, pushing back and sighing contentedly. "Thank you, Peter."

"Dessert?"

"Just coffee, please."

"Brandy?"

"Thank you, no. Peter, I've been so busy eating and talking, I haven't asked about you. How is your, ah, business?"

"Going great."

She lowered her head so the long chestnut hair shadowed her face. Then she raised her eyes to look directly at me.

"Peter, you're happy with what you're doing?"

"Oh yes," I said. "A lot of dull, routine stuff, but it's easier when you're working for yourself. You're limited only by your own ambition. It's the free enterprise system."

"What?" she said.

"Like you starting your own studio. It's wonderful when you think of it. The opportunity! Every man and woman entitled to the fruits of his or her labor. It's the pioneer spirit that made this country great."

"I think I will have that brandy," she said.

After we left the restaurant, we went to a cabaret on West 72nd Street and listened to a group of youngsters sing Cole Porter. We drank a bottle of champagne and Jenny let me hold her hand.

I took her home in a cab, but she didn't invite me up. She thanked me for a lovely evening and I said I'd call.

The strange thing was that this slow, quiet courtship was immensely satisfying. Could it have been the innocence? All I knew was that I was content to be with her.

If it went on for years and years, I wouldn't mind. I wasn't driven by any great passion to get her into bed. I knew she would never, ever, approve of what I was doing. I think what I wanted from her was just acceptance.

102

Martha's voice crackled with excitement.

"Come right over," she ordered. "There's something I've got to tell you."

"Can't you tell me now?"

"Not on the phone."

"You're getting as paranoid as Futter," I told her. "I'll be there in half an hour. Need anything?"

"Could you pick up a jug of chablis? Gallo's fine. Nikki's here and we're down to dust."

The two women were sitting sprawled in that forest of ornamental elephants. They had their shoes off. The air was swirling with cigarette smoke. I switched Martha's air conditioner to Exhaust and poured us all chablis on the rocks.

"I did what you told me," Martha said, "and asked my guy about Susan Forgrove. He didn't want to say anything at first, being very clubby, you know, but he finally told me. Her parents are four-square and true-blue, but they've had trouble with the girl for years. She went through a drug rehab treatment someplace upstate and she's still going to a local shrink."

"I told you I saw old track marks on her arms," I said.

"That's only the half of it," Martha said. "Nikki knows her!"

I turned to look at Nicole Radburn. "You're kidding?"

"I told you I do occasional substitute teaching at private schools in Manhattan. Well, this Susan Forgrove has been kicked out of the best. Peter, the kid's a slut. At one school she was caught in a closet with the ballet teacher, a woman, and at another place she was dragged out of the laundry room where she was having a round of corn-on-the-cob with the guys who worked in there. I mean, she's *sick.*"

"Oh, that's great," I said angrily. "What do we do now?"

"Nikki had an idea," Martha said. "Tell him, Nikki."

"Well . . ." she said, "about a year ago I had a regular customer, good for a trick a week. A sweet guy. His wife got suspicious about where he was sneaking off to, and hired a private detective to find out. This gumshoe got into my apartment and rigged up a TV tape camera in a ventilator duct in the bedroom. Believe me, that film would have filled the Music Hall. The henry liked to wear my lingerie. The kicker is this: After the private detective had the proof, he didn't take it to the wife; he told her that her husband was spending one evening a week at the Metropolitan Museum. Then he took the tape to my customer and sold it to him for five grand."

"Beautiful," I said. "And the john paid?"

"Sure he paid."

I wagged my head. "Crazy," I said. "Now don't tell me your customer still comes around?"

"No," Nikki said with a secret smile. "But I got the private detective. He visits me a couple of times a month."

"And tries on your lingerie?" I asked.

"No, he's straight. But, Peter—this guy is good at his job. I suggested to Martha that the two of you hire him to see what he can dig up on Susan Forgrove. Maybe he can get some film of her."

I began to get a little nervous. "Suppose he does get some film," I said. "Then what?"

"Dummy," Martha said. "We go to Lester Forgrove and tell him to drop his charges or we send still photos of his daughter blowing a donkey to all his friends."

"Hey, come on," I said. "That's a little rough, isn't it?"

Martha looked at me. "Want to go to court?" she said. "Hire an expensive criminal lawyer and fight it out in public?"

"Nooo," I said slowly.

"Because if you do," she went on, "we can kiss that Caesar deal goodbye. We'll be out of business and maybe in the clink."

I was silent.

"Peter," Nikki said gently, "can you think of any other way to stop Forgrove?"

"No," I admitted, "I can't."

"Then we can go ahead with this?" Martha said.

I nodded.

"Look," Martha said. "Maybe it won't work. But it's a chance, and the only one we've got."

"All right," I said.

"Nikki," Martha said, "will you act as go-between on this? We'll take care of you."

"Sure," Nikki said. "I'll call him tomorrow. Come on, Peter, don't look so down. It's just business."

"I told you that you're a softy," Martha said.

"I was," I said, aggrieved.

103

The dining room was completely filled that day, and a party of four was waiting in the living room. Meanwhile, they were drinking up a storm which, at two dollars a belt, made me happy.

I wandered into the kitchen, trying to keep out of the way of Patsy and Luis. I made myself a baked ham and Swiss on sour rye, slathered with Dijon mustard, opened a can of Heineken, and ate standing up in a corner. The swinging door to the dining room opened. King Hayes came in and headed toward me.

"King," I said, "how's it going? Hungry? Want a sandwich?"

"Naw," the big black said. "Thanks anyway. Got a minute?"

"Sure."

"I want your take on something," he said.

He leaned against the wall next to me. I waited.

"Maybe I'll have a beer," he said.

"In the fridge," I told him. "Help yourself."

He came back popping the tab. He took a gulp that probably drained half the can, then leaned against the wall again, looking straight ahead.

"It's Louella," he said. "She wants me to quit studding and move into her pad."

"Oh-ho," I said. "Seems to me you had an offer like that once before."

"Yeah, but that was a white chick, and I didn't really have the hots for her."

"But Louella is different?"

"Sort of, yeah."

"Better tell me more about it, King. If you're not working, who pays the bills?"

"Oh, she pays; she promised that. Until I can find something."

"Like what? Acting? Modeling? You tried that and got nowhere."

"I know, but Louella, she wants—you're going to laugh at this."

"I won't laugh."

"Well . . . she says I've got potential. That's the word she used: 'potential.' She wants to educate me, tell me what books to read, how to dress, how to talk right. Culture—you know?"

"I know. And how do you feel about that, King?"

"I don't know what to do," he said miserably.

I began crushing my empty beer can between my fingers, pressing dimples in it all around.

"Are you in love with her, King?"

"I don't rightly know," he admitted. "I admire her greatly. She is one smart lady and sure keeps herself nice. But I just don't know if I love her."

"Does she love you?"

"She says she does," he said, staring down at his huge hands.

"Well, if she really loved you, she'd take you the way you are, wouldn't she? I mean, she wouldn't pull all this crap about educating you so you can realize your potential or whatever."

He was silent, his head lowered. I thought I had convinced him. I didn't want to lose this guy. He was one of our most popular and profitable studs.

"Then you think I should forget about it, Peter?" he said in a voice I could hardly hear.

I was about to reply when I saw Martha motioning to me from the door to the foyer.

"Excuse me a sec, King," I said. "I'll be right back."

Martha drew me out into the foyer and leaned close.

"Nikki just called," she said. "That private detective will take it on. A hundred a day plus expenses. Okay with you?"

"Do we have a choice?"

"Don't be such a grump," she said, patting my cheek. "We'll come out of this smelling like roses. You'll see."

I went back into the kitchen.

"What did you ask me?" I said to King Hayes.

"You think I should forget about it?" he said.

"No," I said, "don't forget about it. Quit this business and move in with Louella."

He looked at me with surprise.

"I'll think on it," he said.

104

We had a meeting with the PI, Casper Meerjens, at Martha's, figuring the penthouse might be under surveillance following Lester Forgrove's charges.

Meerjens looked like an old, old basketball player. He might have been six-and-a-half feet tall at one time, but now he was so bent and round-shouldered that he was no taller than I. He had a floppy way of moving, arms and legs flinging out in all directions. His sunken cheeks were pitted and his fingers were stained yellow with nicotine.

He wore horn-rimmed glasses, one earpiece wound with dirty adhesive tape. But his eyes were alert enough, and for an ugly man he had a smile of unexpected charm. I liked his voice: a deep rumble with good resonance. During the half-hour we were with him, he popped three Tums.

We figured it was no time to play games, and laid it all out for him: the business we were in, the name and address of Susan Forgrove, her father's name and the charges he had made. We also told him what we knew about the girl and what we had learned from Martha's boyfriend and from Nikki.

"You want to set her up?" he asked.

"Only if we have to," Martha said quickly. "We're hoping you can come up with something dirty to take to her father to convince him to call off his dogs."

"Can you move on this?" I said nervously. "We don't know how long we can stall the investigation."

"I'll get on it," the detective promised in his throaty rumble. "Don't call me; I'll call you when I've got something."

"And then what?" Martha demanded.

"Then we'll go for a frame," Meerjens said, shrugging. "With a whacked-out kid like that, it shouldn't be hard. You want to give me a retainer now? A thousand would be nice."

So we paid him and hoped for the best.

That was during the first week in October. Then, as if we didn't have enough trouble, we got another knee in the groin.

Martha had taken a few hours off to go shopping, and Yancy Burnett was filling in at the reception desk. He came into the den shaking his head.

"Peter," he said, "you better come out to the foyer. We've got a problem."

When I got out there, I saw what he meant. There was a bum leaning forward across the desk, propping himself on grimy knuckles. And I mean a *bum*. Unshaven, bleary-eyed, wearing a crusty overcoat held together at the neck with a safety pin. Greasy hair hung over his collar, and you could smell him at twenty paces.

He was a young guy, no more than thirty, but he looked like he had come directly from the Bowery.

"What do you want?" I asked him.

"Stud," he said in a drunken mumble. "Guy tells me you're hiring."

"Who told you that?" I demanded.

"Guy I met in a bar," he said, leering. "Said you paid good money for screwing."

I was breathing through my mouth by then, not wanting to inhale his aroma.

"This guy," I said, "was he short, heavyset, with a droopy face?"

"Yeah, yeah. He said he was a friend of yours."

"Not anymore he isn't," I said. "We're not doing any hiring. Thanks for coming up."

I gave him a couple of bucks and made sure he got on the elevator, practically pushing him. Yance called down to tell the doorman to get him out of the building. I went back to the den, took some money out of the safe. I grabbed my new gabardine topcoat and stormed out.

Fifteen minutes later I stalked into Sol Hoffheimer's office and caught him pouring whiskey from a pint bottle into a paper cup. I threw the cash onto his desk. Two of the bills skidded off onto the dusty floor.

"That's what we owe you," I said furiously. "Plus a hundred good-bye money. You're fired."

He looked up at me dimly. "What the hell?" he said.

"I met your friend," I told him. "The guy from skid row. Thanks a lot."

"Can't you take a joke?" he said plaintively.

"No," I said, "I can't. Not stupidity like that."

He staggered to his feet. "I got—" he said, choking. "I need— Peter, we been friends— I can't— You made—"

"So long, Sol," I said. "You're just not the right type for the part."

By the time I got back to the penthouse, Martha had returned and Yance had told her what happened.

"I canned Sol Hoffheimer," I said. "Since he started hitting the sauce, he's just not dependable."

"Best thing," she said, nodding. "Who needs that bullshit? But now what do we do for studs?"

"We're in pretty good shape. We're beginning to get some by word-of-mouth; the studs we have are telling their friends and so forth. And if worse comes to worst, I'll find some other theatrical agent who'll work with us."

I went back to my schedules. But I had to have a stiff belt—Sol and I had been together a long time. But business is business.

105

What with all this aggravation, it was an absolute delight to spend a quiet evening with Nicole Radburn. It was intimacy without responsibility—which is what it's all about, isn't it?

She came over on Sunday night and, working together, we constructed an enormous chef's salad with everything in it but the kitchen sink. It tasted great (the secret is crumbled blue cheese). We drank a bottle of muscadet and did a lot of laughing. Then we watched television. A charming domestic interlude.

Then we showered together, but it was nothing like that scene with Susan Forgrove. This was just innocent pleasure.

Later, in the bedroom, I told Nikki that our relationship was the first time I had been so *private* with a woman without becoming aroused.

"Maybe it's me," she said.

"Oh God, no," I said.

"You think you're becoming jaded?"

"I don't think so. Nikki, I love women. I really do. Maybe I just need some time off. I don't know what it is. But I do know I'm happy with you, walking around bareass and not having to prove anything. You're not ready for sleep, are you?"

"Not quite yet."

"I've got a half-bottle of Cordon Rouge in the fridge."

"Just right," she said.

When I came back with the bottle and glasses, she was sprawled naked in the chair, one knee hooked over the padded arm. I set to work uncorking the bottle and pouring.

"It beats me," I said, shaking my head. "Looking at you sitting like that with your bits and pieces exposed, I should be ready to pole-vault out the window. But as you can see, my dear, I am not ready. And I can't see that you're suffering from uncontrollable passion either."

She shrugged. "I'm not a very sexy woman, Peter," she said. "I told you that."

"Well, considering the business you're in, that makes you one hell of an actress."

"Oh yes," she said, nodding.

"It's all performance?"

"Sometimes I get carried away," she admitted. "Rarely. I don't like losing control."

I found a radio station playing country-western and we lounged naked, sipping champagne and listening to those silly, sentimental songs of loves lost.

"I think," Nikki said thoughtfully, "if we ever boffed, it would be a mistake."

"A failure?" I asked.

"No," she said, "it might be great. But it would change things."

"I know what you mean."

"You don't want to, do you?"

"I'm happy with things just the way they are," I said, determined to be as cool as she.

"So am I," she said. "I love just sleeping with you. I like you, Peter, and I know you like me."

"I do."

"I look forward to seeing you," she went on. "To being with you. You're very kind."

I considered that. "I think that generally I'm kind. But sometimes I'm not nice. Usually it's dictated by circumstances. I can't be nice if I want to survive."

"I'm not a very nice person," she said.

"Come on, Nikki. That's not true."

"Maybe I'm nice to you, but you should see the way I treat some of my johns. Like shit."

"But they keep coming back, don't they?"

"Yes."

"Well then . . ."

"Peter, I take advantage of their weaknesses. I profit from it. I wouldn't call that kindness."

"I'm not so sure," I said. "If you're making them happy . . ."

"You're beginning to think like a whore," she said.

Later, in bed, lights out, with her snuggled up against my back, she said, "Don't make a play for me, Peter."

"I wasn't planning to."

"Good," she said. "Let's keep it special."

106

Detective Luke Futter was slumped in the armchair in the den. He was holding a glass of Jack Daniel's and staring at me broodingly. It made me nervous.

I told him we had hired a private investigator in the Susan Forgrove matter and explained what we hoped to accomplish.

"It might work," he acknowledged. "If this guy can come up with something. What's his name?"

"Casper Meerjens."

He shook his head. "Never heard of him. But that don't mean anything. Don't drag your feet on this, sonny."

"How much time have we got?" I said miserably.

"Two, three weeks. A month tops. Then we'll have to close you down."

He straightened in his chair and took a deep gulp of the bourbon.

"Another thing," he said. "What I really came up to talk to you about. I hear you're making a big expansion."

"Where did you hear that?" I asked curiously.

"Oh . . . the word gets around. It is true?"

"In the planning stage," I said.

"Uh-huh. The way I hear it, it's going to be a fancy townhouse. A private club for rich women. Very nice. Lots of money there. I hope your budget includes a nice raise for me and my friends. For a big East Side joint, you better figure ten grand a month minimum."

"Ten?" I cried. "My God, that'll ruin us!"

"Nah," Futter said with his smarmy grin. "Just lump it in with overhead. It comes off taxes. You're planning to pay taxes, aren't you?"

"Of course."

"Well, there you are. When do you open?"

"First of the year," I said. "Hopefully."

"I'll be around before then," he promised, "and we'll talk bottom line." He drained the remainder of his bourbon and got to his feet. "By the way," he said casually, "I know you're doing okay, but I can't see you coming up with the bucks to finance a townhouse. Who's the angel?"

I wasn't too happy about telling him, but I figured he'd find out sooner or later.

"Roman Enterprises," I said. "Ever hear of them?"

His lips pursed in a whistle, but I didn't hear anything.

"You're traveling in the big leagues now, sonny," he said. "Let me give you a piece of advice: When you're in business with guys like that, for the first six months they say, 'You count the money and give us our share.' Then for the next six months they say, 'Let's both count the money.' After that, *they* count the money and give you just what they want to give you."

"We've got a good lawyer," I said defensively.

"Sure you do," Futter said. "Lots of luck."

107

October proved extremely profitable. If it hadn't been for Lester Forgrove's accusations, we wouldn't have had a worry in the world—or at least none we couldn't handle.

That month was also memorable for the number of freakish customers we serviced. At least, I thought the proportion was high; Martha said it was low compared to the percentage of male kinks patronizing bordellos and call girls. Still, she admitted, we had our share of kooks.

For instance:

. . . One of our clients, a top-flight executive in an advertising agency, developed a penchant for simulated rape. She brought a cheap rayon dress in an attaché case to every scene. She donned it in the bedroom and the stud was required to rip it off with horrendous threats and vile insults.

. . . In answer to a phoned request, we sent a call boy to a posh mansion on the north shore of Long Island. He returned, somewhat shaken, to relate that he had arrived the day before a funeral. The scene had taken place on a velvet couch in a room in which the client's deceased husband reposed in a bronze casket.

One of our oddest experiences occurred that month. Martha reported that a customer was willing to pay $500 for a virgin. Most of our studs were in their twenties and early thirties, and none of them looked especially virginal. But we hated to lose that fee.

Yancy Burnett said he might be able to help.

"I know this kid named Tommy Bostian," he said. "He's going to ballet school, but he's a better actor than a dancer. He's twenty, but you'd swear he's no more than sixteen. I think he'll do it for half of the five hundred. Like me, he swings both ways."

"You're sure he's twenty?" Martha said suspiciously. "We don't want another Susan Forgrove."

"I'm sure," Yance said, smiling. "I lived with Tommy for a few months, and I'm very careful to avoid jailbait. If you want to take a look, I'll ask him to bring his birth certificate."

Tommy Bostian turned out to be perfect. He was short, slender, small-boned, with fair skin and hair so blond it was almost white. He really did look like a fifteen-year-old, but his birth certificate and driver's license said he was twenty. We decided to take a chance.

We coached him in the part. He was to be shy, embarrassed, a little fearful, and maybe even shed a few tears. Luckily, he was a quick study and understood exactly what the role called for.

We asked him to wear jeans, sneakers, and a clean T-shirt under a denim jacket. We added a few props: a big comb in his hip pocket, a black leather bopper's cap, a cheap gold-plated chain around his thin neck. He would carry a small transistor radio.

The scene turned out to be a big success. The client even gave Tommy a fifty-dollar tip. Then she asked if we could find her another virgin.

It's all fantasy, innit?

108

Oscar Gotwold and Ignatz Samuelson hammered out a tentative agreement with Roman Enterprises. Late in October, Martha and I met with them to go over details of the deal.

Briefly, Peter's Place, Inc., would be a chartered corporation, privately held. Martha and I would own 52 percent of the 1000 shares of stock. The remainder would be owned by Justice Development Corp., a subsidiary of Roman Enterprises. Michael Gelesco and Anthony Cannis were the chief executive officers of Justice Development.

Martha and I would each invest $104,000 in Peter's Place, Inc., for a total of 520 shares at $400 each. Justice Development would put up $192,000 for 480 shares. The remainder of the funds needed to purchase, refurbish, and equip a townhouse would come in the form of a 1.2-million-dollar loan from Vigor Venture Capital, Inc., another Roman Enterprises subsidiary. The loan would carry an interest rate of 10 percent.

The townhouse would be purchased from Marble Properties, Inc., another Roman Enterprises subsidiary. A 10 percent mortgage of 1.75 million would be provided by Daring Financial Corp., which was, as you may have guessed, another Roman Enterprises subsidiary.

By this time, my eyeballs were glazing over. The first thing I questioned was why so many subsidiaries of Roman Enterprises were involved.

"Strictly bookkeeping," Iggy said tersely. "Take money out of one pocket, put it in the other. Tax advantages. These are very smart people."

"Would it make any difference if you dealt with independent companies?" Oscar asked. "And where else are you going to get a ten percent cash loan and a ten percent mortgage?"

"What it really comes down to," Martha said, "is that we've got no choice, right?"

Oscar shrugged. "In my opinion, this is the best deal you can possibly make. If you think you can do better, try. But you'll be sorely disappointed."

"What I want to know is," I said, "how Martha and I come out personally."

"In return for your one-oh-four grand," Iggy said, "each of you will own twenty-six percent of the outstanding stock in Peter's Place, Inc. In addition, each of you gets a two-year employment contract. Seventy-five thousand per annum."

"They wanted to give you one-year contracts at fifty," Oscar said. "We compromised at two years and seventy-five thousand."

Martha and I looked at each other.

"Do we get that no matter what?" she asked.

"No matter what," Iggy assured her. "Off the top. But it's a straight salary. Withholding and other taxes deducted. Strictly legal."

"Much less than we're making now," she observed. "Not counting profits."

"What about the profits?" I asked. "How are they cut up?"

"Before there are any profits," Oscar explained, "loan payments have to be made to Vigor Venture Capital and mortgage payments to Daring Financial. Then any excess funds, other than a small financial reserve, will go to the stockholders. Which means that you and Martha will get fifty-two percent of the net and Justice Development gets the rest."

I stared morosely at that stack of documents piled in front of Gotwold and wondered if I would ever understand it all. The only thing I could grasp was that it was our only chance.

"Something else you should know," Iggy said. "There are two townhouses being offered by Marble Properties. Either one will be satisfactory to Roman Enterprises. The choice is yours."

That I could understand. "Where are they?" I asked.

"One is in Murray Hill," Oscar said. "The other is on West Fifty-fourth, right off Fifth. The price on both is the same: two million five. I'll leave you the addresses. Take a look at them. I'll also leave copies of all these agreements. I suggest you go over them carefully."

He sat back, fingers laced across his vested belly. He regarded us benignly, shrewd little eyes glittering.

"In my opinion," he said, "you would be foolish to pass up this opportunity. Don't you agree, Iggy?"

Waving his porcelain cigarette, Samuelson jerked about, stabbing at the documents. "Take my advice. Grab it."

So we grabbed it.

109

Now that we were so close to signing with Roman, clearing up the Susan Forgrove business became even more urgent. If Octavius Caesar got wind of it, he'd not only call off the deal but spread the word around that we were unacceptable financial risks.

So it was a relief when Casper Meerjens said he was ready to meet with us. He wouldn't discuss any details on the phone; when he arrived at Martha's apartment, we didn't know whether he was bringing good news or bad.

The private detective folded his bony frame into an armchair and accepted a glass of club soda. He took one sip, then set the glass carefully on the floor. He lighted a cigarette. He put on his tape-patched spectacles. He pulled a tattered notebook from his jacket pocket. By that time, my palms were sweating.

"Susan Forgrove," he said in his rumbling voice. "Nancy Drew she ain't. She's run away twice. Kicked out of half a dozen schools. Got into hard drugs when she was thirteen. Said to be clean now—but who knows?

She's supposed to be seeing a shrink three times a week, but she misses appointments. She also stays away from home overnight or two or three days at a time. Then she won't tell where she's been. It drives her parents crazy."

"Where did you get all this?" I asked.

"Here and there," he said vaguely. "She hasn't got a legit driver's license, but she swiped her mother's Toyota and totaled it. Also, she clips money from her mother's purse. And she steals stuff from her home and sells it. Silver candlesticks, small paintings, ceramics—portable things like that. According to my sources, she's still a heavy pot smoker and probably snorts. She's got the reputation of being Miss Junior Roundheels of Manhattan, the easiest bang in the city. All you have to do is ask."

He fished in his other jacket pocket and came up with a flat packet wrapped in a length of toilet paper. He unfolded it carefully, then handed Martha a stack of Polaroid photos.

"She got in with a street gang on East Ninety-sixth," the detective said. "Stayed in their basement clubroom for two days. They took turns with her and called in all their friends in the neighborhood."

I silently thanked God I had had a Wassermann just a week ago, and resolved to have another tomorrow.

"Anyway," Meerjens went on, "they had these pictures taped to the clubhouse walls. I bought the set for two hundred. They weren't smart enough to make copies."

I watched Martha's face as she inspected the photographs. I had never seen such sadness; she aged before my eyes. She handed me the pictures wordlessly.

It was Susan Forgrove; no doubt about that. And what had been done to that poor, sick girl made me want to be a dog or a cat or a bird. There was one shot of three young hoodlums using her from all angles. The only way I could deal with it was to make it a joke.

"A great vaudeville act," I said. "What do they call themselves—the Aristocrats?"

"You think those shots will do?" Meerjens asked.

"They'll do," Martha said tonelessly. "So now you take them to her father and persuade him to drop the charges?"

Casper Meerjens finished his club soda. He burped softly and patted his lips with a knuckle.

"Not me," he said, lighting another cigarette. "Sorry. Ordinarily I would, but this is different. Lester Forgrove could get my license pulled before I got out of his house."

"Hey," I protested. "Wait a minute—you were hired to clean up this mess for us."

Meerjens shook his head. "Nope. I was hired to get evidence. That's what I did."

So we paid him off and he departed. He left the Polaroid photos and the toilet paper wrapper.

"Do you think *he* made copies?" I asked Martha.

"No," she said. "I don't think he wants anything more to do with this. Did you notice how he handled them by the edges? No prints."

"So what do we do now?"

"Go through with it," Martha said. "Take the pictures to Lester Forgrove."

"Who does all this?" I demanded.

She looked at me.

"Jesus, Martha," I said, groaning. "I can't. I haven't got the balls. You said so yourself. I wouldn't know how to act."

"I thought you were an actor," she said quietly.

"Well . . ." I said, "give me a little time. I'll have to psych myself up to it. Oh God, it's going to be so *awful.*"

"You'll be great," she assured me. "Peter, why don't you stay the night?"

"You think I need comforting?"

"No," she said. "I do. Those pictures made me feel so goddamned empty."

She had turned off the heat in the bedroom and opened the window. It was bloody cold, but that's the way she liked it. We huddled naked beneath a down comforter and she couldn't stop talking.

She told me about her girlhood in a small Ohio town, and how, after her parents died, she had moved to Chicago and gotten a job as a cocktail waitress. Then she had drifted into the game, making a good buck working in a brothel owned by Nikki Radburn's mother.

She always had an interest in clothes and fashion. When she had a stake, she cut loose, came to New York, got a job as salesclerk in a boutique. She banged the right guys and five years later she was managing the Barcarole. Along the way, she married a man who turned out to be a compulsive gambler and a drifter. He split, leaving her with a son to raise.

Now that her money worries seemed at an end, she was faced with the biggest problem of her life: What to do about her boyfriend, the future governor.

"I wish I knew how I *really* feel about him," she said, playing with me. "Sometimes I think I love him. Sometimes I think he's just another john."

"He gives you money?" I asked.

"Things. He gives me things. Jewelry. Stock shares. An antique bronze elephant that cost a mint."

"And what do you give him—the riding crop?"

"It gets him out," she said, her fingers tightening. "People are what they are. We all have our hangups."

"What's yours?"

"Elephants. What's yours?"

"Beats me," I said. "I wish I knew who I was."

"You're an actor," she said. "Not knowing who you are is an occupational hazard. Are you ready?"

"I've never been readier."

"You'll take the photographs to Lester Forgrove?"

"I guess," I said, sighing. "Oh God, Martha, sometimes I'd like to sue for divorce from the human race."

110

King Hayes told me he was quitting. I got his bottle of Manischewitz Concord from the den cellarette and poured him a glassful.

"Louella?" I asked, and he nodded.

I had a brandy, not because I wanted it, but because I felt the occasion called for a toast. We hoisted our glasses. A sweet man. I really liked him. Not so great in the brains department, but sweet.

"No use my trying to talk you out of it," I said. "I'm the guy who told you to go ahead. But I hope you considered it carefully."

"Yeah," he said. "Peter, it's a chance—right? I mean, suppose it don't work out? We split, that's all."

"My God, King, don't move in with this lady thinking it won't work out."

"Oh, I mean to give it my best shot," he said earnestly. "I really do. I'm going to try it her way for a while and see what happens."

"Have you told her yet?"

"Last night. She was real happy. Going out today to buy me towels, toothbrush, a bathrobe—things like that. I've got all that stuff, but if it makes her happy . . ."

"King," I said, "I don't want to put a damper on this, but I never saw you as a guy who would be happy living off a woman. I think you better get yourself a job doing whatever. Even if you make a lot less than she does."

"Oh, I mean to," he said solemnly. "She says she'll pay for food and rent, but I don't want her handing me walking-around money like an allowance."

In a way I envied him. He was making an effort to get out, and I hoped he succeeded. Me, I was in too deep. And I wasn't certain I even wanted to escape.

"If you ever want to come back . . ." I said.

"Thanks, Peter, but I'm not going to count on it. When I'm out, I'm out."

"Well, if you ever get a bad case of the shorts, you know where to find me. We're going to miss you, King. And so are your clients."

"We had some high old times, didn't we?" he said, smiling.

"That we did."

He finished his wine and stood up. We shook hands.

"Take care of yourself, Peter. Sometimes I worry about you."

"Me?" I said, touched. "Not to worry. I've got the world by the tail."

"Yeah," he said, laughing. "I know what you mean."

111

Leaving Yance in charge of the penthouse, Martha and I set out to inspect locations for Peter's Place. We met the Marble Properties agent at a boarded-up brownstone on East 36th Street, just west of Lexington in Murray Hill.

The agent was a bucktoothed lady wearing a belted sealskin coat. She looked like a skinny walrus. She made no effort to sell, so I guess she knew our choices were limited.

"That's it," she said, jerking a long-nailed thumb at the five-story building.

It was a hulk, with sheets of tin nailed over the windows. Maybe it could have been renovated, but nothing could disguise the ugliness of that battered façade.

"It won't do," Martha said firmly.

"Want to look inside?" the agent asked without interest.

"It's hopeless," I told her. "Too far downtown for starters. And it looks like a halfway house for arsonists. Let's try the other one."

We cabbed up to 54th Street and walked west from Madison. Nice neighborhood. Nice street. Well-dressed people. Good restaurants and expensive shops. The air smelled of money.

It was a sharp November afternoon, everything chiseled and clean. A washed blue sky and a sun that had been cut out with a razor. I could see our customers stopping by for lunch and a quickie between trips to Bonwit's and Saks.

The building itself was slender and tall: six stories with a mansard roof. It had bow windows supported by ornate gargoyles. The street-level entrance had carved columns and a stained glass fanlight. The façade was limestone with red brick ornamentation around the windows.

"Looks awfully narrow," Martha said doubtfully. "Let's take a look inside."

"The last owner was a foundation," the agent said. "All the rooms were converted to offices, so it'll need some work."

It was narrow all right, with just the front windows overlooking the street, and the back (north) windows giving a view of a tiny courtyard and the brick walls of commercial buildings on West 55th Street. But the ceilings were high and the first two floors were parqueted.

There was a small self-service elevator that wasn't working, so we walked up. There were a lot of rooms which had, as the agent said, been divided into offices. But we figured we could get eleven or twelve bedrooms out of the available space.

Best of all, in the rear of the main floor was a completely equipped kitchen that had been installed by the previous owner for employee lunches. And the dining room seated thirty or forty.

"Do you like it?" the agent asked.

"For two and a half million," Martha said loftily, "how can we go wrong?"

We closed a week later, in the top-floor conference room of the Barcarole Boutique. The place was mobbed with attorneys and accountants. It looked like a class reunion of the Black Hand Society.

Martha and I had brought our $208,000 investment in cash, and were not thought the less for it. (But we made certain we got receipts.) Michael Gelesco and Anthony Cannis made their $192,000 contribution with a cashier's check drawn on a New Jersey bank I had never heard of. That it was a subsidiary of Roman Enterprises I had no doubt.

We signed and signed. Incorporation, stock shares, loan, mortgage, employment contracts, insurance: There was just no end to the documents. Everything was in blue paper binders. No ink blots or strikeouts. Very comforting. I didn't read a thing.

It took almost two hours to get everything signed, witnessed, certified, and notarized. Papers flew around that table like a snowfall, with Oscar Gotwold and the chief attorney for Justice Development Corp. making little tick marks on their master schedules.

Finally it was finished, and Gelesco invited us all into the next room, where a fully equipped bar with bartender had been set up. I had a stiff vodka on the rocks, shook hands with everyone, kissed Martha's cheek, and didn't give a damn.

I remember talking to Anthony Cannis. We were discussing how much we should charge customers for a membership card in Peter's Place.

"Five hundred?" I suggested.

"Nah," he said, chewing his cigar. "Make it a grand. It'll keep out the riffraff."

112

Martha insisted we make copies of the Forgrove photographs before I took them to Dad.

"Suppose he grabs them out of your hand and tears them up? Or promises to drop the charges and then reneges? Peter, those pictures are the only ammunition we've got."

So we did and put the negatives in the penthouse safe.

Meanwhile I had been planning my performance. My first idea was to come on like Sidney Quink, a creepy-crawlie blackmailer. But then I thought, if I did, I'd probably never get in to see Forgrove.

My second version was to dress all in black and play the part for menace, with quiet authority, hard eyes, and implied threats. I could carry a role like that, generating fear with a posture that expressed barely contained tension and suppressed violence.

Finally I decided my best bet was to avoid panicking Forgrove, but to convince him that I, one of his own social class, regretted bringing this tragic matter to his attention. I would be sincere. And as someone once said, when it comes to sincerity, style is everything.

I phoned him at home one evening around the middle of November. I spoke softly and politely. I gave him my name, told him I had a matter of the utmost urgency to discuss with him, and requested that he grant me a short audience.

"What's this about?" he asked suspiciously.

"It concerns your daughter Susan," I said.

I heard him sigh.

"Can't you come to my office?" he said. His voice was thin and querulous. No resonance at all.

"I don't believe that would be wise, sir."

That seemed to shake him.

"Very well," he said fretfully. "My wife and I are about to go out to dinner, but if you can get here immediately, I can give you a few minutes."

I was at his apartment house on East 79th Street within ten minutes. A nice building, heavy on the marble, with Art Deco lamps in the lobby. I identified myself on the intercom and was buzzed in.

Upstairs, on the ninth floor, the door of Apartment 9-C was opened on the chain and a cold eye inspected me. I was wearing my most respectable costume: vested confirmation suit, white shirt, foulard tie. My shoes were shined and I held my hat in my hand. The chain was slipped, the door opened.

The man in the dinner jacket was, I guessed, about forty-five. Narrow-shouldered and not too tall. A squinched face: small features set close together. His graying hair was brushed sideways. He looked at me without expression. A very frosty piece of goods.

"Mr. Lester Forgrove?" I asked.

"Yes. What's this all about?"

"It shouldn't take long. May I come in?"

He stood aside grudgingly and let me enter. It was then I noticed that he had one hand in his jacket pocket, and I wondered if he was armed. Not a comforting thought.

We stood in a long, brightly lighted hallway. I could see a pleasantly decorated living room at the far end, but he made no effort to usher me in. We faced each other in that narrow corridor.

"Mr. Forgrove," I said, starting my carefully rehearsed speech, "my name is Peter Scuro, and I am part-owner of a school of dramatic arts to which your daughter—"

That's as far as I got. He understood at once. He stiffened.

"I have nothing to say to you," he interrupted savagely. "See my lawyer."

"No, sir," I said. "I don't believe you will wish me to see him after you hear what I have to say—and to show you."

I told him that his daughter had come to us and represented herself as being of age.

I said we were running a legitimate acting school, and we were not responsible for liaisons between our students.

"You're running a whorehouse!" he burst out. "A male whorehouse. And I'm going to close you down if it's the last thing I do."

I replied quietly, all sweet reasonableness, that he had been misinformed. I reiterated it was an academy of dramatic arts.

He looked at me disgustedly. "What are you trying to pull?" he demanded. "I'm going to put you in jail. You're nothing but a lousy pimp. God knows what you do to those innocent young girls."

"Innocent?" I said angrily, insulted and forgetting my rehearsed lines. "Like your daughter Susan?" I took the photographs from my pocket and thrust them at him. "These pictures were taken in the basement clubhouse of a street gang long before Susan came to us. Take a good look, Mr. Forgrove. Don't bother ripping them up. Negatives exist."

He went through the photos slowly, head lowered. He seemed to shrink before my eyes. His collar became too large, his shoulders caved, his entire body appeared to shrivel.

"Where did you get these?" he asked in a voice so tiny I could hardly hear.

"It doesn't matter," I said. "What does matter is that we want you to drop your charges, Mr. Forgrove. What an ugly disgusting thing it would be to force us to send copies of those photos to your family, friends, and business associates."

He made a thick, gagging sound, and for a moment I was afraid he might become physically ill. But then a woman in a black, sleeveless evening sheath appeared in the doorway of the living room at the end of the hallway and moved toward us.

"Lester," she called, "we're going to be late."

He made a convulsive movement, trying to cram the pictures into his pocket. But he was so unnerved that three or four slipped from his fingers and fell to the floor. By that time the woman was up to us. She swooped swiftly and plucked the photos from the rug.

"What are—" she started, then saw what she was holding.

She was sterner than he. She did not crumple. She merely stared at me and said, "How much do you want?"

She was a long-faced woman, young enough not to have all those wrinkles, worry lines, and fret marks. Her hair, too, was graying, drawn back tightly and gathered in a bun.

"We don't want anything, ma'am. No money, that is. We ask only that your husband drop his charges against our acting school."

She drew a deep breath. I could see the blue veins in her splintery arms.

"How can we trust you?" she said scornfully.

"How can we trust *you?*" I asked. "If the charges are permanently withdrawn, the matter will end."

I think Lester Forgrove may have been weeping. His shoulders were bowed, head hanging. His arms dangled limply at his sides. His wife embraced him, almost fiercely, pressing him to her.

"The charges will be dropped," she said crisply. "Please go now."

I nodded and turned away, leaving them the photographs as a reminder. At the door, I glanced back. I knew I was doomed for the rest of my life to remember those two broken people huddled together, holding each other to keep out the darkness.

113

It became evident early on that the Justice Development Corp., although minority stockholders in the persons of Cannis and Gelesco, was going to have a great deal to say in the renovation of our townhouse.

They hired the architect and interior decorator. They made arrangements for refurbishing the kitchen. They decided which contractor got the job. It was true they consulted Martha and me on an almost daily basis, but it was usually to present us with a fait accompli.

Naturally we were angered. But Oscar Gotwold urged patience.

We stopped by the place two or three times a week to see how the work was progressing. It was obviously not going to be the elegant, luxurious private club I had envisioned.

Moldings and paneled walls I wanted stripped to bare wood were painted a cream color. Bedrooms I wanted equipped with Louis Quatorze reproductions got poor imitations of Swedish modern that looked like they had come from a bankrupt motel.

At least it wasn't glitzy, but I thought it plain and uninspiring. However, when I saw the high costs of even this minimal renovation, I muted my protests.

I was able to insist on a large master bedroom on the third floor, which I would occupy and which could be used for scenes when necessary. There was also a comfortable first-floor office, and a room that had originally been a pantry was converted to a cozy bar.

We applied for licenses to serve food and liquor, and were assured that as a private club, not open to the public, we would have no problems. In other matters, such as the prompt delivery of crockery, silverware, linen, air conditioners, paintings, etc., progress seemed magically greased by the influence of Justice Development.

We decided to close the penthouse on December 30 and open the townhouse for business on January 2. Meanwhile we distributed prospectuses for the new club to all our clients, and the response was encouraging. Membership fees were set at $1000. Annual dues were $250. The price of scenes remained at $100, with additional charges for doubles and other specials.

A small, dignified brass plaque was affixed to the stone at one side of the street door. It read simply: PETER'S PLACE. A PRIVATE CLUB.

It wasn't quite like having my name in lights on Broadway, but I must admit it was a source of pride and satisfaction.

114

"Guess who's in town?" Martha asked. And then, before I had a chance to answer: "Grace Stewart. Remember her?"

"Of course," I said. "Your friend from the Coast. The investment counselor."

"She's going to be in New York for two or three weeks and she'd like to see you."

"Why doesn't she come up?"

"She wants an escort for dinner. She's staying at the Bedlington again. Will you give her a call?"

"I guess so."

"You don't sound very enthusiastic, Peter. She's nice."

"She's lovely," I said. "But a little freaky."

"Aren't we all?" Martha said.

Two nights later I greeted Grace in the hallowed lobby of the Bedlington. I was wearing my dinner jacket and carrying a new double-breasted chesterfield over my arm. I had a miniature orchid in my lapel, which amused her.

"So elegant!" she said, laughing, and offered her cheek for a kiss.

She was hatless and wearing a mink coat as ample as a tent. That hard face still showed no lines despite her sixty years. But the shiny gray hair I remembered was now a bronzy red.

"Like it?" she said, turning her head from side to side.

"Beautiful," I assured her.

As before, she had a hired limo waiting for us. There was a new French restaurant in the Village, the Chez Fleurette, she wanted to try. We started off, sitting close together and holding hands.

"Martha told me about the new club," she said. "Congratulations."

"Thank you," I said. "Will you join?"

"Wouldn't miss it for the world. Can guests use my card?"

"Hmm," I said. "Good question. I'd be in favor of it. More business."

"When are you going public?" she asked half-seriously. "I've got a lot of clients who'd take a flier in something like that. Great tax writeoff."

"You talk like a friend of mine," I told her. "She's into tax shelters and money market funds and zero coupon bonds and all that financial stuff I can't understand."

"Oh?" Grace Stewart said. "I'd like to meet her. The great love of your life?"

"Oh no. Just a friend."

She was quiet a moment. Then: "Peter, are you happy?"

The question took me by surprise.

"I must be," I said, "or I wouldn't be doing what I am, would I?"

"That's stupid and you know it. Most people are trapped. Are you?"

I took so long to answer that she gave up and began relating the latest Hollywood gossip. She was an expert anecdotist with a tart tongue and a gift for mimicry. I reflected that I enjoyed her company more in public than in private.

The Chez Fleurette hadn't been "discovered" yet, and they were anxious to please. We had an excellent dinner: pigeon breasts in a green pepper sauce. We drank Mumm's. I saw the bill before Grace paid it. Two years ago I could have lived for a month on what that meal cost.

With the champagne and the after-dinner Rémy, I was in a benevolent mood. As the limousine purred us back to the Bedlington, I reached to caress her calf.

"Bare and shaved," I said. "It's nice to know some things never change."

"What a memory you have," she said, pushing my hand away.

"Only for what's important," I said, realizing I was talking foolishly and wondering if I had fortified myself with alcohol because I knew what was coming.

It must have been that because, in her suite, when she asked if I'd like anything, I said another brandy would be nice. She called down to the bar for two cognacs. Both turned out to be for me. She went to her poppers.

"They give you a lift?" I asked, watching her inhale.

"Not exactly," she said. "More like a delicious dullness. Don't you want to make yourself comfortable?"

"I am comfortable," I said.

"Don't get smart with me, sonny boy," she said, and it was almost a snarl. "You know what I want."

"Sure," I said. "I know what you want. But can we talk a minute?"

"If you like."

"I wish I could understand you, Grace."

"Why I'm a watcher?"

"A voyeur," I said.

"I prefer watcher," she said. "Voyeur sounds like a Peeping Tom. Peter, I don't *lurk*. I just like to watch. I have the largest collection of porn video cassettes in Hollywood. An innocent hobby."

"And you never have any desire to, ah, actively participate?"

"Never. I like to watch bullfights, too, but I have no wish to be a matador."

So I undressed and set about doing what she wanted me to do.

"Peter," Grace Stewart said calmly, "you're putting on weight."

115

Cannis and Gelesco argued persuasively that the size of the dining room and bar operations at Peter's Place required professional help.

So they hired a chef and cooks, a maître d' and waiters. They brought in their own bartenders, busboys, and a bent-nosed doorman-bouncer who looked like a former professional football center who had played too many games without a helmet. He was pleasant enough, but I don't think his elevator went to the top floor.

We were able to keep Patsy, Maria, and Luis, but Justice Development arranged for linen service, food and liquor supply, cleaning and maintenance.

"They're going to make a nice buck on kickbacks," Martha observed grimly. "But we're handling the cash for the scenes, and we can steal them even, dollar for dollar."

Peter's Place would be open from noon to 2:00 A.M., six days a week. Luncheon and dinner by reservation only. Yancy and I would alternate as hosts and do scheduling. Martha would take phoned appointments and collect the fees.

We inaugurated a system by which two unreserved studs would always be available for members who hadn't made appointments. They were called "readies" and were paid $50 a day whether they worked or not.

We also arranged for weekly physical exams of our studs.

Let's see, what else . . .

Well, we established room service so clients could have drinks in the bedrooms. And we kept one large second-floor room available for private parties. And, of course, our call boy and escort services were available to members at the usual fees.

Matches, cocktail napkins, ashtrays, and swizzle sticks were printed with PETER'S PLACE, our address and phone number. Our head bartender even invented a Peter's Place Special, a sweet drink of cranberry, orange, and grapefruit juice with rum, topped with a chunk of fresh pineapple dipped in powdered sugar. I thought it was loathsome.

The holidays were fast approaching, and we raced to put everything in readiness for our Grand Opening. We were spending what seemed to me enormous sums, but I was heartened by the number of membership applications we received, all enclosing the thousand-dollar fee and first year's dues of $250.

Most of them, of course, came from New York, but many were from such distant places as Alaska, Wyoming, Arizona, and several foreign countries. Apparently our reputation had spread by word of mouth.

One letter (written in purple ink) came from a woman in Arkansas who described herself as "Just a lonely old spinster trying to work a farm." She said it was doubtful if she would ever get to New York to take advantage of our services, but "It will give me great pleasure to know I belong."

I wrote her a personal letter, enclosing her membership card, and suggesting that if ever she was able to visit our club, to ask for me.

116

"Who?" I said on the phone.

"Clara," the woman's voice repeated pettishly. "Clara Hoffheimer."

"Oh," I said. "How are you, Clara?"

"I guess you heard about Sol."

"What about Sol?" I asked, knowing it wouldn't be good.

"Sol's dead," she said almost blithely. "God rest his soul. Drove into an embankment on the Long Island Expressway. I guess he dozed off." She added with some satisfaction: "It took them three hours to get him out of what was left of the car."

I felt vaguely nauseated. Dozed off . . . or pissy-assed drunk. Or—just a flicker so painful that I immediately rejected it—maybe he did it deliberately.

"When, Clara?"

"Wednesday night. He was buried yesterday. It was a nice affair."

"I wish you had called me."

"I tried, but you're not listed. When I came to the office, I found your number. Peter, I'd like to talk to you."

"Well . . . sure," I said cautiously. "If you're at the office, I'll come down. Give me half an hour."

I had been getting stuff ready for my move to the townhouse. But I put it all aside and mixed a strong vodka and water. It was 11:00 A.M. and I was drinking. Just like Sol Hoffheimer. The late Sol Hoffheimer.

I couldn't weep for him, but his death was a real bummer. I didn't feel guilty; the choice was his. Still, he hadn't started to hit the sauce until I roped him. But I kept telling myself: All he had to do was say no.

I wasn't looking forward to this meeting with Clara. But I didn't shirk what I saw as an act of Christian charity.

The only sign of her bereavement was a black dress. It was cut impressively low. She was still dripping with rings, bracelets, earrings, necklaces. The purpled hair was whipped high, and her perfume filled the musty office.

"Clara," I said, "please accept my condolences."

"Sure," she said briskly. "Listen, Peter, you were a good friend of Sol's."

"He was my agent for a long time," I said warily.

She was sitting in his swivel chair behind that scarred desk. It was covered with account books, ledgers, stacks of invoices, playbills, and yellowed newspaper clippings.

"I don't get it," she said. "I've been going through his records and it don't make sense. Sol was never rich—you know that—but he always put meat on the table. It was better for the last year, and I thought maybe he was finally clicking. But now I've been through his accounts and they show he wasn't making spit. Where was the money coming from, Peter—do you know?"

"Gambling?" I suggested. "The horses?"

"Sol wouldn't know a saddle from a bit."

"Loans? Maybe he was in to the sharks."

"No," she said. "There's no record of it and no one's called. According to all this paper, Sol was a failure as an agent. But he came up with the bucks. You weren't lending him money, were you?"

"Me? No."

"Sol said you were out of show business," she said, staring at me. "What are you doing now? If you don't mind my asking."

"I'm not really *out* of it," I said. "I meant I gave up looking for stage jobs. I run an acting school now. Peter's Academy of Dramatic Arts. It's in the book."

"Uh-huh," she said. She plucked a thin account book from the litter on the desk and flipped through it. "This is a receipt ledger. It shows dates and amounts. From a couple of bucks to a couple of thousand. And after a lot of those numbers, Sol wrote 'P.S.' That's you, isn't it? Peter Scuro?"

I didn't answer.

"Peter," she said quietly, "my little girl has braces. The insurance isn't all that much after the funeral expenses. I'll have to go to work. What were you paying Sol for? Couldn't I do it?"

I looked at her. My first impression had been of a brass-plated fluff-brain. Now I saw that she was harder than Sol, with chutzpah he never had. She wouldn't be bothered by problems of morality.

I decided to take a chance.

I told her exactly the kind of business I was in and the part her late husband had played.

As I spoke, she rose from her chair and came out from behind the desk. She hung one thick haunch on the arm of my chair and leaned into me. I could feel her warm, solid softness. Her scent almost made me sneeze.

I finished and we sat there in silence for a moment. Then she laughed: a little giggle.

"I think that's wonderful," she said. "A whorehouse for women. And it's successful?"

"Very."

She began stroking the back of my neck.

"I could do that," she said. "Put ads in the trades. Interview young guys. Send you all the studs you need. I'd be good at it, don't you think?"

"You'd be great at it," I said, happy to be doing something for Sol Hoffheimer's widow.

It was a kind of penance.

117

I couldn't believe the wardrobe I had accumulated during my year in the penthouse. (I had also put down reservation money on a bronzy Datsun 280-ZX—but that's another story.)

So the job of moving to the townhouse was heavier than moving from the West Side a year previously. Yancy Burnett assisted with packing and moving chores. That man was rapidly becoming invaluable. A real friend.

They were still working on the renovations, but I insisted my bedroom be top priority, so I was able to spend my first night in the townhouse on December 21. The place was still a mess, but at least I was *in*. Peter's Place was a reality.

There was one phone working, and that first night I called Jenny Tolliver. I was hoping for a Christmas dinner date.

"Sorry, Peter," she said crisply, "I'm working like a fiend so I can get home for the holiday week."

"Oh . . ." I said, disappointed. "That means I can't see you until next year?"

"I'm afraid so."

"Well . . . Merry Christmas and Happy New Year. I hope it'll be a good one for you."

"Thank you," she said, and I thought her voice softened. "I hope the new year brings you everything you want."

So that was that. Martha's son was in town and she was busy with him. Yance had a gay party to go to. I didn't relish the idea of spending Christmas Eve alone, so I called Nikki Radburn and we made a date for dinner.

Meanwhile I finished moving our files, our business records and books (fake and real), and my personal liquor supply. I went through the chest of drawers in the penthouse Rose Room for the third time to make certain I was leaving nothing behind.

I did find something I had overlooked: a wedding band. I remembered who had given it to me—the one-breasted poet. I couldn't think of her name, but I recalled her tenderness. She had never returned to us, and I wondered what had happened to her.

I took the gold band along to my new bedroom in the townhouse, to bring me luck.

118

I was dressing for dinner with Nikki when the phone rang in my townhouse bedroom. It was Grace Stewart.

"Peter!" she said. "Merry the hell Christmas!"

"And the same to you!" I said. "You're still in town? I thought you'd be back in the land of fruits and nuts by now."

"Decided to stay on for a few days," she said gaily. "It's been so long since I've seen a white Christmas."

"You're seeing one now. They're predicting six inches."

She laughed lewdly. "My favorite number," she said. "I know

you've been busy, but I was hoping we might have dinner tonight. I'm scheduled for a very boring business party—you know: quiche and fondue —but I'd junk it in a minute if you have the evening free."

"Ah," I said. "What a pity. I do have plans."

There was silence a moment, then: "I'd make it worth your while."

"Oh, Grace," I said, "the eve of Christ's birth is not a working night for me. It's just a dinner with a lady friend."

I should have stopped there, but I didn't. I suggested that she join us —my treat. She accepted.

I wasn't quite sure how this was going to work out, so I fortified myself with a couple of raunchy vodkas before getting into the rented limo. I was wearing a tobacco-colored suede jacket, twill bags in a fawny shade, cordovan loafers. I also admit to a silk ascot.

I picked up Nikki first. She looked smashing in white silk blouse and black silk slacks. She accepted the news about Grace without objection.

When I told her our guest was an investment counselor, her interest grew. Then we picked up Grace. I knew almost immediately they were going to hit it off and the evening was going to be a success.

Nikki and I had chosen a rib joint, a garish place with plywood, checkered tablecloths, and paper napkins. The ribs were great, as were the french fries, onion rings, and cole slaw. We had a pitcher of ice-cold draft beer.

We ate and drank up a storm, not caring that all three of us spotted our fronts. Outside, the snow was still coming down softly and steadily. But inside, it was warm, redolent, and happy.

"Oh my God," Grace said, groaning contentedly. "Best Christmas Eve dinner I've ever had."

"Ditto," Nikki said. "Peter, could we have another pitcher of beer?"

"Of course," I said. "You ladies are with the last of the big-time spenders."

From then on, they started talking stocks, bonds, tax shelters, municipals, no-load mutual funds, etc. I sat there, the token male between two smart, vivid women, and drank beer, trying not to belch audibly.

It was almost eleven before we left. It had stopped snowing. The sky was jet black and showing a zillion stars. The air was so keen it was painful to breathe.

"Perfume," Nikki said.

"Poppers," Grace said.

She insisted we come back to the Bedlington with her. The radio was playing "Silent Night." We sat around with our shoes off, sipping Rémy and trading limericks. The radio carol was now "O Little Town of Bethlehem."

Then Grace went into the bedroom and came back with her filigreed silver box. She offered the poppers around, but Nikki and I declined. Grace took a snort, smiling at us.

"Merry Christmas, all," she said.

"Merry Christmas!" we chorused, raising our brandies.

"Nikki," Grace said, still smiling, "you in the game?"

"That's right," Nikki said levelly.

"I thought so," Grace said, still smiling. "Would the two of you like to put on a private show for me? Five hundred for the two of you."

The radio was playing "Rudolph, the Red-Nosed Reindeer."

Nikki turned to look at me. "Peter?" she said.

Everything changed. Just flopped over. Up to that moment the evening had been laughs, good food, friendship. Now it was all different.

But not only that evening. I stared at Nicole Radburn and saw her face working and things going on in her eyes. I guessed she was thinking, as I was, of our "special" thing and reckoning what it was worth.

Oh, it was a turning point, no doubt of that. Not only in my relationship with Nikki, but in my relationship to myself, me, who I was and what I was, and where I was going. The odd thing was that this knowledge didn't come later, after reflection. I knew then, that moment.

"Well?" Grace Stewart said.

"Why not?" I said, and Nikki nodded.

I remember the radio was playing "White Christmas."

119

I must give credit to the Justice Development Corp.; by December 31 our West 54th Street townhouse was completely renovated, painted, furnished, cleaned up, and ready to open for business. The staff had been hired, the kitchen equipped, the freezer stocked with food, and the bar had an adequate supply of potables.

On the afternoon of New Year's Eve, we held an open house for our studs. Free food and booze. We let them wander around the premises, inspect the newly decorated bedrooms, and acquaint themselves with the layout of dining room, bar, and the loos.

The studs' reactions were almost completely favorable. They particularly appreciated the fact that the whole place was wired for sound, with switches in every bedroom to control mood music from a tape player in the bar. They also liked the idea of room service.

We cleared them out by five o'clock. From seven to whenever on New Year's Eve we planned a second open house for a more select group. Martha, Yance, and myself, of course. Michael Gelesco and Anthony Cannis, with their bedizened ladies. Detective Luke Futter. A few of the designers and contractors who had worked on the renovation. Clara Hoffheimer. Oscar Gotwold and Ignatz Samuelson. And, to the surprise of everyone, Mr. Octavius Caesar.

He had been invited as a matter of courtesy, but no one had expected him to attend. But there he was, wearing a rusty, old-fashioned tuxedo, beaming and shaking the hands of all the men and gallantly kissing the cheeks of all the ladies.

It was a pleasant, decorous pre-dinner cocktail party. No one drank too much, no one misbehaved. And no one stayed too long. Futter had one drink, wished us the best of luck, and disappeared. Cannis and Gelesco slapped me on the back, assured me that we were all going to make a mint, and took off.

Martha and I embraced, wished each other a Happy New Year, and then she left to meet her boyfriend, who had promised to spend an hour with her before he returned to his family. Yancy and I shook hands and he drifted away.

Finally, at 9:30, only Clara Hoffheimer and Octavius Caesar remained, sitting together at one of the little bistro tables in the bar. I was supervising the cleaning-up chores of Patsy, Luis, and Maria, who had served at both cocktail parties.

By ten o'clock they were ready to leave. I gave all three a nice bonus, wished them Happy New Year, then locked the front door behind them and went back to the bar.

Clara Hoffheimer and Octavius Caesar were leaning close to each other. She was wearing a strapless sheath of some red metallic stuff. Her bulging bosom looked like a fleshy heart, and his bright nose was practically tucked into the cleft.

I went behind the bar and built a big brandy and soda with a lot of ice, put on a tape of "My Fair Lady," and turned the volume low. I sipped my drink and surreptitiously watched Clara and Caesar.

That old fart and that brassy tart . . . it tickled me. And, I figured, it wouldn't do us any harm if our top moneyman got hooked by the woman supplying our studs.

He patted her hand. He patted her bare shoulder. Finally he patted her knee. I wondered if her musky perfume was getting to him.

When I called over to ask if they'd like another drink, Octavius Caesar looked up in surprise. He stared around the room.

"My goodness," he said. "Has everyone . . . ?"

"Yes, sir," I said. "But stay as long as you like."

"Oh no," he said hastily. "I must be . . . The company of this charming lady has been so . . . I really must be . . ."

They left together. Clara gave me a fast wink.

I locked up again and went back to the bar to finish my drink. And then I had another while I listened to "Why Can't a Woman Be More Like a Man?"

I was tired but content. The thought of spending New Year's Eve alone didn't dismay me. In fact, I welcomed it. It would do me good to be by myself.

When I heard the front door chimes, I thought it was one of our guests who had forgotten something. But it was a woman I had never seen before. Short, plumpish, a little nervous. She thrust a membership card at me.

"I belong," she said abruptly.

"So you do," I said, smiling. "But we don't open for business until January second."

"Oh," she said, her face shrinking. "I thought . . ."

"Unless," I said, "you'd be satisfied with me."

She stared. "All right," she said breathlessly. She fumbled with her purse. "I have the fee."

"Nonsense," I said. "You're our first customer. It's on the house."

120

By the second week in January, everyone connected with Peter's Place realized we had a success on our hands. Luncheon and dinner reservations had to be made several days in advance. The bar did a brisk business from opening to closing.

But, of course, it was the bedrooms upstairs that provided the profit. Those and our call boy and escort services continued to grow slowly but steadily.

During those first few weeks we had a number of visitors without membership cards. The gorilla who guarded the door was instructed to turn away men and couples, but women were allowed to inspect the accommodations. Many became members.

While most of our customers still preferred to pay cash, we now took all major credit cards. For clients who preferred monthly billings, we accepted signed tabs. The fee for a scene was listed as a luncheon or dinner bill, of course.

Male guests were allowed to use the first-floor facilities (dining room and bar), but only if accompanied by a member.

Our clientele continued to be of two general classes: bored wealthy women (mostly married) with a lot of time and money to spend, and busy professional women (mostly single) who were too engrossed in their careers to contemplate marriage and child-raising. For both groups, Peter's Place became a haven and a solution.

Martha correctly observed we were at the right place at the right time with the right service. A cynic might say we were running a hot-pillow joint, but I honestly felt we were meeting a need.

121

Yancy Burnett and I greeted guests after they were admitted by the simian doorkeeper. We checked their reservations, then escorted them to the dining room, bar, or the little self-service elevator that took them to the upstairs bedrooms. Yance worked from noon to 7:00 P.M., when I would take over until 2:00 A.M. Each week we reversed our working hours.

One afternoon during that first hectic week in January, I was in the first-floor office, struggling with the schedules when Yancy came to tell me Nicole Radburn wanted to see me.

I hadn't spoken to her since Christmas Eve, and I really didn't want to. Yance must have seen my indecision, because he said gently, "I can tell her you're busy, Peter."

"No," I said, sighing. "I can't have you doing my dirty work. I'll see her."

She looked very smart in a tailored suit and carried a mink-trimmed raincoat over one arm. I had never seen her before with her hair up. The style made her face sharper and harder. We tried to smile at each other.

"Would you like something to drink?" I asked. "I can order from the bar."

"No, thank you," she said.

Silence.

"Nice club you've got here, Peter. What I've seen of it."

"Thank you. I can give you a tour."

"No. I've only got a few minutes."

Silence.

"Grace Stewart is going back to the Coast tomorrow," she said. "She wants me to go with her."

"Oh?"

"Join her business. She says I've got a good money brain and that I can be making a hundred grand within a year."

"Sounds good."

"If it doesn't work out, I've always got a trade I can fall back on."

"You don't think Grace may just want you for shows?"

"No," Nikki said, looking at me directly. "Not for shows."

It took me a few seconds to understand.

"Oh-ho," I said. "You've converted her from a spectator to a participant."

"Something like that. This could be my big chance, Peter."

"Sure. You'd be foolish not to grab it."

She rose suddenly. "I've got to run. Peter, I . . ."

"Yes?" I said, standing.

"It was sweet. Don't you think it was sweet?"

"You and me? Yes, it was."

"But it couldn't be anything more, could it?"

"I guess not," I said. "Still, it was special."

Then we locked stares. Suddenly her face twisted.

"We blew it, didn't we?" she said.

"What does that mean?"

"You don't know?"

"Yes," I said sorrowfully, "I know. It was the brandy, Nikki."

"It was the money, Peter."

"I guess," I said.

Suddenly we embraced. Not kissing. Just holding each other tightly. No sobs, no tears.

"If you ever get out to the Coast," she said, "look me up."

"Of course," I said.

122

I always awoke at eight in the morning. Struggled down to the kitchen in my robe, had juice, coffee, perhaps once slice of unbuttered whole wheat toast. (I was on a diet—again.)

I smoked two cigarettes, popped a handful of vitamin pills, and planned the day's work. Occasionally—but only occasionally—when I had

had a lot to drink the night before, I would belt a single ounce of cognac at breakfast. Just to settle the old tum-tum.

I was usually in the office by 9:30, phoning my boys to remind them of appointments. Then I worked on scheduling for the coming week, using job orders Martha had left on my desk. These included requests for call boys and escorts, which would be handled by Yancy Burnett.

If I had the first shift as host, I'd be out on the floor by noon. I skipped lunch and sometimes went out for dinner when Yance took over at seven. In the late evening, I frequently returned to the office for more pencil pushing.

When I worked the late shift, I had an early dinner. Then I relieved Yance and worked straight through to 2:00 A.M. I didn't eat anything at night, but drank more than I should. Clients insisted on buying me drinks, and it was difficult to refuse. I tried to stick to Perrier or white wine. I didn't succeed.

Occasionally, when I locked up at two in the morning, I'd walk down to Sixth Avenue to an all-night deli. I'd have a toasted bagel and a cup of tea, or something just as innocuous, while I unwound.

This place, the Friendship Deli, catered to the night people. It was a Losers' Place without booze, and I liked it. I listened to the talk and picked up some great shticks. Then, around 2:30 or 3:00 A.M., I went home to bed.

This regimen didn't dismay me—I could handle hard work—but it was a real downer when I got my first paycheck from Peter's Place, Inc. At $75,000 a year, with all the taxes taken out, it appeared that I'd be clearing about $700 a week.

That may sound like a lot, but you must realize that for the past two years I had been living off undeclared income and I was used to carrying several thousand in cash.

My Datsun 280-ZX had been delivered, so I had payments to make. With insurance, garaging, upkeep, etc., the expenses were horrendous. Fortunately I was paying no rent, and I could get all my food and booze at Peter's Place.

Still, I wasn't as affluent as I had been with the West Side cribs or the East Side penthouse. Martha admitted she was in the same situation; the money was good, but not half as good as it had been.

We convinced each other that because our new club was flourishing, we could look forward to the division of spoils at the end of the year. Then I might take a few weeks off and cruise the Greek isles.

I had a dream of Jenny Tolliver coming with me—but I knew it was only a dream.

123

One of the mistakes I made with the club was underestimating the volume of scenes. I should have realized that with the quadrupled number of bedrooms, the number of studs would also have to be increased.

I was on the phone to Clara Hoffheimer almost every day. She had increased our advertising campaign and made arrangements with several other theatrical agents and employment agencies. Eventually, I was certain, our work force would be adequate.

Meanwhile, Yancy Burnett and I filled in as often as we could. Late in January I had a personal scene with a woman named Norma. She arrived on time at my own bedroom and declined anything from the bar.

She looked around the room. "Very nicely done. Did you decorate it?"

"I made a few suggestions," I said modestly.

"It's very feminine," she said, looking at me closely. "The colors, the fabrics."

"For our clients," I assured her.

She continued to stare at me. "I should tell you," she said, "I am a psychotherapist."

"Are you bragging or complaining?" I said, smiling.

"That's a very interesting comment," she said. "What did you mean by that?"

I knew I was in for trouble.

She had a pallid, gawky body. There were stretch marks on her soft abdomen. Armpits and legs were unshaved. Her bush was extensive.

"You must realize," she said, "this is hardly a normal occupation for a man."

"I suppose not."

"It could be an Oedipal conflict," she said, "or perhaps the Don Juan syndrome. You're obviously intelligent. You must be aware of an unresolved personality disorder."

"To tell you the truth," I said, "I hadn't been aware of it."

She began to rub her hands over my naked body.

"You have a very silky ass," she said. "Silkier than mine."

"Thank you."

"Unless," she said thoughtfully, "it was a childhood psychic trauma. Do you recall any dreadful thing that happened when you were a boy?"

"My pet frog died," I said.

She turned to the full-length mirror affixed to my bathroom door. She went over to it, got down on her hands and knees, and turned her head to stare at her reflection.

"What are you doing?" I said.

"I don't want to cause any anxieties," she said. "If you're able to cope with your condition, to function as a reasonably well-adjusted adult without feelings of guilt or remorse, then there is no reason for apprehension or fear. Sit on me like you were riding a horse."

"I'm heavy."

"That's all right. I'm used to it."

I sat astride her bare back, trying to support most of my weight on my bent legs. It was damned uncomfortable. She kept her head turned, staring at our image in the mirror.

"Let's pretend," she said. "I'll be your horsey."

I swayed back and forth. I smacked her rump. "Giddap," I said.

"Go faster," she said.

I rocked away, a berserk dragoon. She began to move under me, still staring at our image.

"The important thing," she said, panting and beginning to sweat, "is to make an effort to understand why you have opted for this occupation. It may be a painful exploration, but you may achieve a certain measure of self-knowledge and, if not happiness, at least contentment. Faster! Faster!"

I gripped her with my knees. I grabbed a handful of her wiry hair, pulled her head up. I slapped her backside enthusiastically. She bucked and reared, beginning to snort.

Suddenly she collapsed, just fell facedown on the rug. I was left crouching over her, my knees trembling from the strain.

"Have you ever thought about seeking professional help?" she asked.

"Frequently," I said.

124

Martha and I had given a lot of thought to making the second-floor banquet room profitable. It was large and well-proportioned and could accommodate thirty at a sit-down dinner or seventy-five to a hundred at a buffet or cocktail party.

We sent a mailing to all our members reminding them that our Mardi Gras Room was available at a reasonable charge for private luncheons and dinners.

We sent a similar mailing to women's clubs, groups, sororities, associations, and organizations in the New York area, suggesting the room for business meetings, seminars, lectures, reunions, etc.

The initial response to both mailings was encouraging. Martha handled the reservations and made arrangements for flowers, favors, live music, etc. We also installed a public address system and made available a portable dais and lectern. These gatherings frequently garnered new members who had never before visited us.

Late in January the Mardi Gras Room was hired by a professional society of about fifty women real estate agents for a cocktail party. Judging by the noise they made, the party was a success.

When I came on the floor at 7:00 P.M. the party was breaking up, and women were streaming down the stairway from the second floor, laughing and talking brightly. Most of them departed, but at least a dozen found their way to the bar.

When I looked in about a half-hour later, I saw a disquieting sight. Women occupied all the tables, and a few were sitting at the bar. But four barstools were occupied by Anthony Cannis, Michael Gelesco, and two other male companions.

I watched from the doorway as the thugs chatted up the women at the bar. I walked over to Cannis, tapped him on the shoulder.

"Could I talk to you a moment?" I said. "In private."

He looked up in surprise, but swung off the barstool and followed me out into the hallway.

"Look," I said. "This is a private woman's club. We allow men in here only when they're guests of members."

He shrugged. "No harm intended," he said in a hoarse voice. "We just wanted to show our new place to a couple of pals."

"You're coming on to the women," I said. "This is not a pickup joint or a swinging singles bar. If the women want a bang, we have studs available. That's how we make our money."

"Okay, okay," he said, holding up his palms. "We'll finish our drinks and be on our way."

The four men came out of the bar about fifteen minutes later. They were all chunky, overdressed, flashy, and loud. Rings on their pinkies, and complexions made florid with facials and Chivas Regal.

They departed without bothering to say goodnight. I was disturbed. I had bad vibes from that confrontation with Cannis. I could have told him that just his presence lowered the tone of Peter's Place—but what did he know about class?

125

I had a date with Jenny Tolliver. She had just landed a new account and was in the mood to celebrate. The evening was a delight.

I picked her up in my new Datsun. It was the two-plus-two model with a T-bar roof. Very plush interior with all the options. Jenny was properly impressed.

We went to Lello's for dinner. Belon oysters and a rack of lamb, with a half-bottle of chablis for Jenny and a half-bottle of a new beaujolais for me. Grand Marnier soufflés to finish. I threw money around like there was no tomorrow.

"The important thing," I said pontifically, "is not to give a damn."

"You're drunk," Jenny said.

"I'm trying," I admitted. "How do you feel?"

"Floating," she said with a giggle. "Let's go dancing."

We drove downtown to a funky disco in Greenwich Village. I hadn't danced in a long time, but with the aid of a couple of vodkas, all my old cunning returned.

Jenny could get around all right, but she danced the steps, not the beat. She just wouldn't let go. I didn't tell her that. We went back to our table with me blowing like a grampus.

"And don't tell me I've put on weight," I said. "I know I have."

We looked around the crowded room, at the crazy costumes and the crazy makeup.

"You know what?" Jenny said. "We're the oldest people here."

I took another look. "You're right," I said. "Let's go."

We drove slowly uptown on Sixth Avenue. It was cold but clear, a diamond of a night.

I put on a Noel Coward tape and we listened to "Someday I'll Find You," which may be the greatest song ever written.

"You cad," Jenny said. "You know that always makes me cry."

"Weep away," I said cheerfully. "You don't want to go home yet, do you?"

"No," she said, her voice surprised, "I really don't."

"Do you know what I'd like to do?"

"Yes."

"No, you don't," I said hastily. "I'd like to take a carriage ride through the Park."

"You're insane," she said, laughing. "All right, I'd like that."

"One stop first," I said.

I pulled up before the first liquor store I found open, dashed in, and bought a half-pint of brandy.

"I think we're going to need it," I said.

But our brougham came equipped with a thick fake fur blanket we put over our laps and tucked in around our legs. It was cold enough, but the brandy saved us. We handed the bottle back and forth, taking little sips.

"I didn't tell you," Jenny said. "Arthur may get his play produced. Off Off-Broadway."

"That's wonderful!" I said enthusiastically, a marvelous bit of acting.

"If he can make the changes they want, they may do it this summer."

I didn't want to talk about Arthur. Successful Arthur.

"It's been a great evening, Jenny," I said. "But all our evenings were great."

"Not all," she said quietly.

"Almost all," I protested. "Until the last."

"Yes, she said. "Peter, are you happy doing what you're doing?"

"Can't we talk about us?" I said.

"What about us?"

Is there any intimacy more intense than traveling in a closed vehicle at night? Inside, all warmth and closeness. Outside, the dark, cold world held back.

When the carriage passed through the pale wash of streetlights, I caught brief glimpses of Jenny's face, shadows moving like moods. I saw the well-remembered serenity, the completeness. And the chestnut hair I loved falling like soft wings.

"What will it take to get us back together again?" I said. "What are your terms?"

"Stop doing what you're doing," she said promptly.

"And then what—become a failed actor again?"

"Peter, you're a clever man. There are a lot of things you could do."

Demonstrate potato-peelers at Woolworth's, sell ascots at the King's Arms, drive a cab, serve mushburgers at a health food restaurant, become a professional dog-walker—a lot of things.

"You know," I said gently, "please don't be offended, Jenny, but I must tell you this: If you became a hooker, God forbid, I would still love you and want to be with you. Or if you got hooked on drugs or had some horrible disease, I would never desert you."

She turned to look at me and took my hand. "I believe you, Peter. But if you'd make those sacrifices, why won't you stop doing the awful things you're doing?"

"If you truly loved me," I said, remembering what Martha had told me, "you wouldn't care what I was doing. I could be a thief, even a murderer, and you'd still love me."

"No," she said, shaking her head. "There's no way I can separate a man from what he does. I could never love a thief or a murderer."

"Or a pimp," I said bitterly.

She was silent.

"I make so much money," I said piteously, seeking to corrupt her, "and I have no one to spend it on."

She made no reply.

"Look," I said. "You may change."

"I don't think so, Peter."

"Can we at least see each other occasionally?" I said testily. "Tonight wasn't so bad, was it?"

"Tonight was grand," she said.

She leaned forward and kissed my cheek. That was more like it.

I spent the rest of the carriage ride doing new shticks for her that I had picked up at the Friendship Deli.

They broke her up.

I reclaimed my Datsun from the side entrance to the Plaza and I drove Jenny home. We double-parked in front of her place, finished the brandy, and had a cigarette.

"What's going to happen to you, Peter?" she asked.

"You keep trying to plan ahead," I told her. "You just can't do that. Two years ago, never in my wildest dreams could I have imagined I'd be doing what I am today. It's all up for grabs, Jenny. All you can do is go with the flow."

"You say that all the time," she said sadly. "Well . . . I better go up. Heavy day tomorrow. Thank you, Peter. It was fun, wasn't it?"

"It was."

Suddenly she said, "Please don't stop seeing me. Not yet."

Then she kissed me on the lips, whirled quickly, and was gone.

I sat for a few moments, alone in my jazzy new car. I really thought I was getting to her.

126

Early in February, we booked a feminist group into the Mardi Gras Room for a dinner and business meeting. It seemed to be a quiet, serious gathering. When it was over, several of the participants adjourned to the bar.

When I looked in about 10:30 P.M., a few guests were still there. Also present were Anthony Cannis and Michael Gelesco, both wearing dinner jackets, both being obnoxious.

This time I drew Gelesco into the hallway.

"Look," I said, as temperately as I could. "I asked you guys once before not to do this. You're ruining our reputation as a safe, pleasant, well-run establishment."

"We weren't doing nothing," Gelesco said.

"You're making fools of yourselves," I said. "The last thing in the world these women want is to be annoyed by a couple of hard-ons."

"Listen, Pete," he said. "We—"

"The name is Peter," I said stonily.

"Sure," he said. "Peter. Well, we own a nice piece of this joint— right? And you're telling me we can't come around and inspect our property?"

There was no mistaking the menace in his voice. I do not believe I am a coward, but I admit physical violence is not one of my favorite pastimes. Martha had called me a softy—that still rankled—but I preferred to think of myself as intelligently cautious.

"Michael," I said, "let me explain something to you. Most of our members are single women who come here for dinner, a drink, or to get laid, because they don't want the hassle of going someplace where guys are going to come on hard. If they want a drink and lunch or dinner and then go home —fine. If they want a scene, they can have that, too. They pay for everything, and in return they expect to be treated as a valued customer—which is exactly the way we try to treat them. It doesn't help when they go into the bar and find a couple of guys trying to make time with them. As I told Anthony, if our members want a bang, studs are available. All you're doing is cutting into our profits."

Gelesco stared at me. "Blow it out your ass," he said in the friendliest way imaginable, then turned and marched back into the bar.

127

I hadn't seen Arthur Enders since our dinner at Blotto's, and the last I'd heard of him was Jenny's announcement that his play was to be produced. I wasn't particularly happy when he called; the success of friends isn't the easiest thing to endure.

But I played my part and congratulated him.

"Jenny told me," I said, hoping it would stun him to hear that I had been seeing her.

"Yes," he said mildly, "she told me. It isn't a sure thing yet, Peter. I'm still working on rewrites. But if they're okay, the producers say they'll put it on this summer."

"Best of luck," I said, "and be sure to send me two on the aisle. How is Jenny?"

"Gee, she's great," he said warmly. "What a woman!"

"Yes," I said.

"The reason I called, Peter—have you seen King Hayes lately?"

"King? No. He's not with us anymore. Hasn't been for a couple of months."

"I know. He told me. Have you heard from him?"

"No. Why? Is anything wrong?"

"Well . . ." Arthur said in a troubled voice, "did you know he was living with a woman named Louella?"

"I heard about it."

"Well, he turned up at Blotto's about a week ago and said he had broken up with her. Gosh, he looked awful. He was practically falling-down drunk."

"On Manischewitz?"

"No, he's switched to warm gin. I mean, he was dirty and unshaved and staggering around. They kicked him out and told him not to come back."

"Banned from Blotto's? My God, Arthur, that's like being black-balled by McDonald's."

"Well, I got him back to that fleabag hotel on Broadway. I've gone over there a couple of times since. I thought maybe I could lend him a few bucks—you know? But I can't find him. You haven't heard from him?"

"Not a word."

"I don't know what to do," Arthur said. "He's such a great guy. I don't want him to become a bum."

"Arthur, he's not your responsibility."

"Peter," he said, shocked, "he's our *friend*. We just can't let him go down the drain."

I took a deep breath. "King has his problems to work out by himself."

"Golly, Peter, at least we can help him out with money. And let him know we care. That's *something*, isn't it?"

"I guess so, Arthur."

"Well, I'll keep trying to find him. If he gets in touch with you, will you let me know?"

"Of course. And best of luck with the play, Arthur. What's it called?"

"*Sunset at Dawn.*"

"I hope it's a sensational success," I said, lying in my teeth.

That call bothered me. It wasn't King's fate that was so disturbing; it was Arthur's reaction to it.

I wondered if I was lacking in something as simple as mercy. I didn't like to think that. I resolved henceforth to be kinder, more compassionate—to everyone. Like Lewis Stone in the "Andy Hardy" movies.

That was a role I could play.

128

Martha's first-floor office was smaller than the one Yancy and I used, but it was more cheerful, with house plants and some elephant figurines from her apartment. I was amused that she had placed them with raised trunks pointing at the door—for good luck.

When I entered, she was seated at her desk, reading a front-page story in *The New York Times.* She saw me, folded the paper quickly, put it aside. She needn't have bothered; I had read the article she was trying to conceal.

It concerned an announcement by Wilson Bowker that he intended to run for governor on a law-and-order platform. That included restoration of the death penalty, stiffer sentences, more jails, beefed-up state and local police forces, and a new law under which juveniles accused of felonies would be tried in adult courts.

Accompanying the article was a photograph of Mr. and Mrs. Wilson Bowker. There was absolutely no doubt that she was the woman I had met on 82nd Street.

"Got a minute, kiddo?" I asked Martha.

"Sure," she said. "Pull up a chair."

I sat alongside the desk. She leaned back in her swivel chair.

"Martha, I'm having trouble with Laurel and Hardy."

She and I always referred to Cannis and Gelesco as Laurel and Hardy.

"What's the problem?"

I told her how our partners were dropping by two or three nights a week and coming on strong with our customers.

"Not only are they not the type we want hanging around," I said, "but the bastards have actually scored a couple of times. The next thing you know, they'll be wanting to use the upstairs bedrooms. Martha, this has got to stop."

"I couldn't agree more," she said. "I thought I smelled cigar smoke in the bar the other day. Have you talked to them about it?"

"Twice," I said. "They told me, in effect, to fuck off."

"What do you want to do?"

"I want to go to Octavius Caesar, explain the situation, and ask him to order them to stop treating this place like a makeout joint. They'll listen to him. Will you back me up?"

"Absolutely," she said at once. "You and I own a majority interest; what we say goes. You want me to go to Caesar with you?"

"Do you want to?"

"No—but if you want me to, I will."

"I think I can handle it myself. I just wanted to make sure you were behind me on this."

"All the way," she assured me.

I started to rise, but she put out a hand to stop me, then flipped open the morning *Times.*

"You see this, Peter?" she said quietly, pointing to the Bowker article.

"Yes," I said.

"You know who he is?"

"Your fun-and-games boyfriend?"

She sighed. "I figured you'd see the picture of his wife and put two and two together. How long have you known?"

"Since last summer."

"Why didn't you tell me?"

"First of all," I said, "it's none of my business. And I thought that if you knew that I knew, it wouldn't help your peace of mind. The fewer people who know, the better, Martha."

"I know," she said. "But I'm glad you found out. I've got to talk to someone about it. I thought I could handle it, but I can't."

"Have you offered to leave him?"

"*Offered?* I *told* him I was splitting. He started crying again. He said if I left him, he'd leave his wife and kids. Or blow his brains out."

"Jesus!" I said. "You think he would?"

"He just might," she said sadly. "Peter, I like the guy, and he's given me some nice things. But I don't want to ruin his life."

"It sounds to me like he's running an emotional blackmail game on you."

"I guess," she said. "But I can't figure out how I can get loose. Give all this up? Go back to Chicago and start all over again?"

"Don't you do it," I said sternly. "Why should *you* make the sacrifice? You've got to think of yourself—first, last, and always. Look, I don't want to get personal, but you told me once that you're the only one who can pull his trigger. Maybe you should cut him off in the sex department. Throw away that riding crop."

She looked at me queerly.

"Did it ever occur to you," she said, "that I might be hooked too?"

129

To the best of my knowledge, Peter's Place was the first establishment of its kind in the Free World. We had to learn by trial and error, but fortunately most of the inevitable mistakes could be remedied.

For instance, the chef and kitchen crew brought in by Justice Development had experience in general restaurants and taverns. Initially, the menus we offered were standard male-oriented fare: fish, steaks, chops, stews—big portions with thick sauces.

After a flood of complaints from members, we realized that we were catering almost exclusively to weight-conscious women. So our menus were changed to feature light soups, omelets, salads, toasted sandwiches, and low-cal desserts. That was fine with us; prices remained high but our profit margin increased.

Still, the largest part of our income came from scenes in the upstairs bedrooms; now the rooms were beginning to yield peripheral profits; several members needed a discreet place to meet their lovers or to take a man they had just met for a quickie.

The bedrooms were made available at the usual hundred-dollar fee for an hour's use. Yance called us the No-Tell Motel.

In addition, we frequently had requests from out-of-town members to sleep alone overnight. If bedrooms weren't needed for late scenes, we rented them out at fifty dollars a night.

This necessitated special permits, licenses, inspections, etc., since we were operating as a commercial hotel. Justice Development Corp. obtained all the needed authorizations in record time. The grease demanded by the city departments was carried on our books as "Miscellaneous operating expenses."

By early March, Yancy Burnett and I had a file of more than a hundred studs, half of whom were regulars. The others, mostly aspiring actors or models, were available occasionally when in town, out of a job, broke, or bored.

We could now provide an almost infinite variety of colors, races, accents, proclivities, and eccentricities.

We had two midgets and a seven-foot-two basketball star. We even had an agile chap, much in demand, who could perform fellatio on himself. And, as you might expect, we had one stud called the Elephant Man—and not because his nose was long.

With this enormous increase in our stable, Martha had stopped auditioning each new addition. As she said, "I don't want to spend my entire day staring at the ceiling."

130

The prime motivation of our studs was, naturally, financial. But I suspected we offered another attraction for would-be actors. Frequently Peter's Place provided pure theater. It was a stage on which hopeful players could develop and hone their skills.

This concept of whorehouse as theater was not original with me, of course. (I once auditioned for a role in Genet's *The Balcony*, but I was rejected; they were looking for a younger type.) But the theory was proved out almost every day in our upstairs bedrooms.

Yancy Burnett agreed our business was as much concerned with illusions, masks, and fantasy as the theater. He told me the following story:

We had a regular named Edith, who made an appointment about once a month. She never requested any particular boy or type. She was a timid woman with large, pleading eyes and wore what looked like thrift shop clothes. I had never serviced her, but all the other studs called her Mrs. Gobble.

Yance said that while we were still at the penthouse, he had a scene with Edith. Her body was slack, shapeless and, for want of a better word, faded.

When they were both naked, she said in a faint voice, "Please tell me you love me."

Yance is a kind, gentle man. He said at once, "I love you, Edith."

"A lot?"

He knew then what she wanted, and played his part.

"I love you more than any woman I've ever known," he vowed.

"Yes!" she said. "More!"

"You're the sweetest, loveliest woman in the world," he said.

"Darling," she said, "I love you, too."

"I wish we could spend the rest of our lives together," he told her. "Just the two of us."

"Alone," she breathed. "Together. Forever and ever. Oh, my sweetheart."

They did not touch as they exchanged endearments. Yance admitted ruefully that after ten minutes he found it increasingly difficult to think of new and different ways to say "I love you." But this mousy woman, driven by want, made no objection to repetitions of his passion for her.

Eventually she asked him to sit in an armchair and knelt in front of him.

"I love you," he kept saying. "I love you so much."

Later, while they were dressing, she gave him a twenty-dollar tip, thanked him, and told him he'd done very nicely.

After Yance told me this story, he said, "There's theater for you. All illusion and dreams."

Early in March, Mrs. Gobble called for an appointment. I told

Martha I'd take it. Just curiosity, I suppose. I met Edith in my third-floor bedroom.

When we were both naked, she said in her soft voice, "Please tell me you love me."

131

After my conference with Martha concerning Cannis and Gelesco in our bar, I had called Octavius Caesar. His spinsterish secretary-receptionist had said the great man was absent for a few weeks, attending business meetings on the Coast.

I told her I'd like to see him as soon as he returned. She coldly informed me that she would call me back if Mr. Caesar wished to see me. The summons didn't come until the ides of March; an appointment had been approved for the next day at 3:00 P.M.

When I entered Caesar's office, I noticed a faint scent in the air. It was heavy, musky, and I was certain I had smelled it before, but I couldn't identify it.

"Well, young man," Octavius Caesar said, beaming and proffering a white flipper. "What a pleasure it is to . . . You're looking very . . ."

"And you, too, sir," I said, taking the chair he indicated. "I hope your trip was enjoyable."

"Most," he said. "Most." He gestured toward a file folder lying atop his ornate desk. "I returned to find . . . It contains the numbers for the first two months of Peter's Place. Encouraging. Definitely encouraging."

"Thank you, sir. We hope to do better as we gain experience."

"Of course," he said. "Hard work and stick-to-itiveness. Nothing like it, eh? Eh?"

I couldn't understand why he scared Martha. To me, he was an old fart, sliding into senility. He certainly didn't scare *me*.

There was silence while I wondered if I should launch into my complaint immediately. Meanwhile, Caesar smoothed the lapels of his pin-striped suit and touched the white piping on his vest.

"Well?" he said suddenly.

"Mr. Caesar, we have a problem which my associate, Miss Twombly, and I feel threatens the future of our enterprise. We bring it to your attention because we feel you are the only one who can solve it."

"Ah?"

I then explained our troubles with Michael Gelesco and Anthony Cannis. "I don't mean to insult them," I added hastily. "I am sure they are good, solid businessmen of excellent character. But their appearance and manner simply do not fit our concept of Peter's Place or the image we try to project to members and potential members."

He stared at me, expressionless. His plump white fingers drummed slowly, lightly, on the desktop.

"Who *are* your members?" he said finally.

"Moneyed women," I said promptly. "They shop at Bendel's and dine at Lutèce. About half are married, half are single, widowed, or divorced. Many have executive positions of great responsibility. They are elegant women, and the vulgar and the uncouth turn them off. If they are to patronize a private club, they want it to reflect their own refinement. Our members have class and they want their club to have class."

All that wasn't the exact truth—but it was close enough.

"Have you conveyed your objections to the . . . ?"

"I have, Mr. Caesar. They ignore me. That is why I am bringing the matter directly to you."

He made no direct response. Instead, he leaned forward over the desk, drew the file folder toward him. He flipped open the cover, peered down at the top document. Then he raised his head and looked at me with eyes of milky blue.

"You are a clever young man," he said with his wintry smile. "Do you have any suggestions for improving the profitability of Peter's Place?"

He had switched gears on me. But I am nothing if not glib, and I went along without missing a beat.

"Increasing the income of the Mardi Gras Room has number-one priority," I said. "I have several ideas on that which I hope to implement soon. Also, we should have a cloakroom near the entrance where members can check coats and packages. With an attendant, of course. The tips to be added to our gross revenue. Similarly, we should have an attendant in the ladies' room on the ground floor."

He stared at me. "I like the way you think," he said.

"Thank you, sir," I said modestly.

"What other improvements can you . . . ?"

"Well, sir," I said, "the size and physical layout of the club make it extremely difficult to develop the kind of facility I had in mind when I first conceived of Peter's Place."

"Oh?" he said. "And what did you envision?"

I made the most of this opportunity. I must have talked for ten minutes, nonstop, and I believe I had his full attention.

I told him that in my original concept, Peter's Place was to be an exclusive private club with Oriental rugs, antique furniture, crystal chandeliers, objets d'art, and standards of service equal to that of the finest hotels.

I said I wanted to have a beauty shop on the premises, a boutique, perhaps a flower shop and candy store. Maybe even a health club, a sauna, a masseuse. I wanted to offer every convenience an affluent woman might require.

"And upgrade the quality of our studs," I added. "Select younger, more attractive boys so we could raise our fee without losing customers."

Having gone that far, I decided to go all the way. I told Caesar that I had such faith in a class-act club that I could foresee an international chain of Peter's Places.

They could be wholly owned or licensed under a franchise arrangement.

When I finished my monologue, I sat back, crossed my legs, and looked for Caesar's reaction. There was none. Slowly his eyes rose until he was gazing into the air over my head.

"Regarding the original matter," he said. "Mr. Cannis and Mr. Gelesco. I agree with your assessment of . . . I will take care of the . . . Thank you for bringing it to my . . . And thank you for taking the time to . . ."

He rose to his feet, held out a soft, white hand. I pressed it and that was that.

132

I was in my office when Martha entered. It was a little before noon.

"I have Louella on the line," she said. "Remember her? The black woman who had the hots for King Hayes. She wants to talk to you."

I groaned. I hesitated. "All right," I said. "Switch it, will you, please."

"Mr. Scuro?" Louella said: a low, quavery voice.

"Yes."

"We've never met, but I'm a friend of King Hayes'. He spoke of you frequently as his best friend."

"Well . . ." I said cautiously, "I've known King for several years."

"Have you seen him, Mr. Scuro? Or heard from him?"

"No," I said. "Not for months."

"I've been trying to find him," Louella said, her voice beginning to break. "He just seems to have disappeared. I can't— I don't—"

And then she began to sob. It was dreadful listening to her. I closed my eyes, held the phone to my ear, and waited.

"Mr. Scuro," she said finally, sniffling, "are you still there?"

"I'm still here."

"Please forgive me. I shouldn't burden you with my troubles."

"We've all got troubles," I said. "That's what life is all about. Did you and King have an argument?"

"We broke up," she said, her voice cracking again. "He couldn't get a job and I didn't want him to . . . to . . ."

"To work for me?"

"That's right," she said. "I didn't. But I love that man so much, Mr. Scuro. Now I realize I don't care what he does as long as I can be with him."

I wanted to give her Jenny Tolliver's phone number and say, "Please call this woman and give her lessons in love."

Admiring that love so much, I said, "I'll tell you what I'll do: I'll try to find King. I really will. If I locate him, I'll tell him you want him back. Okay?"

"Would you do that?" she breathed. "Oh, thank you, thank you. And tell him no strings. He can work at any job he likes. I just want him back."

"I'll tell him that," I promised.

I had to serve as host until seven o'clock that night. When Yance relieved me, I got my Datsun out of the garage on 53rd Street. I drove over to the West Side and found a parking space about a block from Blotto's.

It was the same crowded, noisy, smelly spaghetti joint. I talked to the bartender and the maître d'. Neither had seen King since he was kicked out.

I left the Datsun where it was and walked over to Broadway. It started to drizzle, a mean, shivery drizzle. That was all I needed. I turned up my coat collar and plodded on to King's fleabag hotel.

The fat slob behind the desk said that King had checked out. No forwarding address.

I turned away, but he called, "Hey!" and I turned back.

"I know where maybe you could find him," the slob said.

"Where?"

He stared at me. I got out my wallet and gave him a five.

"Sometimes he hangs out at McDuff's. That's two blocks uptown, west of Broadway. Maybe you can find him there. Gassed to the eyeballs."

McDuff's was a boilermaker joint, but reasonably clean. I had a double vodka that tasted like water—and probably was. The bartender said that King had been in during the afternoon, but he'd finally kicked him out. For five he gave me the name of another place to try. Same story. King had run out of money and been booted out. For yet another fiver, the bartender suggested I try a shelter on the Bowery.

On my way back to the Datsun, I stopped at a liquor store to buy vodka. I just sat in the car, the heater going, until I stopped shaking. Then I had a belt. That was nice; now I was drinking from a liter bottle. The next thing you know, I'd be taking it intravenously.

I drove slowly downtown, leaning forward to peer through the misted windshield. At that very moment I could be in Peter's Place, warm and dry, maybe taking a jolly scene. I tried to imagine what the woman might look like. Jenny Tolliver.

The Bowery on a rainy March night is not exactly Acapulco. I drove around Third, but had to go down to First to find a place to park. Leaving my new Datsun there did not fill me with confidence. It wasn't the hubcaps I was worried about; it was the *wheels*.

The lobby of that shelter was something. There, but for the grace, etc., etc. I had a maniacal notion of recruiting our studs from that collection of derelicts and misfits. I had to make a joke about it if I wanted to survive.

The man in the cage looked through his records and said they had no King Hayes registered. While we were talking, some of the broken ghosts shuffled up and stood in a respectful semicircle. When I turned to leave, one of the skeletons put out a bony hand to stop me.

"A big black buck?" he said in a wheezy voice. He had no teeth at all. Just puffy gums.

"You've seen him?" I asked eagerly.

"Don't know if it was *him,*" he said, giving me a horrible grin, "but I saw a guy like that 'bout an hour ago. On the street. Bowery and Houston."

He could have been scamming me. But I peeled off the fourth fiver of the night and passed it to him. He stared at the bill in wonder, smoothing it in his grimy fingers. Then he looked up at me.

"May the good Lord bless you, sir," he said.

That made me feel better.

Well, anyway, I found King. Lying in the doorway of a shuttered pawnshop, covered with sodden newspapers. Next to him rested an empty half-pint bottle of gin. When I bent over him, his eyes opened and he recognized me.

"Peter?" he croaked.

"Don't move," I said. "Stay right where you are."

I trotted back to the Datsun, brought the car around (wheels intact), and pulled up at the curb alongside King. I finally got him on his feet. God, he weighed a ton, and the stink was indescribable.

Once he was in the car, I lowered the windows, preferring freezing to suffocation. We headed uptown on First. He was more coherent than I had expected.

"I really did it," he said. "Didn't I?"

"You really did."

I double-parked in front of Peter's Place and went inside. There were no customers in the bar or dining room, and Yancy said all bedrooms were free.

Yance helped get King inside. He could walk, but barely, and we both had to support him. We took him upstairs in the elevator, into my bedroom, and dumped him on my bed. He either went to sleep immediately or passed out.

Yance stood alongside the bed, hands in his pockets, looking sadly down at King Hayes.

"Poor fellow," he said. "What are we going to do with him?"

"Damned if I know."

"Well," he said, "no use trying to clean him up tonight. Let him sleep it off and get some solid food into him tomorrow. You can sleep in one of the other rooms, can't you?"

"Sure," I said. "No sweat. Thanks for the help, Yance. I'm going to garage my car. Meet you at the Friendship Deli for coffee and a bagel?"

"Good idea," he said. "In about twenty minutes."

I drove back to the garage, reliving the search for King Hayes.

I didn't know what I was doing. Oh, I knew what I was *doing,* but what was my motivation?

133

Once a month, usually on a Thursday night, Martha and I met in the Mardi Gras Room with Cannis and Gelesco, Gotwold and Iggy, and an attorney and accountant representing the Justice Development Corp.

Following my complaint to Octavius Caesar, Cannis and Gelesco had stopped appearing at the bar of Peter's Place. But at the March meeting, their manner toward me was completely affable, even genial. Caesar must have issued shape-up orders and they were obeying.

We went over the books for the current month to find we were clearing *thousands* every week. Peter's Place was a money machine; there seemed to be no end to the golden flow. And the call boy and escort services showed a gratifying increase, too.

I presented my suggestions for attendants in the front cloakroom and in the first-floor ladies' room. We agreed to try it for a few months until we could decide if it was sufficiently profitable.

Then we got down to a more serious matter. About a month previously, Peter's Place, Inc., had received a letter from an attorney threatening a lawsuit on behalf of his client, a woman. She claimed she had contracted herpes after a scene with one of our studs. That would be a difficult claim to prove in court—but who wanted the publicity?

We called in Casper Meerjens, the private investigator who had helped us out on the Susan Forgrove business. We figured the plaintiff, a married woman, might be so promiscuous that there was no possible way she could prove that she had caught a venereal disease from a single contact with one of our boys.

As it turned out, the lady wasn't promiscuous at all—but her husband was. That guy was some cocksman! According to Meerjens, he'd bang anything that moved. It seemed obvious to us that the wife had contracted the disease from her husband, who transmitted it from one of his bimbos.

So Oscar Gotwold had a meeting with the complaining attorney and laid out the evidence collected by our investigator. The result was that the lady signed a release and we paid her a grand for her trouble and lawyer's fees.

"In my opinion," Gotwold said, "there is absolutely no way we can protect ourselves from nuisance suits of this kind."

"I asked around," Iggy Samuelson said. "If you're thinking about insurance, forget it. No one will touch it."

We finally agreed there was no solution. Lawsuits were just one of the risks we'd have to live with.

But the accountant for Justice Development sensibly suggested that if we were vulnerable to lawsuits, the smart thing to do would be to keep our cash reserves absolutely minimal.

That way, if we lost a suit, our assets would be as low as possible. There was a simple way to do that.

We were obligated to make annual payments on our loans from Vigor Venture Capital, Inc., and Daring Financial Corp. With unanimous approval, these could be converted to monthly payments, thus keeping our current bank balance low.

Gotwold and Samuelson assured us that it was the smart thing to do. So we signed the papers.

134

The moment I walked into the room, I recognized Clara Hoffheimer's scent as the one in Caesar's office. It was rather vulgar, I thought.

My second reaction was to her office. It had been completely redone:

the whole place painted, wall-to-wall carpeting installed, drapes hung at the glistening window. Sol's battered wooden furniture had been replaced by glass and stainless steel. Everything gleamed.

We had been paying Clara a nice buck for the studs she supplied, but there was no way she could have financed that renovation on what she was getting from us. I figured she was giving Octavius prune juice enemas—or something just as outlandish.

"Beautiful," I said, looking around.

"You really like it, Peter?" she asked.

"I really do. You've done wonders, Clara."

"I may hire an assistant," she said casually. "Business has been good."

"Glad to hear it."

She still looked like a Christmas tree, with dangling jewelry and some feathered ornament stuck in her frothy hair. And she still overflowed her tight dress. She was the only woman I ever met who made anorexia attractive.

I handed over her stake in an envelope.

She took out the cash and counted it, then took a small ledger from a desk drawer and checked the total. Sol never would have done that in my presence. He had class.

"Right to the penny," she said, putting the money and ledger away.

"Glad to hear it."

"How's your business?" she asked.

"So-so," I said, flipping a palm back and forth.

"That's not what I hear. I hear business is booming."

"Oh?" I said. "Where did you hear that?"

"Here and there," she said. "Need more studs?"

"Always," I said. "You know how unreliable those boys are. We'll always need new studs."

"Peter," she said, "I've got a crazy idea I want to try out on you."

"Sure."

"Last week a kid comes in here. A Marine, in uniform. He's getting out in a month and he's decided he wants to be an actor. If he's an actor, I'm the Queen of Sheba. Anyway, he wants to go to acting school, but he hasn't got the money. He wanted to know if he could get bit parts, crowd scenes, extra work—stuff like that—to help him out while he was going to school. I explained the facts of life to him—the competition, the unions, and all that —and then I pitched him on working at your joint. He was agreeable. He's a nice, big kid with a peaches-and-cream complexion and red hair I'd give my left tit to have."

"He sounds fine," I said, nodding.

"And he gave me my crazy idea," she said. "The ads we're running aren't bringing in the volume we need. But what about the armed forces? There are a dozen army, navy, and Coast Guard bases around here. And ships in port with hundreds of sailors. If we spread the word that they can pick up an easy buck for getting their rocks off, we should have a new supply source."

"Clara, you're a genius," I said admiringly.

"And these kids are clean," she went on. "They can get court-martialed for the clap."

But something bothered me. "Do they wear their uniforms?" I asked her. "The last thing in the world we need is fifty sailors lined up outside Peter's Place."

"No problem," she said. "They can wear civvies on liberty."

I pondered a moment. "Some women go for uniforms."

"So they bring their uniforms in a little bag," she said, "and put them on before they meet the customer."

"And medals," I said. "They should wear their medals and ribbons. Clara, it's a great idea. We'll have all the studs we need."

"And you can put up a sign in your bar or dining room," she said, grinning: "THE FLEET'S IN."

135

Detective Luke Futter came to see me during the first week in April. I called in Martha, and the three of us sat in my office. I ordered a double bourbon for Futter. Martha and I didn't drink anything.

Since we had moved to the townhouse, the bagman had been collecting $10,000 a month in cash. From the looks of him, his share of the shmear had gone on his back. He was a symphony in gray and blue, with a new Concord wristwatch and a bracelet of silver links heavy enough to anchor the *QE2*.

"I've got bad news and I've got bad news," he said with his loopy smile. "You're going to get raided."

"Hey," Martha said. "Wait a minute. We're paying you ten grand a month to avoid that."

"It's coming out of a different division," he said, shrugging. "Apparently some of your ladies are running up big bills here, and their husbands are screaming bloody murder. They want the place investigated."

"We've got all the permits and licenses we need," I told Futter. "And an army of lawyers making sure we're clean."

"Have you got a license for running a disorderly house?" he said. "That's what they're going to try to pin on you."

"All right," Martha said. "What's it going to cost us?"

"Not much," the detective said, running a palm over his marcelled hair. "I can't stop the raid, but for a measly grand I can get maybe a day's advance notice of when they're going to hit. You'll be able to empty out those upstairs bedrooms and make it look like you're running a nice, quiet private club."

"Who gets the grand?" Martha demanded.

"A guy who works in the division I mentioned. I've used him before, and he's straight."

"We don't have much choice, do we?" I said.

"That's the way I see it," Futter said affably.

We told him we'd add the extra thousand to his April take, and he was satisfied with that. After he left, Martha and I looked at each other.

"We're getting a royal screwing," she said wrathfully. "For all we know, he suggested the raid himself."

"Even if it's legitimate," I said, "I'm certain the other guy won't be getting the whole grand. A couple of hundred if he's lucky."

"Futter's getting greedy," Martha said, shaking her head. "I'm beginning to get bad vibes about that guy."

"What can we do about him, Martha? He's got us by the short hair. And you've got to admit so far we haven't had too much trouble with the law."

"So far," she said darkly. "But if he puts the arm on us again, I think we better let him deal with Cannis and Gelesco."

"What can they do?"

"Oh . . ." she said vaguely, "they'll think of something."

136

All the old bromides—"Nothing succeeds like success," "Money goes to money," "The rich get richer and the poor get bupkes"—were proved by the growing prosperity of Peter's Place. Much of our success was due to hard work and imagination. But part of it, I admit, was just luck.

For instance, a few members asked if they could meet in the Mardi Gras Room for an evening of bridge. We said sure, and even provided cards, bridge table, and chairs. The players ordered drinks steadily from the downstairs bar.

That started in the middle of February. By the middle of April, we had six tables of bridge and three of poker, plus backgammon, going in the Mardi Gras Room every Friday night. Apparently that was the night many husbands "went out with the boys," and their wives were happy to attend what we called Game Night at Peter's Place. There was a lot of heavy betting.

We still didn't charge for this added amenity, but the number of drinks consumed by Game Night players rose to the point where we had to set up a small bar in the Mardi Gras Room. We also offered a limited sandwich menu. And it wasn't unusual for players (especially winners) to hire a stud following the evening's activities. We even had one member dash upstairs and have a quick scene while she was dummy in a bridge game.

We also increased the income from our downstairs bar, due to a simple improvement that was my idea.

"We need an attraction in there," I said to Yancy Burnett. "Something to pull in customers before and after their scenes, or even when they just want to relax and unwind."

"Like what?" Yance said.

"A piano player," I said. "A guy who knows all the old songs and can sing romantic ballads. It would be great if he was young and good-looking, but we don't want him competing with our studs."

"Gay," Yance said at once. "You want a handsome, talented, gay piano player who can sing."

"Can you find a guy like that?"

"I'll try."

He came up with a gem. The boy's name was David, and he had a warm, growly voice that was great for Cole Porter tunes. He was beautiful in a juvenile way, and our customers loved him. We got him a baby grand, and he performed nightly from 9:00 until 1:00 A.M.

We named the bar the Dream Room, hung heavy drapes over the painted walls, and dimmed the lighting. David built up a faithful following and our liquor sales almost doubled. Clients knew he was gay, but it only added to his attraction. We paid him minimum scale, but he did very well with tips and was frequently hired for private parties.

"David's a winner," I said to Yance. "Where did you find him?"

"In my bedroom," he said.

137

The rehabilitation of King Hayes took longer than I figured. It was a week before he was completely off the sauce and another before the shakes stopped.

Meanwhile he was sleeping in my bedroom. Then, after he was sober and reasonably presentable, he moved into one of the other bedrooms. I gave him money for shaving gear and clean clothes; he had sold everything he owned for booze.

"I don't want your goddamned charity," he said roughly.

"Charity hell!" I said. "It's a loan, and if you don't pay it back, I'll take it out of your black hide."

Louella called every day, but he refused to speak to her, and he continually bemoaned the fact that he hadn't been able to get a job.

Finally I said, "You want a job? They need help in the kitchen. Mopping floors and carrying out garbage. Minimum hourly wage."

He promptly took it.

LAWRENCE SANDERS

I didn't know why I was doing this. I liked King, of course, and I felt sorry for Louella, but, in the back of my mind, I may have been thinking of getting him back to studding.

When I worked late as host, he'd usually go over to the Friendship Deli with me for coffee-and. We spent a lot of time just talking, and he told me what had happened with Louella.

"She's so much smarter and finer than I am," he said. "After a while I began to hate her for it. Not that she tried to lord it over me. She was just her, and I was me, so I took it out on her. Once I even belted her. That's when I walked out. Because I was scared I might really hurt her. She was making me feel disgusted with myself. She was paying for everything and I couldn't make buck one."

"She wants you back, King; I told you that. No strings. She doesn't care. She just wants *you.*"

He was silent.

"Do you love her?" I asked him.

"I guess," he said in a low voice. "I know I admire her greatly. But that was the reason I walked out. Jesus, Peter, I'm all mixed up."

"Aren't we all?"

Suddenly he stared at me. "You want me back doing scenes, don't you?"

"It's entirely up to you."

He groaned. "I don't know what to do."

"Go with the flow," I told him.

I remembered the time, not so long ago, when I thought my life was being determined by chance and accident. Or I was being manipulated by people with more money or power or resolution.

Now I was doing the pushing.

138

When the studs finished their scenes, they stopped at my office to pick up their fees and get their next assignments. I heard some weird tales from them about clients, but none as unusual as the one I myself serviced late in April.

It started when Martha buzzed and asked if I'd come into her office for a moment. When I went in, I saw a woman seated at the side of the desk. Martha introduced us.

The visitor was, I judged, about forty. Steely-gray hair drawn back in a bun. A high, smooth brow. Pinched features. Thick glasses in horn rims. She was wearing a black suit so severely tailored that it looked like a uniform. A tight, controlled lady.

"Would you explain to Mr. Scuro exactly what it is that you require," Martha said.

"It is not something *I* require," the woman said crisply. She turned to me. "Mr. Scuro, I live and work in Washington, D.C. I am employed as executive aide to—well, let's just say she is one of the three most important and influential women in government. If I told you her name—which I will not—you would recognize it immediately. If you saw her, you would identify her. I am here to explore the possibility of my becoming a member of this, ah, association. I feel your charges are high—but that's neither here nor there. The purpose of my joining is to lend my card to my employer. That is permitted?"

"Yes," I said cautiously, "provided the privilege is not abused."

"It won't be," she said grimly. "And I have no intention of using the card myself."

"Let me get this straight," I said. "You want to purchase a membership in your name. But the only purpose is to lend your card to your employer. Is that correct?"

"Yes."

"Why doesn't she purchase her own membership?"

"If I told you who she is, you would understand. Complete discretion is absolutely necessary."

"I explained that complete discretion can't be guaranteed," Martha said. "The lady may be seen entering or leaving. And the boy assigned will probably recognize her; we can't swear he won't talk."

We all stared at each other. Then I had an idea.

"Do you think I'd do?" I asked her.

She inspected me coldly.

"Yes," she said. "I think you will be satisfactory."

We talked for another twenty minutes and this is what we arranged:

The VIP would drive up from Washington in a modest car. She would be dropped off at Peter's Place at 3:00 A.M., when I would be the only one in the building. (I didn't bother mentioning King Hayes. He'd be asleep anyway.)

At 4:00 A.M., after the scene was completed, the car would pick up the famous lady and ferry her back to the nation's capital.

"Can *you* keep your mouth shut?" our visitor said, giving me a chilly stare.

"If you don't think I can," I said, "then forget about the whole thing."

"Very well. But I insist on the right to inspect the, uh, chamber for hidden cameras and recording devices before . . ."

We assured her that she could. Then she paid the membership fee, dues, and the price of the scene, all in cash. After she left, Martha and I spent time speculating on who the VIP was and ended up making a ten-dollar bet.

The whole thing went smoothly. Martha was alerted from Washington: "This is Cupid. Tomorrow night."

The car pulled up about 3:15 A.M. Two women scurried across the sidewalk and the car pulled away. I unlocked the door, then locked it again when they were inside.

The executive aide went up to my third-floor bedroom to inspect the premises. Back downstairs, the VIP was standing absolutely motionless in the little foyer. She was wearing a full-length mink coat, a floppy fedora, and dark sunglasses.

"My name is Peter," I said, smiling. "May I offer you something from the bar?"

"Thank you, Peter," she said in a musical voice. "A cognac would be nice."

When the VIP took off her hat and sunglasses, I recognized her immediately. Martha and I had both been wrong. She was a *very* important lady.

In her early fifties. A big, masterful woman. A direct gaze; a face drawn more from weariness than age.

I poured us each a Rémy and we sat quietly, chatting until the executive aide reappeared.

"All clear," she reported.

I told her to help herself to anything she wanted.

"Shall we take the bottle of brandy with us?" I asked the famous lady.

"Splendid idea," she said.

I locked the door of the bedroom behind us and helped her off with her coat. She was wearing a dress with too many flounces and ruffles.

She held out her glass. "I think I'd like another cognac."

I poured her a stiff jolt and she knocked it back like a longshoreman. Then we undressed.

She looked down at her ruined body. "I wish you could have seen me thirty years ago," she said. "I was something."

"You're something now," I said, and she gave me a wry glance.

But the second brandy had lifted her spirits, if not her flesh, and we had fun in bed. I thought she'd be the "Do this, do that" type, but she wasn't. I guess successful executives learn to delegate authority.

"My God," she said once. "I remember doing that on the Cape when I was eighteen. And I haven't done it since, dammit!"

I gave a good performance, being tender and loving when I sensed she wanted it and rough when she wanted that.

When we finished, she held my face in her palms and said, "Thank you, doctor."

When we went downstairs, the executive aide was sipping a glass of Perrier. She jumped to her feet when we entered.

"Are you all right?" she asked her boss anxiously.

"Divine," the famous lady said. "I may adopt this young man."

"Take me," I said. "I'm yours."

We laughed, but the aide wasn't amused. When the car pulled up precisely at 4:00 A.M., I turned off the burglar alarm and unlocked the door.

"Have a safe trip back," I said. "Keep up the good work."

The lady had put on her fedora and sunglasses. She stepped close to me.

"If I had met . . ." she said. "Things might have been . . ."

Then she laughed musically and bent forward to kiss my cheek.

She never appeared at Peter's Place again. I figured she was either dissatisfied with me or fearful of running the risk. I preferred the latter.

But about a week later, I received a package postmarked Washington, D.C. No return address. No card inside. It was a gold money clip in the shape of a dollar sign.

139

I received a phone call from the gorgon who guarded the office portal of Octavius Caesar. The great man wanted to see me at 3:00 P.M. I was scheduled for hosting that afternoon, but Yancy Burnett said he'd switch shifts with me.

So I started downtown at 2:30, not a little concerned by Caesar's summons. Had I offended him?

But when I entered his private office, I knew at once that I wasn't to be spanked. He was all beams, his jowls quivering with geniality. He had me pull an armchair close to the side of the desk.

I thanked him for taking care of the problem of Cannis and Gelesco so quickly and efficiently. He waved my thanks away and assured me that I should always feel free to seek his advice and/or assistance.

Then he got down to business. He said he had been much impressed at our previous meeting with my elegant vision of Peter's Place. He said that I was dreaming big, but that he did not think my dreams were beyond the realm of possible fruition.

That was the word he used—"fruition."

This stroking continued for several minutes. Then he withdrew a folder from his top desk drawer and slid it across to me.

He said that he had put my ideas in written form and wanted to present my proposals to his associates. He hoped this presentation would produce sufficient investment funds to make my dream a reality.

He asked me to look over what had been written to be certain it accurately reflected my thinking.

Either Octavius Caesar or someone in his employ had done a good job. He had encapsulated my ideas in five typewritten pages: how the places were to be decorated, the customers sought, the extra services offered.

The stud, call boy, and escort divisions were to be the basis of the enterprise, but food and beverages, shops, health club facilities, etc., would provide additional income. He had even included my suggestion for an in-house masseuse.

"Before we go further," he said, "I want you to know . . . This is your idea, and nothing will be done . . . But you must realize that without sufficient financing, the best idea will remain just a . . ."

He said that in the event sufficient venture capital was available, and Peter's Place, Inc., underwent an enormous expansion, Martha and I would both be assured of high executive positions, greatly increased incomes, and a hefty share of the stock in the chain.

I told him he certainly had my permission to discuss the proposal with his associates. He then asked me what I thought of the presentation and if I would suggest any changes or additions.

I said it read very well to me, but that there were two new developments of which he should be aware.

I told him about the popularity of David, our pianist in the Dream Room, and suggested entertainment could eventually include small bands, singers, and comedians.

Then I told him about Game Night in the Mardi Gras Room, and how it had grown so rapidly, with bridge, poker, and backgammon players making heavy personal wagers.

"At the moment," I said, "we are not charging admission to Game Night. I know nothing about gambling, sir, but couldn't the house take a percentage of the winnings, or provide dealers in the poker games, or set up some system to profit from the betting?"

"Clever," he said. "Very clever. I shall certainly include these . . . And I shall keep you informed as to . . . And speaking of time . . ."

He withdrew a handsome gold hunter from his waistcoat pocket, flipped open the cover, glanced at the face, snapped the watch shut, and slid it back into his pocket, all in one swift, fluid motion.

He rose to his feet, held out a white flipper. "So good of . . . I appreciate your . . . Please keep in . . . We must have . . ."

I closed the door of the outer office and headed toward the bank of elevators. An ascending elevator stopped and two men got out and walked toward me.

One was short, dumpy, wearing a bowler and chomping on a cigar. He had a face you see in hundred-year-old cartoons in which politicians were made to look like dogs and donkeys. This one looked like a mournful baboon.

The other man was tall, stalwart, handsome. He was dressed with casual elegance and I recognized him immediately. He was Wilson Bowker, would-be governor and Martha's bed-partner.

I stared straight ahead as I passed them. The baboon was muttering, so I didn't hear a thing. At the elevator bank, I punched the down button. Then I turned to look back.

The two men entered the offices of Octavius Caesar.

140

On May 2, Detective Luke Futter called to say the raid would take place at 1:30 P.M. on May 4.

Martha and Yance went to work, canceling all the appointments for May 4. I alerted the maître d', bartender, chef, and kitchen help, telling them we anticipated an inspection, so the premises had to comply with all the health and sanitary codes.

Then Martha and I dug out all our licenses, permits, and authorizations. We put them in order and displayed those requiring posting. We sent our daily records to Iggy and our files and most of our cash to Oscar Gotwold.

By 1:30 P.M., May 4, Peter's Place looked like a stodgy private dining club for women. Luncheon was being served at four or five tables, and there were half a dozen customers drinking quietly in the Dream Room. Cannis and Gelesco had been alerted and were wise enough to stay away.

Yance calmly came into my office to tell me they were here.

I went out to the foyer, followed by Martha. The police captain in command showed us his identification and handed me a search warrant.

I told him we had nothing to hide but to please try not to disturb our guests.

They were inside for almost an hour. The plainclothesmen in charge headed first for the upstairs bedrooms, moving fast, to find all the rooms empty and the beds neatly made. Then they went through the Mardi Gras Room, the offices, the Dream Room, the kitchen and dining area. After they saw the empty bedrooms, their search was perfunctory.

When the plainclothesmen departed, a police captain came into my office and requested we show him our licenses and permits, which we did.

"Why all the bedrooms?" he asked casually.

"Sometimes our members like to sleep over," Martha said. "They come in from the suburbs to see a show, and then they have dinner and a few drinks. It's easier to sleep here than drive home at two in the morning. Or try to catch a train or bus."

"Uh-huh," the captain said, rising to his feet. He was a big, porky man with a perpetual smile. He poked at our stack of licenses.

"Looks like everything's in order," he said. "Sorry to have bothered you folks."

"That's quite all right," Martha said.

He started for the door, then stopped and turned back.

"Who tipped you?" he said, smiling.

"I beg your pardon?" I said.

"If I find him," the police captain said, still smiling, "I'll have his balls."

141

Game Night took care of the Mardi Gras Room Friday evenings, and Martha was able to book two or three meetings or parties a week. But on most afternoons and nights, the room was a frustrating waste of space.

Then Martha came up with the great idea of having the Barcarole Boutique sponsor a fashion show to be held in the Mardi Gras Room at 11:00 A.M. Admission was free to all members and to Barcarole customers who had received invitations.

The show was a success. It was covered by fashion reporters, and gave the Barcarole a lot of free publicity and increased sales. And we got substantial new memberships. More importantly, we benefited because many of the women who attended the performance moved on to the Dream Room after it was over.

Inspired by this, Martha began to book more fashion shows, sponsored by stores, boutiques, and designers. We booked fur shows, a jewelry show, a perfume show. A cosmetic company tried a combination product-presentation and makeup demonstration. It was so successful that they signed up for six months of weekly shows.

It seemed to Martha and me that the marketing possibilities were almost endless. We were tapping a segment of the buying public that apparently had never before been treated as a distinct demographic group.

We knew we were on the right track when we were approached by a company that sold sexy lingerie by mail order. They made a generous offer for our membership list. We were tempted, but finally turned them down, feeling we would be sacrificing our clients' discretion and privacy.

Yancy Burnett was present at this discussion, and he laughed.

"What's so funny?" Martha said

"Oh," he said, "all this talk about marketing possibilities, demographic groups, and merchandising our mailing list. Peter's Place is just a glorified crib, isn't it?"

Even if he was right, he shouldn't have said it. Who can live without illusions?

142

Luke Futter called again.

"I hear you made out like a bandit," he said, laughing.

I didn't appreciate the comparison.

"I think maybe it's time we had a talk," he said.

He didn't want to be seen visiting Peter's Place too frequently, so we had to meet elsewhere. Martha and I finally decided on her apartment.

"He wants more money," she told me.

"How much, do you think?"

"Another couple of grand at least."

We met at ten o'clock. I brought Futter a tumbler of bourbon. There was no need to psych him, so Martha and I had white wine spritzers.

"Well now," he said with his customary smirk. "That cockamamie raid went off just fine, didn't it?"

"No strain, no pain," Martha acknowledged.

"Sure," Futter said, inspecting his manicured fingernails. "Well," he went on, "you got a friend in high places. Me."

He looked at us as if expecting to be showered with gratitude. When none was forthcoming, he continued . . .

"The trouble is, I don't do all this myself. There are the squad guys, the precinct guys, and then we have the uppers, the brass. Everyone gets a taste. So that ten-grand pad a month don't go too far."

"How much?" Martha asked stonily.

"How much?" he said. "Well, now that I proved I can deliver, I figure twenty-five Gs a month would be about right."

"You're crazy!" I burst out.

"No," Futter said thoughtfully. "I've got a pretty good idea of what you're netting from that hot-pillow joint of yours, and you can go for that much easy—if it means keeping open. Which it does."

His smarmy grin had suddenly disappeared. Now his face was chilled, bloodless, the same person who engineered the disappearance of Sidney Quink.

"Look," Martha said. "You're leaning too hard. Maybe a couple of grand extra. But you're talking about a pad of three hundred thousand a year."

"Well . . ." the detective said, inspecting his gleaming fingernails again, "I can talk to my people. Maybe I can squeeze the pad down to twenty a month. But I can guarantee you that they won't go below that."

"Twenty grand a month?" Martha said furiously. "No way!"

"Hey," he said. "Wait a minute. You people have been nice to me and I've been nice to you. We're friends—right? I hate to muscle friends. So when I tell you that twenty thousand a month is the price for staying open, believe me. Listen, there are guys involved in this you don't even know about. I mean, it goes all the way up. Me, I'm getting a nibble. That's all—a nibble."

"Who gets the rest?" I asked.

The detective looked at me pityingly. "You expect me to name names? Look, you haven't been hassled, have you? I mean, street cops, health and fire inspectors, and all that shit. So your grease is working, right? And you want to keep it that way. Twenty big ones a month won't break you. Write it off. You can lose it somewhere in your tax return. Think of it as insurance."

Martha's reaction was unexpectedly mild.

"Put that way," she said, "it makes sense. But we can't give you a yes or no right now."

"Oh sure," Futter said, his loopy grin returning. "Talk it over with those swell guys from Roman Enterprises. I'm betting they'll tell you that the way to get along is to go along. As the old saying goes, you can't fight City Hall."

He rose, gathered up a ridiculous feathered hat and a coat that looked like it had been cut from a horse blanket.

"Ta-ta," he said. "Talk it over. Take your time. But twenty Gs is the bottom line. I'll be in touch."

After the detective departed, Martha made me lock and chain the door behind him.

"Well?" I said.

"Peter, do you still have a copy of that tape I made when Futter agreed to take care of Quink?"

"Sure, I have it. In my safe deposit box."

"And I have mine. I think we better meet with Oscar Gotwold and play it for him."

"You're figuring to lean on Futter?"

"Lean on him?" she said wrathfully. "Remember what that police captain said after the raid? If he finds the guy who tipped us, he'll cut off his balls. We're going to do it for him."

143

I had been seeing Jenny Tolliver two or three times a month. I invited her out more often than that, but she was working twelve hours a day at her new business, and some nights she was just too tired to go out.

But she always asked me to try again. I thought she was definitely thawing.

Around the middle of May, she finally agreed to have dinner with me. And on a Saturday night! But my elation was dampened when she explained:

"I usually see Arthur on Saturday night, but he's busy with rehearsals."

"Oh?" I said. "His play is being produced?"

"Yes, it's opening in July. Isn't that wonderful?"

"Wonderful," I said.

We went to Christ Cella which, for my money (and it takes a lot), is the best steak joint in Manhattan. I had a rare sirloin and Jenny had sliced filet. We consumed enough protein that night to keep a tribe of aborigines dancing for a month.

"By the way," I said, "when you see Arthur, tell him . . ."

Then I explained that I had found King Hayes, who was off the booze and in good condition.

"Oh, I'm so happy to hear that," Jenny said. "I really like King, and I know Arthur was worried. What is he doing now?"

"Working in our kitchen."

Jenny stopped eating and looked at me. "You have a kitchen?"

"Of course. With a dining room, naturally. And a bar with a piano player. We also put on fashion shows and have a Game Night for card players."

"Oh," she said confusedly. "I thought . . ."

So I gave her a short lecture on what Peter's Place was and what it was going to be: an international network of exclusive private clubs for moneyed women, offering entertainment and shops and health facilities— all under one roof.

She listened intently. I knew she was fascinated.

"What do you think?" I asked when I had finished.

"I had no idea it was a place like that."

"Do you want to join?" I asked, looking at her. "I can get you a free membership."

"No," she said. "Thanks."

"Well, would you like to come back to see it? Maybe have a drink at the bar?"

"No," she said. "Thanks."

So we went instead to the Stanhope, sat in a corner banquette, shared a bottle of Heidsiek, and popped salted peanuts.

"Tell me more about Peter's Place," Jenny said.

So I did.

She sighed. "Peter, do you think you'll ever get out of it?"

"Jenny, if all our plans go through, it's going to be a huge, huge organization. I'll be a top executive. They need me. I'll never have another opportunity like it."

"What about your acting?"

"I do more acting in one day at Peter's Place than I did in a year of looking for theater work. I'd be a fool to give this up. I'm making a lot of money at something I'm good at."

"And something you enjoy," she stated flatly.

"Yes," I said defiantly, "I do enjoy it. Every day is different, with new problems and new solutions. The whole place is really my idea—and it's a thundering success."

She twisted sideways to stare at me. "Look," she said. "Isn't it a place where women pay men to go to bed with them?"

First Yancy Burnett and now her.

"That's part of it," I admitted, "but not *all* of it."

"I'm getting awfully sleepy," she said. "Could you drive me home now, Peter?"

I double-parked the Datsun outside her apartment house and turned to look at her.

"Jenny," I said, "one of these days I wish you'd draw me a blueprint of your moral code."

"You don't need one," she said. "It's very simple: Some things are right and some are wrong."

"We have almost a thousand members," I told her. "Are you going to tell me that you're right and all those women are wrong?"

"They're them," she said, "and I am me."

"Just tell me who's getting hurt," I said, falling back on my old argument. "Tell me what's so terrible."

In the pale glow of the dashlight, she looked infinitely sad and infinitely beautiful. Sometimes she infuriated me just by tempting me to throw it away and live the way she dictated. That sacrifice lured.

"What's so terrible," she said quietly, "is the quality of life. You're cheapening it, making a commercial joke of something fragile and precious."

"I don't know what you mean."

"Yes, you do. You know exactly what I mean. Thank you for the dinner, Peter."

She swung out of the car and ran into her lobby. I sat there and smoked two cigarettes. Then a squad car pulled alongside and the cops told me to move on.

144

On the Monday night following my dinner with Jenny, I worked late, and after I closed up, King Hayes walked over to the Friendship Deli with me. We sat at a table against the tiled wall. I was hungry, and had scrambled eggs with lox and onions, hash browns, toasted English, and a pot of tea. King just had coffee.

"Peter, I'm splitting. I mean, I'm moving back to Louella's," he said, looking down into his coffee cup. "We finally talked, and I agreed to go back."

"I hope you're doing the right thing."

"I know it's a gamble," he said, lifting his eyes.

"You want to keep working in the kitchen?"

"No," he said. "Can I start doing scenes again?"

"Sure. Happy to have you. Did you tell Louella?"

"She says it's okay with her."

I continued forking food into my yap, and he sipped his coffee. I envied him—having a woman who loved him that much—she didn't care what he did.

I finished my food in record time, pushed the empty plate away, dunked my tea bag.

"Look, King," I said. "I don't want to put the whammy on what you're doing. God knows I'm all for it. I'm getting a popular stud working again. More money in the bank. But have you considered that Louella might change her mind?"

The big black stirred restlessly. "You think I haven't thought of that? I told Louella that's what probably would happen."

"And what did she say?"

"She didn't say, 'Oh no, that's impossible.' She says she couldn't guarantee as to how she'll be feeling six months from now, but she says meanwhile she wants to try it. Just to see if it works."

"I hope it does work, King."

"Yeah. Me, too."

I paid the bill and bought two cigars. I hadn't smoked one in years. King and I lighted up and we strolled back through the tender night to Peter's Place, puffing importantly.

"You know," King said, "we all make mistakes. Then we say, 'Well, if I had it to do over again, I sure wouldn't do *that.*' But there's no second chance, is there? I mean, you got to learn as you go along."

"We're all amateurs, King. At living I mean."

"Louella, she says that all her life she's been planning how to get a good education, go to college, get a big degree, land a job and work her way up. Well, she's done all that and it isn't enough. So now she's going to live day to day."

"Smart lady," I said.

"Well . . .," he said cautiously, "maybe. But then again, on her dying day she might say, 'My goodness, that was a terrible mistake, and I must remember not to do those things the next time.' But there's no next time, is there? I mean, Peter, no one really *knows* if what he's doing is right for him."

"I sure as hell don't," I said.

145

It had been a long time since I had gone to bed with Jenny Tolliver, and there didn't seem much likelihood of it happening in the immediate future. And after Nicole Radburn left for the Coast, I was deprived of her physical intimacy, too—which, in a crazy kind of way, I had cherished.

So I took one or two scenes a week, because I was working hard and wasn't all that randy. But I wanted to keep my hand in—you should excuse the expression.

Early in June, one of our studs didn't show up for his scene—not an unusual occurrence—and I told Martha I'd take it. The client's name was Mabel, which is far from being my favorite name.

She came up to my third-floor bedroom. She looked like a big Little

Orphan Annie, wearing a calico dress with the skirt in tiers and lace trim on the cap sleeves. It was godawful. But she was young and fresh-looking. In her middle twenties, I judged.

She ordered a diet cola, which was served in an ornate pressed-glass goblet with a slice of lime hooked over the rim. Mabel held it up to the light.

"Fab," she said admiringly.

When she shucked her clothes, I admit I stared. Not because her body was so beautiful, but because it was so bizarre.

From the navel up, she was slender: small breasts, narrow shoulders, whippy arms. Her hair was a cap of tight blond curlicues on an egg-shaped head atop a stalky neck. The whole effect was one of youthful fragility.

But from the navel downward, she was a totally different woman: broad hips, a pushy bottom, massive thighs and heavy calves. Her hands were small and delicate; her feet were big and sturdy as hooves.

She really looked like two women sawn in half by a depraved magician who then joined the disparate halves. From the front or back, she looked like a large, golden gourd.

After I had undressed, she inspected me and said, "You have a marvy bod."

She wasn't very practiced in bed, but she was a willing student. "Fab," she kept saying. Or, "Marv."

She had the strength and springiness of a teenager. Even those bulging hips, thighs, and assertive behind were firm. Like Sally, my ex-wife, she was particularly sensitive to tickling.

We had a lot of fun together. As she became aroused, her face, then her throat, chest, torso got rosier and rosier. The bottom half of her body remained creamy, which just accentuated the dichotomy. It was quite a sight.

It took a long time to get her off, but I finally managed.

When she was able to speak, she said, "That was super."

"For me, too," I said—which is standard whores' talk.

"I really came, didn't I?"

"You really did," I said, then looked at her more closely. "You never have before?"

"Maybe. I'm not sure. But nothing like that."

While we were dressing, she said, "I have my own apartment. I'm a marvy cook."

"Mabel," I said, "we're not allowed to see clients on the outside. They're very strict about it."

"Oh," she said, disappointed.

"You can always come back again," I pointed out. "Ask for me."

"I know. But it would be nicer if we . . . Can I give you my number? Just in case?"

"All right," I said. "If you want to."

She had a little memo pad and gold pencil in her purse. She wrote out her address, phone number, and full name—Mabel Hetter.

"Don't lose it," she said.

"I won't," I assured her, folding the note and slipping it into my wallet.

"You never know," she said.

146

We met with Oscar Gotwold at Martha's at 9:00 A.M. Even at that early hour, the little man was alert and beautifully groomed, his bald pate and wingtip shoes gleaming.

As he sipped coffee and nibbled Danish, I told him how Detective Luke Futter had demanded we double his take to twenty thousand a month. Oscar merely nodded.

Then Martha took over. She told him how Sidney Quink had tried to shake us down when we were just getting started. She said we had gone to Futter for help and he had come through. Then she played the tape.

Those scratchy voices were from another world, another time. We all listened intently. When the tape ran out and Martha turned off the machine, Oscar finished his coffee and dabbed at his lips with the paper napkin.

"Correct me if I'm wrong," he said, "but I gather you wish to use the recording to keep this man in line. Am I right?"

"Right," Martha said angrily. "Futter wouldn't care to have that tape made public."

"Oh?" Gotwold said. "And how do you propose to make it public? In a court of law? Television news programs?"

We stared at him.

"In my opinion," the lawyer went on, "you would be wise to burn that tape and all copies. It implicates *you* and comes perilously close to suborning a felony. If this detective is as smart as you describe him, he'll know that you wouldn't dare go public with that tape."

"Shit," Martha said. "What does that mean? That we've got to roll over and play dead for that gonif?"

"Not necessarily," Gotwold said. "Did he give you any reason for doubling the amount of the pad?"

"He said he was sharing it with a lot of other guys," I said. "Higher-ups who got a bigger share than he did. He made it sound like there was a big organization and he was just a lowly bagman."

"That may be true," the attorney said, "and it may not. In any event, this is not a legal problem; it is a muscle problem. My advice to you is to take it to Cannis and Gelesco."

"Do we have to do that?" I asked.

Gotwold looked at me with mild surprise. "What is your objection?"

"I just don't like the idea of admitting we've got a problem we can't solve and running to them for help."

"Amen," Martha said.

"A very understandable and human reaction," the attorney said. "But you must understand that Cannis and Gelesco have a very significant investment in Peter's Place. Anything that endangers the enterprise endangers them. And they are, you must admit, much better, ah, qualified to deal with a matter like this than you are. I urge you most strongly to turn the whole thing over to them."

He glanced at his watch, rose, and picked up his black Homburg and gray suede gloves.

"I must run," he said. "Please think it over. Your partners are experienced businessmen. It would be silly not to take advantage of their expertise."

"We'll think about it," Martha said.

"Do that," he said. "Or meet Futter's demands. I can't suggest any other solution."

147

Martha had been wearing a terry robe and mules during our meeting with Oscar Gotwold.

"I've got to shower and dress and get down to the club," she said. "Come in with me while I get ready. There's more coffee if you want it."

She went into the bedroom while I took the dishes to the kitchen, then went into the bathroom and sat on the closed toilet seat.

"What do you think?" I yelled.

"I guess we'll have to go to them," she yelled back. "I hate it."

"Me, too," I said.

We didn't speak again until she came dripping out of the stall. She grabbed a towel and began rubbing herself.

"I'm getting fat as a pig," she said. "Do my back."

I stood, took another towel, began to dry her broad shoulders and back.

"Oscar is right," she said. "It's a muscle problem, and Cannis and Gelesco are better equipped to handle it than we are."

"I suppose," I said, swabbing away. "But they'll start wanting more voice in how we run the place."

"That's the kind of guys they are," she agreed.

We moved into the bedroom. She began to pull on pantyhose. I sat on the edge of the bed and smoked a cigarette.

"I wouldn't want those guys for enemies," I observed.

"All their clout comes from Octavius Caesar." She held up two dresses. "The pink or the black?"

"Black. The pink's too girlish."

"If it wasn't for Caesar," she went on, "they'd be pussycats."

I considered a moment, then finally decided.

"Martha," I said, "remember last month I told you I had a meeting with Octavius Caesar?"

"Sure, I remember. About launching the chain."

"Right. Well, what I didn't tell you was that when I came out of his offices I saw your boyfriend, Wilson Bowker, going in."

She had been putting on lipstick. Suddenly she stopped and whirled to me. Her eyes were wide.

"Wilson?" she said. "You're sure?"

"Absolutely. He was with a short guy who wore a derby and was chewing a cigar."

"McMannis," she said dully. "His campaign manager. And they went into Caesar's office?"

"No doubt about it."

"Son of a bitch!" she said bitterly. "That's all I need."

She turned back to the mirror and tried to complete her makeup. But she couldn't manage.

"Caesar isn't going to say anything about you," I told her. "He's not the kind of man who talks about his business. And Bowker sure as hell isn't going to mention you to *anyone.*"

"I know, I know," she said. "But I still don't like the idea of those two guys getting together. Peter, there's so much riding on this. If Wilson makes it to Albany, in another four or eight years he could go right to the top—just like his wife dreams."

"President Bowker?" I said. "Maybe he'll make you Secretary of the Interior."

"Shithead!" she said angrily, and I didn't make any more jokes about it.

I had driven up in my Datsun, and after Martha had carefully double-locked her door, we went downstairs to the street, where I found a parking ticket neatly tucked under the windshield wiper.

"Send it to Octavius Caesar," Martha advised. "He can fix anything."

We drove downtown in heavy Fifth Avenue traffic. Martha said, "You're sure it was Wilson?"

I sighed. "I shouldn't have told you."

"No," she said. "That's all right."

"Are you going to ask him about it?"

"Wilson? Christ, no! I'd have to explain how come I know the old man."

" 'Oh, what a tangled web we weave . . .' "

"Cut the bullshit," she said, "and watch the lights."

148

I parked the Datsun in front of Peter's Place and told our doorman-guard—known to the staff as Godzilla—to keep an eye on it. Martha went to her office to start taking reservations for luncheon, dinner, and scenes.

I went through my usual morning routine of checking the bar, kitchen, dining room, bedrooms, to make certain all the staff were present and the club was ready for business.

Yancy Burnett showed up to take the first shift as host. He was wearing a three-piece suit of soft gray flannel, striped shirt with white Windsor collar, and a mellow Sulka cravat. There was a small carnation in his lapel.

"Very impressive," I said, nodding approval. "What's the occasion?"

"I think I'm in love," he said.

"Who's the lucky man?" I said, and he laughed. "Yance, I'm taking Clara Hoffheimer's loot down to her. Be back in about an hour. Hold the fort."

Clara's idea of supplementing our supply of studs with members of the armed forces on liberty or leave was working out very well. Would it surprise you to learn that we also had a number of moonlighting New York policemen and an FBI man?

On that morning Clara was wearing a triple strand of pearls, and they weren't Chiclets. Good-quality cultured, I guessed. And I noted a new topaz ring, the stone large enough to qualify as a knuckle-duster.

I watched her carefully count the money.

"All there?" I asked.

"Just right," she said, not bothering to add "Thank you."

"You're looking very prosperous these days, Clara," I said casually. "Things going well for you?"

"Couldn't be better."

"It shows," I said.

She grinned lasciviously.

She was as beefy as Martha, but coarser, with a worrisome predatory streak. I wondered how Octavius Caesar coped with her rapaciousness. Then it occurred to me that it might be what attracted him.

She stood up behind her desk and came around to plump one soft haunch on the arm of my chair. She put a hand on the back of my neck.

"I like working with you, Peter," she said throatily. "You and I are a lot alike."

That wasn't the most comforting news I had heard that morning.

"I like working with you, Clara," I said. "It's profitable for both of us."

"I could lock the office door," she offered with a giggle.

I had a horrid image of her spreadeagled atop the desk, rolling about on pencils, rubber bands, and paper clips while I hunched over her, puffing and grunting.

But that wasn't what stopped me. I wasn't about to endanger the future of Peter's Place by putting horns on Octavius Caesar. I thought quickly.

"Clara," I said sorrowfully, "I'd like to have a closer relationship with you. But Sol and I were such good friends . . . When I think of you and me—well, I see Sol looking down at me sadly from the great beyond. As if I had betrayed him—you know? I just couldn't do it to Sol's memory."

I carried on like that for some time. After a while she got off the arm of my chair, went back and sat down behind her desk. I thought I saw tears in her eyes.

"Peter," she said, choking, "I want you to know I understand—and I respect you for it."

It was one of my better performances.

149

There was one lamp burning in a corner of the Mardi Gras Room. In the center, Cannis, Gelesco, Martha, and I sat at a card table. Cigar smoke was thick. In the semidarkness, you could see it billow like fog moving in.

I explained to the two shtarkers that Detective Luke Futter was now demanding twenty thousand a month grease.

"If we want to stay open," Martha added.

"That prick!" Gelesco said explosively.

"It's just greed," Cannis said, shaking his head dolefully. "If there's anything I can't stand, it's a greedy guy. I mean, we got a nice thing going here and he's been doing okay. But now he smells money and wants more, more, more."

"He says it's not for him," I said. "He claims he's got to spread it around. He swears most of it goes to higher-ups."

"He says," Gelesco said disgustedly. "He claims. He swears. Who the hell knows? Maybe he's pocketing it all himself. I think we better get the skinny on this guy."

"Yeah," Cannis said. And then, addressing his partner, "We could put Lou on it. He's a real diplomat."

"Sure," the other man said. "Let's do that. Let's find out where our money's going. We should have done it long before this."

Against my advice, Martha had insisted on bringing along her portable recorder and the tape she had made of Futter agreeing to take care of Sidney Quink for a fee. Now she explained to Cannis and Gelesco how Quink had tried to shake us down and how we had gone to the detective for help.

Then she played the tape. The raspy voices echoed in that dim, smoky room. We all listened closely until the tape ran out.

"And then this Quink just disappeared?" Cannis said.

"We never heard of him again."

"He's feeding the fishes right now," Cannis said.

"Maybe he's a highway," Gelesco said, and both men laughed.

"The point is," I said quickly, "we can't use that tape to lean on Futter. Oscar Gotwold says if we go public with it, it's just as damaging to us. I mean, we're offering a bribe to an officer of the law to get rid of a guy."

"Yeah," Cannis said slowly. "You put him in the soup but you're right in there with him."

"Look," Gelesco said. "There's more than one way to skin a cat. For instance . . . This cop says he's been spreading the pad to the higher-ups—right? He probably has. The only hassle we've had so far was that raid, and he tipped us to that. But these top guys don't want no trouble. Believe me. No front-page stories in the *Post.* So they've got to have a bagman they can trust. But they hear this tape, and they say, 'We got a guy we thought was smart, and he's so fucking stupid that he takes a contract and lets himself get bugged. This yutz has got to go.' "

"Yeah, Mike," Cannis breathed. "That's beautiful. We get Lou to find out who Futter has been paying off. Then we play the tape for them and let them take it from there."

"Right, Tony," Gelesco said. "That way our hands are clean. Listen," he added, turning to Martha and me. "You should have come to us right away. I mean, Tony and me, we know a lot of people. We got a lot of friends who owe us. So anytime you get socked with something like this, just give us a call. We want to work a lot closer with you folks. Am I right, Tony?"

"Right," Cannis said.

150

I had been doing some heavy thinking about Jenny Tolliver, wrestling with the problem of how to get her back without sacrificing $75,000 a year and 26 percent of the profits. I came up with what I thought was a splendid solution.

I would continue working at Peter's Place, but I would restrict my duties solely to the bar, dining room, and social events. No more booking studs. No more taking scenes myself.

In effect, I would become a restaurateur. Martha and Yance could take over my responsibilities as studmaster.

Surely that decision would answer all of Jenny's moral objections. It would be as though I were a maître d'. A maître d' can't be held responsible for what his patrons do after they leave his dining room, can he?

Another factor that led to my determination was the meeting with Cannis and Gelesco. I had the uneasy feeling that I was getting in over my head. All that light-hearted banter about grease to higher-ups and enemies becoming part of a highway . . . It shivered my timbers.

As I have said before, physical violence is not my cup of tea. I was quite willing to leave the illegal part of our operation to those bolder than I. Well . . . Martha had said I was a softy.

I finally wangled a date with Jenny about the middle of July, planning to present my decision to her during dinner. And then I would ask her to marry me. Yes, it had come to that.

I designed that evening like a production of *The Glass Menagerie*. I was to be the gentleman caller—only I wouldn't leave. I made a reservation at La Folie. I sent flowers to her office. I bought an engagement ring. A small stone, but elegant.

I dressed with special care, donning a white dinner jacket with black formal trousers and a wine-colored cummerbund. I was floating on high hopes and Halston Z-14.

But when I picked up Jenny at her apartment house, I knew immediately it was not going to be an enchanted evening. She was wearing a man-tailored shirt with the sleeves rolled up above her elbows, denim wrap-around skirt, and espadrilles.

It wasn't the costume that dismayed me so much as the way she looked. Her hair hung damply about her shoulders. Her face was devoid of makeup, and she seemed to have gone forty-eight hours without sleep. Either that or she had been weeping; there were dark smudges beneath her eyes.

"Something wrong?" I asked when she slid into the car.

She shook her head, not replying.

"I made a reservation at La Folie," I told her. "Is that all right?"

"I'm sorry," she said, "but I can't make it. I was going to call you, but then I thought that wouldn't be fair. I had to tell you face-to-face."

"Tell me what?"

"Could we drive around a while?" she said. "Through the Park. Anywhere."

So I started up the Datsun and headed for the 72nd Street entrance to Central Park.

"I've got something important to tell *you,*" I said.

"No, Peter. Listen to me first. I'm going to marry Arthur."

I didn't slam on the brakes or run into a jogger or anything like that. But I felt my hands grip the wheel so tightly that my elbows ached.

"Arthur?" I cried. "Why?"

"He's a fine, decent man."

"I know—but *Arthur?* I mean, he's sweet and gentle and all that, but he's got no pizzazz. He's not the man for you."

"He told me exactly what you're telling me," she said evenly. "He knows himself as well as you know him. But he said he loves me and will work hard to make our marriage a success, and I believe him."

I groaned. "Jenny, he'll bore you to death in six months."

"I don't think so. We've been seeing each other regularly for almost a year now and he hasn't bored me. We're comfortable together. We don't always have to be doing something or going somewhere. We just like being with each other."

We were making the great circle through the Park's interior roads: south on the West Side to 59th Street, east, then curving north. I drove slowly enough to miss the lights. I needed time.

"Look," I said. "Before you make up your mind—"

"I've already decided," she said firmly.

"Let me say what I wanted to say . . ."

Then I told her of my plan to give up the studs and the scenes. "No bedroom stuff," I vowed. "I sincerely mean that, Jenny. Here . . ."

Driving with one hand, I fished in my pocket, pulled out the little velvet box. I thrust it at her.

"Take it," I said, but she wouldn't.

"It's an engagement ring," I said. "I want to marry you. I know you love me. I *know* it. And if I give up the kind of work you object to, I don't see why—"

But then she began to cry, turning her head away so I wouldn't see the tears. But I heard her soft sobs.

"You won't," she said, her voice thick. "You can't."

"What are you talking about?" I said angrily. "I can walk away from that business anytime I like. It would be foolish to give up my financial investment. But I'll have absolutely nothing to do with the bedroom stuff."

"You'd go back to it," she said, snuffling. "I know you would. In a month, six months, a year . . . you'd be at it again."

"The hell I would!" I bellowed, and I continued trying to persuade her of my staunch resolve. But nothing I said could convince her.

Finally there was nothing more to be said. We finished the ride in silence. I brought her back to her apartment house.

"Best of luck to you and Arthur," I said formally, staring straight ahead through the windshield.

She leaned to me suddenly and kissed my cheek.

"You were right, Peter," she said. "I do love you. But there are more important things."

Then she was gone.

I slammed the car into gear and went roaring down the street.

"Go fuck yourself!" I screamed.

I double-parked in front of Peter's Place. I didn't care if I got a hundred tickets or if they towed the damned thing away.

I stalked into the club. Yancy Burnett looked at me without expression.

"Back early," he said.

I went into my office and slammed the door. I fell into my swivel chair, leaned back, put my feet on the desk. I took the velvet box from my pocket, opened it, looked at the ring. Then I threw it at the far wall. Screw the world!

Yance came in with a snifter of brandy.

"Here," he said, handing it to me. "You look like you could use it."

"Thanks," I said gratefully. "I can."

I drained it in two gulps and caught my breath.

"Better?" Yance asked.

"Not much. How's the action tonight?"

"Fine. Six scenes going on right now. Five more scheduled before midnight."

"All the studs show up?"

"Right on time."

"Shit," I said.

He gave me a commiserating smile and left the office. I thought a moment, then straightened up at the desk and pulled out my wallet. The folded note was still in there: Mabel Hetter, phone number and address. The young lady who looked like a gourd.

She picked up the phone on the second ring.

"Hi!" I said brightly. "This is Peter from the—"

"I know who you are," she said. "Fab! Come right over."

151

It was July 24; I remember it very well. I came down early in my bathrobe and slippers. They were setting up in the kitchen, so I took my coffee into the Dream Room and sat at one of the little bistro tables.

I hadn't been there more than a few minutes when Anthony Cannis and Michael Gelesco walked in, came up to my table, and loomed over me.

Their expressions were grave. Cannis put down the morning edition of the *Daily News.*

"Page four," he said.

I stared at him a moment, then flipped the paper to page four. Gelesco pointed. I followed his stubby finger. It was a small item:

DETECTIVE A SUICIDE. The body of Detective first grade Luke Futter, a twenty-year veteran of the New York Police Department, was found late last night on the front seat of his car parked near Eleventh Avenue and 54th Street. Futter had a single bullet wound in his temple. His service revolver, with one round fired, was found on the seat alongside him. Pending an autopsy, the death has been tentatively labeled a suicide. Authorities stated the detective had been depressed lately, apparently due to personal problems.

I read the item twice, then looked up slowly at Cannis and Gelesco.

"That's terrible," I said in a low voice.

"Terrible," Gelesco agreed, shaking his head.

"He didn't seem like a suicidal type to me," I said.

"Like the newspaper says," Cannis said, shrugging, "he was depressed."

"Yeah," Gelesco said, "he had personal problems. Hey, how about a cup of coffee? Black for both of us."

I went into the kitchen and asked one of the waiters to bring two coffees. I knew I couldn't carry them; my hands were trembling too much.

We didn't speak until the waiter left. The two villains sat down, sipped coffee, sighed, leaned back.

"We had our guy looking into this Futter," Cannis said. "He was sharing all right, but not as much as he said. He was skimming something awful."

"Greedy," Gelesco said.

"The extra ten was going right into his pocket," Cannis said. "How do you like that?"

Gelesco took a tape cassette from his pocket and slid it across the table to me.

"Here's Martha's tape," he said. "We never even got a chance to use it."

"The guy bumped himself first," Cannis said. "Can you beat that?"

"So what happens now?" I asked nervously.

"We talked to some people," Gelesco said. "We agreed to twelve-five, which is a hell of a lot better than twenty—am I right?"

"And from now on," Cannis said, "Mike and me will handle that end of the business. Okay, Peter?"

"Thank you," I said faintly. "And it's okay with me."

"We'll take care of the pad," Gelesco said, "and any other heavy problems like labor relations and security. Why should you have all the worries? You make a good cup of coffee here."

They finished and stood up, but lingered, staring down at me.

"You went to Mr. Caesar," Anthony Cannis said, "about me and Mike dropping by at the bar now and then just to show the joint to our friends."

"I—" I began.

"That's okay," Gelesco said. "Tony and me aren't sore—are we, Tony?"

"Nah."

"But sometimes," Gelesco said, "we think you don't show us the right respect."

"It's very important to show respect," Cannis said virtuously. "We show respect to Mr. Caesar. It's due him."

"And we think you could show us a little," Gelesco said. "After all, we're partners—right?"

"So . . ." Cannis said, "you show us respect, we show you respect."

"Fine with me," I said as bravely as I could.

"That's a good boy," Michael Gelesco said, reaching out and pinching my cheek.

It hurt.

152

On the night Jenny Tolliver told me of her intention to marry Arthur Enders, I had called Mabel Hetter, rushed over, and exhausted my frustration and hostility on an oak four-poster in her bedroom.

"Super!" she said happily.

I was back at Peter's Place before midnight, but in gratitude for

Mabel's generous compliance, I agreed to come for dinner the following Friday night. I insisted on bringing the wine: a bottle of chablis and a '78 Pommard.

Mabel lived in one of those battleship apartment houses on West 57th Street that have seventy-five years of city grime encrusted on limestone gargoyles and cherubs carved into the façade. The elevators were cages and all the bathtubs crouched on four legs, ready to pounce.

It was really a marvelous old building, built originally to provide artists' studios. Parquet in the living room and ceramic tile floors in the bathrooms. Twelve-foot-high ceilings with plenty of walnut paneling. Sliding doors with chunky brass knobs and locks. Velvet-covered window seats, of course.

Mabel had a one-bedroom apartment and told me she was paying $1250 a month rent. So there was money there—right? And since she wasn't working, I figured it had to be coming from Mommy and Daddy in Kansas. She told me her father owned some grain silos or something like that.

She had furnished the place in Salvation Army Traditional—big chairs and couches, almost as old as the building itself. There were a lot of slipcovers in chintz and cretonne. Some good bric-a-brac, but mostly junk. Plenty of fresh flowers, which was nice. A battered upright piano. The single air conditioner was a window unit in the bedroom.

She had told me she was a "marvy cook," but I figured her as the quiche and spinach salad type. After I got a look at her kitchen, I knew she was serious about food.

It was almost as large as the kitchen at Peter's Place, and an overhead rack held enough pots and pans to feed the South Bronx. A double sink, long butcher-block working counter, refrigerator and separate freezer, a commercial-type gas range, a microwave oven.

"I just love to cook," she said.

"I just love to eat," I said, giving her my best Groucho Marx leer. But she didn't get it.

She served halves of chilled avocado heaped with big chunks of crab meat and tiny bits of roasted almonds. The salad was a tossed mixture of arugula and watercress with Japanese mushrooms and a few spikes of endive. The dressing had an unusual flavor. Pistachio maybe?

The main course was medallions of veal, paper-thin, sautéed in butter and shallots with just a hint of marsala. The slivers of fresh green beans were served cold with dime-sized slices of Canadian bacon. There was a dish of mixed white and sweet potatoes, no larger than marbles, boiled and then dipped in something that gave them a crust when they were fried.

Mabel had baked the bread herself—miniature French baguettes served with sweet butter.

Dessert was sinfully rich chocolate ice cream, doused with Kahlua, sprinkled with crumbs of double-bitter chocolate, and topped with a toque blanche of freshly whipped cream.

It was a memorable meal. There was only one thing wrong: It was so bloody hot in that cavernous room that I was acutely uncomfortable. The big windows were wide open, but New York was sweltering in a midsummer heat wave, and it was like dining in a sauna.

I finally persuaded Mabel to snuff the candles; more heat we didn't need. We finished the chilled chablis first, and ended up putting ice cubes in the Pommard, which was a grievous offense against a noble wine.

So I was just as happy when dinner was finished and I could rise and get my pants unstuck from my seat. I helped clear the table, and while Mabel was putting the food away and stacking the dishes, I went back into the living room.

All I could think of was how soon I could decently lure her into the bedroom. Not because I was especially randy, but because I knew it was air conditioned in there. Meanwhile, I wandered about, lifting my arms and twisting my neck in a sodden collar.

The piano was old and scarred, but when I struck a few soft chords, it seemed in perfect tune. Mabel came in while I was noodling around.

Alongside the piano was an open cabinet filled with sheet music. I flipped through the stacks. She seemed to have every song written by Victor Herbert, George M. Cohan, Rudolf Friml, Sigmund Romberg, and Jerome Kern.

"What's all this?" I asked.

"I came to New York to study singing," she said. "I haven't appeared professionally yet, but I belong to this marvy amateur group that specializes in operettas. We put on free performances at churches, nursing homes, schools, hospitals—places like that. It's really fun."

"I imagine it is," I said, not much interested. "Mabel, do you mind if I take off my jacket?"

Without waiting for permission, I doffed the jacket, loosened my tie, unbuttoned my collar, turned up damp cuffs.

"I don't know how you stand it in here without air conditioning," I told her.

"I usually walk around naked," she said, giggling. "It's a crazy habit I have."

"Don't let me stop you," I said, making the mechanical male response.

I never thought she'd do it, but she skinned off all her clothes in record time, flinging dress, bra, pantyhose, and shoes in all directions. Then she posed, hands on hips, cocked her head, and gave me a sappy grin.

"Isn't that better?" she said.

The big windows were wide open, shades up, drapes drawn back. There was a darkened office building across 57th Street, but if there had been a platoon of guys watching with binoculars, she wouldn't have cared less.

"Would you like me to sing something for you?" she asked hopefully.

"Sure," I said manfully. "I'd like that."

I sat on the edge of a couch, not wanting to put my wet back against the upholstery. She bent over and began to shuffle through the stacks of sheet music.

"Here's one I like," she said.

She sat at the piano, propped up the music. I saw the egg head balanced on the stalky neck and topped with a cap of blond curls. Narrow shoulders, slender arms, slim waist. And then those awesome buttocks spread over the piano bench like plump pancakes.

She began to sing "Ah! Sweet Mystery of Life."

I'm not going to tell you she was a lousy singer; she wasn't. But it was a very small soprano, strictly a parlor voice, not even strong enough for light opera. Her teacher should have been prosecuted for obtaining money under false pretenses.

"That was lovely," I said when she finished.

It was the gentlemanly thing to say, but it condemned me. I had to sit there, sweating, and listen to a concert that included "Mary's a Grand Old Name," "Indian Love Call," "One Alone," and "Lover, Come Back to Me."

She ended her recital with "Why Was I Born?"—which caught my mood exactly.

When she turned to face me, her face was flushed with her exertions.

"Let's go in the bedroom and cool off," she said.

"I thought you'd never ask," I said.

As if to make up for the inferno in the living room, she had the air conditioner in the bedroom turned up so high that you could have hung sides of beef on the walls. But I made no complaint.

We took a shower together, standing up in that crazy bathtub and taking turns under the spray from a pipe that seemed to have been added at the end of the tub as an afterthought. Then we went to bed and I paid for my dinner.

It wasn't a chore; she was young, willing—and very vocal. I didn't mind the "Fab!" "Marvy!" and "Super!" I could even appreciate the cries, groans, yelps, and whimpers. But I thought she went too far when, after we finished, she insisted on crooning a chorus of "Can't Help Lovin' Dat Man."

About two in the morning I awoke with an insatiable thirst. Probably the highly spiced food, the wine—whatever. I slipped stealthily out of bed and went padding naked into the kitchen. The heat out there was a slap in the face.

I poked around in the refrigerator. Finally, in the freezer, I found a bowl containing what was left of our dessert: chocolate ice cream, Kahlua, chocolate bits, and whipped cream. I stood at the kitchen counter and wolfed it all down.

Like most people, I had long believed in the old cliché that the way to a man's heart is through his cock. Now I began to wonder it if might be through his stomach. Could that be true?

153

I wasn't invited to the wedding. That was all right; I could understand why Jenny and Arthur might find my presence embarrassing. Still . . .

King Hayes went, and told me all about it. He said the bride was absolutely beautiful and the groom looked like a scared rabbit. They had a small reception in the back room of Blotto's, then went right back to work.

Arthur's play opened during the first week of August. The *Times'* review was the only one I read. It said *Sunset at Dawn* was clumsily crafted and, in places, excessively sentimental. But it also said the playwright was obviously a writer of natural talent and showed great promise.

Arthur did remember to send me two house seat tickets to his play. I invited Mabel Hetter, but she was appearing in a performance of *Babes in Toyland* at Rockland State and couldn't make it. So I went to see *Sunset at Dawn* by myself. It was the first time I had been to the theater in two years.

It was a wrenching experience. The play itself was a revelation. It was totally different from the script Arthur had been working on when we were roomies. Now it dealt with outsize emotions. It really should have been an opera.

The *Times'* reviewer had been correct: The play was awkwardly constructed and mawkish, but there was no denying its power and plangent appeal.

It concerned a farm lad dissatisfied with the restricted life of a small Nebraska town. He leaves home to explore the world and explore himself. A series of vignettes present his experiences in love, at war, rich, poor, betrayed, betraying, triumphant, and defeated.

Finally he returns home. Most of the audience (including me) expected the conventional ending: The hero realizes that everything he has been searching for is contained within that little Nebraska town. "East, west, home's best." But the playwright has one final sharp arrow in his quiver.

The hero, returned from his journey into the big world, finds his small town as dissatisfying as everything else. In a final, bitter scene, he renounces the possibility of discovering his personal grail and accepts the truth that we are all doomed to discontent.

It was a very disturbing play—which is what a good play is supposed to be. Not only was I shattered by Arthur's perception and talent, but I longed for a chance to play the lead. It was a complex role that offered a dozen subtle interpretations.

A few years ago, Sol Hoffheimer had told me that if I surrendered, I was fated to spend the remainder of my life wondering what might have been. It was already beginning.

I assured myself that I had a good-paying job, a car, a splendid wardrobe, a bed-partner who was also a marvelous cook, and a bright future. So why the weltschmerz? I didn't know.

All I did know was that I felt the spring of my life was over, and all I had to look forward to was a dying autumn with no happy surprises.

154

A few weeks previously, Seth Hawkins had come tottering into my office looking like he had been mashed by a steamroller. His hands were trembling and there was a twitch in his right leg he couldn't control. Also, he had a wild look in his eye, as if he had just seen something monstrous and couldn't believe it.

"What the hell happened to you?" I asked anxiously.

He groaned and told me his sad tale.

His customer was in her early thirties. Her name was Sybil. She was tall, broad-shouldered, with a tiny waist and narrow hips. When she undressed, it was immediately obvious to Seth that the lady was a physical fitness freak. Probably a weight lifter.

"Peetuh," he said despondently, "she even had muscles in her titties."

The client posed for Seth, showing off her biceps and triceps. Then she insisted they arm wrestle so she could demonstrate her strength. She won.

"She like to broke mah ahm," Seth mourned.

But worse was to come. When Sybil insisted on Indian wrestling, she turned Seth upside down, balanced on the back of his skull, and tangled like a pretzel.

She bounced up from this victory and, before he could object, grabbed his shoulder and thigh and, after a few grunts, lifted him over her head.

The acrobatics continued after they got into bed.

"There ain't a part of me that don't ache," he complained. "She stretched mah laigs like ah was a wishbone and she was hoping for something. Ah damned near *split!* But the wust thing, the absolute *wust,* was when it was all over, she shakes my hand, cracking mah knuckles, and says, 'See you soon.' Peetuh," Seth Hawkins said piteously, "don't do it to me again. *Please.*"

I assured him I wouldn't and ordered a brandy from the bar to steady his nerves before he departed.

Around the middle of August, Sybil returned. But it wasn't for another scene. The first I knew about it was when Martha came into my office.

"There's a woman at the bar," she said. "A member. She wants to talk to someone in charge."

"Can't you handle it?" I said.

"I don't understand what she wants," Martha said confusedly.

I looked at her. Both Yance and I noted that she hadn't appeared well lately. She seemed to have lost her spark. She had always been well-groomed, but recently she had become almost slovenly, wearing dresses with stains and hose with runners. And the gray roots of her red hair showed through.

"Are you all right, Martha?" I asked. "You haven't been looking so perky lately."

She managed a wan smile. "I'll survive," she said.

"Same problem?" I said. "The next governor?"

She nodded.

"Get out of it, darling," I advised.

"How?" she asked, and I couldn't tell her.

"All right," I said, sighing. "The lady at the bar. What's her name?"

"Sybil Headley."

"Sybil?" I cried. "Oh lord!"

"Do you know her?"

"I've never seen her, but she almost killed Seth Hawkins. Is she looking for a scene?"

"I don't think so."

"Thank God," I said. "I'll live to play the violin again."

There were several women in the Dream Room, but mostly in groups of two, three, or four. The only woman by herself had long, sandy hair falling about her shoulders. She was wearing big aviator sunglasses tinted yellow. There was a goblet of diet cola in front of her. I sauntered over.

"Miss Headley?" I said.

"That's me," she said. "Who are you?"

"Peter Scuro."

"Are you the boss?"

"One of the bosses," I said, smiling determinedly. "How may I help you?"

"You can sit down for starters," she said. So I did.

We stared at each other. I don't know what she saw, but I saw a handsome woman with skin as soft and fine as butterscotch Ultrasuede. She was wearing a sleeveless sundress and her long legs were bare. Her skin was absolutely flawless.

"You have a marvelous tan," I told her.

"Cut the shit," she said sharply.

She fished in a small lizard and snakeskin purse and came up with a business card. She slid it across the table to me. Sybil Headley. Contributing Editor. *Madhatter* Magazine.

"You know the *Madhatter?*" she said.

"I know it, yes," I said.

"Do you read it?" she demanded.

"Occasionally," I said cautiously.

"We specialize in investigative journalism," she said rapidly. "The story behind the stories in the New York area. Exposés, scandals, where the skeletons are hidden, where the bodies are buried. More than a million readers every week. They love us because we don't pull any punches. No puff pieces. We've got three libel suits against us right now and we'll win them all."

"Glad to hear it," I said.

"Now the bad news . . ." she said. "You're running a whorehouse here—only the whores are men and the customers are women. A great story. A two-parter, at least. I've got all the facts and figures. I've even got some photos I snapped with my trusty Minox when no one was looking. I'm giving you a chance to make a statement. We're fair; we'll print your defense."

I sighed. "How much?" I said.

"What?" she said. It was a bark.

"How much to kill the story?" I said wearily.

"You turd!" she said hotly. "You think you can buy us off?"

"Yes," I said.

"Well, sonny, you're in for a shock. We're not for sale."

She glared at me and I gave her my best cool, amused William Powell look.

"If you're interested in the big gorilla who guards the door . . ." I suggested.

She blushed, jerked to her feet, grabbed up her purse.

"I suppose that mush-mouthed farmer told you about our scene," she said accusingly.

"He did. Fascinating. Kinky but fascinating."

"You prick," she said and marched out.

I went into Martha's office and started to tell her what had happened, but she interrupted me.

"Please, Peter," she said. "I can't be bothered. You take care of it."

So I went to my own office and tried to call Anthony Cannis and/or Michael Gelesco. Their secretary told me they were both on a junket to Las Vegas and wouldn't be back for a week. I asked her to have them call me as soon as they returned.

155

After Clara Hoffheimer came on to me, I tried to make my visits to her office as short as possible. I'd pop in, pass the time of day, hand over her pourboire, wait till she checked it, and then get out of there as quickly as I could.

But late in August, I didn't make my escape in time. She stopped me.

"Peter," she said, "I have a problem."

"Welcome to the human race," I said lightly.

"And I think maybe you can help," she continued. "I have this gentleman friend. Let's call him Mr. C."

"Let's," I said.

"Well, he's got this wife who doesn't understand him. So we've got no place we can go—you know? I mean, it can't be where he lives, and I live way out in the sticks with a daughter and all. And he doesn't want to check into a hotel where maybe someone might recognize him. He's a very important person."

"Sure," I said. "I can understand that."

"So what I was wondering—the club closes at two in the morning?"

I nodded.

"And there's no one around then except you—right? So I was wondering if maybe . . ."

She was beginning to dangle her sentences just like Octavius Caesar.

I didn't like what she was proposing. I would have said no immediately except that it occurred to me that it might have been Caesar's idea. I didn't want to cross him. Not with the future of Peter's Place depending on his benevolence.

"Perhaps it could be worked out," I said slowly. "For all night?"

She laughed merrily. "Oh no. An hour should be more than enough."

I thought so, too.

"What about transportation?" I said. "A car, parking, and all that?"

"I'll arrange that. If you could just let us . . ."

"And then make myself scarce?"

"I knew you'd understand," she said, giving me a demure smile.

So there I was, two nights later, waiting nervously inside Peter's Place, peering through the little judas in the locked door. About 2:30 A.M., an old black Lincoln pulled up, just slightly shorter than a hearse. Clara Hoffheimer got out first, then assisted Octavius Caesar to alight.

I unlocked the door, stood aside as they entered, then locked the door after them. Caesar wasn't wearing a hat. His billowy hair gleamed whitely in the gloom. He shot me a sharp glance.

"Good evening, young man," he said, offering a pale palm.

"Good evening, sir," I said, pressing it. "Would you care for some refreshment?"

"Veuve Clicquot?"

"Of course," I said. "Immediately."

I got the champagne from the bar, twirled it in an ice-filled bucket, brought it to Clara.

"Any room on the fourth or fifth floor," I whispered to her. "I'll be down here when you're ready to leave."

She nodded and the two of them tottered to the elevator.

I spent a lachrymose hour sitting behind the bar, drinking Perrier.

I heard the elevator come down and got to my feet. Clara Hoffheimer came rushing in. She was almost hysterical with laughter: giggling, snorting, hooting, trying to cover her nose and mouth with her hand. Her eyes were streaming.

I got her calmed down enough to hear the story. Octavius Caesar had been dressing, and the zipper on his trouser fly had become entangled with the fly on his boxer shorts. Endeavoring to yank it free, he had jammed the zipper, and now his trousers yawned wide open with the length of white underpants protruding.

"It looks so *funny!*" Clara said, still heaving and sputtering. "Peter, what are we going to *do?* He doesn't want you to see him like that, and then there's his chauffeur, and what happens if his wife is awake when he gets home and sees him like that?"

"Look," I said. "I've got an old raincoat he can have. He doesn't have to wear it; he can carry it over his arm, hanging down in front to cover him."

So that's what we did. About five minutes later, Octavius Caesar appeared with my raincoat clasped tightly to his front.

"Good night, sir," I said, my voice carefully empty.

He didn't even look at me.

Clara gave me a quick, frightened smile. Then they were gone, and I locked the door behind them.

I had agreed to stage-manage this assignation, thinking to please Mr. C. But I had a nagging suspicion that the night's events had yielded me no Brownie points.

156

Michael Gelesco called to say he had received my message. I told him I'd like to see him and Cannis as soon as possible.

"Where do you want to meet?" he said coldly.

When I said I'd be happy to come up to the Barcarole Boutique, he thawed immediately. I presume that's what they considered "showing respect." We made an appointment for 4:00 P.M. the following afternoon.

We sat at one end of the long table in the conference room. They smoked their stogies and I tried not to cough. I told them about Sybil Headley and the planned article in *Madhatter* Magazine.

"She claims she's got photographs," I said. "And, in her words, 'all the facts and figures.' Where she got them I have no idea."

"*Madhatter* Magazine?" Cannis said. "Mike, we advertise in that rag, don't we?"

"Sure," Gelesco said. "A little two-inch ad every week. Just our name, address, and phone number. Very dignified."

"I guess I got off on the wrong foot with this Sybil Headley," I confessed. "I asked her how much she wanted to kill the story and she blew her stack."

"Peter," Gelesco said in a pitying way, "you've got to learn that with things like this, you go right to the top. Otherwise you get stiffed along the way and end with your thumb up your ass."

"Well . . ." I said helplessly, "what do we do now?"

"Don't worry about it," Gelesco advised. "It'll come out all right; you'll see."

"Thanks," I said gratefully and rose to leave.

"Hey," Cannis said. "How's old Martha these days?"

"Fine," I said. "Busy as ever."

"Fine, huh?" Cannis said. "That's not what we hear. We hear she's been looking like a bag lady lately, and she's not paying attention to her work."

They had put the entire kitchen staff, doorman, and bartenders in their jobs, so I had no doubt they had a sufficient number of spies reporting back to them.

"Martha's doing a great job," I protested.

"Yeah?" Gelesco said. "I hope you're right."

"She's indispensable," I added, but I went too far with that.

"Peter," Cannis said portentously, "no one is indispensable."

157

I had been seeing Mabel Hetter two or three times a week, usually sleeping over. She insisted on serving five-course dinners every time I visited. I couldn't resist those rich sauces and freshly baked pastries. I mean, I was getting truly *gross.*

"You should open a restaurant," I told her.

She looked at me, offended. "Oh no," she said, "I have my singing career to think about."

I could have told her the truth about her voice—but what was the use? She wouldn't have believed me.

Finally, over the Labor Day weekend, I persuaded her to have dinner out. We went to a restaurant that featured nouvelle cuisine. The prices were horrendous and the food was not as excellent as Mabel's. That was the first and last time we dined out. She was content and so was I.

I don't wish to be mean and bitchy about Mabel—she was never anything but generous and loving to me—but I must say that she was far from beautiful. Not ugly, but extravagantly plain.

Still, she had a pleasing smile, and her manner was so ingenuous that it was impossible to take her seriously. She seemed to have lived her twenty-four years avoiding corruption and with everlasting faith in her dreams. Perhaps it was her innocence that kept me coming back.

That and her roast duck with ginger.

I brought her gifts. Mostly small things because I just didn't have the cash to play the big-time spender. But she accepted everything with the same childlike delight, and especially cherished a teddy bear with a music box up its ass. It played "Look for the Silver Lining."

By September, I had moved shaving gear and toilet articles into her bathroom, and was keeping fresh shirts, underwear, and socks in the bedroom dresser. She bought me a bathrobe—what else?

Our evenings together were quite domestic. After dinner, I helped her clean up and stack the dishwasher. Then, while I sucked on a beer or sipped a glass of wine, Mabel favored me with a recital.

I never quite understood why such a young woman should be enthralled by hokey operettas written sixty years ago.

Following the obligatory concert, we adjourned to the bedroom. For an innocent she quickly developed some very sophisticated sexual skills. "One Kiss" might have been her favorite ballad, but she learned to expect more than that in bed.

Our coupling was important to me, I think, because the pressure of having to please a paying customer was absent. Perhaps that was why I was able to perform so successfully. And she was grateful for everything.

Also, for the first time since Nikki Radburn had left for the Coast, I was able to enjoy intimacy with a woman. Part of it was physical, I knew, but the postcoital comfort and coziness were just as precious. And if she wanted to end our sexual joust by singing "Stout Hearted Men" *a cappella,* I could endure that.

"Mae," I said to her (I just couldn't bring myself to address her as Mabel), "suppose the worst thing happens and, because of circumstances over which you have no control, you're not able to have a professional career on the stage?"

"Oh, that'll never happen," she said blithely. "One of these days I'm going to be famous."

Her resoluteness was breathtaking.

"But so much depends on luck," I argued. "With being in the right place at the right time."

"I think you make your own luck," she said.

I told myself I wanted to save her from hurt—but perhaps I was trying to justify my own life.

I liked to think of myself as a kind man. But a problem I had faced before arose again: Where was kindness? Should I be brutally honest or conspire in perpetuating an illusion? My only comfort was that wiser men than I hadn't solved that ethical dilemma.

I suppose I am an intellectual lightweight. To me, heavy introspection is a waste of time that rarely leads to positive action. So I left Mabel Hetter to her dreams and clasped her yummy, misshapen body closer. She really felt good.

If her theme was "Make Believe," mine was "Every Day Is Ladies' Day to Me."

158

After Labor Day, our business increased enormously. And just about then, Martha began taking days off, calling in sick or simply not showing up.

It was rough on Yance and me because we had to take over her duties in addition to our own.

"Look," I said to him. "I don't know what's with Martha, but we've got to do something before the place falls apart."

"I can do the bookings when Martha's not here," Yance said slowly. "But I can't do that *and* schedule the call boys and escorts *and* work as host seven hours a day."

"Of course you can't," I agreed. "Suppose you take over the reservations when she doesn't show up, and schedule the call boys and escorts as usual. But forget about hosting. We'll hire another guy."

"Who?"

"What about King Hayes?"

Yance lifted his eyebrows, but then considered it a moment. "You know," he said, "he just might do. He's big, handsome, personable. And he's had experience in the kitchen. You think he'll go for it?"

"He'll be on salary and won't have to take any scenes unless he wants to. I'm guessing he'll jump at the chance."

"You'll have to dress him up."

"No problem. He'll get a kick out of it."

So I took King to Brooks Brothers and we picked out two vested suits—one a gray flannel with a chalk stripe and the other a navy blue tropical worsted. Shirts, ties, and shoes: all traditionally elegant. King couldn't stop laughing.

He was an instant success as a host. Ingratiating without being servile, he had a good memory for names and handled complaints with disarming humor. He stopped taking scenes, and I got a tie from Sulka's with a card that read: "Thank you. Louella."

On the days when Martha came in, she was so distraught that Yance had to sit with her to help keep appointments and reservations straight. With their espionage system, I was sure that Cannis and Gelesco were aware of all this.

Around the middle of September, I was hosting the late shift. It was a Friday night and we were busy as hell. At one point in the evening every bedroom upstairs was in use—including mine.

I was happy when, by 2:30 A.M., everyone—customers and staff—was gone, and I could loosen my tie, let my belt out a notch, and relax. I decided to go over to the Friendship Deli for a cup of tea and a toasted bagel.

I was on my way back, about a half-block from the club, when two men stepped out of the shadows and into my path. I thought it was a mugging.

But one of them said, "Mr. Scuro?" and I looked at them more closely.

Two small, dapper Latin types wearing black, shiny suits. They both had little mustaches, but one also had a scar that ran from forehead to chin. Neither had a visible weapon, but they obviously weren't the kind of men you'd invite to your nephew's bar mitzvah.

"Yes," I said, wondering if I should start shrieking.

"A moment of your time," scarface said. *"Por favor."*

He gestured to a big, gleaming Mercedes sedan parked at the curb. The door opened, the interior light came on, and a man in the back seat leaned toward me, nodding and beckoning.

Although the two little men were careful not to touch me, I had the conviction that if I tried to bolt, they would have my heart sliced out before I hit the sidewalk.

So I climbed into the back of the Mercedes. The seated man was as small as his two henchmen. I could just make him out in the dim illumination of a nearby streetlamp. About fifty. Very well groomed. Hand-tailored suit. Iron-gray hair in waves. A sad, thoughtful face. His cologne filled the car. Fruity.

"Please accept my apologies, Mr. Scuro," he said in a high, fluty voice, "for this unconventional method of arranging to meet you. But I thought it better than visiting your club. My name is Ivar Gutierrez," he said, not offering to shake hands. "I am the proprietor of several things, including the chain of Kwik Kleen drycleaning shops. Perhaps you have heard of them. More than a hundred stores in the New York area."

"Mr. Gutierrez, Peter's Place already has a drycleaning and laundry service. It's contracted for."

"I know," he said. "I know a great deal about your establishment. For instance, I know that you personally own twenty-six percent of the stock. I would like to purchase that stock at an agreeable price. Cash."

It took my breath away. I had no idea how he had discovered the exact extent of my holdings in Peter's Place.

But what amazed me most was his offer to buy. It made me realize the value of what I had and my determination to hang onto it.

"I'm sorry, Mr. Gutierrez," I said, "but my shares are not for sale."

"Don't say no so quickly," he chided me gently. "Think about it. You paid, I believe, one hundred and four thousand for your twenty-six percent. I am prepared to offer a quarter of a million dollars. Isn't that a nice profit, Mr. Scuro?"

And three years ago I had been eating spaghetti and meatballs at Blotto's! I would have signed an agreement to sell that minute if it hadn't been for the possibility of a worldwide chain of Peter's Places. That dream made a quarter-million seem like pocket change.

"Naturally," Gutierrez went on smoothly, "I do not expect you to come to a decision this moment. But you will consider it? A young man such as you could do many things with so much money. Is that not true?"

"Yes," I said hoarsely, "that's true."

"Then I may expect to receive your decision shortly?" He suddenly whipped a business card from his side pocket and thrust it into my hand. "You may call this number at any hour. Day or night. If I am not present, feel free to leave a message. Yes or no. I really believe you would be wise to say yes."

"I shall give your kind offer very careful consideration," I said formally.

"Hokay," he said, smiling for the first time and revealing one gold tooth.

I climbed out of the car and the two little thugs let me leave. I walked away quite steadily, not looking back, and it was only when I was inside Peter's Place, the door locked, bolted, and chained behind me, that I realized I was sodden with sweat.

159

When Martha didn't show up for work the next morning, I called her about eleven o'clock.

"I don't think I'm going to make it," she said in a dull voice.

"I guessed that," I said. "But I've got something important to tell you. How's about if I pop over for a few minutes?"

"I'm really not in any condition to entertain visitors."

"So I'll entertain you. Feeling peckish, dear? I could pick up a jar of calves'-foot jelly."

"Make it Armagnac," she said.

I think I expected to find a frowzy slattern, hair down and eyes bleary. She would be wearing a smelly robe and trying to cure the shakes with a Bloody Mary. The apartment would be furred with dust and littered with cigarette butts.

It wasn't like that at all. She was dressed with reasonable chic, hair done and hands steady. The apartment was neat, the ashtrays empty.

"I got all gussied-up and ready to go to the club," she confessed, "and then I couldn't move. Peter, what's wrong with me?"

"The megrims," I said. "And possibly the fantods. What you need is a wee bit of the old nasty."

I uncorked the Armagnac and poured us each a small tot. I sat alongside her on the black leather chesterfield and put an arm about her shoulders. I really liked that woman, and it hurt me to see her all torn up over some shithead politician.

I did a new bit I had invented: impersonations of Anthony Cannis and Michael Gelesco discovering the glories of the Venus de Milo.

"Hey, Tony, this cunt ain't got no arms!"

By that time I had her laughing so hard her eyes were streaming.

"Jesus, Peter," she said, gasping. "You're just what the doctor ordered."

"And I make house calls," I said.

Then I described my previous night's encounter with Ivar Gutierrez, including how much I had been offered for my stake in Peter's Place, Inc.

"Forget it," she advised. "He sounds like a small-time crook trying to muscle his way into easy money."

"You think so? For a small-time crook he's doing all right. And he travels well escorted."

"A couple of barrio louts he picked up for an hour's work. Just give him a call, Peter, and tell him you're not interested. That'll be the end of it."

"I'll do it," I said. "Now let's talk about you. . . . Martha, I don't like to see what's been happening to you lately."

"I know," she said. "I just don't seem to have any zap anymore. I realize I'm not pulling my weight at the club. Do the goons know how many days I've been out?"

"I didn't tell them," I said, "but they know."

"Oh yeah," she said bitterly. "They would. Well, fuck them."

"But what about Yance and me?" I said. "Even with King filling in as host, we're working our tails off. Doing *your* work. It's not fair to us."

"Pour me another brandy," she said.

We both sipped our new drinks reflectively, not speaking. I looked around that room, cluttered with trumpeting pachyderms, and thought of all the times I had been there and all the important changes in my life that had started there.

"Anything new with Mr. Bowker?" I asked casually.

"Yes. Remember I told you he threatened to commit suicide if I left him? Well, now he says that if I leave him, first he'll kill me and *then* he'll commit suicide."

"Jesus Christ!" I burst out. "Martha, this guy is a nut."

"He's a politician," she said, shrugging. "You think any normal, sane man gets into that line of business?"

"Well, you've got to get rid of him," I said sternly. "He may be just talking about murder and suicide, but it's not worth taking the chance."

She sighed. "You're right, Peter. It's not only myself I've got to think about, but there's my son. What I've decided to do is this: I'll move back to Chicago. I'll walk out on my employment contract—no one's going to sue—

but I'll hang on to my twenty-six percent of Peter's Place. That should bring in enough loot so maybe I can open a small boutique in Chi. What do you think?"

"Well . . ." I said, "I hate to see you go, dear, but I can't suggest any other solution. When are you figuring on leaving?"

"The first of the year. That'll give Yance or someone else a chance to learn my job. I own this apartment and I'll get a nice price for it, so I won't be hurting in the money department. I really think it's the best thing to do. I've got to get rid of this guy one way or another, just for my peace of mind, and this seems the best way."

"What's *with* him, Martha?" I asked. "As a matter of fact, what's with you? I mean, what's the attraction between you two? Is it love or sex— or what?"

"Oh, honey," she said. "It's only in movies and books and plays that people have one motive. In real life we all have a dozen motives, all at once, for the way we act, and who the hell can sort them out and say I did this because of that? Look at you. You're in the flesh game because you like easy money, you enjoy sex, you like women, you like to be on, you like to live by your wits, you can't stand the thought of a regular nine-to-five job, and so forth and so on. You've got a million motives for what you're doing."

"Yes," I said thoughtfully. "You're right. I guess the thing is that everyone thinks he's so goddamned complex and everyone else is simple."

"I feel better now," Martha said. "Just talking to you. Thanks for coming over. Maybe I'll come back to the club with you. Knock me a kiss."

So we kissed. She hung on to me tightly.

"You're really a sweet man," she whispered. "Rotten, but sweet."

When we got back to Peter's Place, I went immediately to my office. I found Gutierrez's business card and called. I was shifted from extension to extension, but I finally got him.

"Mr. Gutierrez," I said, "this is Peter Scuro."

"Ah, yes," he said in his warbling voice.

"I've considered your offer, Mr. Gutierrez, and I have decided that now is not the time to sell my stock in Peter's Place."

"I disagree," he said immediately. "I think now is the best time. The price may come down in the future. It is even conceivable that your holdings may eventually be worthless."

"I don't believe that," I said firmly. "I've given this matter a great deal of thought, and—"

"Think some more," he interrupted. "Think very long and very carefully. Perhaps you are not aware of what is involved here, Mr. Scuro. I urge you strongly to give my generous offer every possible consideration."

"I'm sorry," I said, beginning to get angry. "I've made up my mind. No deal, Mr. Gutierrez."

"I think you may change your mind," he said. "I'll be in touch, Mr. Scuro. You'll be hearing from me."

The menace in his words and tone was real, but at least I had the satisfaction of hanging up first.

160

Late in September I came up with an idea that netted the club at least another thousand a week.

It was a lottery and worked like this: Interested members bought numbered tickets at five dollars each. They could purchase as many as they wished. Every Friday night at midnight, in the Dream Room, we held a drawing. The winner was entitled to a scene the following week with the stud of her choice.

This weekly lottery (called Bango!) was only one factor contributing to the phenomenal financial success of Peter's Place. Bookings for the Mardi Gras Room were on the rise, David and his piano were attracting crowds almost every night, and the upstairs bedrooms were so busy that on one Saturday night we actually had a waiting line.

"It's like a bakery," Yance said, marveling. "Maybe we should make the customers take numbers."

Martha and I no longer attended the regular business meetings unless specifically requested; we felt we were well represented by Oscar Gotwold and Ignatz Samuelson. But I saw the total of each day's receipts and knew how well we were doing. I couldn't wait until the year-end divvying of the spoils; I could use the cash.

I was in my office on the last day of September, checking monthly bills for liquor and food supplies, when suddenly the door was flung open. I looked up and there stood Sybil Headley, the weight-lifting lady. She glared at me so wrathfully that I scrambled hastily to my feet.

"You prick!" she shouted.

"Hey," I said, holding up my hands. "Wait a minute. I don't know what your beef is, but there's no need for language like that."

She came into the room, slamming the door behind her.

"You really screwed me, didn't you?" she said fiercely.

"Look," I said. "I haven't the faintest idea of what you're talking about. But if you'll just calm down and tell me, maybe we can solve your problem."

She looked at me, face twisted. "You really don't know?"

I held up a palm. "I swear I don't. Now why don't you sit down."

She flounced into the armchair alongside my desk, crossed her bare, muscular legs. She really did have extraordinary skin. I think I mentioned that it looked like butterscotch Ultrasuede. She had a deeper tan now; it looked like pie crust. Succulent.

"Would you care for a drink, Miss Headley?" I asked politely. "On the house."

"No," she said sharply. "You really don't know what happened?"

"I really don't."

"Who did you tell about my article in *Madhatter?*"

"Ah . . . my associates."

"Are they the power boys?"

"Sort of."

"Well," she said bitterly, "they killed the whole thing."

"Oh?" I said, interested. "How?"

"Signed up for six months of full-page ads in four-color. For the Barcarole Boutique. So the publishers canceled the story on Peter's Place."

"I thought you said your magazine is not for—"

"I know what I said. Was I ever wrong."

She twisted in her chair, stretching and clenching her fingers, making hard fists. I watched her sympathetically. Learning how the overworld worked had obviously hit her hard.

"Did you scream?" I asked her.

"Did I ever!" she said with a wry smile. "I yelled my head off. I made such a fucking nuisance of myself, they finally told me that was the way it was going to be, and if I didn't like it I could resign."

"Did you?"

"No," she said quietly, "I didn't. I need the job. Oh God," she cried, "what a lousy world this is."

"It's the only one we've got," I reminded her.

She was silent a while, then sighed. "I think I've just lost my halo."

"You're more human without it," I assured her.

She stared at me. "You don't like me much, do you?"

"I didn't," I said. "I do now."

"Listen," she said, looking over my head. "Do you take scenes?"

"Now and then," I said. "But never with Arnold Schwarzenegger." She laughed. "I promise to behave."

"Let's go," I said.

161

Perhaps because of my stage training, I thought of clothes as costumes. (It is, I think, a feminine trait.) My wardrobe was enormous, but I never had enough changes. They were, I suppose, disguises.

One October morning I took a few hours off from the office to go shopping on Fifth Avenue. I didn't intend to spend a lot of money—I didn't have a great deal to spend—but thought I might pick up a few shirts, a sweater, and something small and funny for Mabel Hetter.

It was topcoat weather, brisk and blowy. The flags were snapping on Fifth Avenue, and all the pedestrians seemed to have that added hustle that increases as Christmas approaches. The clear sky was a postcard blue, and I saw the first roast chestnut vendor of the season.

Manhattan looked like a stage set. Someone clever had designed it and the curtain had just gone up to applause. There was an open, shining glory about it and I was indecently happy.

I wandered about, looking in shop windows, buying a few inconsequential things. I considered getting a haircut, but it seemed too serious a decision to make on such a pleasant, indolent day. So I just strolled.

I bought Mabel a miniature chocolate piano, complete with white keys, and had it delivered. I enclosed one of my engraved personal cards. Just my name in small script. How elegant can you get?

I had lunch at the Plaza: Belon oysters and a small bottle of muscadet. I overtipped because I wanted everyone to be happy. Then I walked back to Peter's Place.

King Hayes was hosting that afternoon. He was wearing his chalk-striped gray flannel, to which he had added a tattersall waistcoat. He really looked great and I told him so.

"Like you always say," he said, grinning, "go with the flow. Hey, a package came for you."

"Oh?" I said. "Who from?"

"No return address. A messenger delivered it and then took off. Didn't even wait for a tip. It's on your desk."

King followed me into my office. The package on my desk was about the size of a shoebox. Wrapped in brown paper and tied with twine. It reminded me of the package filled with cut newspaper I had thrust into the hands of Sidney Quink.

I bent over to inspect it. Just my name printed in block letters. I picked it up and held it to my ear.

"It's not ticking," I told King.

"Shake it," he said. "If it gurgles, I'll help you drink it."

We were laughing as I slid off the cord, unwrapped the paper, lifted the lid. We leaned down to look.

The box had a layer of white cotton batting. Nestled in the center was an oversized soft plastic penis. One of those grotesque things you can buy in a novelty shop. I don't know what they're used for. Perhaps as a dildo or just a gag gift.

But this one had been neatly sliced in two. With a razor blade, I guessed.

We both stared down at that severed schlong.

"Sick joke," King Hayes said.

"Sick," I said, "but no joke."

"You know who sent it?"

"I can guess," I said, hardly hearing my own voice.

I didn't panic or get hysterical, but I admit to a paralyzing numbness. King must have seen it, because he brought me a double brandy that got my heart pumping again.

I showed the thing to Martha.

"Jesus Christ!" she said.

"My friend, the drycleaner," I said.

"Oh God, Peter. You better call Cannis and Gelesco right away. They'll know what to do." Then she looked at me more closely. "Sit down for a minute—you look shook. I'll call them for you."

But they were gone for the day and couldn't be reached. Martha was very firm with the secretary and told her that I'd be at the Barcarole Boutique first thing in the morning; it was of the utmost importance that I see them.

After she hung up, I said bitterly, "Why didn't you tell her it was a matter of life or death?"

"Peter," Martha said, "do you want to come home with me tonight? You can sleep over."

"No," I said, trying to smile. "Thank you, but I can cope."

162

But I found I couldn't cope. Oh, I did my job, but it was all automatic. I couldn't forget the implied threat of that bisected plastic cock.

When the club emptied out, I decided against going to the Friendship Deli. Gutierrez obviously knew of it, and I had no desire for another meeting. So I locked, bolted, and chained the outside door. I left most of the lights on and went into the bar for a vodka.

The snaps, creaks, and soft thuds of the old townhouse had never bothered me before, but now those normal sounds corroded my nerves. I imagined all sorts of things, none of them pleasant.

Finally, around three in the morning, I phoned Mabel Hetter. Woke her up, of course. I told her I was so lonely and wanted to be with her. Could I come over?

"Fab!" she said. "Hurry up."

I called my garage and offered twenty bucks if they'd bring my car around. It was there in ten minutes, and ten minutes after that I was parking only a half-block from Mabel's apartment house. During the drive up Sixth Avenue, I had kept an eye on the rearview mirror to make certain I wasn't being followed. What a way to live!

Mabel was wearing white batiste shorty pajamas embroidered with little bluebells. She smelled sweetly of soap and sleep, and wasn't at all annoyed by my unexpected appearance. She seemed so genuinely pleased to see me that I vowed on the spot to be kinder and more considerate of her.

She fetched me a tumbler of ice and I filled it with vodka I had brought from the club. She sat on my lap and I started her talking about what she had done the previous day. Sipping my drink and listening to her artless prattle eased me.

As she nattered on, I wondered what an entire life would be like with this innocent. Boring, I supposed, but it would have its compensations. She was good-hearted, a skilled cook, enthusiastic in the sack. Simple virtues, true, but after what had happened to me, they seemed estimable.

"Peter, are you all right?" she asked anxiously.

"Jim-dandy," I assured her. "A little tired maybe. It was a rough day."

"You seem sort of depressed."

"Nah," I said. "Just relaxing. You were a dear to let me come over."

"You know," she said giggling, "when you called, I was having a marvy dream about you. It was so crazy!" she said, blushing. Then she squirmed around to whisper in my ear. "In my dream, you had *two* things!"

I drained my vodka, just drank it straight down.

"Isn't that wild?" she said.

But it wasn't so wild in bed. I wanted it to be. I wanted to find total memory loss in her complaisant body. But I discovered to my chagrin that I was unable to perform. It was not the first time in my life, of course, but it was terribly frustrating at that moment.

I couldn't delude myself: It was fear that was defeating me. I had a horrific vision of my career in ruins, all because of a stupid little man who was smart enough to threaten my most cherished conceit.

So, to conceal my shame, I was uncommonly tender and loving, and had the satisfaction of seeing the upper half of her bifurcated body begin to glow with a rosy flush, a sure signal of her arousal.

I finished by introducing her to what the studs called "bushwhacking." It was obviously a new and unimagined practice to her, but she accepted this service gleefully, crying "Super! Super! Super!"

One advantage of stage experience—you learn to ad-lib.

The best part, for me, came when Mabel fell asleep in my arms and I could hold her soft, young warmth and feel safe. I almost wept with the peace that she unwittingly provided. I put my lips to a little rosebud nipple and she groaned contentedly in her sleep.

163

We were in the conference room of the Barcarole, and the box containing the sliced penis lay on the polished table. Anthony Cannis motioned toward it with his cigar.

"Plastic," he said. "A toy. You'd think he'd have sent the real thing."

"The guy's got no class," Michael Gelesco said. "Everyone knows that."

I looked at them in astonishment. "You know Ivar Gutierrez?" I asked.

Cannis: "Sure, we know him."

Gelesco: "A putz. Tell us again what he said."

I described once more my encounter with Gutierrez.

Gelesco looked at me narrowly through a billow of cigar smoke. "You weren't tempted to sell?"

"Hell, no!" I said forthrightly. "One of these days my share of Peter's Place is going to be worth more than that."

"Attaboy," Cannis said. "If you wanted to sell, me and Mike would buy you out for more than that. Wouldn't we, Mike?"

"In a minute," Gelesco affirmed. "That joint is a fucking gold mine."

"And then," I continued, "when I called him to turn down his offer, he wouldn't take no for an answer and said I'd be hearing from him."

"Tony," Gelesco said, "we better get things moving."

"I'll get on the horn," Cannis said, rising. "Peter, you stay here for a half-hour. By then we'll have things organized and you can go back to the club."

He left the room. I was alone with Michael Gelesco. He leaned back in his chair, chomped on his cigar. He jerked his head toward the box on the table.

"That thing spooked you, huh, Peter? Let me tell you something about hard guys. You got no experience with them, so it's natural you wouldn't know. Real hard guys don't threaten; they *do*. It's the cheapies who try to throw a scare into you. All you got to do is call their bluff."

"How do we do that with Gutierrez?" I said nervously.

"Well, right now Tony is on the phone to our security service. They'll send muscle over to the club. It'll be guarded inside and out, twenty-four hours a day, just in case that bum gets some cute ideas about busting up the place."

"Guards in uniform?" I asked, horrified.

"Nah, these boys will be young and well-dressed. Very polite and well-behaved. You won't even know they're there."

"I hope they won't try coming on to the customers," I said, trying to smile.

"They won't," Gelesco said. "They'll have their orders."

"How long will they be there?"

"Not long," he promised. "Two, three days maybe. Until we convince Gutierrez that he doesn't want in."

"And how do we do that?"

He stared at me coldly. "You really don't want to know, do you?"

"No, no," I said hastily. "Whatever you decide is all right with me."

"Don't worry," Gelesco said with heavy good-humor. "Your schlong is safe."

Anthony Cannis came back in and nodded to his partner. "All set," he said. "Five guys around-the-clock. You tell Peter what we're doing?"

"I told him."

"They'll be there by the time you get back," Cannis said to me. "They'll eat in the kitchen, one guy at a time. If I was you, I'd stay inside for the next couple of days. It won't take that long; that scuz will get the word —you'll see."

"I hope you're right," I said.

"You gotta trust us, Peter," Cannis said, coming over to pat my shoulder. "You just keep running the club and making us all rich. Leave stuff like this to us."

"Right," Gelesco said. "Remember Timmy O'Neill and how he tried to move in?"

"I remember," Cannis said, smiling reminiscently. "I wonder where Timmy is now."

"You know this new onion-flavored liverwurst?" Gelesco said. "I think he's in that."

They laughed uproariously.

164

Cannis and Gelesco did exactly as they had promised. By the time I returned to Peter's Place, the security guards were there. They were sedately dressed young men, a few of them quite handsome. One stayed outside the door. The others moved about the interior. I presumed they were armed but saw no unsightly bulges.

There wasn't a moment of the day or night when Peter's Place wasn't protected. As I had been told, they were quiet, polite, and made no effort to cozy up to the customers. But I did see a few clients come on to *them*.

I took Anthony Cannis' advice and didn't set foot outside the club for three days. By late October, I was beginning to suffer from cabin fever. But then one morning I leafed through a late edition of the *Daily News* brought in by King Hayes and saw it: a short item reporting that six Kwik Kleen drycleaning stores had been firebombed the previous night.

Two had been totally destroyed and the others badly damaged. There were no deaths or injuries. The owner of the chain, Mr. Ivar Gutierrez, was quoted as saying that he had been having labor troubles recently.

I showed the newspaper story to Martha and she smiled knowingly.

The next day I searched the morning papers eagerly. Four more Kwik Kleen stores had been firebombed; three of them were completely gutted. That afternoon, our security guards were suddenly withdrawn and I got a phone call from Michael Gelesco.

"All clear," he said tersely. "We've come to a friendly understanding with you know who. You can go out now."

"Thank you," I said humbly.

I went into Martha's office to give her the good news.

"I'm glad I'm getting out," she said. "Peter, our problem is that we're just too successful. Mostly from your ideas. It was too much to hope that the overworld wouldn't move in. The rich and the politicians and the mob guys—they can smell money a mile away, so they're taking over."

"You think Cannis and Gelesco are mob guys?"

"You mean like belonging to the Mafia? No, but I'm sure they have an understanding with them. Maybe they pay off. That goes for Octavius Caesar, too."

"It's hard to think of that dotty old man being part of a criminal conspiracy," I said.

"Is it?" Martha said indifferently.

I sat down alongside her desk and lighted cigarettes for us. We smoked in silence a moment. Then . . .

"I'm really going to miss you, babe," I said.

She leaned forward to pat my cheek. "You're the only reason I'll regret leaving," she said. "We had a crazy time together."

"That we did."

"Sometimes I wish we had stayed small," she said. "With just those two West Side cribs. They were all ours and we were making a nice buck. Now look what's happened: We're a million-dollar corporation, and every few weeks we have to run to the shtarkers to get us out of a jam. I warn you, Peter, it's going to get worse. Those guys will find some way to take over the whole shooting match."

"Over my dead body," I said.

She looked at me. "If necessary," she said.

"Jesus, Martha, don't talk like that."

"It's the truth. That's one of the reasons I'm getting out."

"Have you told Wilson Bowker you're leaving?"

She stirred restlessly. "No, and I don't intend to. I'll write him a letter the day I leave. With no forwarding address."

"He'll find you if he wants to."

"Maybe," she said, sighing wearily. "But I'm hoping with me gone and his political campaign heating up, he'll come to his senses. Peter, I really believe you better start thinking about getting out, too."

"What would I do," I said, "sell Jockey shorts at the King's Arms?"

"If you hang on to your stock, they might send you enough money to live comfortably."

I was silent.

She stared at me with a crooked smile. "You really like this business, don't you?"

I nodded. "I like the excitement. The chance to make big bucks and maybe build something famous. Also, you've got to remember I'm a failed actor. If I run away from this, it would be another failure. How many times can you flop before you lose your chutzpah?"

"Well . . ." she said, "I tried. Just watch out for Laurel and Hardy.

If they get a chance, they'll throw you to the wolves and call you a shmuck for letting them."

"They wouldn't do that," I protested. "They think I'm doing a great job."

"You may be pushing forty," she said, "but you're so young you've still got dimples in your ass. Peter, believe me, you're playing in the big leagues now. Promise me you'll think about getting out."

It was my turn to pat her cheek.

"I promise," I said.

165

On the evening of November 9, King Hayes was working as host and I was in my office. I finished what I was doing before midnight and told King I was turning in. He said he'd lock up and turn on our new burglar alarm before he left.

The club was busy, but I knew the noise wouldn't bother me. I went up to my bedroom, took a hot shower, and crawled into bed. I was asleep almost instantly. The ringing of the phone awoke me. I thought I had been sleeping for hours, but the bedside clock showed it was only 1:05 A.M.

"Peter? Yance. Did I wake you?"

"That's all right."

"Bad news, Peter. I was just listening to the news on the radio. A woman's body was found in an apartment on the East Side. Identified as Martha Twombly."

Silence.

"Peter? Are you there?"

"I'm here," I said faintly. "Yance, are you *sure?*"

"That's what the announcer said. Martha Twombly. East Eighty-third."

Silence.

"I'm sorry, Peter."

"Did they say how it happened?" I asked, wiping my eyes. They were dry.

"No. Just that her door was open and a neighbor found the body."

"Oh God."

Silence.

"Yance, you think I should go up there?"

"I don't know. Maybe you should stay away."

"I think I'll go. I think I should."

"You want me to meet you there?"

"No, but thanks anyway."

"Take care of yourself," Yance said anxiously. "Call me if you like; I'll be up for a while."

I pulled on a sweater, slacks, a sport jacket. I took a topcoat. I went downstairs. There was laughter and music coming from the Dream Room.

"Ah-ha," King Hayes said. "Going to do a little tomcatting to-night?"

I gave him a bleak smile.

There were police barricades in front of Martha's apartment house. But no mob scene; just a few curious pedestrians trying to peer into the lobby. A uniformed cop stood inside. He opened the plate glass door when I went up.

"You live here?" he asked.

"No, but—"

"Sorry," he said. "Only residents allowed in."

"I'm a close friend of, uh, the woman who was . . ."

"Yeah?" he said. "And?"

"I don't know," I said confusedly. "I thought I might be able to help."

"Sarge," he called over his shoulder.

Another policeman, mustachioed, with chevrons on his sleeve, walked over.

"My name is Peter Scuro," I said. "I am—was a close friend of the, uh, victim. I thought maybe I could . . ."

Again my voice trailed away.

"Sure, Peter," the sergeant said affably. "Come along with me."

We rode up in the elevator together.

"Smells like snow," the policeman said. "Did you notice that?"

"It's raw," I said, nodding.

The door to Martha's apartment was open. The sergeant ushered me in ahead of him. I looked about nervously.

"That's all right," the cop said. "They took her away. You come in here."

He took my arm lightly and led me back to the bedroom. The apartment was a shambles: lamps upset, drawers yanked open, porcelain elephants broken.

There was a tall, exhausted man with pitted cheeks slumped on the edge of Martha's bed. He was in mufti. He was going through the bedside table. He looked up at us through wire-rimmed glasses.

"This here is Peter Scuro," the sergeant said. "Says he was a close friend of the recently deceased."

The man nodded, climbed to his feet, held out a hand.

"Detective Jules Slotkin," he said. "What was that name again?"

"Peter Scuro," I said, shaking the bony hand.

"You knew Martha Twombly?"

"We worked together," I said. "At Peter's Place, a private club for women on West Fifty-fourth. Can you tell me what happened here?"

"Sit down for a minute," he said, gesturing toward the bed. "This must be quite a shock for you."

"Yes," I said, "it is."

We sat side by side on the bed.

"You know her long?" he asked casually.

"About three years."

"But she lived here longer than that?"

"I guess so," I said. "She was living here when I met her."

"It's not important," he said. "The super will know—if we can ever find him. Was her apartment broken into before—do you know?"

"Not to my knowledge."

"Was she careful about locking the outside door?"

"Always," I said.

"Uh-huh," he said. "Someone jimmied the lock. Splintered jamb. The chain hook busted off. Must have made a hell of a racket."

"Didn't anyone hear anything?" I asked.

"No one we talked to heard anything," he said. "The closest people to her went out to the theater. They were the ones who found her."

"How was she . . . ?" I asked, my mouth dry.

"Skull crushed," he said, looking at me. "With a bronze elephant. She liked elephants, huh?"

"Yes. She collected them."

"Do you know if she kept a lot of cash on the premises?"

"I don't know," I said. "I do know she had some good jewelry."

"Uh-huh," he said, peering at me. "You her boyfriend?"

"No," I said. "Just a business associate. You think robbery was the, uh, motive?"

He ignored my question. "Did she ever get any dirty phone calls?"

"I don't know."

"Ever threatened by anyone?"

"Not to my knowledge."

"Enemies? Personal or business?"

"Not that I know of."

"She have any fights with anyone? Business or personal?"

"She never mentioned any."

"You're a big help," he said, a tired smile taking the sting from his words. "Would she let someone in she didn't know?"

"Never," I said.

"That's what I figured," he said, nodding. "The way I see it, it went like this: The perp, probably a junkie looking for a quick score, gets into the building by the front or back door. The locks on both of them are a joke; you could spring them with a nail file. Why he picked her apartment, we'll probably never know. So he knocks on her door. No answer, so he figures nobody's home. He jimmies the door and starts to take the place apart, collecting whatever he can fence. She comes home and finds her door open. Right then she should have started screaming or run to a neighbor's apartment to call the cops. But she's not thinking straight. Not many people do in a situation like that. So she goes barging in. She and the perp fight. That's when the lamps get knocked over and stuff broken. She was a big, heavy woman?"

"Yes."

"She looked like it. So she puts up a good fight and the guy has to bash her head in with an elephant. Maybe he didn't intend to waste her. Just knock her out. But she's down and he takes off. That's the way I see it."

"It sounds likely," I said slowly.

"You buy the part about the perp being in the apartment when she comes home?"

"It sounds logical."

"Yeah?" he said wearily. "Then how come the chain fastening is broken? If she wasn't home when the guy got in, the chain wouldn't be on and so it wouldn't be broken, would it?"

"Some chains you can put on from the outside," I said.

"Not the kind she had."

I was silent.

"It's all bullshit," Detective Slotkin said, staring at me through his wire-rimmed glasses. "I don't know what happened here and maybe we'll never know—unless we get lucky. We get a lot of these things. Most of them go in the file. Who was her next of kin—do you know?"

"She has—had a son in a military academy in Virginia."

"I found his address in her desk. What about the aunt in Chicago?"

"I never knew she had an aunt in Chicago," I admitted.

"I thought you were a close friend of hers."

"I was, but she never mentioned the aunt."

He took a small notebook from his side pocket and had me spell my name. He also wrote down my address and phone number.

"Good-looking woman," he said. "Any boyfriends? Or was that another thing she never mentioned to you?"

"I guess she dated," I said. "She rarely talked about her personal life."

"Uh-huh," he said. "Was she divorced?"

"I never got it straight," I told him. "I think she was separated. That's the feeling I got—that her husband just took off, and she didn't know where he was, and didn't care."

"So it goes," the detective said, snapping his notebook shut. "If I think of anything else, I'll give you a call. Thanks for coming by. Most people don't want to get involved. Here's my card in case you think of something I should know."

"She was a fine woman," I said foolishly.

"I'd love to know how that chain got busted, wouldn't you?"

I didn't answer.

"Crazy," he said, shaking his head. "If she was inside, and the chain was on, you'd think she'd scream bloody murder when someone started breaking down her door. Wouldn't you think she'd do that?"

"I guess so."

"Unless," he went on, musing aloud, "it might have been someone she knew. She lets him in. And suddenly, before she can defend herself, she gets snuffed. So the perp tries to make it look like a B-and-E. You know—breaks things, takes her jewelry, upsets lamps, and all that. Then, on his way *out*, the perp jimmies the door to make it look like a break-in. Only he goes too far and busts the chain, not realizing it'll prove she was inside the apartment when he arrived. That's pretty nutty, isn't it?"

"Yes," I said, "it is."

"Sure," he said. "I've been watching too many crime shows on TV."

"Uh," I said, "did she—was she, ah, *wounded?* I mean, did it appear that she fought with her—with the guy?"

He looked at me admiringly. "You're all right," he said. "You got more on your neck than a hat rack. No, she had no defensive wounds.

Nothing like that. Just the hole in the back of her skull that killed her. That's why I like the story of her letting in someone she knew, someone who broke her head when she had her back turned and wasn't expecting it. I appreciate your dropping around."

I started out of the bedroom. But he called, "Mr. Scuro," and when I turned around, he was beckoning me with a splintery forefinger. He went to Martha's closet, picked up the riding crop. He walked over to me, swishing it through the air. It made a *wheesh* sound.

"Ever see this before?" he asked me.

"The whip? No, I never have."

"Any idea why she had it here?"

"No."

"Uh-huh." His eyes glittered through his wire-rimmed glasses. "Interesting case," Detective Jules Slotkin said. "I might spend some time on it. Just for fun—you know?"

166

Mabel Hetter finished a rather tremulous rendition of "Wanting You" and turned around on the piano bench to face me.

"I have this marvy idea," she said brightly. "Why don't you move in here with me?"

At any other time I might have greeted such a proposal with a shout of laughter. But it was the day after Martha's murder and I was in a somber mood. Nothing like sudden death to concentrate your mind on wasted days and noble resolves.

So I didn't reject her suggestion immediately.

"Oh, Mae," I said. "That's the nicest thing anyone's said to me for a long time, and I appreciate the invitation, I really do. But it's a big, important step, dear, and we should consider it carefully."

"Don't you want to live with me?" she said in hurt tones.

"Of course I do," I said, "but look at it this way: We've been seeing each other two or three times a week and getting along wonderfully. But that's no guarantee we could be with each other every day and maintain the same relationship. I might drive you right up the wall."

"Never," she vowed. "And you could have as much independence as you wanted. You could go out with other women if you liked and I could see other men."

That surprised me. I was egomaniacal enough to assume she wanted me exclusively.

"Let's think about it," I urged. "I'd hate for us to rush into a steady relationship and then find we've made a mistake."

"All right," she said equably.

I spent the night with her and our lovemaking was a smash success. I was awed by my repeated prowess, and if Mabel's barks of delight were to be believed, she was too.

I knew the reason, of course. Just as I had been frightened into impotence by Ivar Gutierrez's threat—the sliced dork—so now did Martha Twombly's violent end spur me to a frantic desire to clutch hot life, hold it close and drain it.

After she slept, snoring quietly with little burbling sounds, I went naked into the living room, sat slumped in an armchair, and nursed a small brandy. Deep, deep thoughts . . .

Mabel was not the woman for me; that I knew. Not as beautiful as Jenny Tolliver nor as intriguing as Nicole Radburn. That is not to put her down. She would be perfect for another man—but not for me.

I sat silently, staring into the darkness, seeking. And wondered what I was longing for.

167

Martha's aunt came from Chicago to make arrangements for shipping the body back. I persuaded her to let us hold a memorial service in a funeral chapel on upper Madison Avenue. She agreed when I assured her Peter's Place would pick up the tab for everything.

Yancy Burnett, King Hayes, and I went to work on the studs to ensure a good turnout. We also put up a notice in the Dream Room and a lot of clients promised to come. Clara Hoffheimer said she'd be there, and so did Oscar Gotwold and Iggy Samuelson. We closed the club until 2:00 P.M. so the staff could attend.

Anthony Cannis, Michael Gelesco, and Octavius Caesar said that unfortunately they could not be present, but they all sent large and expensive flower arrangements. The studs chipped in for their own floral piece. Yance and I had flowers delivered. The small chapel looked and smelled like a hothouse.

The Chicago aunt was a grim, gaunt woman whose dentures clacked. She hung on to the arm of Martha's son, a tall, skinny boy wearing his military academy uniform. He looked pale, bewildered, and nervous. The two of them sat down front, facing the coffin.

The casket was on a draped gurney before the podium. On the closed lid was a bouquet of roses from Martha's son. The service was conducted by a minister provided by the funeral chapel. Organ music was piped in via a loudspeaker. I think it was recorded.

The minister, an earnest, totally bald young man, had asked me for details about Martha's life that he might include in his eulogy. I told him what I thought he should know—it wasn't much—and he worked it all into a sorrowful address to the assembled mourners that was mercifully brief.

I had stationed myself against the rear wall near the door. It was sheer cowardice; I figured that if it got too much for me, I could make a quick unobtrusive exit. But I stayed for the entire service.

During his droning sermon, the clergyman said this "splendid, vital woman" had been "plucked from life" by one whose "violent and ungodly philosophy" made a mockery of "all we hold dear" and threatened the very existence of a "peaceful and loving city."

He sounded like he was cribbing from one of Wilson Bowker's campaign speeches, and I wondered what the reaction of the audience would be if I suddenly shouted out that the apostle of law-and-order had put that "splendid, vital woman" in her coffin.

I really believed it. I was convinced, as Detective Jules Slotkin obviously was, that Martha had not been the victim of a street villain. No, she had known her killer and admitted him. Or her.

Because if it wasn't Wilson Bowker who had crushed Martha's skull, it was his wife Alice. She was capable of it.

Both of the Bowkers had enough motive. Either would be admitted to Martha's apartment. And both had the intelligence to try to cover up their crime by making it look like a common burglary-homicide.

The moment the service ended, I ducked out and found a public phone near a basement room with a windowed door. It revealed two long rows of waiting caskets, ranging from simple pine to ornate bronze.

I took the card from my wallet and called Detective Slotkin. The man who answered said Slotkin wasn't there but could be reached at another number. He gave it to me and I dialed that one.

"Slotkin," a weary voice answered.

"This is Peter Scuro," I said. "I met you the other night at Martha Twombly's apartment. The woman who was killed on East Eighty-third."

"Oh yeah," he said. "Sure. I remember."

"I've just come from her funeral service," I said. "I thought you might be here. Isn't that what the police usually do—attend the funerals of murder victims in case the killer might show up?"

"Yes," he said, "we do that sometimes. But I've been taken off that case."

"What?"

"I've been taken off that case," he repeated patiently. "That's why I wasn't at the service. I've been transferred. To community relations."

I didn't know what to say.

"In East Harlem," he went on. "I *hablar* the language pretty good."

"Well, who's handling the case now?" I demanded.

"The Twombly kill? I really don't know, Mr. Scuro. They probably divided my case load amongst three or four guys. Why? Have you got anything new?"

"No, nothing new," I said slowly. "I was just wondering how the investigation was coming along."

"These things take time," he said. "If there's any break, you'll read about it in the newspapers."

"Yes," I said, "I guess I will. Good luck on your new assignment."

"Thank you."

"Was it sudden? The transfer?"

"Well . . ." he said warily, "I wasn't expecting it. It came as a surprise."

"Uh-huh," I said.

168

Yancy Burnett moved into Martha's office and took over all her duties. I gave up my hosting chores and devoted all my time to scheduling studs, call boys, and escorts. Yance recommended a friend of his as host and he worked out well. A very nice guy. Flitty, but nice.

Within a week or so it was as if Martha had never been. Yance removed all her personal things from his office and brought in a few Aubrey Beardsley prints to decorate the walls. The clients learned to call him personally for scenes, and there was no indication that business was suffering because of Martha's death.

I asked Oscar Gotwold what had happened to Martha's twenty-six-percent share in Peter's Place, Inc. Did she bequeath it to her son? Her aunt? Oscar was very vague about it; I got the feeling he was stalling me.

Then, early in December, Octavius Caesar's secretary called and requested my presence in his office at 10:00 A.M. the following morning. I breezily assured her that I'd be there. I swear I had absolutely no premonition of what was to come.

I arrived a few minutes early, but Caesar's office was already crowded. He was seated behind his desk as usual, and Anthony Cannis and Michael Gelesco were sharing the couch. Two straight-back chairs had been brought in for Ignatz Samuelson and Oscar Gotwold. The armchair alongside Caesar's desk had been left vacant—apparently for me.

No one stood up when I entered, and no one offered to shake hands. But they all returned my greetings pleasantly enough. When I was seated at the side of Octavius Caesar's desk, he began without preamble:

"We thought it best, young man, to have this conference before the end of the year to . . . In view of the recent sad events . . . I refer particularly to Miss Twombly's untimely death. Mr. Samuelson, will you begin?"

Iggy had a thick folder on his lap, but he didn't open it up or consult any documents. He spoke rapidly in his staccato style, looking directly at me. I listened closely, trying to follow the numbers he was spouting.

He said the income of Peter's Place during the current year, and projected for the final month, was gratifying. However, because of start-up costs and unforeseen expenses—such as the recent extraordinary security precautions—plus monthly payments on our mortgage, cash loan, renovation costs, and so forth, Peter's Place would end the year showing a very modest profit.

"How much?" I said hoarsely.

He answered immediately: "Total annual profit as projected is eleven thousand, six hundred fifty-two dollars and thirty-six cents. Your share will be approximately three thousand and twenty-seven dollars."

I stared at him, not believing what I had just heard. Martha and I had figured we'd each clear a hundred grand at least.

"That's bullshit!" I burst out. "We've been setting records. Every month with a higher take. I see the receipts; I know."

"True, Peter," Samuelson said, nodding. "Income has held up well. But you're not aware of overhead, salaries, expenses, and so on. For the first nine months we had a negative cash flow."

"Impossible!" I cried.

"All here," he said, tapping the folder on his lap. "A copy for you, of course. All legitimate. To the penny."

"I know," Octavius Caesar said smoothly, "that you anticipated a larger . . . Quite natural that you . . . However, one cannot argue with numbers. Peter's Place, I might say, has been an unexpected success. We projected two years of losses before we turned the . . . But here you've done it in nine months! I congratulate you, young man."

He beamed at me, and the other idiots smiled and bobbed their heads like Chinese dolls. Three thousand lousy bucks above my salary for a year's work! Even our laziest studs did better than that.

I remembered what Detective Luke Futter had said when I told him Roman Enterprises was backing our new club. He said that eventually they'd be giving me just as much of the profits as they wanted me to have. It was happening sooner than he predicted.

"Of course," Caesar went on, "we can expect higher profits in coming years as the club . . . And you will retain your stock and so share in the . . . Which brings us to another matter. Mr. Gotwold?"

I turned to look at Oscar. He was intent, almost sympathetic. Just the right manner for a serious assassin—"This hurts me more than it hurts you."

"Peter," he said, "as I am sure you are aware, the original corporation agreement included a clause stating that in the event of the demise of one of the original investors, his or her shares had first to be offered at book value to the remaining partners before those shares could be offered to outside investors. You were aware of that clause, were you not?"

"Like hell I was!" I yelled.

"Peter," he said in a mildly reproving tone, "it was included, not once but twice, in the documents you signed. Didn't you read the agreement?"

He knew goddamned well I hadn't read it. And neither had Martha. Because we believed he was looking after *our* interests. Now it was obvious to me that he, and Ignatz Samuelson, too—those crooks!—were creatures of that devilish Santa Claus sitting behind the desk.

"In my opinion," Oscar Gotwold went on, "this is a perfectly legitimate agreement."

"Are you prepared to exercise your option?" Octavius Caesar asked, rocking back and forth gently in his swivel chair.

"Wait a minute," I protested. "You mean I've got to come up with a hundred and four thousand if I want to buy Martha's stock?"

"That is correct," Gotwold said.

No way did I have that kind of cash. And what bank would give me a loan to buy 26 percent of a whorehouse? Oh, Ivar Gutierrez, where are you now that I need you?

"I can raise it," I said desperately.

"The clause heretofore alluded to," Gotwold continued, "allows thirty days from the demise of one of the partners for the remaining shareholders to exercise their purchase option. Martha's tragic death occurred thirty days ago. Do you wish to exercise your option at this time?"

I didn't answer.

"Mr. Cannis," Gotwold said, turning to the couch, "Mr. Gelesco, does Justice Development Corporation wish to exercise its option to purchase the twenty-six percent of Peter's Place, Incorporated, formerly held by the late Martha Twombly?"

"We do," they chorused like an imbecilic couple getting married.

So that left Justice Development Corp. (Cannis and Gelesco)— which was, I was certain, a subsidiary of Roman Enterprises—the owner of 74 percent of Peter's Place. I suppose I should have been thankful they left me the fillings in my teeth.

"And now," Octavius Caesar said, patting his soft hands together, "let us move on to happier . . . Young man, I am delighted to tell you that my associates have agreed to . . . Peter's Place will become a chain, just as you envisioned, with establishments in several other . . . And you will play a key role in this expansion, beginning with a second Peter's Place in Beverly Hills, California. We want you to go out there after the first of the . . . You will be completely in charge of . . . With an annual salary of a hundred thousand. How does that strike . . . ?"

"Beverly Hills?" I said, dazed. "California? Me?"

"Yancy Burnett will take over the Manhattan club," Cannis said briskly. "He can handle it."

"And we'll do a complete renovation job after the holidays," Gelesco said. "Make a real classy joint out of it. We got a dynamite designer."

"It's going to be real elegant," Cannis assured me. "Crystal chandeliers, big vases—the works."

"And of course," Octavius Caesar said blandly, "as a stockholder, you will continue to share in the profits of the New York club as you will in the profits of the Beverly Hills establishment and in any other branch opened by Peter's Place, Incorporated."

Share in the profits—that was a laugh. After they siphoned off the big money to their subsidiaries for mortgages and loans, they'd toss me a bone and pat my head. It was all my idea, but essentially I'd be a salaried employee and I knew it.

I looked at them all and wondered why they didn't kiss me. When you get fucked, you deserve a kiss.

169

I stalked into Yance's office and slammed my hat onto his desk.

"*You son of a bitch!*" I screamed at him. "You knew about it all the time."

He looked up at me. "For about a week," he admitted.

"Well, why the hell didn't you tell me?" I demanded. "I thought we were friends."

"Friends?" he said with a squinched smile. "Oh, Peter—you meet people and then you unmeet them. Life is all short takes and quick cuts—isn't it? Nothing lasts. The only important thing is not to give a damn."

I didn't have to force a laugh. "You're absolutely right," I said. "Let's have a drink, old buddy."

Yance opened his bottom desk drawer and pulled out a liter of vodka. We drank it from paper cups shaped like dunce caps. We added a little water from the office cooler.

I sat slumped in an armchair alongside his desk, still wearing my new tweed Burberry. I told Yance they wanted me to go to the Coast and open a Peter's Place in Beverly Hills.

"You're going?" he asked.

"Do I have a choice?" I asked bitterly. "They've got me by the balls. If I walk away from the whole thing, I can kiss my investment goodbye; I'll never see a cent of profit."

"You'll love California," he told me. "Great climate and all the women you can eat."

"Maybe I'll bump into Nikki Radburn," I said. "That would help. As I understand it, Yance, they're going to close this club after the first of the year and redecorate. I'll probably leave right after we close. Are you going to live here?"

"Probably," he said. "The lease on my apartment is up in April and I'll move then."

We drank more vodka and talked in a desultory way of changes that might be made when the club was renovated. Yance wanted to convert one of the bedrooms to a private gambling room for high rollers. Another could be converted to a projection room for porn flicks.

I liked both ideas and told Yance I'd probably incorporate both features in the new Peter's Place in California.

We drank more vodka and began recalling crazy things that had happened since we had been working together. I wasn't sore at him anymore. He hadn't put the blocks to me, and I could be happy that at least he was benefiting from my banishment from New York. I told him that.

He smiled his sad, sweet smile. "You know, Peter," he said, "I had eyes for you from the start."

"You never made a move, Yance."

"I could tell; you weren't interested."

"You never know," I said.

But that was the vodka talking.

I think.

170

That was the best holiday season ever. We had so many luncheon and dinner reservations that we set up tables in the Mardi Gras Room to handle the overflow. The Dream Room was crowded every night, and we had to stop selling tickets to our planned New Year's Eve party, we had so many orders.

The bedrooms got a phenomenal play; it wasn't unusual to schedule a hundred scenes a day. I was on the phone constantly to Clara Hoffheimer, calling for more warm bodies. But we were hard put to find enough studs to meet all the requests.

I filled in occasionally and so did Yance. I even persuaded King Hayes to go off the wagon a few times when we had an emergency.

One of the scenes I had about a week before Christmas was memorable. The lady's name was Tammy, and I recognized her the moment she walked into my bedroom. Her photo, biog, and interviews with her had been published in all the local papers and news magazines.

She had appeared as second lead in a comedy that opened on Broadway in November, and she stole the show. The reviewers were ecstatic, hailing her as the greatest comedic talent since Carole Lombard and Kay Kendall. She had already been signed to a big movie and a TV series. She was twenty-three.

What she was doing paying for a scene at Peter's Place I'll never know, but I suspect that at this point in her career she just didn't want the emotional hassle of a relationship with anyone she knew. And women as publicly successful as she always have the problem: Does this guy want to screw the star or does he want to screw *me?*

She was on from the moment I met her. I admit she was funny as hell, and had a great repertoire of quirky smiles, fake snarls, moues, grimaces, operatic gestures, and gawky body movements. You knew the charm was an act, but you couldn't resist it.

"Look at you!" she cried. "Your ass is *fat!*" And she plumped her cheeks, rolled her eyes, waddled to the bed.

"You can't drive a nail with a tack hammer," I said with a glassy smile.

"More like driving a tack with a sledgehammer," she said, giving me an exaggerated expression of imperious disdain.

She didn't let up for a minute, not even on the sheet. The gags kept coming. One-liners mostly, but also shticks and bits that had clearly been rehearsed. Some of them were quite good; some were so hammy I wanted to throttle her.

To put it as kindly as possible, she was a lousy lay—but I've never met an actress who wasn't. I think it's got something to do with narcissism and role-playing. Very few actors and actresses can go deeper than deliberate and practiced craft on the stage or in bed. They simply will not or cannot surrender.

That hour with Tammy was a chastening experience for me. I saw myself in her: the shticks, the bits, the clowning; but more distressing, the constant artifice, the performance that substitutes for living.

Anthony Cannis and Michael Gelesco were who they were. They were rude, slimy boors and made no effort to pretend otherwise. I thought they were evil men, but they didn't put on the manners of monseigneurs. That troubled me; it made them superior to me.

How often had I bored Jenny, Arthur, Martha, Nikki, Mabel, Yance, and all my other friends and acquaintances by constantly being on? It was wearying; the hour with Tammy taught me that. It was like being constantly beaten over the head with a burlesque bladder.

But even worse was what it had done, was doing to me. When your whole life is a performance, you lose the ability to distinguish illusion from reality. Who the hell *was* I? Peter Scuro. That much I knew. And that's all I knew.

So I made another of my noble resolves. I decided that henceforth I would be my natural, sincere self, acting from instinct tempered by thoughtful consideration.

I suspected that Octavius Caesar (and Gotwold and Samuelson) thought me a clever lightweight, good with profitable ideas and inspirations that could be used, but not a *serious* man. Not someone worthy of respect.

I decided that my days of playacting were over. I would no longer be a mummer. The people I would deal with on the Coast would meet a man of quiet poise and restrained confidence. A stately man who thought before he spoke, a distinguished man of sober earnestness. Perhaps even staid.

No more make-believe.

171

Two nights before Christmas, on a Sunday, the studs gave me a farewell party. It was organized by Yancy Burnett and held at the club. All the food and booze were provided by Peter's Place, Inc., but the guys gave me a great assortment of gifts—some funny, some useful, some elegant and expensive.

I had worked with these boys for almost three years and, as I told them in a short thank-you speech, I only hoped I could organize as good a stable on the Coast. During the evening's festivities, several studs came up to say they planned to move to Hollywood, looking for movie or TV work, and would contact me there.

My goodbyes to Yance, King Hayes, Seth Hawkins, and a few of the others were more personal. We promised to keep in touch, knowing we wouldn't. Then we all got drunk. Some of the studs paired off and went to the upstairs bedrooms. So?

Christmas Eve, Mabel Hetter was taking a night flight to Kansas to spend the holiday week with her parents. I hadn't yet told her I was leaving and in all probability would never see her again.

Parting was not only such sweet sorrow, it was also a pain in the ass. I knew she was madly in love with me, and the problem was to let her down easily so she could retain her self-esteem. What I feared most was that she would weep uncontrollably. Women's tears shatter me; I usually end up crying along with them.

I made elaborate preparations for the farewell. First of all, I bought her an antique Victorian brooch as a Christmas present. It was a filigreed rose set with garnets—really a stunner—and it cost me almost a grand.

Then, because she had a nine o'clock flight and wouldn't have time to cook, I ordered up a gourmet dinner from the Brasserie and had it delivered to her apartment. When I showed up, I brought two chilled bottles of Dom Perignon '71. I had, I admit, lifted them from the wine cellar of Peter's Place.

Mabel absolutely loved her Christmas gift and pinned it on immediately, vowing she would wear it on her trip home. She gave me a gold money clip in the shape of a dollar sign, exactly like the one the VIP had sent me from Washington. I told Mabel it was just what I wanted, but she shouldn't have done it.

Then we opened the champagne and toasted each other. We laughed a lot and sang a duet of "Make Believe." Mabel was so lighthearted and happy that I cravenly postponed telling her the bad news until after dinner.

We had braised endives, medallions of duck breast, broiled mushrooms, a ruby lettuce salad, and petits fours for dessert. Those we sprinkled with a little Cointreau, just for the hell of it.

But finally the moment of truth arrived. I took Mabel onto my lap and told her that I had been transferred to the Coast, and this would be our last meeting for a long, long time. I held her tightly, ready to kiss her tears away.

She was silent a moment. Then: "Is it a promotion, Peter?"

"Sort of."

"Will you be making more money?"

"I suppose so."

"Then you've got to go," she said firmly. "It's just fab that they think so much of you that they're giving you an opportunity like that."

It wasn't going exactly the way I had anticipated.

"Mae, I'll really hate to leave you," I said sorrowfully.

"Don't even think of that," she said, laughing merrily. "My daddy always says to go where the job is. When are you leaving?"

"I'll be gone by the time you get back to New York," I said hollowly. "This will be the last time we see each other."

She turned my wrist to look at my watch. "Goodness," she said. "Not much time. Can we have a quickie?"

"Sure, Mae," I said manfully. "Why not?"

Later, when we were dressed again and gathering her luggage to take down to my car, she said, "Peter, a girl I know who's a member of the club, well, she told me she met this super boy there. This girl has got like arthritis in her hip, and she said after one scene with this boy it cleared right up. His name is Seth. Do you know him?"

"Seth?" I said. "Sure, I know him."

"Do you think I'll like him?"

"Of course you will," I told her. "He's marvy."

172

Peter's Place was closed for alterations on January 2. The decorators, painters, and carpenters moved in and I retired to my third-floor bedroom to start packing for my move to the Coast. I was taking only two suitcases. Yance would ship the rest of my stuff when I got settled.

I had been doing a lot of heavy thinking since I had been shafted at that meeting in Octavius Caesar's office. I finally decided what had happened. I think the scenario went like this:

Neither Alice nor Wilson Bowker had murdered Martha. Her death had been planned by Caesar and carried out by his minions, maybe even Cannis and Gelesco. She would have let them into her locked apartment.

Roman Enterprises had a heavy cash investment in Bowker's campaign for governor, and somehow learned of his relationship with Martha. So she had to be removed before the political career of the Great White Hope went down the drain.

At the same time, Octavius Caesar knew that Martha's death—and my stupidity—would ensure his majority ownership of Peter's Place, Inc. The joint was coining money, and a chain of Peter's Places would make umpteen millions. So Caesar wanted complete control, with me as a hireling, bowing and scraping every time they tossed me a few extra shekels.

There was more than one reason why he decided to send me to the Coast. First of all, he knew I was a clever lad who could organize and manage a profitable establishment in Beverly Hills. And he wanted me out of New York, where I might get curious and start asking questions about Martha's murder.

A crafty scoundrel like Octavius Caesar, who undoubtedly engineered the transfer of Detective Jules Slotkin, would foresee a danger like that and take steps to prevent it.

There was another reason why he wanted me gone—and you may smile at this, but I really believe it. I knew about his making nice-nice with Clara Hoffheimer. Even worse from his point of view, I had been witness to his embarrassment when he got his undershorts stuck in his zipper during his scene with Clara at the club.

Octavius Caesar could probably endure a lot of things, but being thought ridiculous was not one of them. I had seen him scurry out, clutching an old raincoat to conceal his shame. After that, he knew he could never expect me to show sincere respect.

That's the way I think it all came about. I may be wrong, of course, but I doubt it. It doesn't make any difference anyway.

Poor Martha was so right when she talked of the overworld and how it works in mysterious ways. She was a problem to the lords of money and power and so she had to die. I was luckier (I thought); I was exiled to Beverly Hills. Which meant they felt they could still get some use out of me.

By the evening of January 4, I was packed and ready to go. We had locked up the club's liquor supply before the decorators came in, but I had thoughtfully kept out a few bottles to see me through the last days at Peter's Place.

I mixed myself a vodka and water and wandered around the ground floor of the club. Most of the furniture had been removed for sale, but we kept the few good pieces we owned. Now these were covered with dropcloths to protect them from paint splashes.

It was like walking through a graveyard. The draped furniture loomed like burial monuments, and the few lights still working pushed shadows back into corners. It was a ghostly place without music and laughter, without greeds and passions that drove customers and studs upstairs.

I stood at the sheeted bar in the Dream Room and thought of my future.

I saw myself, a pudgy ponce, standing on the terrace of a house overlooking the Pacific. I'd be wearing a maroon cashmere sport jacket, raw silk slacks, Gucci loafers—without socks, of course. A gold Concord Mariner on my wrist, a diamond pinkie ring, and at my throat a billowing silk ascot.

And my arm would be about the smooth waist of a tanned nubile toy in a string bikini. Blond, sun-streaked hair down to her bum. She would have one of those California names—Candy, Astra, Bliss.

"Daddy," she'd say, "I need money for my guru."

But that image did not dismay me. I could play that role.

The front door chimes sounded. I went to the lobby and peered through the judas. A single woman. I unlocked the door.

She was tall, cool, quite lovely. Bundled up in ranch mink.

"I am a member," she said crisply, displaying her card. "May I—"

"I am sorry," I interrupted, "but we're closed for alterations. We'll open again in two weeks."

"Oh," she said. "That *is* a disappointment."

"However," I said, turning on the charm, "if I can be of service . . . ?"

She looked at me.

"Sorry," she said, giving me a chilly smile. "I'm looking for a younger type."